An Unconquerable Spirit

By Catherine Smith

To my Husband Dennis and our daughters Gillian and Lauren for their encouragement and patience in letting me realize my dream

MARSOC CSO CREED

My Title is Marine, but it is my choice and my choice alone to be a Special Operations Marine. I will never forget the tremendous sacrifice and reputation of those who came before me.

At all ranges my fires will be accurate. With surprise, speed, and violence of action, I will hunt enemies of my country and bring chaos to their doorstep. I will keep my body strong, my mind sharp, and my kit ready at all times.

Raider and Recon men forged the path I follow. With Determination, Dependability, and Teamwork I will uphold the honor and the legacy passed down to me. I will do the right thing always, and will let my actions speak for me. As a quiet professional, I will not bring shame upon myself or those with which I serve.

Spiritus Invictus, an Unconquerable Spirit, will be my goal. I will never quit, I will never surrender, I will never fail. I will adapt to the situation. I will gain and maintain the initiative. I will always go a little farther and carry more than my share.

On any battlefield, at any point of the compass I will excel. I will set the example for all others to emulate. At the tip of the spear, I will teach and prepare others to seek out, dismantle, and destroy our common enemies. I will fight side by side with my partners and will be the first in and last out of any mission.

Conquering all obstacles of mind, body, and spirit; the honor and pride of serving in special operations will be my driving force. I will remain always faithful to my brothers and always forward in my service.

Chapter One

Each branch of the Armed Forces has an elite squad of operatives that comprise a special forces unit. Selection into these units invites the best candidates to participate in training and skills development that will challenge the candidates both mentally and physically to the test of their limits. In the Marine Corps this squad is called Marine Corps Forces Special Operations Command, or MARSOC. The MARSOC Raiders are trained and educated in individual, basic, and advanced special operations to carry out highly specialized covert operations in the most volatile and dangerous regions of the world.

Like all Special Forces teams, or spec-ops, only the most highly skilled Marines are chosen. Attrition in The Raiders is not as high as the Navy Seals or Army Rangers since Marine Corps training already demands mental and physical toughness. To enter the Raider Battalion, candidates must demonstrate attributes and personalities compatible with the stresses of working in a close independent unit. Nine months attending Marine Special Operations Individual Training Course (ITC) at the Marine Special Operations School in Camp Lejeune North Carolina and a three-week Assessment and Selection Preparator and Orientation course (ASPOC) determine those that enter the ITC training. The four phases of ITC training determine which Marines have what it takes to become a Raider. The Basic Skills, Small Unit Tactics, Close Quarters Battle, and Asymmetric Warfare culminate all the training and skills acquired throughout the course. Graduates are then assigned to one of the three Marine Raider Battalions.

The three Marine Raider Battalions, MRB, are comprised of four Marine Special Operations companies, MSOCs, that contain four Marine Special Operations Teams, MSOTs, in each. These teams deploy to Marine Corps forward positions to support ground troops and aid in military training to friendly foreign nations. 2dMRB 5th Marines MSOT comprised of companies Alpha, Bravo, Charlie, and Delta MSOTs out of Camp Lejeune North Carolina are aiding in locating and eliminating insurgent groups assisting ISIS from Camp Delta in a classified location in Afghanistan.

Monday, 0300 hours Gunnery Sergeant Kristian Cole holds the team on the edge of the village with a hand gesture while he readjusts his night vision and scouts the area. The Marine looked too young to be heading the mission. His five-foot ten-inch frame was solid with a tough stance backed by lean muscle. The blonde standard Marine buzzcut under his helmet highlight hollow cheek bones and slightly chiseled chin. The sharp golden-brown eyes look over the area under straight dark brows. Kris heard all his life he was a pretty boy. His model good looks made women take more than one long glance and gave the men in the division constant fuel for razzing. He never let it bother him. He was a Marine.

The three buildings opposite them show the scars of a previous mortar attack. The top right corner of the right one gone. The alley they are concealed in smells of rotting Kabuli Palaw and goat feces. The wind stirs the dust and brings the smell of smoke from a nearby barrel fire. A man and women several houses down yell in Pashto; too far away to make out the argument. Reedy Arabic pop music drifts faintly from the window above them. The eight-man team has been sent in to locate and exfiltrate a family belonging to the Tajik tribe who were taken hostage and threatened with execution to force the tribes to cease opposition with the Taliban and aide insurgents backed by ISIS to continue to escalate the instability of the area.

"Base, this is Raider One-over." A tinny voice responds in Cole's headset; "Copy Raider One, this is base."

"Base, Alpha Company in position- over."

"Affirmative Raider One, hold for confirmation of Bravo Company."

Cole, the Intel Specialist and Tactical leader, sweeps his gaze over the other seven members of his team. All in position. The team's XO Major Justin Alario the Special Operations Officer, Captain Javier Juarez IT Support Specialist, Master Sergeant John Reineke Logistics Specialist (or better known as the scrounger), Lieutenant Davis Gentry Communications

Specialist, Master Sergeant Michael Tomball Reconnaissance Specialist and translator, Sergeant Daniel Jenkins EOD Specialist, and Staff Sergeant Jack Jeffries Fire Support Specialist. All tough heavily muscled men who were ideally suited to their jobs.

Spec-ops teams do not necessarily hold to a ranking structure of command, rather a command structure based on merit and experience. Kris was young for a team leader at 29 years old, but he and Alario at 38 years old had 7 years as a Raiders. Kris's teams nominated him consistently as team leader for the last six and a half years; ever since the poorly executed mission in Jordon where he saved the life of his Lieutenant and team after the op went sideways trapping them in a firefight and certain death inside an insurgent commune. Cole's knack for problem solving and ninja-like ability to get out of difficult situations earned him a well-deserved reputation for success and was a highly prized member of the team. The men refused to allow anyone else to lead them into or out of the shit. Kris always made sure everyone made it through and came home no matter what the odds. Everyone on the team encouraged Kris to attend Officer's Candidate School but he didn't want to break from the team.

"Raider One, Base. Bravo Company in position."

Cole turned his head back to the building caddy corner from them. "Affirmative Base. Alpha Company engaging." Cole signaled the men. Like shadows the team crossed the street and surrounded the building; covering exits and watching for enemy combatants. Cole quietly opened the door and two by two the team entered the hall sweeping the rooms. The sound of shots fired in the headset indicated Alario and Reineke engaged in the rear. That meant combatants were headed back toward the rest of the team. Turning the corner shots connected with the wall just off to his side.

"Base, contact. Team is under fire. Objective still at large." The tinny voice responded; "Affirmative Raider One, contact."

Cole shot the two men firing on them and stealthfully made his way into the room to the door on the far side and down another hallway. Behind him Juarez watched his six as he made his way to the room in the southwest corner where intelligence confirmed the family was being held. Cole signaled Juarez to stop as things suddenly got very quiet.

"Raider One, Raider Two copy." Alario's voice in the headset answered, "Raider Two, copy." Cole remained still. "Raider One, my dick twitched."

Kris had a sixth sense for danger and traps that was legendary in the Raider teams. Reineke used to give Kris a hard time being the youngest Raider to command a team; saying his sweet little baby face couldn't grow a decent beard because his balls hadn't dropped. They also gave Kris a hard time about never beating off in the showers because he was too young to know what his dick was for. Some of them joked that Kris only got a hard on for regulations. No one was more by the book. Anytime anyone had a question Kris quoted regulations. He was always reading a manual. Kris had every new regulation that came out before the ink dried. He had memorized the Marine Corps regulations manual and the Uniform Code of Military Justice as well as the general guidelines used by SOC for rules of engagement. The guys joked that Cole had the regulations tattooed on his dick. Juarez stuck up for him by saying Kris didn't need to beat off in the shower, he really got off in the field when everything went to shit, and he had to use that famous ninja skill to save their asses and complete the mission. If Cole's dick twitched, the shit was about to hit the fan.

Cole and Juarez slowly made their way to the room in the southwest corner and kicked open the door. A family of five huddled in the corner; a man trying to shelter his wife, daughter, and two young sons. Cole addressed them in Pashtu.

"We are 2dMRB 5th Marines Alpha Company. What is your name?" The man answered Samir Kabiq. Bingo. Just who they were looking for.

"Mr. Kabiq we were sent to get you and your family to safety. Come with us and stay close. How many men are here?"

"We have only seen five men, but we hear many others. Maybe 12?" Cole frowned. Reports from the other team members had five men down, plus the two he killed. That left five unaccounted for. "Bring your family Mr. Kabiq. Raider Two we have the objective, coming out."

"Copy Raider One."

The team met up in the middle of the building after both floors had been cleared. That was too easy, something was wrong. Cole signaled to Alario and Jenkins.

"Raider Two, get the family to safety. Raider Six, call our ride."

Just as they were exiting the building Jenkins spotted a 10-year-old boy coming down the main hall and darting into the room on the left they just vacated. Jenkins called after the kid and turned back into the building. Kris told the others to get back to the rendezvous point and went after Jenkins. Kris caught up with him and tapped the other man on the helmet. "Leave the kid, let's go." Just as they were turning to leave the kid ran by them holding something in his hand. Kris realized it was a detonator. He looked Jenkins dead in the eyes, "Run!" Jenkins didn't hesitate and ran out the back. Kris caught something out of the corner of his eye and stopped. In the corner sat an IED on a timer. It was not there when they came through before, so it must have been concealed. He knew looking at the timer and size of the charge the team would not be able to get far enough away to get out of the blast radius, and there was no time to disarm it before it blew. He had 12 seconds to act. He gathered the pallets and mattresses off the floor in the adjacent room and surrounded the device to absorb the shrapnel.

"Clear the area, IED!" He turned over a large cabinet blocking the device in the corner and propped the remaining mattresses in front. He had 6 seconds on the counter. Two seconds later he was climbing over the last bed when the device exploded, and everything went black.

Chapter Two

The explosion shook the building covering everyone in rubble and dust. Alario shook the dust off and crawled out from under a section of wall that had covered his lower legs. He checked on Gentry who was still down but stirring. "Alpha team, report."

Each member checked in except Cole. Alario entered the building coughing from the dust in the air.

"Raider One, report."

He continued to make his way into the building to the last area Cole was known to be in. He swept back and forth looking for danger but all he met was silence. He paused before entering the doorway. He took a knee and pivoted bringing his weapon forward meeting an identical image in the opposite doorway-Reineke. The middle of the room was nothing but a pile of rubble still smoking.

"Where's Raider One?"

Jenkins looked startled. "He went back that way, we split in different directions."

"He didn't come out that way."

They looked at the pile of rubble and started tearing through it. It didn't take long to uncover a boot and a leg. They worked furiously to uncover Kris's body. They fought like demons to get their fallen team mate out. They grabbed his arms and dragged him from the debris. Alario immediately started assessing him for injuries. It wasn't hard to see where Kris was the most injured. The blast seemed to be concentrated on his lower half.

"Hold on man, we got you. You hear me, Gunny? We got you!" Jenkins sounded a bit panicked. Alario was feverishly pulling triage gear from his pack.

"Raider Four!" Alario signaled to Juarez.

"Roger, Raider Two."

"We need a chopper and a med unit. Now! Raider One is down."

The men could hear their communications specialist radioing in their position and situation report. Alario was opening packs of gauze to stop the bleeding from Cole's badly torn up torso.

"Hold on man." He looked at Jenkins who looked like he was going to be sick. "You need to hold this tight here to stop the bleeding. Remember your triple c training! Hold it together Marine!"

Jenkins pushed the gauze into the meat that used to be the Gunny's groin. "Jesus man, did he...?"

"Yeah, just hold that tight or he's gonna bleed out before help arrives." Kris groaned when the men pushed down on the injuries trying to stop the flow of blood copiously flowing from his wounds.

Kris's weak voice piped up, "Better to bleed than to have the rest of this building on our heads. Let's take this outside." The building started to groan around them, and they all knew what that meant. The blast had destroyed the structure's integrity and they probably only had minutes before it collapsed.

"Don't be gentle, just get me outta here." Kris opened his eyes and looked at his brothers who both wore an identical look of horror at his condition.

"Hold tight man, we're gonna move you. Alpha team, three out, one ambulatory."

The team met outside the building and carried Cole to the LZ in standard ambulatory carry. The men carried Cole and made their way to the edge of town with their five civilians in tow. A boom and crash behind them showed the building collapsed sending a cloud of dust that covered them from any snipers that may still be in the area. A click outside of the town was their landing zone and they could already hear the chopper incoming. The men ran as fast as their burden would allow to meet their transport. Once the UH-1N Iroquois touched down the men lifted Cole inside.

The corpsman immediately started working on stabilizing Kris. Alario jumped in while the rest of the teams filed into the second Huey. He grabbed scissors and cut away the younger man's pants while taking more gauze packs to staunch blood flow. A fountain of blood poured out.

"Need compression, we've got an artery here. Forceps!" Alario reached out for the scissor like tool used to clamp of bleeding in surgery and applied it to the open artery staunching the blood flow. "Hemostat!" as he held his hand out for the second tool trying to save his friend's life. "I need 3.0 silk to sew off this bleeder or we are going to lose him." The corpsman, recognizing the skill and training the Major was displaying and got all the necessary instruments ready and waiting. Alario fought furiously to close some of the bad areas as the corpsman in the chopper looked on in awe.

"You a surgeon Major?" asked the corporal assisting him.

"Yeah, general and emergency surgery."

"What the hell are you doing out here, Sir?"

"I figured I could save more lives preventing wounds then treating them. More suction!"

Alario's fingers flew as he continued to work at a breakneck pace. "ETA?"

"Two minutes, Sir."

All he could think of is that Kris may not have two minutes. The corpsman radioed in Cole's status and injuries to the field hospital, so they could have a medical team standing by. The younger man lay still and pale in the red light of the cabin. The chopper finally made its way to the landing strip at Camp Delta and Kris was loaded on a stretcher. His team right behind him as they entered the emergency medical treatment building. Kris was wheeled into an operating room as Alario and the Corporal gave a report to the surgeon on duty as to Cole's condition. The surgeon, a Lieutenant Commander Campbell, tried to order Alario out.

"I am not leaving Lieutenant Commander. Right now, my hand holding his femoral artery is the only thing keeping him alive."

"The Major is an emergency surgeon, Sir" the Corporal added in.

Lieutenant Commander Campbell looked at Alario, "I am not leaving my team leader."

"Where did you intern Major?"

"Northwestern Memorial and the Southside streets of Chicago."

Campbell looked at Cole's wounds and didn't really see any way the kid would make it; but he could see the fierce determination in Alario's face and figured he could use all the help he could get. He pulled on gloves and told Alario to scrub in.

Alario threw off his gear and shirt scrubbing his hands and arms in the practiced way that surgeons do and held his hands up to be gowned and gloved. Then moved back into position as a nurse placed a surgical mask over his face.

The Lieutenant Commander was cutting the rest of Cole's clothing away as the anesthesiologist moved in to put Kris under. Just then Kris came to and started fighting.

"Hold him!"

The Lieutenant sitting behind Cole's head trying to wrestle the mouth cup over Cole was having a hard time succeeding. Cole was fighting him furiously.

"Calm down Kris we have to put you under to fix you up man, stop fighting!"

Kris shook his head and mumbled something Alario didn't get.

"What Kris?"

Kris kept fighting the anesthesiologist as someone called to tie him to the table. He kept moving his head from the mouth cup and Alario finally caught was he was saying.

"Anaphylaxis...."

He grabbed the Lieutenant's arm and held the cup away.

"Say again, Kris!"

"Anapha...." The younger man was struggling to talk from the pain and exertion.

"Do you have an allergy to anesthesia?" Kris nodded weakly.

"Shit!" Alario looked up to Campbell. "If we put him under it could kill him."

"Do you suggest we try to operate while he is awake?!"

Alario looked down at his best friend. Kris opened his burning eyes and stared into his friend's tense gaze.

"Get it done!" Kris's head fell back on the table as the two men trying to save his life stared at each other for a brief second coming to a decision. They forged ahead without anesthesia.

"Get something for him to bite down on!" A nurse ran to find something to use. The team just outside the room started rummaging through their packs; Reineke pulled a leather strap out of his bag and placed it in Kris's mouth. Kris bit down hard. Just then Colonel Stirling came into the room; his pallor a startling contrast to his ordinarily swarthy complexion. Fit and tough and looking far younger than his forty-nine years he stood to the side of Alario taking in Cole's condition. Kris had been a substitute child for him from the moment they met.

Alario worked feverously searching out shrapnel. Campbell doing the same. The metal bowl made a rhythmic pinging sound each time another piece of metal was located and removed. The man's lower abdomen was peppered with it as were his thighs. The worst wound was the area where Kris had been castrated by the blast. Alario noticed that the bleeding wasn't as bad as it should be considering the wound. He commented as such to Campbell.

"Yeah. I noticed that too. I think this might have something to do with it." He pointed to another metal bowl with what appeared to be what was left of a prosthetic device in it. It was hard to see what it had been before the explosion. "I pulled that from out of his pants."

Alario took a second to look at it, then shut down that line of thinking. He could worry about that later. Just then the monitors started beeping. Kris's pressures were down.

"We have to open him up, we have a bleeder in there."

The Lieutenant Commander looked grim. Cole looked at him with fiery eyes. He could see the strength and tenacity in Cole's eyes. This Marine wasn't not going to quit fighting. He sighed. Then neither could he. He looked over his shoulder to the men just outside the room. He pointed at them and said, "You! Come here!"

They filed in. "Hold him down."

Juarez, Jeffries, Tomball, and Jenkins came in taking point.

"You two hold his arms, and you two his feet. Don't let him move!" Campbell looked at Cole, "Stay as still as you can Gunny. Yell, scream if you want, but don't move!"

Alario's dark brown eyes met Kris's lighter ones and gave a Kris a hard stare. Kris lay clenching his teeth over the leather strap and nodded to Alario.

Alario looked at the nurse and ordered, "Scalpel."

As the two men made incisions in Kris's abdomen the Gunny yelled through the strap in his teeth, but he didn't move. The two doctors continued exploring Kris's abdomen looking for where the bleeding was coming from. Kris spit out the strap and started yelling. Harsh words with a liberal amount of swearing kept the younger man focused on something other than that savage pain that was ravaging his body. Jenkins stood holding Kris's arm with tears rolling down his face as he fought to keep it together. Juarez commented to Jeffries holding his feet wondering why he didn't just pass out. Tomball on the other arm just shook his head looking grim; his dark cocoa complexion ashen. He kept closing his eyes willing himself to be anywhere but here while praying that Kris took Juarez's suggestion. Meanwhile he started reciting scripture aloud, praying for Kris.

Alario kept looking for shrapnel and areas of bleeding to see why Kris's pressures kept falling. He called for suction and found the area that was causing the trouble. At first, he couldn't tell what the tissue had been, it was so badly damaged. He rooted around looking at the area trying to make sense of what he was seeing when the truth of it slammed into him. He raised startled eyes into that of Campbell who had come to the same realization.

"It's too badly damaged, you have to remove it."

Alario looked at Campbell, torn. "It's the only way to stop the bleeding Major."

Kris lifted his head and said, "What.... what?" His head fell hard against the table with eyes closed...still.

Just then all the monitors went nuts. Nurses were yelling out stats and both doctors rushed into action.

"Kris! Kris! You listen to me! Hang on there, Gunny. Do you hear me?! Hold on!"

Campbell moved in to remove the damaged organ while Alario fought to stitch up the vessels leading to it. Kris's vitals continued to drop. There was no way he was going to let Kris slip away. He stopped working, pulled aside his mask, and grabbed Kris's face. He bent down and kissed the Gunny right on the lips, hard. The men all had looks of incredulousness on their faces. Kris's eyes fluttered open. Kris looked at Justin with alarm and confusion.

"Keep your eyes open Marine! Don't you dare give in!"

Kris looked at Alario's blazing face as the beeping died down and became less rapid. Kris nodded. The anesthesiologist grabbed gauze and cleaned off Kris's blood smeared face as Alario went back to working on saving Cole's life. The two surgeons called out orders for suction, retraction, clamps, and a score of other commands to nurses assisting. Alario finished the surgery and finished sewing Kris up as Campbell continued finding small pieces of shrapnel from Kris's thighs. Three hours after starting on Kris they were done. The Gunnery Sergeant was very pale, but still conscious. The Lieutenant placed an oxygen mask over Kris's face and checked blood pressure. He looked up to the Lieutenant Commander and nodded. Alario looked at the men who were wearing nearly identical grim, terrorized expressions. The emotional and physical fatigue of the night had caught up with all of them.

"Thank you, men. All of you get showers and chow. Then write up your field report and get some rack time."

The men all left after telling Cole to keep fighting, saying prayers, and holding the younger Marine's hand. They filed out slowly; the weariness of the day weighing upon them.

Alario stripped off his gown and gloves and gripped Kris's hand. Kris's eyes fluttered open.

"It's all good Gunny. You are going to be fine. Just don't pull any of that stupid shit you tried before, huh?"

"Look who's talking, Sir! Permission to pass out now?"

"Stand down Marine."

Kris's eyes closed again, but this time the vitals stayed strong and even. Kris finally passed out. Heaving a strong breath Alario looked at the Lieutenant Commander.

"I owe you big time Lieutenant Commander ...?"

"Campbell. Lieutenant Commander Nick Campbell. Not as much as I owe you Major..."

"Major Justin Alario."

"Alario? Any relation to Salvatore Alario?"

"Yeah, my old man."

"Well that explains a lot. I wrote a paper once on him for school. He's been a hero of mine for quite some time. I read he had a son that was a Marine."

"Yeah he's a hero of mine too."

"Where did you attend medical school Major?"

Alario laughed wryly. "U of C. I read all my dad's medical books by the time I was 12. Then he took me with him in a retrofitted ambulance he used to treat people in the areas cops and ambulances wouldn't enter because of street violence. I interned at Northwestern but learned more with OJT on the streets of South Chicago. I passed the surgical boards when I was 19. After a couple of years running a street clinic out of the back of a retrofitted ambulance getting shot at every day, I figured I'd get shot at less in the Corps! I decided I wanted to save lives another way."

"Well I have worked with my share of surgeons, and you are by far the most skilled I have ever seen. I don't know of any that could have done surgery on a patient without anesthesia in these kinds of conditions. Especially on a friend and after a firefight during a combat mission. I think you get the award for being the toughest SOB I have ever met!" Campbell said laughingly.

"No Campbell, the toughest SOB you have ever met is lying right here." Alario said after pulling up a chair next to the bed holding onto Kris's hand. After speaking with the team, Colonel Stirling the Company Commander, walked in.

"Both of you, come with me." Alario and Campbell followed the Colonel out of the hospital to a building several yards away. They walked inside, and the Colonel closed and locked the door.

Colonel Nathan Stirling was a strongly built man the same height as Justin at six foot. His thick dark hair was cut into a typical Marine buzz cut showing the chiseled features and lean face of his Latino mother with the slightly darker skin tone of his black father. His light brown eyes were piercing against his swarthy skin tone. At 49 he looked far younger owing to his rigorous fitness regime of martial arts. He was a six-degree black belt in Aikido and he and Kris often performed a demonstration at local, state, and national martial arts competitions with nun chucks and staff fighting. The Colonel was passionate about working with at risk kids as was Kris.

After gesturing for the men to sit, Stirling pulled a bottle out of the locked bottom door with three glasses and filled them halfway. Alario raised an eyebrow; liquor in camp was strictly against regulations.

"I think after that we can all use a stiff belt." The Colonel rubbed his hands roughly over his face. "That couldn't be rougher if that was my own kid lying there."

Alario smiled. "Colonel we all know that IS your kid lying there."

Campbell looked confused, "Cole is your child Colonel?"

"Not by blood. I never had kids, never married. Cole has been son to me since day one."

Alario and Campbell glanced at each other over their glasses and looked away.

"What are you not telling me gentlemen?"

Campbell started to speak, but Alario held up a hand. "That is a conversation for later Colonel. I need to check on my men, make sure they are ok. This was rougher than most. I need to see what Colonel Meyer was able to learn from the family about that attack, and I need to get some down time. Campbell just got off a full night rotation and needs to get some sleep."

"Thank you for the drink, Colonel."

"Don't mention it Campbell, I mean that-Don't mention it!"

"Yes, Sir!"

Campbell and Alario walked out and the doctor grabbed Alario by the arm.

"We have to tell him."

"We will. First, we need to get some more information. Prosthetics all have serial numbers. We need to research Kris's, find out where it came from. Second, we need keep this between us two only. Cole is a Raider, and this is a delicate situation."

The Lieutenant Commander's face lit up with understanding. "I see."

"I have a contact I can tap for the prosthetic. Get me that serial number and I will find out everything I can. I am going to place a couple of calls stateside."

"Say 'hi' to your dad for me!" Campbell said with a smile as he walked back into the hospital. Alario went back to Special Operations command to place those calls. The sun was coming up and yesterday wasn't even close to being over yet.

Chapter Three

At 1100 hours Justin Alario headed to the Colonel's office armed with a folder of information. He'd only had four hours of sleep, but it was enough to clear his head. Surprisingly he slept well and was not plagued with any nightmares like he expected. Strangely the traumatic experience eased his mind of a few worries he'd been harboring the last several months. He was still worried about Kris, but his check in with the hospital eased that some. Kris was sleeping under the influence of pain medicine and vitals looked good. Kris still had a long road ahead, but prognosis was good. He knocked on the Colonel's door and was let in. Lieutenant Commander Campbell was already seated. He saluted the Colonel and was gestured to sit down.

"Lieutenant Commander Campbell was waiting until you arrived before going into detail, but he did give me an update on Cole."

"I just stopped by the hospital, Sir. Kris was resting."

Alario got up and poured himself a cup of coffee from the Colonel's coffee pot.

"About Kris, there is something that we discovered in surgery that we need to discuss with you Colonel."

"What was that Major?"

"Sir I don't know how to say this, so I'll just say it: Kris is female."

Stirling set back in his chair resting his elbows on the armrests and touched his fingertips together in front of him. "I see. And you know this how?"

"As you know from Lieutenant Commander Campbell's report, we had to do invasive surgery on Kris without anesthetic to get to shrapnel and stop internal bleeding. During the course of that surgery we discovered some anatomical anomalies. The source of the internal bleeding was damage to an organ that should not have been there. We had to remove it, as the damage to it was severe and Kris's life was at stake. We did not have the luxury or time to try to repair it while Kris was suffering."

"What was this organ you removed?"

"Kris's uterus."

Stirling sat thoughtfully weighing his next words. His brown eyes and swarthy face impassive.

Alario continued. "I have some information I asked my father to collect for me. Being an eminent surgeon, he could make inquiries without raising any flags. What he sent to me was several files; a medical file and two court case files. Cole vs. Cole and Cole vs. Standish. The medical file was regarding a prosthetic device we found surgically attached to Kris; a prosthetic penis and scrotum. The serial number is for a prototype developed by Innovative Prosthetics and says it was attached 19 years ago when Kris was 10. This ties to the court case file of Cole vs. Standish. Dr. Anthony Standish was a plastic surgeon and pioneer prosthetic designer who lost his medical license after performing an experimental procedure on a minor without both parents consent and without FDA approval. That minor was Kris. The prosthetic was a prototype for a fully functioning penis for both urinary and sexual functions. Designed as a replacement for men wounded in battle. Standish was working to get a contract to supply cutting edge prosthetic devices to the VA. His company, Innovative Prosthetics, was trying to get a government contract to propel his startup company into a major rival in the prosthetic industry.

One of his major investors and backers aiding him in getting in with the VA was Major Marcus Sheldon Cole. Kris's father. The second court case is the divorce proceeding between Jenna Cole, Kris's mother, and Major Cole. Kris's mother got custody after the police charged Major Cole with depraved indifference in the life of a child, reckless endangerment, collusion in an illegal medical procedure, and gross neglect. He did not serve any time but was discharged from the Army. He was 2nd Battalion, 75th Ranger Regiment, stationed at Fort Lewis, Washington. They retired him after 18 years with half benefits. He didn't suffer as the company took off and as a major investor he became a millionaire after about four years. He is now a facilitator who works with civilian companies making products for military. He acquires government contracts through his Pentagon connections. Jenna Cole died when Kris was 18 in a traffic accident.

Standish was required to pay damages to the Cole family which went to Mrs. Cole and Kris. The initial payment was a 5-million-dollar award for a malpractice suit. Then an additional amount undisclosed to cover Kris's medical expenses for life. Reasoning being that because of complications during surgery in which Kris ended up in a coma from a previously unknown anesthesia allergy doctors could not remove the prosthetic device.

There is a mention of a condition I have never heard of: Gender Dual Chromosomal Zonation or they abbreviate it as GenZ. According to my father's information it is a genetic condition where children are born with no gender; or rather as XXXY, but with no sexual or reproductive organs. Research is still being done, but what they know is that children with this condition are both male and female, yet neither. Some children develop a gender around puberty when the body is triggered by the pituitary gland to start producing hormones. The body 'chooses' either male or female and starts development as it should have in utero; but its stilted. Development must be aided by hormone therapy which rapidly develops the genitals and sexual organs. Some cases the body stays truly androgynous with no further development. It was believed Kris had the latter form based on the little information available at the time.

   According to Jenna Cole's testimony, Major Cole would not accept Kris's condition and insisted on listing male on the birth certificate. Kris was raised as a boy. Mrs. Cole testified she hoped she could change Major Cole's attitude regarding their child, but over time he became angrier and more abusive toward her and Kris when it was mentioned, so she worked behind his back to get answers while he was deployed. She had scheduled appointments with several genetic specialists to examine Kris, but before they could go her mother had a stroke, and she had to leave to care for her. Major Cole was recalled from assignment to be with Kris while she was away, and an argument ensued. While Mrs. Cole was gone Major Cole contacted his buddy

Standish and figured once it was fait-accompli she would let it go. While Kris was in the hospital the doctors ran tests to determine Kris's gender. During the trial the judge gave Kris a sealed envelope with the results. Kris took the envelope and tore it into pieces and dropped it into a garbage can then grabbed the judge's lighter and set it on fire. Kris said since the prosthetic could not be removed, and would have to live life as a male, it was better to just let it alone. Kris did not want to be put in the position of having to lie or evade because of the physical characteristics supported by the prosthetic. Kris accepted living life as male regardless of what the truth was."

"Did they make any mention of being able to remove the device once Kris was older?"

"The allergy made that highly unlikely a possibility, according to the doctor's testimony, but not impossible. They made sure not to be definitive as to not get Kris or Jenna's hopes up if it did not come to pass."

"Court files regarding minors are sealed to protect the minor. How did your father get them?"

"My uncle Antonio is the Attorney General for the State of Illinois."

Alario handed the file to the Colonel. The Colonel started to flip through the file while Lieutenant Commander Campbell asked to read the medical file on GenZ.

"This is fascinating. The doctor who discovered this disorder pioneered gender research. 1 in 43,000 children are born without gender due to various developmental irregularities. He said this one differs from other gender disorders as the child does not identify with a gender role due to a lack of dominant gender specific hormones in childhood. In many cases they identify as both male and female having an unusual affinity toward both. They are truly androgynous, assimilating the roles of both genders to the best benefit. They identify with both genders and tend to be able handle gender specific problems easily and work as a type of liaison between genders."

Alario and Stirling both laughed. Kris was always acting as a mediator when it came to getting men and women working together to the best advantage in the field. Kris was admired by the female Marines for being able to understand their unique challenges in battle and helping them overcome prejudice within the ranks. Male Marines admired Kris for both being tough and no nonsense, a born leader and a fearless fighter.

"Oh, yeah. Kris is well known for that. Last year Kris bought, and secretly donated, portable female stand up urinal devices like campers use in the wild to the division for all the forward deployed female Marines because of the vulnerability of female troops losing sight lines when squatting to urinate in the field. This put the men and women at risk. Several casualties ensued when snipers and insurgents opened fire on mixed gender teams either targeting the females while they were vulnerable squatting in the sand or targeting the males who moved in to protect the females; so, Kris leveled the playing field. Only, everyone knew it was Kris. It made Kris a hero with the women. The only guy not threatened by them being there."

Campbell laughed. "Fascinating!"

Colonel Stirling smiled at Campbell's enthusiasm but looked severely at Alario.

"The shit is going to hit the fan when Division gets a hold of this."

"Yeah, that's why I wanted to have as much information as possible before we spoke. You know what they'll say about Cole not knowing--Bullshit."

"What's the big deal? So, Cole is female? That doesn't change anything."

Stirling and Alario looked at the doctor shaking their heads.

Stirling answered. "You have a lot to learn about the bureaucracy and politics of combat doctor. We do have women in combat and forward deployed, but women in Special Forces is a sticky subject. Only since 2013 have women been allowed in spec-ops units. Only a handful are able to pass the strict and rigorous training. Kris joined the Raiders in 2009. No way anyone is going to believe Kris didn't know. Someone out there is going to make this a big deal saying it's some sort of political statement or publicity stunt to prove women can compete in the combat arena. Many people think women do not belong in such units. The standards are brutal, most men cannot pass the training. Then there is the gender bias that exists between men and women. It is both physical and social. Men are physically stronger; women have proven to be psychologically stronger. Socially the gender roles tend to educate males to protect and defend females, which can be a liability in the field. If they stop fighting to help a female it can jeopardize their safety. Also, if a male gets wounded; can a female carry them out? Then there is the need for females to prove themselves as capable, tough, and skilled as the males which makes them take unnecessary risks to show they deserve to be there. It is quite simply a shit storm. Something like this stirs the pot for both sides of the argument. At any rate they will be in a tug of war with Cole as the rope. Each one using Kris as an example of why they are right without taking into consideration the special circumstances. This could mean an end to a promising career. If Kris is allowed to continue what will it be like? Kris will have to work with men once called friends who will look at Kris as a freak. They won't know how to treat her. She'll be ostracized. Anyone who sides with her could find themselves in the same boat."

"I can't believe people would be that inflexible. With all the information people have now and the education they can get on subjects online that kind of ignorance is misplaced!"

Alario added, "Doctor, you understand this. Let's use this in a medical analogy; AIDS."

The doctor nodded, while Colonel Stirling looked questionably.

"When AIDS was first diagnosed people were terrified. No one really knew anything about the illness or how it really was transmitted. Anyone with the illness was a pariah. Everyone was told it was a death sentence. If you had it, you would spread it. If you had it, you would die. People hid the truth for years to maintain a normal life. You could lose your job, your insurance benefits, your relationships; everything out of ignorance and fear. Many still hide it for the same reasons. Medical science knows more now, but the old fears persist. I fear it will be similar for Kris. Marines for all their toughness are rather narrow minded. They are warriors, not scholars or philosophers. They won't look at the details, just the result. Kris pretended to be a man. We know that's not the case, but the rumors and bullshit will carry like a brush fire and the truth will be lost underfoot. "

"Right now, I am ordering you two to keep this to yourselves. For Cole's sake. I will need to talk to Command about this. Your report, Lieutenant Commander Campbell, said Cole will be sent to Landstuhl Hospital at the end of the week for additional treatment?"

"Yes."

"Well when you send the paperwork, list Cole as female and don't say anything of this condition. Only the straight medical facts of the injuries. What they don't know won't hurt Cole. In the meantime we need to tell Kris."

"Sir with your permission I'd like to be the one to tell Kris. We've been best friends for eight years. I think Kris will take it better from someone trusted."

"Agreed. Give it a day or two. Let Cole rest up. I don't know how she'll take it and I don't want to set her back."

"Agreed Colonel."

"Dismissed."

The two men saluted the Colonel and left the office.

Stirling opened the bottom drawer and pulled out a worn picture frame showing a younger Stirling with a beautiful blond woman and child at a martial arts competition. The child was missing two front teeth and holding up the coveted black belt with a huge smile. Stirling had his arm around the woman who was holding the child. The child who was now lying wounded across the compound.

"Oh Jenna. I let you down. I promised you I'd keep Kris safe. It looks like you have a little girl now baby. I know you'd be so proud of what she's accomplished. I miss you." He placed the photo back in the desk drawer.

Stirling gathered up all the information Alario brought with him, the doctor's reports, all of Kris's PER and fitness reports and loaded them into his briefcase. He would read everything through in quarters. He was interested in learning what Jenna had been hiding from him. He knew there was more to Kris's so called 'injury' she wasn't telling him that resulted in the prosthetic. He began thinking of the next step; all the while praying he was able to make the powers that be see reason and keep Kris where she belonged. Leading a Raider team.

Chapter Four

Kris floated in and out of consciousness for several days. There were times she could feel someone holding her hand. She heard bits and pieces of conversation and slipped in and out of dreams. Sometimes they were separate, but sometimes they morphed together.

***

"Stop coddling the boy. He needs to toughen up."

Kris was breathing shallowly out of his mouth trying not to cry. The boys in his class took special delight in tormenting him at recess and after school. Today several older boys ganged up and knocked Kris around. The six-year-old was terrified to go to school. Jenna held Kris's hand while dabbing at the blood on his fat lip and bloody nose. His father looked on disgusted at Kris's red eyes and pale face. He left the room and went into the den to sit in his chair and watch the news.

"I hate him."

The calmly stated statement shook Jenna and she looked concerned into Kris's golden-brown eyes.

"I had a friend once who said the best way to keep kids out of trouble and to build confidence is to learn martial arts. You can learn to defend yourself and build your confidence. What do think, Baby?"

Kris nodded, thinking of beating the bullies to a pulp. Over the next several weeks Kris worked like a Trojan to learn. He checked books out of the library and read about all the disciplines and settled on Aikido. He researched different schools and found one with a teacher who was a former military officer who studied Martial Arts in Asia. Kris started by attending classes twice a week building skills. By the time he was in a year he trained daily and had surpassed many of the older students and started competing on a state level. He learned discipline and patience. He did not beat the bullies to a pulp, but deflected all attempts to bully him. Eventually they gave up.

They also grew to fear him as his skill compounded. The proudest day in his life was the day he earned his black belt at age eight. The youngest his sensei had ever taught to do so. The more he learned and the more skill he amassed the less his father picked on him when he was home. It didn't make him love Kris more, but made him more like invisible to the Major. Invisible was good. If the Major didn't see him, he couldn't belittle him.

Sheldon Cole was intolerant of Kris's condition. Having a son that had no genitals was an embarrassment to the large muscular man who felt having a son just as tough as he was just what he deserved. He felt it was a slight to his manhood that his son was small and deformed. As an Army Ranger he was feared. He tended to be short of temper and brutal which did not earn him respect in the ranks. He had stalled out as a Major and it did not appear that Lieutenant Colonel was in his future. He ruled his family with the same disregard and disdain he had for anyone junior to him. He ruled with an iron fist and no one gainsays anything the Major said. The couple had few friends and the few friends Kris made were never invited over to the house.

Kris's greatest joy was when his father was deployed. Then it was just him and his mom. She made his life amazing. Jenna Cole was as compassionate as her husband was intolerant. She taught Kris that it did not matter how you looked on the outside, but how you were on the inside. She taught Kris the meaning of the word strength. She raised him gender neutral and taught him how to be a strong person without needing to rely on gender. She taught him to use tools and cook, to build and sew, and to rely on instinct and self over anything else. She encouraged him to study and be smart as well as athletic. Kris tended to be a bit of a loner, but still managed to have friends and be popular. As Kris grew his confidence grew as well.

***

"Kris honey, I have to go away for a little while. Your dad is coming home to take care of you." Nothing his mom could have said would have put terror in the ten-year old's heart but that. Kris hated his father and was scared to death of him. Just prior to this last deployment his mom and dad yelled like he had never heard. They were fighting over him. He didn't understand it all, something about his mysterious condition; the one that made him different from other boys. His mom only stood up to his dad when it was about him. They had been talking about seeing some doctors, specialists, to find out more about his 'condition'. His dad wouldn't allow it. The day his mom left to care for his grandmother after her stroke Kris wondered if he would ever see her again. He had a sinking feeling and wanted to cry.

 Two days later his dad told him he had a doctor's appointment, and he wouldn't be going to school. The doctor's office wasn't like any other doctor he had seen. No one here looked sick. Everyone was pretty and dressed in expensive clothes. The pictures on the wall made Kris blush. They were parts of naked people. Everyone smiled too much, and Kris was very nervous. His father shook the hand of the doctor like an old, trusted friend and they went back into an exam room. The doctor made Kris take off his clothes and put on a gown. The doctor examined him, and he talked with his father in low tones Kris couldn't hear. Then they both left, and a nurse came in with a tray.

"This will only pinch a second honey," as she lifted a syringe and examined the fluid inside. Just then his dad came back in with the doctor and Kris wanted to run. He didn't want a shot. While he was distracted the nurse jabbed his arm. He jumped and flinched. Pinch my ass, that hurt! He was going to tell his dad he wanted to go, but everything got really blurry and everyone sounded like they were talking from far away.

The next thing Kris heard was his mom's voice. She was upset, and it sounded like she'd been crying. He couldn't open his eyes. His head felt heavy. When he got his eyes open nothing made sense. There were police in the room and his mom was sitting on the side of the bed. She had tears on her face and in her voice. The police were asking questions. Kris didn't know what happened. Everything faded out and he went back under.

When he woke up again he was alone. His mom was outside of the room talking to a doctor. Kris looked around his head and there were machines beeping and buzzing all around him. He had hoses connected to him everywhere. He looked around and shifted a little. There was a strange feeling from between his legs. It felt heavy. He lifted the covers and saw bandages around his hips and between his legs. He tore at them and stared in horror at the appendage that now lay there. He'd seen pictures of penises and his dad's getting out of the shower but now he had one attached to him. The skin on it was shiny and pink. It was too large for his small body and he was disgusted by it. He tried to pull it off and the pain made him scream almost as much as the horror. His mom and the doctor came at a run and restrained him as he screamed and thrashed. The nurses tied his hands to the bed as his mother begged him not to fight and to please let the doctor help. He continued to scream until a nurse put a needle in the tube going into his arm and the world got wavy and dim again.

When he woke this time, his mom was sitting next to the bed. She explained to him that his dad had a surgeon attach a penis and scrotum, so he would look like other boys. That he did it without asking was a crime. The doctor that performed the surgery committed a crime and they would pay for what they did.

"Can they take it off?" Kris asked weakly.

"No baby, they can't. You almost died in the surgery. If they tried again you may not wake up. The doctor said maybe in a couple of years when you get bigger and stronger they can try again. But right now, it has to stay." Jenna started crying when she saw the tears leaking out of Kris's eyes. The hopelessness in her child's face filled her with rage. The only bright light was the information the doctor inadvertently gave her. Kris's blood type was B+. Her blood type was A+. She held onto what that meant like a talisman.

The publicity around the trial made school difficult so moving from Washington to California enabled Kris to start over where no one knew him, and he could have a clean slate. California was great. It was warm, it didn't rain all the time, and he met his best friend ever. He became a skater and grew out his hair. Learned to surf. He was finally in a place where he could be himself. When his mom took in his best friend when he was twelve he had shed the last of the fear of nonacceptance and learned to live his life freely. She changed everything.

***

Amalia El Moufas was a small shy girl who was raised in a strict
Middle Eastern family. She had attended an all-girl boarding
school in London with many Eastern girls like herself. American
culture was a shock to her. California was as far from London as
you could get, and not in just miles. Here was a culture shock
from the insulated Muslim community she had always known;
the first coed school she had ever attended and did not know how
to interact with boys. She sat apart from other kids at lunch and
kept to herself. They made fun of her traditional dress and head
covering. Kris recognized another lost and scared soul and asked
to sit with her. She refused at first since Kris was a boy and there
were rules in her culture against it, but Kris did not give up.
After a while she gave in and they became friends. He helped her
navigate American slang and she taught him Pashtu. He gave
her her first nickname. After a few weeks they were inseparable.
She was a year older than him, so they didn't have any classes
together, but met for lunch every day and hung out both before
and after school. By the end of the school year, he noticed a
change in her behavior. She would get scared and withdrawn.
He figured something was going on at home, but she refused to
say what. One day she did not come to school and wouldn't
answer when he called. She had a spare Firaq partug and tsadar
in her locker, so Kris picked the lock and took it out and put it in
his backpack. When he got home he changed into it and went to
her house which was two miles away. He rang the bell and said
he was her friend from school and was bringing her homework
from today's lessons. He was let in and sent to her room. She
was sitting in the corner crying. When he came in she was
terrified.

"You can't be here! If my father finds a boy in my room he will
beat me!" She tried to push him out of the door.

He put his hand over her mouth and pushed the smaller girl back
into the room and closed the door.

"The woman who answered the door thinks I'm a girlfriend from
school. It'll be ok."

Just then her door opened, and a handsome charismatic man came in. Amalia bowed her head as did Kris knowing this was her father.

"Who is this?" Amalia kept her head down as she answered him. Kris responded in passible Pashtu the traditional greeting.

"This is Faith. We go to school together. She brought me my homework from school. She is my friend."

Her father looked Kris up and down then left the room. Amalia just about fainted from relief.

"Kris you must go, you can't be here."

"Tell me you are ok. I won't leave you here alone."

"I am scared. My father is arranging my marriage to an old man. I started my woman's time and he said it is time to be married. I won't marry him. My mother just ignores my pleas. She spends more time at the water pipe than ever and she doesn't hear me. She won't stand up to him. I don't know what to do!" She started to cry again.

"You can come live with us. We will take care of you. I'll tell my mom and we'll come get you!"

"You can't! If he knows I told anyone he will kill me. Girls are not allowed to disagree with their parents. Our only worth is in how good a marriage we can have to bring honor to our family."

Kris was disgusted. He thought his father was bad. Kris wrote down his address and phone number in the back of one of Amalia's books. "If you ever need a safe place, you call me, day or night. If you run away, you come to me. We will hide you and keep you safe. Please promise me Amalia, I can't leave you here otherwise."

"I promise Krissy. I will."

Kris went home and told his mother of the situation at Amalia's house. They agreed to help her anyway they could. Kris went to Amalia's house every day after school and throughout the summer dressed as a girl to watch over Amalia. He learned a great deal about the family. Kris was smart and cautious. He watched everything the family did knowing that something was off with all of them. Amalia's uncles would come from Afghanistan to stay and when they did many men would patrol the grounds and all of them were armed. Kris started carrying a portable recorder and kept a small camera on hand to photograph any papers or items of interest. They never paid any attention to him and didn't realize he was gaining intel on them that would come back to haunt them. Jenna became certified for emergency foster care so if Amalia needed somewhere to go, she would be able to stay with them. Within the next year that promise was put to the test. Amalia showed up beaten and bleeding from several rapes. Her father had sold her virginity to a man of great influence to gain favor. After the man had fallen asleep Amalia had climbed out the window and ran the two miles to Kris's house barefoot and in only a t-shirt and underwear. Jenna and Kris took her to the hospital where she was examined, and the police called.

When they arrived at her father's house several more underage girls were discovered to have been raped by several men there. The man Amalia described as her attacker was an Afghan diplomat with diplomatic immunity. He was released. Her father however was arrested for facilitating an auction of seven ten to twelve-year-old girls, including his daughter, and for the large number of drugs discovered under the search warrant. Amalia's mother was arrested on drug charges and for depraved indifference. Amalia testified at their trials.

Aziz El Moufas, Amalia's father, was well connected in Afghanistan. He was the youngest son of Nadir El Moufas who was a tribal leader and on America's watch list as a suspected terrorist. His father and brothers Amir, Saiyid, Farouk were arms dealers disguised as successful businessmen and suspected to be ranking members in the Taliban. They were clever and knew how to cover their tracks. They did not take very kindly to American authorities incarcerating one of their own. He was an embarrassment with his drinking and partying which brought unwanted attention to them; but his ability to make contacts and give the authorities someone to concentrate on allowed the rest to quietly gain wealth and power. That he squandered so much of that in his hedonistic lifestyle angered them. Not enough to cut him loose as he still had his purposes. He was also the only one with a child. Amalia was the tribal heir.

After the trial the Justice Department placed Amalia in protective custody, but the convoy of U.S. Marshalls bringing her to the safehouse where she would stay until she was put in witness protection were ambushed and slaughtered. Amalia was able to get away and hide in a drain yards from the carnage. She recognized the men as her father's and knew if they caught her, her life was over. She stayed hidden for three days. She hitchhiked with a trucker to Utah where she called Kris.

Only one person in the Justice Department knew of Jenna and Kris's place in Amalia's life. He redacted their names from the official reports to protect them. They informed him of Amalia's survival and he arranged for them to have documents for Amalia El Moufas to have a new identity. Papers that would hide her as Kris's sister. He told them not to contact him again as there was a mole in the US Government and Amalia's life was in danger. They drove to Utah to pick up Amalia and kept driving east. Jenna drove east with a mission. Get Amalia as far away from California as possible and lose themselves in the rest of the country. They moved several times over the next couple of years. Kris felt it was wise to stay on the move and off the grid as much as possible. They stayed in areas where people came and went and no one questioned or cared. The hopped around the Southwest for two months. Jenna home schooled the kids. Mostly they taught themselves. Kris and Amalia were dedicated students and studied much harder and longer than they had to. The longest was on a ranch in Texas for four years.

***

Kris walked very quietly behind the man he was stalking. He'd taken off his boots so as not to make a noise. The ranch that Kris and his family were staying on was the coolest place ever. Kris had never seen land stretch out so far that towns couldn't be seen in any direction. There were no roads either. This area of South Texas was close to the border so that most everyone spoke Spanish and English. Kris and Emily were learning. They could already talk with the Mexican cowboys and be understood. They got to ride horses every day and the chores they were assigned were so much fun it wasn't like it was work. Mucking out stalls and feeding the horses and chickens was fun. Kris's mom got a job on the ranch as a domestic foreman. A fancy way of saying housekeeper. She made sure the women who came to clean twice a week were getting the job done and run any errands needed by the owners. They didn't go into town often because it took two hours to get there. Most of that was on the ranch and only a little was the road for town. It was one of the largest ranches in all of Texas and an 11-year-old boys dream. Kris loved roping and riding and listening to the cowboys tell stories. His favorite was Buck. an old tough leatherneck who ran the bunkhouse and bossed the cowboys around.

He followed the old man out of sight of the bunkhouse and into the bush. Kris liked to stay late and listen to the cowboys but his mom was getting mad at the salty stories and language Kris came back with. He promised to be in by 8 o'clock but he wanted to know where Buck went every night. He thought he stayed in the bunkhouse, but he didn't. He walked into the wild and disappeared. Kris held back so Buck wouldn't hear him, but he started to lose sight of him in the dark. He stopped to see if he could hear the older man walking but he couldn't hear anything. The lights of the bunk house were getting dim and he didn't want to get lost. He was debating whether he should turn back when an arm came around his neck holding a knife.

Kris didn't hesitate. With skill honed in martial arts he hit a pressure point on his assailant's arm above the wrist and disarmed him while spinning around and capturing him in an arm hold with the knife hand behind his back and pinned. He realized quickly the man was Buck and let him go. He jumped back as the man lunged for the knife that had fallen to the ground.

"What in the hell are you doing boy? You want to die? You don't sneak up on man out hear in this country. That is how you get shot or worse. You got a death wish boy?"

"No Sir."

"Then explain yourself."

"You don't stay in the bunkhouse. And no one knows where you go. I wanted to see."

"That's my business kid. People around here stay out of one another's business. Another lesson for you."

"Yes Sir."

"I will say one thing for you. You are smart. Ain't no one figured out that I go. You are quiet too. If I wasn't trained to hear a flea crawling on a dog I wouldn't've heard you. You work hard and you don't sass. You're smart and you learn fast. Faster than I've ever seen. What's your name boy?"

"Kris Sir."

"You got hair like a girl, boy."

"Yes Sir."

"We have never allowed that in the Corps."

"The Corps Sir?"

"The Marine Corps boy."

He looked Kris up and down.

"You know how to shoot boy?"

"No Sir."

"Why not?"

"My mother won't let me Sir. She says it's dangerous."

"Only dangerous if you don't know how. Something you need to know out here. Not all predators are on four legs here. You want to learn?"

"More than anything Sir. Yes Sir."

"Well we'll make a Marine outta you yet. You come to the corral after chores and I'll settle it with your Ma."

"Yes Sir!!"

Kris's smile lit up in the pitch black so even Buck could see it.

"Now you go back to the ranch and you wiggle that porch light when you get there. Don't let me catch you following me again. I like my privacy. One day if I learn to trust you I may show you where I go, but you ain't there yet. Now git."

"Yes Sir."

Kris made his way back to the ranch. Being quick but not running since that was a good way to break an ankle. When he got back to the porch he flickered the light to let Buck know he got back ok. He couldn't wait for the next day.

Buck showed him how to use a gun. Then a rifle. He taught Kris how to site stationary targets and moving targets. Buck was a sniper in Viet Nam. His stories of kills fascinated the young boy. The more Buck showed him the more Kris was determined to learn. Kris's days were chores, school with the ranch tutor, more chores, and shooting. He barely missed his skateboard.

That first April on the ranch the rains were horrible. Floods everywhere. No one went out that didn't have to. Kris hated being inside. He mended tack and did extra barn chores but still ran out of things to do. He walked to a barn on the far edge of the compound that wasn't in use. It was huge; at least three stories tall and as big as a football field. The roof was rotting in spots, so it leaked in several places. The owners only used it for storage and kept talking about tearing it down. The old structure was solid though and would cost more to demolish than a new building would to build so it stayed. Kris got permission to practice martial arts there. He had several videos that showed him advanced techniques so he didn't lose skill. He still competed in several tournaments a year but it was hard to get away with his mom's job. Also he didn't want to leave his sister behind and she was finally not scared anymore being on the ranch. She loved it. It offered her the first security she'd had in a long while.

Kris and Emily earned money for chores and Kris banked his not needing anything on the ranch. One day the rain got to be too much and he headed in for the ranch business office. He waited for the ranch manager to finish on the phone before he spoke.

"What can I help you with Kris?"

"I was wondering if I could build something in the old storage barn."

"What were you thinking on building in there?"

"A skate park."

"A what?"

Kris laughed at the man's confusion.

"A skate park. It's a series of ramps and turns used by skaters Sir."

"What would you build it out of?"

"Lumber. I was going to draw up a plan and get some idea of how much I need and how much it'll cost to see if I have enough saved. But first I need permission. No sense in doing the work if the answer is no."

The man looked at the boy. He didn't wheedle or whine. He wasn't sullen or smartass like a lot of boys his age. He worked hard, never complained, always asked for extra duties, and never gave sass when he was asked to help the women. In fact, he always checked with them before going out to the men to work. It was a rare quality to see in a person of his age. Instead of getting into trouble, the kid would practice martial arts in the old barn. He'd asked to put up bags and obstacles and never complained when they needed to be taken down when the barn was in use.

"Would this be something that could be moved when the barn is needed?"

"Yes Sir. I could build it in sections that could be moved with a four-wheeler if the barn was needed."

"Well then I'll say yes."

"Thank you, Sir. I'll work out what I need for lumber so we can add it to the monthly order. Thanks again."

The next day Kris had a working plan. A list of materials and cash money on the manager's desk for the order. Two weeks later the shipment came in and his lumber and materials were placed in the barn. Kris asked for everyone to stay out while he was building. The cowboys thought he was crazy. Two weeks later he was done and invited everyone on the ranch over after supper to see what the crazy boy was up to. They were stunned. The boy had built an amazing set up. A long straight run went into a curved angled run that fed into several small jumps. Two ramps set ten feet apart facing one another leading to a half pike. The area to the side had raised plywood decks with metal pipes on long runs for stunts and tricks. Kris already had the area to the back set up with varying bales of hay to practice Parkour. A tough street training discipline that required strength and balance moving from different elevations and using running, climbing, swinging, vaulting, jumping, rolling and balance. Kris saw it in Nevada during their brief stay and decided to try it. It aided with martial arts and helped Kris keep up his balance. Kris climbed the ladder for the first ramp which stood a full story tall. He put on his helmet and pads and shot a cocky grin at the cowboys. Jenna just shook her head. She worried Kris was going to break his neck.

He leapt off the top grabbing air while grabbing his deck and performing a full 360 flip over the jump to the opposite ramp. He jumped from the ramps to the level course and took the curve at breakneck speed. He jumped his deck to ride the low pole all the way down and performed a bull flip. He picked up his deck and followed the ramp to the full pike where he ramped up his speed to make the top and hit a 360. He hit the downslide and went up the opposite to hit a Japan Air. He kept on the pike for a bit showing off then got down to walk over to the crowd who was hooting and hollering very loudly. He was flushed with heat and happiness. He really had missed catching air since coming to Texas. No sidewalks or roads to hit on the ranch.

Buck stood off the side taking in the young man. He didn't say anything but nodded to him once and left. That hurt Kris a bit, as the old man's opinion really mattered to him. Kris's happiness dimmed a little with Buck leaving.

The next day it was dry enough to work outside and Kris got to work. His muscles were sore from skating. He hadn't done anything like that in close to a year. But he never complained. Buck grabbed him about halfway through the day and took him out into the ranch. They rode for a long while before Buck stopped. He dismounted and signaled to Kris to do so. He pulled a long leather bag out of the side holster of his saddle.

"C'mere boy. This is a Model 70 Marine Corps sniper rifle. This baby was mine during the war. A finer firearm does not exist. I have 74 confirmed kills with this weapon. It is a precision firing solution and not a toy. I am going to show you how to use this weapon with skill and accuracy. Normally I wouldn't waste time showing a boy how to use this fine weapon but you are not a boy. What I saw yesterday was the steel of man. Pure nerve and grit. You tackled that crazy course you built with strength and confidence. You built it to challenge yourself. You built it yourself so you would have the pride of ownership. Then you offered to let the other kids use it. But only if they got their own skateboard. You protected your equipment. When you were done you cleaned and oiled that thing like it was a classic hot rod car. You put it in a case to protect it from the dirt and you put it away. Just like all the tools you used. Every one put away and cleaned after use. That is man's mind, not a boy's."

Kris sat there stunned. He thought Buck left. To hear his hero was impressed with him made Kris work hard to earn the accolade. He listened and learned. After a year Kris was able to hit a moving target at 600 yards. By the end of the second year he was able to hit a target in high wind at a 1000 yards. He soaked up everything that Gunnery Sergeant Arlon Buckley had to teach him. Buck had been a sniper in the field and after being wounded went home to teach at the Marine Corps Sniper school. Every sniper he trained had the highest skill ratio in the Corps. Many were record holders. By the time Kris was 14 he was a fully trained sniper. He read all of Buck's Corps training manuals and every book on weapons he could find. Buck finally trusted him enough to show him his home.

Buck lived in an underground bunker on land he purchased from the ranch. The parcel was ten square acres of rock and scrub. Not suitable for grazing or anything. He built his home himself and it was built to withstand a nuclear blast. He had tunnels that let out on the far side of the property hidden by natural brush. He had enough supplies to live down there for six months. It had its own water supply and air supply and was completely self-sustaining. Kris was amazed at the engineering. He thought Buck's reasons for it were a little wild. He was one of those extreme guys that gave survivalists a bad name. One convinced the government was going to come for him. They might at that.

He had every type of firearm ever made. Handguns, long guns, rifles, machine guns, semi-automatic, automatic, manual, and selective fire. Every make and model, every manufacturer, and some homemade ones. Every caliber was represented. The walls of the bunker were lined with enough firepower to start a war. Hundreds. Kris was shown how to break down, clean, and operate every one of them. Only half were registered. Kris didn't know that the other half were illegal. Some because they were military, some because they were bought on the black market, most because they weren't legal to import into this country. Kris learned everyone to the point where he could recite all the specs and details of the weapon including its perks and flaws. He learned to recognize the sound they all made so that he could pick them out blind folded.

When Kris was about to turn 15 he started to get restless on the ranch. He withdrew from everyone. Jenna finally called him on it and he confessed what was bothering him. He wanted to leave the ranch. They'd been there four years and even though he learned a lot he wanted to go to high school. He knew if he was going to join the Corps, ROTC would make a difference and gain him rank. They discussed it the over the summer. Emily agreed that Kris should go. The hardest part for Kris was saying goodbye to Buck. He couldn't keep the tears at bay. Even though Buck said Marines don't cry he could see Buck wiping his eyes with his kerchief as they drove away.

They felt enough time had passed and Amalia had sufficiently changed in appearance for it to be safe to return to a populated area and enter into a traditional school. After Texas they went to Georgia. Kris had researched schools and found one adjacent to a Marine Corps base that had an excellent ROTC program. Once they rented a house and settled in Jenna started some research of her own. Jenna was looking for someone she had lost touch with long ago; a man who would become a pivotal part of all of their lives.

***

Kris felt a hand holding his hand again. The hand was familiar. Justin. Justin was holding his hand. He hadn't left. He'd been a great friend since the beginning. That fateful day eight years ago in Major Benson's office.

***

Kris had drawn corridor duty and was standing guard outside General Sacks office. Major Benson, his aid, was meeting with an Afghan General and his staff. Justin was serving as the Major's aide as he had trained in several Afghan dialects. The man had brought his own translator, but the division head wanted someone there who could verify the communications.

They stood outside the corridor talking for several minutes. Justin caught the expression change on Kris's face. Cole's features tightened, and his eyes grew flinty. A muscle in his cheek twitched as his stance which was alert before became taught. He did not betray his change in demeanor to the men around him; Justin was trained to see imperceptible details. He noticed how Kris's hand kept twitching as he worked hard to keep his hand from making a fist. Kris's eyes quickly darted to the men and his face darkened even more.

Just then the General let of a long string of sentences that ended in him referring to the Major with a word the Marine Corps had ordered members of color to remove from their vocabulary. Kris wiped all emotion from his features and tried not to look at Major Benson's face. The large heavily built black officer was staring at the man trying to figure out if he was trying to be insulting or if he should address the comment at all when the translator explained that he heard it was considered a term of solidarity among men of color and since the General was also of dark skin, he was trying to affect a bond of friendship between himself and the Major. Justin, like Kris had wiped his face of all expression. While the Major was struggling with a response, Second Lieutenant Alario tried to explain to him that the relaxed slang term was not something the Marine Corps encouraged as it was not necessarily used as a positive connotation. Kris knew the comment was meant to bait the Major but stayed still and continued to glare at the wall. Kris held his ground as they concluded speaking and Justin walked them out to the waiting staff car that would escort them off base. When he came back to Benson's office, Kris was summoned inside.

"Staff Sergeant Cole, you seemed rather upset at the General and his men. Care to tell us why?"

Kris turned to Alario and answered, "I do not like assholes, Sir. And assholes who deliberately insult their host to their face thinking no one will understand them are not to be trusted. They have no respect for the Major, the Corps, or Americans, Sir. They are not here to make peace, but to make trouble, Sir."

The Major looked to Justin and he nodded that Kris's assessment was correct. The Major asked Kris to relate to him what was said. Kris repeated the entire conversation verbatim including their own responses. Two of the men spoke in a different dialect from the General and Kris translated that as well. The Major was impressed. Not only could Kris recognize and translate several dialects but obviously had a photographic memory which allowed him to act like a human tape recorder.

Major Benson reassigned Kris to work under Justin. Kris was being wasted holding down a corridor. As Kris left with Justin to fill out paperwork for his reassignment the two Marines walked silently down the hall until they reached the end of the corridor and entered the elevator. As soon as the doors closed the two Marines looked at each other both recalling the look on Benson's face at the meeting. They burst out laughing nearly collapsing with mirth. They were in tears by the time they reached the first floor and exited into the admin area. After an hour long debriefing and several forms in triplicate the two bonded. After work they grabbed a beer. It didn't take long for the two to become inseparable. The next year Kris informed him of his plan to enter into Special Forces training. Justin decided to further his career by going with him.

***

Kris drifted again and heard a woman's voice. Mom?

"Kris, I want you and your sister to be home tonight we are having company for dinner."

"Ok Mom. Who is it? We finally going to meet this guy you've been sneaking around with?" Kris said with a teasing smile. His sister, now known as Emily, walked in and punched Kris in the arm for teasing their mother.

Jenna looked shocked. She had been very careful to hide her relationship from the kids. She didn't want to upset them.

"How did you know about that?"

"C'mon Mom! You are as stealthy as an elephant! We have known for months you've been seeing someone. So, do we finally get to meet him or what?"

"Yes. I am sorry Kris; I didn't hide it from you exactly. We knew each other a long time ago and reconnected a couple of years ago, but he has been deployed a lot and every time he seemed to be home you would be away at martial arts camp or a youth retreat and just missed each other. I've wanted you to meet for a long time. Please be here. It is very important to me. I have something very important to talk to you both about."

"Deployed, so he is military?"

"Yes, he's in the Marine Corps. He is Special Forces. I figured that would upset you being Sheldon was...."

"Oh please, Mom! The Major was a dick, that doesn't mean every spec-ops guy is one too. He is the exception, not the rule. Like Lieutenant Colonel Stirling. He's a badass! He's cool and smart and kind and he's special forces. You taught me that every person should be measured on their own merit and to never paint anyone with someone else's brush."

Jenna walked over and pulled Kris into a hug. "I'm sorry I didn't confide in you sooner. I seem to have wasted a great deal of time. Dinner is at 7! I am going to pick up a few things. When you get home from Aikido shower and clean up the bathroom for company." She rushed out into the rain to her car and left.

Kris looked at his grinning sister. "She seems nervous, she must really like this guy."

"I wonder what the important news is? Oh, I bet she is going to marry him! Wow. I always wondered why she didn't date after your dad. She always had guys after her. I bet that's it! What do you think?"

Kris was quiet and thoughtful. If that was it, he hoped this guy measured up. He wanted his mom to be happy but didn't exactly trust her taste in men after his father. That he was military, and spec-ops meant he was tough, but he hoped he was a good man as well. Kris didn't like to borrow trouble, so he would wait and see.

Unfortunately, he would never get the chance to meet this man or hear the important news his mother wanted to tell them. He came home from Aikido to find a police car outside of the house. The rain which had been falling steadily throughout the day had caused several accidents. Jenna was killed in a collision when a car in the opposite lane lost control on the slick roads and crossed the center line. She swerved and hit a light pole dying instantly.

Kris's world came to a crashing halt. Jenna was the heart of their home and they were devastated when they lost her. Then just one week later, Child Protective Services showed up at the door. Since Emily on paper was only 16, she'd be seventeen in two weeks, the state made her a ward of the state and determined to put her in foster care. She was terrified. Really she was 19 but no one knew that and they couldn't tell them. Her small size allowed her to pull off being younger which gave her added protection. Kris was given 30 days to remand her to Child Protective Services. Kris's mom did not have a will that they could find. Kris researched like a man possessed another solution to keep her out of the system. Kris discovered a full proof legal recourse.

Kris had been going around and round with Jenna about joining the military. Kris only returned to public school to take ROTC.

ROTC seemed to fit him like a glove. He loved the structure and rules as well as the comradery. Jenna balked at his joining the military because of his gender condition. Since Kris had never found out what gender he truly had, Jenna felt that entering the military would be asking for trouble. That Kris should find out prior to joining if that is what Kris wanted to do. Kris confided about the prosthetic device in his mentor Lieutenant Colonial Nathan Stirling who assured Kris that it would not be an issue. He told his sister his intention to enlist. She knew how badly he wanted to serve. His plan allowed his sister to complete high school and enroll in college without having to go into foster care. He would keep her safe like he always promised. Always.

***

Kris floated in a cloud of pain. He could hear a radio playing. It sounded like a fight. It was an MMA fight. Ranson VS Lopez. He listened for a couple of minutes before he went under again. Drifting to 9 years ago went he became a big brother to Bobby B Ranson.

Kris loved working with Corps Values a local charity that paired Marines with kids needing a helping hand. The big brother like program helped keep kids who would otherwise be on the streets find positive relationships. Kris's duties at Camp Geiger NC gave him lots of time in the middle of the day which was a key time needed for supervision for most of these kids.

Kris started a charity when he was 18 called the GenZ Foundation. It was an organization that provided information, education, and a forum for discussion for families who had a child or other family member with GenZ. The biggest issue with the condition was the lack of information out there for people to understand it. It was not a well-known gender issue. Families could find doctors who were versed in the condition and read articles regarding hormone therapy and treatments by medical professionals. Parents were able to go and find accurate and relevant information from specialists who knew the disorder and people could share their experiences with others facing the same issues. The forum allowed families to discuss how to handle gender identity issues, how to decide if the child should adopt a gender at an early age, and how to deflect painful questions and ignorance from people unfamiliar with the disorder.

The State of North Carolina foster program had reached out to the foundation regarding a child whose foster family had asked if they had a mentoring program. Bobby Ranson was in the foster system having been born to a teenage mother who couldn't handle the issues of having a child with no gender. Bobby had bounced from home to home never quite fitting in. The ten-year-old was having trouble in school with fights and bullying. They asked if there was anyone they could recommend to mentor the young child during this difficult time. Kris jumped at the chance. He contacted the family through Corps Values and asked if he could be a big brother to Bobby.

When they first met Bobby was sullen and suspicious of Kris. At first the big Marine frightened the young kid a bit after being picked on by so many older boys. Right up until several months into their relationship when Kris dropped a bomb on the kid.

"So I hear you are GenZ?"

The child just looked at the ground not answering. Bobby just gave a shoulder shrug.

"Yeah? Me too."

The kid's head snapped up and looked at the Marine. Bobby was looking for a trick or a joke. There was none.

"Can I tell you something I never told anyone before?"

Bobby nodded.

"When I was born my dad hated me. He told everyone he was having a boy and when I was born not a girl or a boy he hated me. For making him a liar. He couldn't tell everyone he was wrong so he made my mom say I was a boy. She wouldn't. She just learned not to use gender identifiers. She named me Kristian Michel Cole. A gender neutral name. Told my dad 'Michel' was her father's name and that he was French from Quebec. She lied; it was Michael. I was made to dress like a boy and live like a boy. When I was your age he...."

Kris stopped and tried to figure how to say what happened next.

"He made me go to a doctor, a plastic surgeon, who performed a surgery on me to attach a penis to me. He didn't ask and he did it while my mother was out of town. I hadn't gotten old enough for the test so we didn't know if I was a boy or a girl. When the surgery was done he got in big trouble so did the doctor. I almost didn't wake up after the surgery and because of that they can't take it off. When I got old enough for the test I wouldn't have it done. Since they can't take it off I decided to live my life as a male. I still don't know for sure."

The young kid's eyes were about to pop out of his head.

"You're the only person I have ever told. Even my wife doesn't know. Or my best friends. They wouldn't understand. But you do. I can trust you with my secret right?"

Bobby just nodded. He wasn't sure if he believed the Marine or not. But why would he lie? After that the two grew very close. Bobby and Kris spent almost every day together. When Kris joined the Raiders Bobby waited patiently for Kris to finish school and was there when Kris was reassigned to Camp Lejeune. Kris taught Bobby martial arts and how to defend himself from bullying. The foundation gave workshops on how to deal with social issues and stigmas. Bobby took everyone they had. Bobby lived for the days that they hung out. Kris took Bobby routinely to the weight room to workout. Kris's team adopted the kid and Bobby became the team mascot. By the time the kid was 13 Bobby showed remarkable skill in mixed martial arts. So much so Bobby began competing in local and regional competitions. One day Bobby came in to work out and was somber.

"What's up kid?"

Kris could see something was wrong.

"If I wanted to go to the doctor and find out if I am a boy or girl would you go with me?"

"Of course. When are we going?"

The look of worship on the kid's face filled Kris with a warmth and a sense of purpose. Maybe there was a reason for all the difficulties he grew up with. He wrapped an arm around the kid.

"You get your foster mom and dad to set it up and I will be there. I swear."

Two weeks later, just a week before the team was set to deploy, Kris and Bobby's foster parents sat in the hospital waiting room waiting for Bobby to come out. When the door opened he looked at the man who had become his surrogate brother. His foster parents stood smiling.

"Go ahead Bobby. Put us out of our misery."

Kris looked excited and hopeful as Bobby snapped open a t-shirt that said across the front-

Congratulations it's a boy!

They all cheered and Kris lifted the kid up onto his shoulders and carried him around. He laughed at their antics and his hair which was longish in a unisex style was ruffled by large hands giving him atta boy's.

"So Bobby Boy what's next on the agenda?"

"I want to go shopping."

Kris groaned making the boy grin. Kris got it. Bobby was careful to wear clothes that a boy or a girl would wear. Jeans, t-shirts, Converse tennis shoes. Everything gender neutral. Now that he knew he was a boy he wanted to look like one.

"I want to get my hair cut too."

Kris took him over and informed his foster parents he'd be home at a reasonable hour as he took the boy first to the base barber shop for a haircut. Then to the Exchange to pick out some new clothes. He picked out some new high top tennis shoes the guys all liked and some trendy shirts and jackets that were very boy oriented. When they were done they went for a celebratory lunch. The day was full of laughter and good natured teasing. Just before dinner time he got in the car with Kris to go home.

His heart was full and he felt good for the first time in a long time. But he worried about one thing.

"Are you mad at me for finding out?"

Kris looked over at him.

"What? No! Not at all! I am so happy for you Bobby Boy. Kind of jealous though."

Bobby was stunned at the handsome, powerfully built Marine who everyone liked being jealous of him.

"Why Kris?"

"You know. You know what you are and where you fit. I'm still not sure sometimes."

That bit of information rocked the kid's world. Kris was always confident and sure. Everyone went to Kris when they wanted to know what to do. Even the older guys on the team looked up to Kris. Bobby could tell he was their hero too. He thought what that meant. How someone so great and happy still was unsure. How the guy that always knew the answer to everything because he was so smart didn't have the one answer that mattered to him. And couldn't find out either. It made their friendship more important to Bobby. He liked being called Bobby Boy.

As he grew older his skill with MMA grew. He paid it forward by getting a tattoo on his bicep of the GenZ foundation symbol that he and Kris came up with. That way when he fought everyone would see it. He also tattooed the website below it. Kris continued to mentor him and train him in Aikido and Tae Kwando. Any time he started slacking off or not giving it his fullest he reminded him, 'go big or go home.' As his skill grew and he began to fight professionally he gave talks at schools about gender identity. He changed his name to Bobby B Ranson. The 'B' standing for Boy. He also volunteered at the foundation.

At every fight there was a seat in the front row reserved for Kris and his wife Melody. When Kris was down range Melody came alone with a bear that Bobby had given her in a Marine Corps uniform with Kris's badges on it that sat on the chair for Kris. Sometimes Kris brought one of the guys, usually Justin, sometimes it was him and Javier. A couple of times the whole team showed up. Bobby won the title at that match. It was his proudest moment with his whole family present.

Once a month Bobby came to Lejeune to spar with Kris and the 'match' was recorded and aired on Bobby's website. It was such a huge event that the team that sponsored Bobby started setting up a live stream on screens outside the gym for the Marines to watch as the crowd was too large to fit in the gym. Hits on the website were astronomical for the fights because Kris never took it easy on Bobby and Bobby never pulled any punches respecting the Marine too much. Bobby was the number one MMA fighter in the country and Kris was the top in the Armed Services. It was clear to anyone watching them fight that Kris's skill far surpassed that of Bobby. So the fights were epic. Bobby lived for the day he beat Kris in one of their matches. The competitive man who rarely lost in the ring had never beat his mentor. Kris tried to listen to the match on the radio but quickly lost consciousness before hearing the outcome.

***

The team was on a KC-130J heading home after a quick three month deployment. Kris was worried about Justin. The last couple of weeks he'd been moody as hell. He'd picked fights with both Kris and Javier. At one point Javi had to pull them apart. He'd been listening to a bunch of weird music that suited a teenage girl more than a grown man who usually preferred hard rock and hip hop. He usually skyped Trina at least twice a week but hadn't done so the twelve weeks they'd been gone. He said they needed a break. As the transport they were taking home prepared for landing, Kris stared at her best friend. He just stared straight ahead without moving.

When they landed and gathered their gear, Kris could see Mel waiting with the families over in the airfield hanger lounge. Trina was not there.

"Hey guys!" Mel ran up and through her arms around them both. "Justin we'll give you a ride home, ok?"

"Where is Trina?"

"She had to work late. Some sort of project that was supposed to be done last week that has to be in by tomorrow."

"Yeah she mentioned it." He just grabbed his gear and tossed it in the back of Kris's pickup. Mel looked at Kris furtively and handed Kris the keys. They guys got in the truck and they drove home. They dropped Justin off and Mel climbed up into the front seat he just vacated.

"Something is really going on between those two and I don't think it's good."

"Yeah. He hasn't said much but he's torn up man. I hope he talks to me about it soon; before I have to kick his ass."

Mel rubbed Kris's arm and they drove home.

When Justin walked into the house it was empty. Just as he expected. There was a horrible smell from the kitchen. Trina hadn't taken out the trash. He grabbed the bag and walked around to the other trash cans in the house and added them to the bag to fill it up. After dumping the trash and pushing it down to fit the last bit, he noticed a box had ripped the bag. Holding it up to make sure the bag would hold he took a look at the box that was buried in the bottom of the can. It was a pregnancy test. Justin's body got very hot. Then very cold. He had wanted to have a child since the moment they married but Trina did not want children. He took that to mean right then, that she wanted to wait. After a year of marriage he realized she meant never. She wanted to be free and unencumbered and figured she'd talk him around. He wanted the security and joy of watching their family grow and figured he'd talk her around. Five years later they were still circling the subject.

Two nights before the team deployed he woke in the middle of the night as she got up. She went into the bathroom and swore. He got up to check on her and her underwear and t-shirt were covered with blood. He turned back to the bed and saw the dark patch in the dim light. He turned on the overhead light to see the sheets bloody. He stripped the bed while Trina took a quick shower. They remade the bed and went to sleep. Her periods were never regular. Sometimes they lasted for a couple of weeks and others only a couple of days. No hormone or birth control worked to regulate them. It was not the first time they'd woke in the night to a mess to clean up. Justin was secretly relieved. She wouldn't have sex if she was on her period because of the pain during intercourse. He didn't think he could be intimate with her since her mood was so cold to him lately.

"Listen. I think while you are gone we should take a break. Just think about things. I'll email you, but we uh, we'll talk when you get back and see where things are."

"Trina you can't get through a problem by ignoring it. We need to talk about this."

"We have Justin. I just need time to think and I think you do to."

When he left they hadn't made love in two months. The longest they had been apart outside of a deployment since they met. Now he is home three months later and she has a pregnancy test. He fished the box out and pulled out the applicators inside. All three of them had been used. All three said positive. He just sat hard on the kitchen chair and stared sightlessly ahead. A car pulled into the driveway. He heard her shoes on the sidewalk and then she came in. When she walked into the kitchen she stopped dead seeing him holding the tests.

When he looked up at her his eyes were in agony. Then he shut it down and his face grew hard.

"Are you going to try to tell me it's mine?"

She let out a hard shuttering breath as she held her arms around her waist to protect herself.

"No."

"Why Trina?"

"I just couldn't cope with you sleeping with someone else. I got drunk one night and I went out...and...I didn't mean for it to happen."

"Trina. I have never been unfaithful to you. Ever." He heaved a huge sigh. He dropped the tests back into the garbage at his feet and put his head in his hands. When he looked up she could see the truth in his eyes. Behind the hurt. She realized at that moment what she had thrown away in her insecurity.

He stood up. And went upstairs. He came down in jeans and a t-shirt and carrying a gym bag that was stuffed full.

"I'm going over to Kris's. I'll come back tomorrow for my things. If I stay I'm going to say something I can't take back." He walked to the door. Without turning around he said, "Goodbye Trina."

Kris was surprised to see Justin's car pull up in front of the house less than an hour after getting home. When he got out his face scared Kris. He ran out the door to the man who looked as if his life was over.

"Trina is pregnant."

Kris just stood there a second. Not even thinking he grabbed his best friend in a hard embrace as Justin dropped his bag and grabbed onto Kris breaking with the pain he was in. An agonized sob tore from his chest as the two men collapsed onto their knees on the front lawn. Kris holding Justin as he sobbed. Kris's eyes remained strangely dry. He felt the man's grief and pain and wanted to take it from him. But he couldn't mourn the end of a relationship he knew wasn't right for his brother. He just held him promising his brother it would be ok.

***

When Kris's eyes finally opened it was dark. Sitting next to the bed was Justin. She blinked a few times to clear her vision and he was still there.

"Are you awake this time?"

She moved a bit and winced. Her abs felt like someone hacked at them with a meat cleaver. She took a deep breath and looked at him.

"I'm awake."

He was holding her hand. His hand was warm and strong. And the heat from her hand told her he'd been holding it for a while.

"What time is it?"

"It's 0300. Sunday morning."

"So, I've been out of it for a while."

"Yeah."

Justin looked exhausted. He had a full day's growth of beard and hadn't looked to have slept much in the last few days.

"You didn't have to stay with me man, you need to hit the rack."

"I didn't want you to wake up alone."

"The mission; was it completed?"

"Yeah, we got the family back. All the reports are in and the family debriefed."

"What did they..."

"No, that can wait. I have some news for you Kris and it's not easy to say."

"What happened?"

"You don't remember getting hit?"

Kris stopped for a moment and tried to piece together what Alario was saying.

"Wait, is this about the explosion? About the mission? Nothing happened while I was out?"

"What do you remember?"

Kris snorted. "Dude I have a photographic memory; I remember everything!"

Kris smiled that famous shit eating grin. Justin smirked as well, but then his face became very sober.

"Do you remember coming back-the surgery?"

"Yeah. You had to open me up to find the bleeding. Then my mom was there. She hugged me and told me how proud she was, but that I couldn't stay because I wasn't finished. Then I was here and..."

"And?"

Kris seemed to be struggling with what to say.

"I was here, and you kissed me." Kris said with some confusion. "Am I remembering that right?"

"Got your attention didn't it?"

"Humph. Yes, Sir it did! Why? Why did you do it?"

"I wasn't about to let you go, not like that. And I just.."

Justin stopped and slumped over in the chair with his elbows on his knees.

"Kris when we opened you up, you were tore up pretty bad. We had to remove some parts we couldn't repair under the circumstances."

"Remove parts? What parts?"

Justin took a deep bracing breath. "Your uterus. I had to take out your uterus."

Kris just looked at him with no expression for a moment. That famous control keeping her features a blank mask. Her eyes were another story. They were calculating and focused on something inside as Kris wrestled with the news. She closed her eyes and spoke.

"It sounded like you said you had to remove my uterus. I had a uterus. Did I hear that right?"

"Yeah, you heard it right."

Kris kept her eyes closed and breathed very deep. The beeping of the monitor increased for a moment then settled down. Kris opened her eyes and looked into the tormented eyes of the man who was the closest friend she ever had besides Amalia. She squeezed his hand still holding hers.

"You had to do what you had to do man. I know you would have fixed it if it could have been fixed. Don't...That's not on you man."

"Do you understand what that means Kris?"

Justin's eyes were hard on Kris's face, but with concern.

"Yeah, man. I get it." Kris heaved a deep breath that seemed to exhale forever.

"I didn't want you to hear from anybody else. You're female Kris."

"Well yeah, or medical science just found a really bizarre phenomenon!" Kris said with a laugh, then groaned from the pain of the movement.

Justin laughed along. "You ok with that?"

Kris gave Justin a measured look. "It is what it is man." Kris shook her head and let out a wry laugh. "Are you ok with that?"

Justin flashed a lightning quick smile. "Yeah, I am ok with that." The look Justin was giving her was making her heart beat faster, but she didn't know why. He squeezed her hand tighter and held it between the two of his. "The Lieutenant Commander said once you regained consciousness, he was getting you evac-ed out to Germany for treatment. As long as your vitals are good, you'll ambulance out tomorrow. Medical transport leaves for Panzer Kaserne at 1300. Once they evaluate you it's off to Landstuhl. I hate to see you go, but the faster they patch you up the faster we can get you back to the team."

"Will they let me back with the team, Sir?"

"Yeah. Of course. Why wouldn't they?" Justin did not meet Kris's eyes during that statement which told Kris the shit was already starting to hit the fan. Kris sighed and closed her eyes.

"Well then I better rest up. It'll be a long flight. You better get some rest too Sir. You look like hell."

Justin continued holding Kris's hand. "I'm good. You get some shut eye Marine. You need it worse than I do."

When Justin moved to rise, Kris tightened her hold on Justin's hand. Justin sat back down. He put both of his hands around Kris's again and sat with her as she went back to sleep. When first shift came in at 0600 hours. Justin was still there, with Kris's hand safely between both of his and his head on the side of the bed sound asleep.

Chapter Five

Landstuhl Regional Medical Center was a military hospital adjacent to Ramstein Air Force Base that saw more than it's fair of combat wounded. The facility was the largest American-run medical facility outside of the U.S. It specializes in the care of wounded warriors even providing housing for family members visiting the wounded.

Ordinarily the wounded would only stay a few days and move stateside, but Kris was going on her third week now. Her internal injuries were healing, but three more surgeries for skin grafts over her pelvic region had kept her there longer. The doctors did not want to risk infection by moving her. That and some of the finest surgeons in the Military were there providing care for the more than 13,000 wounded personnel that have come through there since 2004. It was hard to find a better group of medical professionals in one facility-even stateside. Kris's case had fascinated them. Despite the Colonel's best efforts, Kris's condition did not stay a secret long. Several Marines in and out of the facility recognized Kris and it did not take long for the talk to start. It only took one corpsman to refer to her as 'she' to several Marines that knew her as 'he' for the rumors and talk to start.

On Kris's third day there, Kris's wife Melody arrived. She was a petite woman with a forceful personality. Her normally dark brown hair was died a light blondish brown. She kept it shoulder length; not too short for a ponytail, but not long enough to get in her way. Her delicate oval face had a medium complexion with a straight nose and strong jaw; she spoke with a slight Spanish accent which suggested Mexican decent. Her almond shaped dark brown eyes were worried seeing Kris in the bed. She hid her curvy shape under a baggy sweatshirt and tight jeans. She was horrified to see Kris so badly torn up. She cried for a solid hour until Kris was able to convince her she was going to be fine. Kris was replaying the scene in her head for the tenth time when the doctor told Mel of Kris's change in gender. He outlined all of Kris's medical history and what lead to the discovery.

"You mean to tell me the balls to the wall never say die Marine with the biggest pair of steel cojones in the Corps is really a woman!?!" Mel had to be treated for a bruised shoulder after she fell off the bed laughing.

"Did you get a good picture of the look on the teams faces when they heard?"

"They don't know yet Mel, its complicated."

"Yes! Say I can be there-promise me Kris! I have to be there when you tell them!" As she dissolved into a puddle of hysterical laughter again. The hospital psychologist sat in the corner with a look on her face that phased between incredulous and indignant from Mel's reaction. After a few minutes of realizing that her services were not needed she left.

"Are you done?"

"For now."

"Well you did say you have always wanted a sister."

"Oooh! That means I can take you shopping for girl clothes and we can get our nails done!"

Kris groaned a heartfelt painful groan and grabbed a spare pillow to hold over her face. Mel didn't let her hide long before yanking it down and smacking her with it.

"Hey! Wounded here!"

"Oh please! You act like getting blown up was less painful than shopping."

"By my experience it is."

Mel snorted. "Please. Big tough guy like you afraid of a little mall. How the mighty have fallen!"

"If you keep threatening me I'm going to send you home."

She said something rude and pointed in Spanish. Both of them had been in a pretty good mood since the day before Kris got a surprise visit from Bobby B. He was fighting in a match in France when the news came that Kris was wounded and being sent to Germany. Bobby told his manager he was forfeiting the fight because he had to get to Kris. His opponent Jean Michel Renault heard and refused to fight Bobby until he was able to see his brother in Germany. They rescheduled the match, which actually increased the hype around the fight, for the following week. Bobby arrived and Mel took him aside to talk to him before he went in to see Kris.

"I want to tell you something before you go in there. Kris was wounded pretty bad, but is going to be ok. But the doctor's found something unexpected."

"What is it? Oh man did Kris lose a leg or something?" Bobby looked sick.

"NO! No. Kris is all good. It's just um. Uh. How to say this. Bobby, Kris is a woman."

Bobby sat and looked at Mel with no expression. He blinked rapidly for a couple of seconds before saying, "What?"

"Kris is a woman."

He fell over grabbing his knees as he let out a huge laugh. He took off his traveling bag and thrust it at her.

"Hold this. I'll be right back."

He ran out of the hallway and dove into the open elevator with a huge grin on his face. Mel just stood there wondering if he had lost his mind. She didn't want to go back in the room without him so she waited. A few minutes later he came back up and when he got off the elevator he was carrying several balloons that said, 'It's a girl' and a pink teddy bear. When they walked into Kris's room she took one look at him with all that crap and busted up laughing.

He handed Mel the balloons and gave Kris the bear as he grabbed her in a huge hug. Then he pulled back and gave her a smacking kiss on the cheek.

"Glad you're ok Sis."

"So Mel told you."

"Yeah. So? How's that going?"

"It's different. I miss peeing standing up."

They both snorted at that. Bobby had undergone surgery when he was 16 for a similar prosthetic to Kris's. That was an interesting time when Kris was helping him understand the ins and outs of the device and how to use it. Kris harped constantly on hygiene and keeping the device clean since she learned the hard way in the field what happened if you didn't. They all talked for several hours. Mel smacked the crap out of Kris when she found out that Bobby already had known about Kris's gender condition. She yelled for several minutes in three languages she was so mad. When Bobby reminded her they shared that gender condition and Bobby only knew because Kris wanted him to feel a little less alone in the world when he was little did she finally calm down.

Kris filled Bobby in on what happened and Bobby told Kris and Mel about his most recent fights. He bunked in with Mel at her apartment for the three days he stayed. Watching Kris go through physical therapy was hard. He always saw the Marine as infallible and indestructible. Seeing her struggle through simple movements tore him up. Kris told him it was ok. Just part of the healing. Just like if you have a bad tear or a break, you have to work it slowly. By the time Bobby left Kris was getting more agile and quicker so Bobby knew she was going to be ok. They made plans to hang out when Kris got back stateside. Bobby would finish his tour in six weeks and Kris would be home then. When he left he was all smiles. Which meant Kris wouldn't have to worry about him during the fight.

Kris grabbed her laptop to check her email. In the nearly four weeks since the day of the explosion Kris had received many emails from the team. She used Mel's laptop to respond and keep in touch. They were still at Camp Delta working with two other teams on a mission that once completed would get them all back stateside. Each member of the team emailed her daily. Only she hadn't received an email from Justin in almost a week. No one on the team seemed to know where he was other than an errand with the Colonel. Which explained why she hadn't heard from him either in just as long. She hoped he'd get in touch soon. She missed him.

The first email was from John Reineke who was the old man of the group. The logistics officer had been in nearly 17 years. The forty-year-old kept saying he was going to transfer out of the team and take a desk. He never did. He was younger than all of them put together. The wiry man with the gray at his temples could out pace every member of the team. The older he got, the younger he got. His ability to ferret out information, people, and gear wherever they were was invaluable. They all joked he could scrounge a lake out of the endless sand dunes of the desert. He sent random news from home. His wife Sue and two teenage daughters were praying for her. They were watching the house while Mel was here in Germany.

Kris read the gossipy message from Gentry. The flamboyant Cajun from Louisiana lived for camp gossip and always knew what was going on. He regaled Kris with all the scandals and juicy stories of the camp. He caught Kris up with his daughter Miracle's activities. She lived with his grandmother when Davis was deployed but otherwise lived with him. She was a product of a youthful dalliance that never should have resulted in pregnancy. He suspected he was gay but was fighting it and she was certain she was too. They decided to have sex as an experiment. Both of them used contraception and she was on the pill. And still she got pregnant. She wanted to get an abortion and even went to a clinic to do so but Davis figured out her intentions, stopped her at the door, and informed her he wanted the baby even if she didn't. When Miracle was born her mother turned her over and never looked back wanting to have a high-powered career. Her mother claimed it was a miracle she got a grandchild at all from her only child and the name stuck. He joined the Marines when she was five. Now at ten she was a complete handful. She competed in dance and routinely attended Kris's hip hop dance classes that she taught at the youth center on base. Thanks to Kris's influence she also was in martial arts. She claimed it helped her dancing and vice versa.

Jeffries typed a quick note with words of encouragement and prayers. The quiet sturdy Midwesterner loved to laugh but was usually very serious. He was short and stocky with a boxer's build but was very gentle and soft-spoken. He was always ready to lend a hand. He passed on bits from forums of other wounded warriors on the best way to come back from a serious injury. He also included links to different sites where Marines shared experiences to help each other recover from combat incidents and wounds. The last link was to a series of really crass cartoons called "Joe Cartoon." Kris clicked on a few and laughed uproariously. Jeffries always found humor in things and loved a good laugh.

Tomball was a man of few words, but writing was a different matter. The large black man with the deep booming voice was as quick to volunteer his opinion and quicker to pick a debate. He loved to talk trash and argue. Nothing thrilled him like a good strong intellectual debate. He was tough and very smart. Suma Cum Laude in college. He regaled bits of the last mission, Bible verses, and a lot of trash talk about the MLB season. He was a hardcore Red Sox fan and Kris supported the Dodgers having fallen in love with baseball in California. He attached an article on the prospects of the Dodgers' pitcher after a slow start to the season. Kris fired one back on the Sox's poor chances of getting the pennant.

Jenkins note asked Kris's advice for a choice between classes to take the next semester. Like Kris, Dan was completing his master's degree. Kris had taken both classes already and listed the pros and cons with their training schedule. The tall thin blonde man with the rodeo cowboy build and demeanor was careful not to mention Kris's injuries or the mission. He was still having a real hard time after the experience. Some of the guys had mentioned it. Even Kris had gotten past it, but Dan was still having nightmares. Justin recommended he get counseling as it appeared he was having some post-traumatic stress from the ordeal.

She opened up one from Javier. Aside from Justin, Kris's other best friend was Javier Juarez. Javier was a hardened Marine and a practical joker with an unashamed passion for Telenovelas. He was a couple of years older than Kris but acted far younger. He was quick to joke, and he never seemed to take anything seriously. The toughly built Latino man looked fierce; he grew up in a bad area of South Texas where Mexican gangs and illegal migrant workers swarmed over the Rio Grande. He grew up with a widowed mother and four sisters in a small house outside El Paso.

He was first generation American, and his mother was determined he go to college. He had a skill at electronics and saved $22,000 working under the table for a pawn shop doing repairs by the time he was 18. Then his girlfriend, now his wife Rosa, got pregnant. He was going to put his dreams of college on hold, but his mother insisted he attend. They lived with her until their son Ernesto was three. Javi only was able to pay for a two year degree in electronics at Texas A&M so he joined the Corps to finish with the GI Bill. They now had four boys; Ernesto was joined by Gabriel, Fernando, and Sebastian. Sebastian was born deaf so the whole team learned sign language. Rosa and Javi were a solid unit. Strong and sure. Other than Justin, Javier was the only other one she truly was afraid of what he would say about her gender change. She hoped he would understand.

Kris's emails were put on hold by the arrival of Colonel Stirling. The older man looked exhausted yet also strangely energized. He hugged Kris for a long time. Kris just held on. She always considered him a surrogate father, so she was thrilled to see him. They spoke for about twenty minutes, and he caught up on her progress with physical therapy and the surgeries to repair the damaged flesh ripped away from the prosthetic. He winced as she described the procedure of removing the skin from her backside and using it to graft on her inner thighs. The Colonel could only stay about a half an hour. He was able to arrange a flight from the states to land there but the next hop was out of Kaiserslautern, and he needed to arrange for transportation. That always took a while. He left and Kris was wondering again where Justin was.

Kris's musings were interrupted as Mel stood up and started packing her bag.

"Listen I have to go back to the apartment for a while. I need to complete and submit my assignment for class. Will you be ok here alone?"

"Yes, mother. I'll be fine. See you later." Kris handed Mel the laptop.

Mel gave her a quick peck on the mouth and grabbed her bag and left.

Kris hated the inactivity. She had two more days of bed rest until the skin grafts on her pelvis and thighs healed enough to continue physical therapy. Once the last surgery was done the doctors started hormone therapy. Everyday a small dose of Estrogen to kick start her body into puberty. Once her levels were up they would start ovarian hyperstimulation. She could already feel the changes. She never had emotional ups and downs with her hormones staying neutral her whole life. It had been hard dealing with the sudden highs and lows wreaking havoc on her system. Her body had started to change as well. Her physique was softening, and she had started to grow breasts. Thankfully the loose gown hid those. She was still finding her new shape a bit of a shock. She asked the doctors what to expect. They said women tend to be built like their moms. Nothing could have horrified Kris more. Kris's mom used to describe herself as 'busty'. That was an understatement. If Kris ended up like her mom her career could be over. As a joke once when they were kids, Kris and Emily put two kids sized soccer balls in one of Jenna's bras. They fit. Kris shuddered at the memory. Next week she was back stateside. Outpatient treatment at Bethesda with a specialist for more specialized hormone therapy and continued physical therapy to rebuild muscle strength in her thighs and abdomen. She was going to have a long hard talk with the doctors regarding that hormone therapy.

The curtain was pulled for her privacy, she hated seeing all the people in the halls trying to get a glimpse into the room, and when she heard the footsteps, she figured it was Mel coming back for something. It was a bit of a shock, but a pleasant one, to see Justin Alario come around the privacy curtain. The six-foot-tall 235-pound man was dressed in travel utilities that barely contained his solid muscular frame. His massive chest strained the garment to its limits, with the sleeves rolled up showing his massively muscular arms. They looked like he could bench press a truck. This topped trim hips and a curvy muscled ass (which turned many female Marines heads) and ended with long heavily muscular legs which crossed the room quickly. His dark brown hair had seen a fresh haircut and his sharp dark brown eyes zeroed in on Kris like a laser. Justin had a classical Italian face; straight nose, high cheekbones, squared firm chin, and creases in his cheeks that turned to dimples when he laughed. Kris thought he looked dangerous, but Mel referred to him as 'ruggedly handsome." He had his go bag over his shoulder which he set down in the chair by the wall and walked over to the far side of the bed and sat down.

"Should have known you'd be malingering in bed, asshole," he said with a grin. "Nice hair, they don't have a barber here? That mop is completely out of regs."

Kris's face lit up as she grinned at Justin. She had started growing out her hair some since regulations for female's haircuts differed from males. It was still short, but not the ridged buzz that had been her standard since entering the Corps. Justin sat down on the side of the bed.

"What are you doing here, Sir?"

"I rode shotgun with the Colonel. You have caused quite the shitstorm with the brass. They are all trying to figure out how to address this and not cause an even bigger problem. We just got in from Washington. Full meeting with SECNAV, SECDEF, the Commandant and the Armed Forces Services Committee. They are all trying to save face and cover their asses. It would be funny watching them spin if it wasn't my best friend's career in the balance."

"What's the scuttlebutt, Sir?"

"Right now, no one is committing to anything. They are all talking, but no one is saying anything. No one wants to do or say anything that may come back to haunt them. They are in a wait and see pattern."

"Can't say that surprises me."

"The Colonel and I both testified on your behalf. Several of them were convinced that you were trying to make a political statement and wanted you dishonorably discharged. We showed them the err of their ways quickly. Thank heavens my Uncle Anthony was able to get me those court documents. That changed the tide for sure."

"What documents, Sir?"

"From the custody trial and the criminal trial against Dr. Standish. My dad sent them when I asked for information on the prosthetic serial number. The Colonel read aloud to get them into evidence and on the record. After that they didn't have a leg to stand on. Then I went on record with your evals and testing scores. All the men submitted a written avadavat since we are still in the field. We didn't tell them why. Only that your ability to command was in question and after your injuries, the division was trying to keep you from returning to SOC. All I asked was in their reports they did not use pronouns at all. I think they should hear it from you."

"What if they don't understand?"

"What's to understand? You were told when you were a kid you were male; you found out the hard way that was not the case. End of story."

"What if they don't want to work with a female. You know there are those out there who just can't or won't look past a Marine's anatomy regardless of their abilities."

"No one on our team is going to hold this against you. Kris you are family. Once they get over their shock, they'll let it go."

"I hope you are right."

"I am always right." Kris busted up laughing at Justin's signature phrase. It was good to have her best friend here; and a greater relief than she would ever admit that he accepted her without reservation. Not only accepted but fought to get her back where she belonged. She wasn't used to having anyone fight for her other than her mom and Mel. They sat and talked for almost an hour barely noticing the time pass.

"I'm glad you came, Sir."

"Yeah, me too." Justin started to get up off the bed and sat back down. He wrapped his hand around Kris' neck and leaned his forehead against hers with his eyes closed. Justin opened his eyes and with a hard-intense look Kris hadn't seen in her friend's face before. He leaned in and before Kris could even react Justin's lips captured hers in an explosive kiss.

At first Kris froze. She'd never been kissed before. Justin's lips moving across hers felt odd then a host of sensation swamped Kris. Feelings she couldn't imagine swarmed all through her body. Her lips felt burned, her head swam, and electricity seemed to be racing from the pit of her stomach then skyrocketed to shoot out of every orifice. Kris's mind emptied of all thought, and she grabbed Justin's wrist tightly. Justin changed the angle of his head and his lips devoured hers. Kris was pummeled with a new set of unexpected feelings. She gasped opening her mouth to Justin's invading tongue. She was shocked to feel his tongue touch hers. It felt alien yet completely right. She inexpertly stroked his with her own. He groaned long and low in response. His other hand came up to run through her hair as the kiss deepened. It was wet and filled with motion. He leisurely explored her mouth from left to right and back again. Tracing the outside of her lips with his tongue and reexploring her mouth.

Justin could not believe how incredible Kris's mouth tasted. Her lips were firm and sweet. Every time he thought he'd tasted her completely a different angle changed the taste, so he was craving her more. He never enjoyed kissing anyone this much before. He'd always felt kissing was just an appetizer to the main course. Not with Kris, he felt he could kiss her all the rest of the day and through the night and it wouldn't be enough. It was all he could do to remember that she was still severely wounded and not pull her firm hard body under his on the bed. Staying apart from her was almost as hard as seeing her on the floor of that stinking building bleeding and broken.

Kris had no experience for the sensations coursing through her body. She didn't even know what to call it. Justin just went on kissing her as if he could go on forever. Finally, after what could have been several minutes or several days, he captured her bottom lip between his teeth and pulled as he moved back. With that a pulsing burst exploded inside her leaving her breathless and panting. Her head was swimming and her vision blurred. She blinked a few times and shook her head slightly to orient herself. When she looked at him lust was all over his face.

It took Kris a couple of moments to get her brain cells functioning for speech. She just took several deep breaths as she looked at Justin.

Justin kept staring at her with the same lustful expression.

"I've been holding that in for a while; I just couldn't hold back anymore. When I realized it shook me up, tore me apart. I didn't know what to say or how to say it. I just know I couldn't leave here without doing that. The scent of you is driving me crazy."

"What.... Wait, how long? What do you mean...." Kris almost didn't want to hear the answer.

"Weeks."

"Justin," Kris paused unclear of what to say. She searched his face.

"You don't have to say anything. I know this is probably all a shock to you."

She could see the uncertainty on his face and him steeling himself for rejection.

"I don't have any experience with this. I've never had a relationship with anyone. I don't know how to approach this." She leaned forward again and clasped his hand. He could see the uncertainty in her eyes, but underneath that he could see the wanting too. His temperature shot up. He brushed his thumb back and forth across the back of her hand. She shivered with desire. Her breath hitched as she leaned back against the pillows. They sat there staring into each other's eyes. A noise outside the room brought them both back and he glanced at the clock next to the bed.

"Listen, I need to get back to the airfield. When we got here the Colonel said our flight leaves in two hours. If I'm late the Colonel will have my head. You're heading stateside in a couple of days, right?"

"Saturday."

"When you get there, I want to hear from you. Let me know you are ok. Let me know how therapy is going."

"So far everything is good. The doctor is pleased with how rapidly my skin grafts are healing."

Justin's eyes moved to Kris's lap covered by the sheet. He moved his hand slowly up the bed to grasp the sheets and pulled them down just as slowly. As if to give Kris the chance to stop him. When Kris didn't move he pulled the sheets down to her thighs and pulled the hem of her gown up over her hips. The bandages had come off the day before. The skin above it was liberally scarred from shrapnel. The look he gave her made her insides turn to liquid and quiver just as it did when he kissed her. He ran his hands down her thighs to her knees and closed her legs. Then pulled the covers back up over her lap. She licked her lips but didn't move. He leaned in and captured her lips in a gentle kiss. She grabbed his head in her hands and pulled him close, running her hands down his arms to clasp his hands as he pulled away.

"You better hit the road if you want to make that flight, Sir."

"Suddenly going AWOL is starting to look good."

Kris laughed and smirked, shaking her head.

When Kris met his eyes the desire in hers echoed his. "I want you to work hard at getting back to duty. I want you to set up a new personal email account I can contact you on once you get out of here."

"Why a new email account?"

"Because the things I have to say to you I don't want intercepted by the Corps or Mel. The things I want to say to you are just between you and me."

Kris's throat went dry with the deep sexy timber his voice took on with that statement. Yet her body felt electrified. As if she grabbed onto a live wire. She nodded minutely. He turned and grabbed his bag and strode out of the room. Kris leaned her head back into the pillows weakly trying to calm her breathing. She had a lot to think about.

Chapter Six

"Oh my goodness, I just ran into Justin in the hall! How long was he here, what is he doing here.......Kris?"

Mel stopped suddenly at the look on Kris's face. Kris was stunned and dazed looking. She dropped her bag on the chair Justin's bag just vacated and came to sit on the bed next to Kris.

"Are you ok? What happened?"

"Um. Yeah. I'm fine. Just, um. Thinking."

"Uh huh. Thinking. Care to share your thoughts?"

"I'm not sure what to...um." Kris looked at Mel for the first time since she entered the room. Mel's face was a mask of concern. Mel took in Kris's face; her lips were swollen and bruised looking. Like someone that had been good and kissed. Her cheeks were flushed, and her breathing was hitched and rapid.

"Justin kissed me."

Mel's eyes grew as big as saucers and her mouth dropped open. She shook her head quickly.

"Wait, what? Justin kissed you. On the mouth? Our Justin."

"Yeah."

"How was it?" Mel had leaned in and grabbed Kris's hand. It was obvious Kris was in a bit of shock.

"It um..." Kris just nodded fiercely. Mel squealed and insisted she tell her everything. Kris took her through the conversation as Mel gasped and squealed over again.

"Mel my body felt um odd. While he was kissing me. I don't know how to describe it really."

"Tell me everything!"

"I felt hot; then it felt as if my blood was boiling. There was a fluttering in my belly, like you get on a roller coaster on that first plunge, then I felt this pulsing inside. At the end he grabbed my lip in his teeth and pulled and it felt like something burst inside, but not painful. More like waves lapping on the shore but inside me."

By the time Kris finished Mel was smiling with her hands clutched over her mouth.

"What!?

"Oh honey, don't you know what happened? I forget how many holes there are in your education! Kris baby, you had an orgasm."

Kris stared at Mel nonplussed until Mel burst out laughing.

"That must have been some kiss. Trina always said Justin was skilled. Man! I have never known anyone who had one just from a kiss. W-O-W! I guess I don't have to ask if you liked it. But I do have to ask how you feel about it."

"I'm not entirely sure I'm not having an out of body experience."

Mel laughed again at the comical look on Kris's face. It was so rare for Kris to come up against any situation that wasn't conquered with minimal fuss, great skill, and cocky arrogance. Mel wasn't laughing at Kris per se but delighted to see Kris need someone else's advice or knowledge to handle it. Even Mel adopted the team's nickname of "know it all asshole" for her. It was refreshing to see one thing Kris couldn't handle.

"I liked it. I'm not sure how I feel about his feelings for me."

"What did he say?"

"He didn't say anything, but the look on his face. It wasn't just lust Mel. That was there, but there was a lot more underneath it. He told me to get a private email account because he had things to tell me."

"Well. You're thinking about that kiss again, aren't you?"

"How'd you know?"

"Your skin got flushed, your breathing got harsh, and pupils dilated. Well that tells me what I need to do."

"What do you mean, 'what you need to do'?"

"Looks like it's time for that divorce."

"Why the sudden rush now?"

"Because you found someone who can look beyond 'all this' as want you as you are. Time to make good on that declaration."

Kris was propelled back to three years ago when the team had returned home from another deployment. They were five days early for a change. He walked into the house he and Mel shared and dropped his bags. He heard noises from the living room and walked in to see Mel naked with an equally naked man reclining on his couch; he knew him to be a Lieutenant but didn't know his name.

"Mel!" Kris stopped in shock and raised his eyes to the ceiling as he turned around shaking his head in disbelief.

"Who the hell is this?!"

Kris looked back at the naked man now standing wanting an answer to his furiously asked question.

"Kris honey I can explain."

"Lieutenant you may want to get dressed and get out of here before I forget you are an officer and beat the crap out of you. Mel- I'm going to Justin's to work on my bike. I'll be back in an hour or so."

Kris walked out of the door as Mel grabbed her clothes and pulled them on. The Lieutenant also began to roughly pull his clothes on.

"Who was that guy?"

"That was my husband. You better get the hell out of here before he gets back. He's Special Forces; I don't think he was kidding about beating the hell out of you. You're lucky he didn't kill you."

"Your husband is a Raider?"

"Yeah. He wasn't supposed to be home until next week."

"Do you think he's getting a weapon?" He dressed faster, looking afraid.

"He's trained to kill with his bare hands. If he wanted you dead, you would be."

The Lieutenant didn't pause once he got dressed, he grabbed his things and bolted out the door without a word to Mel.

She sat down on the couch with half her pants and a bra on and put her head in her hands. "Oh no!"

***

Kris walked across the back yard and down the block to Justin's house one street over. He knocked on the door; Justin answered and invited Kris in. Like Kris, Justin was still in his travel utilities. They stood in the foyer just outside the kitchen. He could hear Justin's wife Trina asking him if he wanted to go out for dinner or stay in.

"Hey, sorry to disturb you, Sir but I'm going to work on my bike for a bit if you don't mind." Kris pointed back to the garage.

"Kris we just got home; don't you want to spend some time with your wife?"

"Uh, yeah. She has a friend over and I felt it best to leave until she was alone."

Just then the sound of breaking glass came from the kitchen as Justin's wife Trina dropped what sounded like several plates.

Justin stuck his head around the door frame, "You ok babe?"

Trina was kneeling on the floor picking up the pieces with a worried look on her face. Her eyes darting from Justin to Kris repeatedly. "Um yeah, the plates were slippery. I guess I didn't dry them all the way. Sorry guys." She ducked her head in a completely uncharacteristic way and quickly cleaned up the pieces. Kris flicked his head to Justin to indicate he wanted to talk outside. Justin told Trina he'd be in the garage and they could see Trina diving for her phone through the window.

They went into the garage and Justin pulled a couple of beers out of the mini fridge and handed one to Kris.

"You want to tell me what's going on?" Kris took a long pull on the beer and Justin's eyes grew sharp.

"This 'friend' she had over happen to be male?"

"Yeah."

"Kris, Mel loves you, she wouldn't cheat on you! Did she say anything about why he was there?"

"No Sir, she was scrambling to get dressed. And no, I didn't misunderstand the situation. The naked Lieutenant on my couch with my equally naked wife was pretty self-explanatory."

"Oh man. You need help hiding the body?"

Kris laughed and sat down on the work bench.

"No Sir, I didn't kill him-or her. I just left."

"What do you mean you didn't kill him? And Lieutenant who? Why is he still breathing perfectly good air after sleeping with your wife?"

Kris just shook his head and drank more beer. "We don't have a typical marriage."

"That much is getting perfectly clear."

Kris snorted, "Thanks for the beer. I'm sure he is long gone. I need to have a talk with my wife."

"Kris, I don't think you should do that now. Why don't you bunk here and wait until tomorrow when you have had time to cool off?"

"I'm good, Sir. Thanks for this, but you need to be with your wife. I am kind of pissed at Trina since she obviously knew something by that little demonstration inside. But I'm glad that she and Mel are close enough that she felt she could confide in her. Mel doesn't let anyone in; it's not healthy."

Kris got up and walked out of the garage and cut back across the lawn. Trina was at the door looking worried. Justin followed behind Kris; far enough that the younger man didn't realize he was being followed. Kris walked up the drive and into the house; walking back into the living room where Mel was sitting on the couch dressed and alone. Justin stayed outside the screen door and listened. He would only go in if things got out of control.

"Oh, Kris I am so sorry!" Mel hopped off the couch to walk up to Kris.

"Dammit Mel we have one rule, just one! No guys in the house! I do not need to see something like that when I get home."

"I know and I'm sorry. I swear I've never brought a guy here before. But I didn't see any harm, everybody we know is at work and you guys were gone..."

"Trina's home! And she obviously knew since when she saw me she grew pale and dropped the stack of plates she was holding!"

"Oh no!" Mel grabbed her phone and saw the missed call from Trina ten minutes ago.

"Ugghh!" Kris flopped down on the recliner chair. He wouldn't go near the couch. "I will never be able to sit on that couch again. We just got it. I've never even laid down on it and I will never be able to touch it after knowing that guy tea-bagged it!"

Mel just stood there biting her lip.

"You know he's married right?"

"Of course! I never would have gotten involved with him if he wasn't!"

"How are you ever going to meet someone you could settle down with if you keep hooking up with married men?! I think we need to seriously talk about getting divorced for real."

"Please Kris! Settle down? I am settled down. I am perfectly happy the way things are."

"You have always wanted a husband-a real husband-and a family. You are not going to get that with these random hookups and staying in a fake marriage to me!"

"I gave up on that fantasy a long time ago."

"Why?"

"Oh, come on! I get married and have a couple of kids and a happy life and one day there is a knock at the door. And my life as I know it is over! My family destroyed! I come home, and they have been tortured and killed! Or I never come home; I disappear, and they spend the rest of their lives in agony wondering what happened because no will find my body."

"Honey that is not going to happen. I made sure of that. His daughter is dead. I saw to it that he believed she is dead, and he will never connect her to you and me."

"You don't know that! I can't pull some poor unsuspecting guy into my life and put him in danger. Someone who doesn't know there is a psychopath out there who will never rest until he finds the answers he wants about his daughter. And doesn't care who he must kill to get to them! You know! You can protect yourself. I can't risk putting someone else I care about in danger." Mel face was a mask of terror and her eyes were swimming with tears.

"But Mel by living in this paranoid fear you are letting him win! What happens when you wake up in thirty years, your life behind you and nothing but regrets because you were too afraid to live your life the way you wanted?"

"Look who's talking! What about you Kris? At least I'm getting out there. I'm having fun. I'm dating I'm living. What about you? When is the last time you had a date? Oh, that's right, you never have! You've never even kissed anyone before or since our wedding! At least I'm getting out there. It may not be serious, but it's something! That prosthetic of yours is fully functional; I know because you showed me when we were 14 and I wanted to know what a man looked like! But you've never even tried to use it! You've never tried to have a normal relationship with anyone. Because you are scared; just as scared as I am about what could happen! You hide in our marriage to protect yourself just the same as I do. You bury yourself in work and hanging out with the guys. What about your family? What about your dreams? It's the pot calling the kettle black and you know it! You are just as guilty as I am."

Kris jumped out of the chair and got in her face. "You want to know the difference? I am not afraid to live! If I found someone who would be able handle all of this," he gestured from his head to his feet, "and be able to look beyond everything and care about me inside and out I wouldn't hesitate! I would grab on to that with everything I have. But who is going to ever be able to look past what they see to get to who I am underneath, huh?"

"How will they ever get the chance when that gold band on your finger stops them before they can start?"

Kris ran his hand over his hair and let out a heavy sigh. Mel walked over to him and wrapped her arms around him. He pulled her close and tucked her head under his chin.

"How many times have we had this same fight?"

"I've stopped counting."

They both laughed. "Do you believe there really is someone out there meant for us?" He almost couldn't hear her with her voice muffled by his jacket.

"Yeah baby, there is definitely someone out there waiting for you."

He knew that he could never get intimately involved with someone until he knew for sure the truth behind his gender. He wasn't attracted to women, or men for that matter, and he never would get involved with someone who didn't know the truth. He also didn't trust anyone enough to ever tell them; even Mel didn't know the whole truth. She only knew about the surgery but not the reason behind it. He was afraid if she knew, she would see him differently. She was right he was scared.

Justin walked slowly away from the door and back across the yard to his house. He was trying to digest what he just heard. He thought he knew pretty much everything about the man he called his best friend, but what he just heard changed that. Could Kris have killed a woman and covered it up? Fake marriage? What the hell had he just heard?

***

Kris sat back in the bed while Mel was online shopping for Kris. She was still scared, but for an entirely different reason now. Now that the truth was out, she didn't worry about her old fears when she had so many new ones. Getting involved with Justin wasn't just scary it was stupid. He was her best friend. He knew everything about her now. They had no secrets. Almost no secrets. But what happened if things went bad between them? They still worked together, and their job required them to be able to trust one another and have each other's back. She would hurt her team and lose her best friend. Then there was the fact that he was a superior officer. Kris being enlisted, any relationship would be fraternization. They couldn't risk it. She would not destroy his career or her own. But the thought of not being with him was like a knife to her chest. In the last hour her entire focus had changed. She went from trying to focus on getting her career back to the way it was to her mind filled with nothing but Justin. Screw it all! She would find a way to have both or die trying. Her life was a series of outer forces directing every move and never making a choice for herself. Mel was right; it was time to make good on that declaration.

Chapter Seven

Kris set up a new email account and emailed Justin with her new email address and waited for a response. She filled him in on the therapy and how well her wounds were healing.

To: Justin.A.Alario@usmc.mil

From: kmcA1raider@mail.com

Subject: New email address

Sir,

Here is the email address you can contact me at out of the field. Therapy is going well. Doctors are increasing my activity and I am getting more into a physical routine I am used to. They praised your sutures and incision skills. No problems rebuilding the muscle. I have been increasing my core toning and hope to be back to my regular workout in a week. What's new in the sandbox? Any interesting stories from downrange? Heading stateside later today. Mel headed back and is getting us an apartment in Bethesda. Most of my treatment there is going to be outpatient. The first week will be in the hospital as they monitor my treatment 24/7 but after that I'll be going in twice a week for five weeks. Got to figure out what to do in my off time. Any ideas?

Kris

To: kmcA1raider@mail.com

From: jaaA2raider@mail.com

Subject: re: New email address

Kris,

New email address for personal use while I'm down range. This is only for topics not cleared for our official email. I will continue to use both. I think it would cause suspicion if we discontinued all communication from the Corps address. Also I wouldn't see any messages if we are out and about. Our regular communications will stay on our official email. Let me know by signing off 'Romeo Whiskey' for reply waiting on the mail address. So I will be sure to check it. It will take some juggling but better to be safe than sorry.

We are working up for the next mission I will fill you in on the other email.

I dreamt about you last night. It was like some of the dreams I had before. We were at home on the couch and you were laying on top of me. You had long hair that was hanging down and we were making out on the couch. I pulled your hair back away from your face and held your head in my hands. We lay there forever kissing while I ran my hands all over you. I seemed so real. When I woke up I could still taste you and I swear I could smell you. I didn't know where I was for a second. Luckily it was close to dawn so I got up and went for a run. I knew I wasn't going to get back to sleep! Figured a good long run and a cold shower would burn off the lust. How are you sleeping?

Horny and Hot

Justin

To: jaaA2raider@mail.com

From: kmcA1raider@mail.com

Subject: Horny and Hot

Justin,

I have had quite a few dreams as well. This is new for me. I've never had dreams like these before. At least not that I remembered. You and I were in a fox hole taking fire. We could hear the enemy moving in the dark. You pulled me in and took off my helmet as well as your own and started kissing me. Everything was blowing up all around us and we just got as close as our gear allowed. Next thing we were home and you were cooking breakfast naked. You turned around and asked me how I wanted my sausage. I woke up laughing because it was so ridiculous, but I thought about you standing there naked for a long time after.

I don't quite know how to feel about that. I never thought about you naked before. It's a new experience for me. I'm not quite sure what to do about how it makes me feel. I've seen you naked so many times in the shower or in the barracks. Just like we all have. I started thinking about the rest of the team. Recalling how they looked naked. It wasn't the same. It was just the guys. When I think about you I feel needy and I want something but I don't know what. I feel unsettled. I hate that you are so far away while I lay in bed even though I wish I was there with you all.

I got some books and manuals to read up. I didn't realize how much I didn't know. I figured listening to you guys, watching porn, and the stuff I've heard from Mel over the years I knew pretty much everything. I think I barely scratched the surface! I guess that is where practical knowledge and academic knowledge differ. I have to make sure I'm not reading this stuff before bed or it makes it hard to sleep. Then I start dreaming about it.

Mel and I have had some talks about sex. She has taken the role of big sister to walk me through all the stuff I don't understand. Most everything I know about sex is from the male perspective. I guess sex for women is different. I am reading up on it. I've also got a few books on health and wellness for females so I can learn more about my body. Watched the wrong film in 7th grade health class! Now I have to start from scratch. It's weird.

Thinking of you

Kris

****

Over the next three weeks Kris got into a basic routine. The first week stateside Kris spent in Walter Reed Medical Center for inpatient hormone treatment. They wanted to monitor her closely to make sure she didn't have any issues. After five days she was discharged for outpatient treatment. Her progress was significant, and she didn't have any issues with side effects or imbalances. Small miracle that. She was grateful. She'd read a great deal of issues posted on online forums of people with severe side effects and complications from hormone stimulation. Most were for males rather than females. Aggression and anger issues causing emotional trauma. She was just dealing with the physical changes and how that affected her everyday life.

She spoke with every woman she came across to get information. All of the nurses and some of the patients. Her quest for knowledge at first was a source of amusement then a source of annoyance for the staff because Kris never ran out of questions. In some cases the nurses didn't have the answers which disappointed Kris and set her into research mode. It amazed her how little the average woman actually knew about her body. Especially the nurses. Mel was a good source of information. She didn't get upset with Kris like some of the other women did. Kris had a lot of unorthodox questions that made some of the women uncomfortable. Kris didn't understand their issues. Mel said it was because many women didn't delve that closely into knowing like Kris did. They were content to just live without knowing all of the hows and whys. Kind of like owning a car. No one really understood how everything worked under the hood. They just drove it and let the mechanics figure it out.

Kris worked her physical training back into her daily routine. She started on the treadmill at the gym in the apartment building she and Mel were staying in. The military had a building of month to month furnished rentals for families of the patients. Once Kris went outpatient Mel went back to North Carolina. Now that she was through the heaviest portion of the hormone regimen she started running outside. First a mile every morning and increasing up to five miles by the end of the second week. The doctors warned Kris about lifting too much as her body adjusted to the change in hormones so she stuck to Parkour workouts.

She found a local dojo and enrolled to use their facilities to train. The owner Tony was a former Army paratrooper. They bonded pretty quick and Kris ended up volunteering there several nights a week to help with the students. It kept her busy and enabled her to get back into condition. She was weak from her injuries and the hormones. It pissed her off. She wasn't used to not being a machine. Tony helped her out having been medically discharged from a back injury. He understood her frustration and need to get back to fighting shape. With his help she slowly built back up to fighting form.

Kris also debated enrolling into some online courses. She was halfway through her master's degree and needed to finish. The training schedule hadn't allowed for a lot of time to dedicate there. Mel solved the debate by showing up with Kris's project car. Since Kris would likely return to duty as soon as she was discharged in a couple of weeks she didn't want to get into classes she wouldn't be able to finish, but she didn't want to waste the opportunity so she enrolled and got to work. She'd work into the late evening and exhausted fall into bed.

Kris woke up in the middle of the night with her chest pulsing with pain. The doctor said it was normal considering the level of growth her breasts had developed in the last few weeks. Mel was sympathetic as she went through the same thing in puberty. Kris remembered filling up the hot water bottle for her and bringing it to her while she lay in bed crying. Mel had developed rather quickly as well. She went from an A cup to a D cup in the course of one summer. She spent a lot of time in bed trying not to move during that time in order to minimize the jarring.

Kris didn't have that luxury. She had PT several times a day and she had to get back into condition. Running was torture. She compensated by wearing several sports bras at once. It was hot, but it kept the bouncing to a minimum. The doctor recommended Ibuprofen but Kris didn't want to start popping meds with all the hormone cocktail swimming in her system. She was very leery of side effects or adverse reactions. She lay there with the hot water bottle but it only made her hot and didn't seem to be giving her any relief.

She decided to get up and see if Justin had responded to her last email. The Colonel had sent her several emails. She was glad he finally started writing. She had become worried that her change in gender somehow upset the man she had as a mentor since she was 16. It had to be a shock for him. The team must have been in the field because she hadn't heard from him or any of the them in the last two weeks. She was anxious to hear Justin's response to her last email. She was a little nervous to open up to him emotionally. It left her feeling vulnerable and uncomfortable. She tended to face things rationally rather than with an excess of emotion. Part of that was her condition. With all the hormones in her system as they stimulated her system she was anxious and irritable. Mood swings were frequent. She handled them but they still made her feel off. Waiting for Justin's response made her edgy. She didn't have the ability to sit and wait like she was used to. She whipped back and forth between anger that he wasn't responding to anxiety that he couldn't respond, to angst

that he didn't want to. She knew that was the hormones talking
though.

To: kmcA1raider@mail.com

From: jaaA2raider@mail.com

Subject: Question

I can help you with anything you want to know. I'd rather show
you than tell you! If there is anything you want to discuss or
don't understand please ask me. Don't be uncomfortable or
embarrassed. You can tell or ask me anything. You know that.
Speaking of questions...

One question I meant ask you in Germany before I was
distracted by your sexy mouth is why you never told me about
your gender disorder. I can guess, but I would like to hear it
from you.

Thinking of you.

Justin

Kris sighed and swore. She knew this question was coming and
had been putting a great deal of thought into what she would say.
She was surprised it took him so long to ask. She wondered why
he waited.

To: kmcA1raider@mail.com

From: jaaA2raider@mail.com

Subject: Gender disorder

Justin,

This isn't an easy thing to go into on email. The explanation is
simple yet very difficult to articulate in text. You need to let me
know when we can Skype. It's better to talk on this one.

Kris

Less than a minute after she sent the message her computer signaled she had an incoming Skype. She saw it was Justin's address and quickly calculated the time difference. It was 9pm there. She answered.

His face popped on the screen and she smiled.

"Hey."

"Hey yourself. Why are you up it's really late there."

"Yeah I can't sleep. I am having chest pain."

Justin looked very concerned and bordered on upset.

"Kris if you are having chest pains you need to call for the doctor immediately. The hormone therapy can cause stress on your heart."

She smiled an indulgent smile at his serious concern.

"I'm not having chest pains doctor; I have pain in my chest. The doctors here say it's ... uh...growing pains."

She followed the statement with a meaningful look. It took him a couple of seconds then he nodded and laughed as he caught the gist.

"Ah. In that case."

"Yeah. I have a hot water bottle but all that does is make me hot and in pain. And I don't want to take anything. So. Figured I'd check the email. Your question was a long time in coming. It's been weeks. I figured you'd have asked that a while ago."

"I was hoping you'd volunteer. I didn't want to press you."

"No pressure. It's just something I never talk about. Not because it's difficult for me. But because it's hard for people to understand."

"Ok. Make me understand. We've been best friends for years and I never knew this about you. I didn't think we had any real secrets from one another."

Kris squirmed a bit at that. She hated lying to people and to Justin most of all. But some things in her life weren't her secrets to tell. This one however was.

"I don't talk about it because I don't think about it. I learned to put it out of my mind a long time ago. I had to or I would go crazy. Once I decided to not find out, when they told me the prosthetic couldn't be removed, I chose to just live my life. I don't think about my gender any more than you do. Who does really? I know that with my condition it's different than it is for everyone else but once I decided to identify as male it just was. Just like I never think of having blonde hair or brown eyes. The only time it was even brought to my mind is when I had issues with my prosthetic. Even then I only thought of solving the issue, not the reason I had the prosthetic in the first place.

A good analogy is your pinky on your left hand. The one you broke on the mission in Kandahar. We couldn't get it set right because we didn't have the right equipment. So by the time we got back to base it had started to set and was bent. The doc chose to leave it since the fracture was healing ok and it might have injured it further to rebreak it. So now your pinky is jacked up. It doesn't change the function of your hand. It doesn't change how you handle a weapon or how you are able to perform surgery. Unless you point it out it's actually pretty unremarkable. Just a broken finger. It doesn't define you. It doesn't change who you are or what you can do.

But what if someone looked at that broken finger and felt that by having it, it made you different? That broken finger wasn't like everyone else. Everyone else's fingers were whole. Straight. By pointing out that finger and focusing on it changes how everyone looks at your hand. At what that hand can do. Pointing out what it can't do by virtue of the injury. They judge you and your abilities just off that one finger. Stupid huh? But that is exactly what people do to me once they know of my gender disorder. I was born not male or female; something everyone is one or the other of. Not like a broken finger. It's not something people are able to understand. It's not something they have knowledge of. That's why I started the GenZ foundation when I was 18. There wasn't any information out there for me growing up. I knew how hard it was to live in that bubble of ignorance that surrounds the condition. I wanted people with gender disorders to have somewhere to turn to get knowledge and be able to connect with others who face the same challenge."

"Wait, you started the foundation?!"

"Yeah. Ignorance is not bliss when you have a condition that tends to isolate you."

"Dammit Kris! I helped with that foundation and we all worked on the fundraising campaigns!"

Every year several men in MARSOC got together to put out a beefcake calendar called the "Men of MARSOC Calendar." Kris, Justin, Davis, Mike, and Dan as well as several guys from a couple of different teams all modelled for the calendar which was a major fund raising tool for the foundation and for the Marine Corps Toys for Tots drive. The sexy calendar was joke at first with the men catching a lot of flak from the Spec Ops community, but it was so popular and such a big seller that the other SOC commands developed their own for the charities and special programs their services sponsored. The men wore concealing camouflage paint to hide their faces but the rest of their bodies were sexily displayed. It was a constant source of razzing on Alpha team that every year Kris was Mr. February. Everyone wanted the coveted month as the hottest guy in the calendar. The foundation committee and the Ombudsman voted on who was placed on each month. With the whole group on December. Kris tended to win the spot as most of the wives and volunteers had the hots for her. Chances are she will not make the position this year! One of the men would get their chance for the new calendar.

"Yeah I know. I didn't not tell you because I didn't think you could handle it or that you wouldn't accept it. As a doctor I know you would have a better understanding than everyone else. I just didn't think about it. And I learned over the years that even when you have people to understand it still makes them look at you differently. After the trial I expected the kids to be cruel. They actually weren't too bad. It was the adults. Teachers, my mom's friends, and adults in the community that I regularly interacted with suddenly didn't know how to treat me or talk to me. People who had known me my whole life. Suddenly I wasn't the same anymore. I didn't want you especially to look at me differently.

Then there was Mel. She didn't know either. I'd have to tell her. She'd drive me crazy. She'd nag me to go get tested even though it wasn't what I wanted. You would have to, but not because like

Mel you were dying to know, but because you would see the medical need as I grew older. The truth is I was considering telling you. Something had changed."

"What changed?"

"When you found out Trina was pregnant and you broke down?" Justin nodded.

"I grabbed you and pulled you in for a hug while you tried to pull it down. You held onto me like I was the only thing keeping you together. And I held onto you too. I hadn't ever been held like that before. I hadn't ever held onto someone like that before either. I liked it. I liked the connection, the closeness. I've never had that. With anyone, even Mel. I wanted that with someone. I wouldn't let myself get that close before because I decided it wouldn't be fair to anyone until I knew my gender for certain and I started wondering. Maybe I should find out. So I could take that next step. I never in a million years would have guessed I would be taking that step with you like this."

"I wonder how much further we'd be now if you had then."

"What do you mean?"

Justin just laughed and shook his head.

"Last year when I was still with Trina when I was struggling so bad? You said you'd be there when I was ready to talk about it."

"Yeah. I forgot about that. I'm sorry man. You never did tell me what that was about."

"Yeah. It wasn't easy. I had figured out something that was eating me alive. I didn't know how to approach it and I didn't know what to do about it. There wasn't anyone I could discuss it with."

"Can you tell me now?"

Justin laughed and rocked back in his chair. "Oh yeah. Kris. Buddy. I know this will be hard for you to hear. It's hard for me to say. But I think you are a woman."

"Geez, ya think?!" Kris said with heavy sarcasm.

"No man, that is what I was trying to get up the courage to say!" Justin just sat there and laughed. "You asshole! If you'd told me about your gender condition before I wouldn't have had such a hard time! I went round and round with myself trying to decide whether or not to tell you. I was so afraid it would destroy our friendship. That you would hate me! I mean come on! How the do you tell a guy you have been brothers with, who was best man at your wedding, who is one of the most important people in your life something that life changing? I figured if you didn't hate me you'd think I was nuts. If I had known, I would have been able to sit you down and talk about it sanely instead of thinking I'd lost my mind!"

Kris sat there with her eyebrows near her hairline.

"That's what you were agonizing over?"

"Yeah. Then Trina convinced herself I was having an affair. I couldn't tell her what I was going through without talking to you first. She wouldn't believe it. I wasn't sure I did. I figured if I hung out with you the time would just present itself. But I couldn't do it. Then something changed. I started looking at you as a woman. I started comparing you to Trina. Then I realized what I was feeling for her was fading. And I started feeling for you what I thought I felt for her. The more I was around you the stronger it got. Then I felt guilty because even though I never cheated on her, I felt disloyal and unfaithful because of what I started feeling for you."

"Oh man, that day you got drunk when you left Trina."

"Yeah. I don't remember much, but I do remember telling you that you were my perfect woman."

Kris had taken Justin out for several beers to talk about what was happening. Kris offered the spare room for Justin to take for a short time while he and Trina were going through the divorce. Justin polished off a pitcher of beer and several shots. Kris realized he wanted and needed a good drunk, so she let him tie one on and made sure to get him home and into bed. While she was putting him down after getting him home he asked her why she can't be a woman. Because Kris would be his perfect woman and if Kris could just be a woman he wouldn't be hurting so bad. Kris just undressed him, made him take a couple of Tylenol and drink a glass of water so he wouldn't be sick in the morning and tucked him in bed. The next day he turned up after work with a couple duffle bags of clothes and moved into the spare room. The room he was still in almost six months later. The divorce was quick since it was uncontested. Because of Justin's family money they signed a prenup. Because of her infidelity and pregnancy she didn't ask for alimony. They just divided up their savings and belongings and walked away. Justin planned on looking for his own place but Mel talked him into staying since they were getting ready to deploy anyway. Why waste the money?

Kris felt terrible that Justin went through such a terrible time because of her secret.

"Man I am so sorry. I had no idea. I hate that you had to go through that. Alone. Because I didn't confide in you."

"I'm not. It opened my eyes about Trina. Made me face what our relationship really was. I am grateful for that. If I had known we might still be together. Then again, probably not. Once I realized you were a woman I don't think I could have stopped what I started feeling for you. I had already realized Trina and I weren't going to last. I just didn't want to own up to it. You tried to tell me before we married. But damn I was happy. I thought I loved her. I realize now though I wasn't in love with her. That makes all the difference. Most of why I was angry and upset wasn't just that my marriage was ending. It was that I was so confused. I looked at you and saw a man that was closer to me than my own brothers. One that every time I looked I felt things I shouldn't have. I didn't know what to do with it. I'm starting to figure it out." He said with a grin.

Kris shifted and grimaced.

"Hurts?"

"Yeah. Nothing seems to work for long. The doc said in a couple of weeks the pain will go away as the tissues relax. But right now it seems like I have hurt forever and will. It sucks."

"Massage them. Lightly at first. The tissues are tight from the unexpected growth. It should help. Epsom salt baths will work too. I'd give you a hand if I were there."

Kris laughed. "Yeah I bet you would. You always were a boob man."

"Why don't you show me what the problem is. Bring those babies out and let me see."

"You are out of your mind. I am not flashing you my breasts over Skype."

"Oh come on! No one is here to see. Lift that shirt and give me a good look."

"No way man! Besides. They aren't done yet. The doctor says they've still got some growing to do. For the first time since all this started I'm getting scared. If they keep growing like this, I'm not going to be able come back."

"What do you mean?"

"They're huge man! If they get any bigger I am not going to be able put on body armor or crawl on my belly. As it is I doubt I could lay down low enough to snipe a target."

"Now I am curious. Pull away from the camera so I can see what we are dealing with."

"Nope. You will just have to wait and see when you get back."

"How big is big? What is your cup size?"

"How would I know! What do I know about cup sizes? Big."

"Big enough to fill my hands?"

Justin had big hands.

"At least. Maybe bigger than that."

Justin let off a long agonized groan. "Looks like I'll need to hit the showers again before I hit the rack."

"Sorry Justin. I didn't say that to get you jacked up. I really am seriously concerned. I am talking with the doctors tomorrow. I seriously think want them to stop the hormone treatments if that will keep them from getting bigger. I'm going to see what they say. It may be too late. I really hope not. You think massaging them will help with the pain?"

"Yeah. Light massage with slow circular motions. Work from the nipple out. Concentrate on the heavy tissue under the armpit and on the bottom of the breast. That is where the tissue is the densest. It should help. I think I'm going to need some serious tissue massage of my own after this conversation. I hope the showers aren't full."

The showers were a popular spot for the men to release sexual tension. Most everyone slaked their lust the shower. Semiprivate and easy clean up. No one really gave anyone a hard time for taking a little time to release the tension unless the lines were long. When they were no one cared about your needs only that you got in and out so the rest could do the same.

"You aren't the only one. If I wasn't so uncomfortable, I think I'd need one too."

"Listen I need to go. Keep up the emails. I want to know what the doctors say."

"Hey listen. Are we good? You get why I didn't tell you right?"

"Yeah. I can imagine what that's like. And I know you. You don't get keyed up about stuff. If you say you locked it down and put it away then that's what it was. One thing you've never done Kris is lie or avoid problems. I do want to talk about this more so I'll email you in the morning. But right now it's 11pm and I need some sleep. You need to get back to sleep too. It's almost dawn there. Massage the breasts and get some sleep. I will be thinking about what you said. Almost as much as I will be thinking about when we'll be home so I can see you."

"Get some rest Justin."

"Roger. You go to sleep, that is an order!"

"Bye."

"Dream of me."

Justin signed off and Kris pushed back from the desk. She went back to the bed and lay down. She lifted her shirt and exposed her breasts. The large mounds were very firm. She did like he said working her way around the tissue. It did help. She continued to massage for a bit then grabbed the hot water bottle and clutched it to her chest. The pain lessening she drifted off to sleep.

Kris and Justin traded emails for several more weeks. They got increasingly more playful and erotic. It was much easier for her now to banter with him. Opening up to him seemed to release something in her. They teased constantly. The missives were ripe with sexual innuendo. He described often what he would like to do to her. She returned the favor. She fantasized often over his form. They talked frankly of their feelings for one another. She was very honest with him in regard to how the change in their relationship was affecting her. He was careful not to rush her feelings. It was hard with them being so far apart. He'd had a great deal more time in examining his emotions in regard to her than she had with him so he was careful to not pressure her into feeling more than she was ready for. When they were together they could figure it out.

She had a visitor earlier in the day and finally had something to talk about other than her body or injuries. The men of her team and several in MSOC nominated her for the Medal of Honor. Two Colonels had come to interview her regarding the nomination. They had been completing a routine examination of her service record, her actions in combat, and her medical condition. They had spoken with the doctors and nurses in the hospitals regarding Kris's recovery and gender change.

One of the Colonels was a man she had met in Germany. Colonel Andrew Tucker. Hardened combat Marine that lost a leg in action. He was in the same wing as Kris in Germany. An area of severely physically and mentally wounded, the staff referred to behind closed doors as the 'suicide squad' meaning they were all at high risk for suicide attempts. Kris befriended the Colonel while sneaking out of her room one night to break into the weight room. They kept it locked down because of the danger of most of the equipment posed for being used in suicide attempts. Cables and weights that could end a life if used improperly. Kris went in and the Colonel was already in there sitting in the dark. He had not handled the loss of his leg well. Earlier that day someone from his division came and offered him a promotion as the Division Chief of Supply. Desk job. For a guy that had spent his entire career downrange that was insult to injury.

Kris didn't see him at first and made use of the mats to start back into basic strength training with pushups and sit ups to rebuild her abs. He just sat in the wheelchair not moving. She stopped and spoke to him and congratulated him on his promotion. He sneered at her and said in a disgusted tone it was an insult. He wasn't going to take it. She asked him to reconsider. It encouraged her to know that a combat veteran was going to head supply. Someone who knew what it was like in the field and the challenges the men faced when their equipment was delayed, lost, or just plain wrong.

Kris told him a story about how one of the divisions received 500 boxes of paper clips instead of 500 magazine clips. The stupid paper pusher in the office in Florida didn't see how that was his problem the requisition had got screwed up. He was sitting in a comfy air-conditioned office back in the states while Marines were getting killed in the desert heat because they didn't have what they needed to get the job done. Knowing a combat trained Colonel would be there to whip those pencil necked paper pushers into shape gave her strength to know when she got downrange everything they needed would be there because Tucker would make sure of it.

As Kris left she turned to him.

"Just make sure you get a nice fully functioning prosthetic, Sir. Don't let them push off one of those Government issue pieces of crap on you. You deserve the best. And don't slack on your therapy Sir. It seems stupid and unnecessary but these guys know what we need. You listen to them."

The Colonel just sat there in the dark when Kris left. An hour later he was back in his room. The next day he gathered up several others in the 'squad' and brought them to the gym where he knew Kris would be. They all talked. All of them, including Kris, ducked out of group therapy. Not wanting to sit and listen to a bunch of Marines whine about their problems. Kris knew it would help most of them, but what could anyone say for her? She talked to all of them. Her commonsense approach and straight forward manner was just what they all needed. Not to be coddled or given platitudes but matter of fact talk. She spoke to all of them on their issues straight forward and clear. Told them to let go of what was and embrace what is and move on. Talking to her pulled all of them out of the brink. They all improved and were able to be discharged or transferred for more treatment.

When the men found out about Kris and what happened to her they were amazed. They couldn't believe it. Most of them admitted they wouldn't be able to handle it. She agreed. Being a woman wasn't for the weak. Good thing she wasn't one! There were worst things. They could be Air Force. The laughter at that comment was genuine and rich. They all left there over the next few weeks grateful to have met Kris. What none of them knew was that eyes and ears were everywhere and all their 'meetings' were observed. Kris had managed what the head shrinkers couldn't; to get the men to accept their injuries and move on. One of those doctors also nominated Kris for commendation. It was the same doctor who had treated and signed off on Tucker's return to duty as the Division Supply Colonel.

Tucker was heavily invested in Kris being confirmed for that nomination. He wouldn't be there if not for Kris. He found the work he did rewarding and challenging. He also worked with other Wounded Warriors in combating depression, PTSD, and transition to civilian life. He was given a new purpose and was determined that the reason he was there would be formally acknowledged for her contributions to the Corps. After interviewing her men, SOC, and others Kris had worked with since joining the Corps he made sure that everyone was aware of how exceptional a Marine Kristin Cole was. His recommendation was so outstanding it was brought to the attention of the Commandant of the Marine Corps who reviewed and forward Cole's nomination to the Secretary of Defense and then personally invited Kris and her team to Marine Corps Birthday ball in Washington DC. The team was released from field duty to come back and attend Kris's awards ceremony.

Chapter Eight

The Marine Corps Birthday Ball held in Washington DC was an exclusive event. Celebrations were held in cities all over the country and all Marines were expected to attend and pay homage to their beloved Corps. The Commandant of the Marine Corps reads a birthday message which is aired to all the celebrations nationwide and to those serving overseas.

When she checked into the Washington Hilton where the event was being held, she was pleasantly surprised to see her room was upgraded to a very large suite. Compliments of the Marine Corps in honor of their Medal of Honor winner. She wandered around the suite taking in the modern upscale furnishings with the dark wood and light materials with appreciation. The living room and dining room was larger than the one in the home she shared with Mel. The bedroom was clean and modern with a king bed with padded headboard attached to a bathroom designed to wrap the user in clean lines and sumptuous luxury. Her three days there were going to be very nice. After stowing her bags and sending her new dress uniform down to press out any wrinkles, Kris took a walk into the sitting area where an envelope sat on a tray on the coffee table. It was addressed to her with the Commandant's seal. Her original pride in receiving a personal message from the head of the Marine Corps quickly turned to seething rage. The letter stated that Kris would not be permitted to wear the Marine Evening Dress "B" or Blue Dress "A" uniforms for the event. Hoping Kris would understand that wearing the Marine Uniform as a female would be an 'affront' to both male and female Marines; and as she was still on medical leave she was technically 'separated' due to her medical status which was still under review making her not entitled to wear the uniform.

Kris had never been so furious in all her life. Even all the abuse her dad put her through did not fill her with the red tinged fury she was seething with. The ability to kill someone with her bare hands was something she never took lightly but was currently something she wanted to utilize on the bureaucrats who were determined to make her pay for something out of her control. It took her a couple of hours to calm down enough to think. She almost destroyed the letter, but instead took it and several sheets of paper down to the front desk. She made copies of the letter and left notes for each member of the team to meet in her room at four o'clock. With Justin's letter was another note to meet her earlier and a key to the room. She did not want her first time seeing Justin since Germany to be with the whole team present. Just then the front desk clerk took a call and called out to Kris as she was walking back to the elevator. The laundry had called to say her uniform was lost, and they were doing everything in their power to find it. Kris knew whoever took her uniform did so with a purpose in mind. Lost? Right.

Those invited to the Washington Event are among the Who's Who of the Marines and Armed Forces. 2dMRB 5th Marines MSOT Alpha Team were among the special invitees to this select event. After a great deal of deliberation and several investigations the Secretary of Defense confirmed Kris's nomination for the Medal of Honor but awarded it in a special private ceremony that was held three days ahead of the joint ceremony. Ordinarily the event is combined with those awarded from each branch of service, but due to the circumstances around Kris, the powers that be decided to award Kris in a smaller private ceremony and reception away from the normal hoopla of the event citing that Kris's current assignment in Special Operations would be in jeopardy from the usual publicity. It was quiet, but not by any means less prestigious than the combined ceremony.

It was politics and pandering. Protecting Kris was a dodge; the Marine Corps or the DoD was trying to hide the embarrassment of having a female Marine that served as male for nearly a decade. There seemed to be a great number of people in Washington that did not like Kris's place in SOC. The campaign by a select few to see her removed from duty was still very much underway. Her team was still in transit from deployment and was unable to make the quickly set up separate ceremony as planned. The only one there from SOC was Colonel Stirling who was able to get to Washington ahead of time to be there for Kris's big moment. She was glad he was there for her. She considered him family. Mel couldn't come and Kris, understanding her conflict wasn't upset. Mel was with her there in spirit. With so many people ready and willing to capitalize over her situation and use her for their own interests and agendas, Kris slipped out of her own reception. It was so skillful no one noticed she was gone for some time. She brooded about what she was going to face when she returned to duty. She hated this stuff.

A knock at the door disrupted her dark musings. The door opened before she could get to it admitting Justin with the key she had left him. Their eyes caught and held as he took in her new form. She still had roughly the same physique; the weeks of lighter activity combined with the hormone treatments slightly softening her hard muscles into muscular curves. The plain white t-shirt clinging to her generous new breasts before flowing down into the waist of her tightly molded faded jeans. She shouldn't have looked seductive, but his blood was racing. He shut the door behind him and walked slowly toward her. She met his look boldly and stepped to meet him halfway. It was all he could do to keep his hands off her. He knew if he touched her he wouldn't be able to stop. This wasn't the time with the team about to arrive; but later he would get her alone with no possibility of interruptions.

Kris was waiting for him to say something. He kept running his eyes over her body and she would swear she could actually feel them touching her. She felt as if someone turned up the furnace as the room was unbearably hot suddenly. She let him take in her new shape and gloried in the unbridled appreciation in his eyes. She would never admit she was worried how he would react to her new form. A small part of her was afraid he would not like what he saw. He not only seemed to like it but seemed to be having a very hard time not exploring it with more than his eyes. His fists kept clenching. She was about to step into his hard form when there was a knock at the door. He walked further into the suite willing his body to cool as she opened the door to room service. They brought in a cart of refreshments she ordered for the team who would be arriving shortly. After signing the slip and letting them out she spoke.

"You look like you could use a beer."

"I think I need something stronger than that, but I won't turn one down."

She smiled that familiar grin he remembered so well and took the top off a bottle and handed it to him. She did the same for one for herself.

"I can't believe the transformation in you. I am having a very hard time seeing the man I have been best friends with for eight years in the sexy woman in front of me. I like that you grew out your hair for me."

Kris's hair was in a pixie cut. It was very flattering to her high cheekbones and strong jaw. Kris snorted, "Who said I did it for you, Sir?" She had. She knew how many fantasies he'd had of her with long hair.

Justin's smile became feral. He closed the distance between them and nearly pinned her against the back of the couch where she was standing. Her nose filled with his scent. His face was so close she could see the dark brown irises deepen until they were indistinguishable from his pupils. His presence enveloped her so there was nothing else in existence but him and her in that moment. He moved in slowly about to capture her lips with his when another knock sounded at the door. Kris was so focused on Justin the sound made her react; a strong jerk upsetting her beer down her shirt front.

"Can you get that Sir? Looks like I need a new shirt."

Justin's eyes grew even darker with desire as the liquid made the material covering her chest practically transparent. The top now see through material. The knock sounded again as she moved from her pinned position against the couch, brushing against Justin boldly as she stared him down with heated eyes and headed into the bedroom. Justin took a deep breath and walked to the door. He opened the door to the remaining six members of the team who had arrived with him an hour before in the transport van carrying them and the two wives who came up for the event.

Tomball and Gentry went over to the room service carts and grabbed a couple of beers and sat down. Juarez looked around and whistled.

"Nice digs! Gunny rob a bank or something?"

The others laughed making other snarky comments regarding the posh upscale space.

"Our Medal of Honor winner was upgraded, compliments of the Corps. Wow! They comped the room and meals for the stay!" Gentry set down the card he had appropriated from the dining table from the hotel. "Maybe we should charge any shit we get to Gunny!"

A familiar voice drifted out of the bedroom, "Don't even consider it, Lieutenant!"

The familiar voice was soon followed by a not so familiar body. The familiar black t-shirt was formed around an unfamiliar pair Double D-cup breasts; breasts which seemed to have everyone's attention.

"So, got some interesting news from the doctor when I was wounded..." Kris stopped and grabbed her beer from the table where she had sat it down and took a long drink.

The six powerfully built men were in varying stages of shock. Juarez kept looking her up and down, shaking his head, then starting over. Tomball choked on his beer and got up and turned his back on the group coughing his dark cocoa skin flushing. Reineke sat paused with his drink halfway to his mouth and stopped. Gentry swore and put his head in his hands. Jenkins sat back on the couch with his arms crossed and a blank expression on his face; which told Kris he was upset and not knowing how to react. Jeffries started laughing; literally falling off the arm of the couch and rolling on the floor laughing.

Kris gave them a second to take it in and then loudly cleared her throat causing all of them to start. Juarez looked at Alario propped against the wall with his arms crossed with no obvious surprise on his face.

"Major, you knew? You knew and didn't tell us?"

The men all looked to Justin with degrees of anger and betrayal.

"I wasn't going to say anything until I talked to Kris."

All eyes turned back to her for an explanation.

"I was born without a gender and raised a boy."

Kris explained about finding out about her condition, the situation with the Major, and went on to explain waking up in the ICU finding out about the surgery.

"Since the prosthetic couldn't be removed, I chose not to find out. I wouldn't live a lie if it turned out I wasn't male. But since nothing during my pubescence indicated I could be female," she indicated her breasts, "I assumed incorrectly that I was either male or completely gender neutral which can happen with my condition.

My mom had raised me pretty gender neutral and always said it didn't matter, it was just a label and I didn't need to worry so much on a label that would limit me but work to become someone beyond labels and limits. I tried to do that. I didn't much care one way or the other. It wasn't like it was a shock to know. I just hoped it wouldn't mess with my ability to rejoin the team. I hoped it wouldn't change how you guys see me. I hoped our unity and friendship wouldn't be jacked up and torn apart. I am the same person I was before."

"Yeah, it's just now that giant set of cojones you had in BVDs; you now wear in your Double Ds."

Juarez always knew how to make them all laugh. Kris almost spit out the drink of beer she paused to drink. Jeffries, who never made it off the ground just leaned his head back cracking up all over again. The rest of them seemed to relax. Reineke threw a sofa pillow at Javier's head. He ducked, and it nailed Tomball in the chest. Kris looked at Justin who was smiling at the team's antics knowing the storm had passed. It would take a while to really accept it, but the anger was gone considering the knowledge that Kris was just as much in the dark about it as they were.

They asked about her Medal ceremony, and she filled them in on the highlights. When they asked her how she enjoyed the reception afterwards she admitted she skipped it and came back to the hotel.

"So, you don't know then, huh Gunny?" Davis Gentry asked.

"Know what?"

"A brawl broke out at that reception. I tapped a buddy of mine who was who's a staffer for the Commission to get info since they rushed us to get here only to go on without us. Colonel Stirling punched a civilian and beat him to a pulp. They had to drag him off. The Colonel left under his own power, but I heard tell that he was severely reprimanded for it."

Justin spoke before Kris could, "Who was this civilian?"

"Retired Army Major Marcus Sheldon Cole. Relation of yours Gunny?"

Kris's face turned to stone at the mention of the Major's name.

"My father."

Justin asked, "What did your guy say happened?"

"Well from what he said the man kept making references to Kris all night. How sorry he was she wasn't there; how sad he was that he couldn't share this moment with his only child. How her mother deliberately kept them apart after their divorce, so he never got to have a relationship with his child. How he reached out to her just last week and she refused to give him Kris's number and let her know he would be in town.

Apparently, he wasn't invited, but weaseled his way in as a plus one. As soon as the Colonel saw him sparks started to fly. Every comment he made the Colonel's face was consumed with fury until he just snapped and grabbed the man by the throat and then beat the daylights out of him. It took four men to pull him off. When they did, the Major was barely conscious. The Colonel blasted him. He looked at the Commandant and told him the Major was a lying sack and a worthless excuse for a human being and an embarrassment to the Army and Spec Ops.

He told the Commandant to look up Cole VS Cole and he would see that he was no father, but a monster who should be caged. That he was thankful that Kris wasn't here to be subjected to this criminal and his lies. That she was a shining example of what it meant to be a Marine and he thought of her as a son since she joined his command. And now that she was found to be female he was proud to think of her as the daughter he never had.

To take note that Cole was careful to say 'child' and not 'daughter' because the possibility of her being female was like bamboo shoots under his nails for as long as she lived. That he is a liar and manipulator and if they were smart, they'd cut ties with him immediately. Then he turned to the Major who was still on the floor bleeding and pulled him up by his collar and said, 'By the way you pathetic lying bastard, Jenna was killed ten years ago when Kris was 18!' Then he hit him again and knocked him out. He picked up his cover, put it on, apologized for his behavior and how it reflected on himself and the Corps, and saluted the room before turning heal and walking out."

Kris was furious her father tried to use her to gain sympathy and favor with the bigwigs who attended the event. It made her happier than ever before she skipped it. She's pretty sure she would have snapped his neck if she saw him face to face. She was having a harder time absorbing the fact that the Colonel not only defended her but told the entire room he thought of her as a daughter. She considered him the father she never had but never knew he felt the same way. Kris moved over to look out the window overwhelmed with emotion.

"No, I didn't know Davis. Thank you for telling me."

"What now Gunny?" Gentry was curious. "When are you coming back? You are coming back, right?"

Kris's face darkened with rage. She handed him the letter she received and sat stone faced while he read it aloud. When he finished the men were all on their feet and swearing.

"This is bullshit!"

"Are you kidding me?"

"Those Assholes!"

"They can't do this!"

Justin came over and took it from him to look it over. He recognized the genuine seal and looked straight at Kris. "What are you going to do about this?"

"I don't know. I made a few calls and the letter did come from his office, but it's possible it was from a corpsman and not the Commandant himself. I can't see the man pulling something like this, he's a straight shooter. "

"Yeah, that awards ceremony was straight shooting," Jenkins said with rancor. The team was pissed that they raced back to the States to make the ceremony only to miss it anyway.

"I don't have to like the politics to understand it, Dan. It's clear they don't want me to come to the ball. If I can't wear the uniform, I am not going."

A new round of swearing ensued.

"If you don't go, you let those bastards win!"

"You can't do that man!"

"I say screw'em! You more than anyone has earned the right to wear that uniform. Go anyway!"

"I would, but the hotel laundry called to tell me the uniform I sent down for pressing earlier was lost. They are terribly sorry. I can't get another, that one had to be special ordered because I am not a standard female size. I say someone is trying to make a statement."

"So, make one of your own." Justin's gaze pierced into hers. "Buy a dress and come anyway. They want to play a game saying you can't wear the uniform, get a gown, and beat them at their own game."

"I wouldn't have the faintest idea of how to buy a dress or even where to get one at this short notice."

Reineke was looking up various sites on his phone. He rattled off the names of four dress shops within a half an hour of the hotel. One specialized in hard to fit sizes. The men all agreed and had Kris pushed out the door in minutes not waiting for her to respond. The Raiders were going dress shopping.

Luckily Georgetown had several boutiques that catered to the needs of the Washington elite and gowns were not in short supply. The difficulty would be in finding one to fit in time for the ball tomorrow night. The first two shops the team hit did not have anything to suit. The third looked to be the charm. The staff seemed to be a bit nervous with the sudden arrival of eight very tough-looking Marines. The team split up and started looking. Reineke, having been married for 15 years had no trouble asking the staff for help. The next thing Kris knew she was being measured and sized.

Thanks to Juarez the team had in their earpieces, so they could communicate effectively throughout the large store. To them, this was just another mission. Kris was warmed at their response, which soon turned to wariness as some of the comments came through the earpiece. She was terrified about what they were going to come up with. Each man decided to pick out a dress for Kris to try. Their tastes ran from gaudy to prudish. She gave up trying to direct them and let them have their fun while she picked a couple of nice, but classic styles the Mel suggested during a rushed call on the drive in.

The staff showed Kris into a dressing room, and she started trying on dresses. Javier had picked a gold-colored slinky metallic dress that almost didn't cover her rear. It had more material in the sleeves than across the front which dipped down to a V halfway to her navel. The comments when she came out were varied.

"Daaamn!"

"Um, no. It's a ball, not Club Spyder in Miami Javi!"

"Gunny, you're looking good!"

Kris just shook her head and went back into the dressing room. Justin signaled to one of the clerks and said something low that had her nodding and smiling.

The next dress was a bit too matronly.

"She looks like your Grandma Gentry!"

"Hey, it's not that bad! At least she's not naked like your dress Javi!"

The next several were better, but not the right color or look. Kris was thinking this was going to be a failed mission. Their first.

Several more and she came to the dress Justin had picked out for her. He always did have style. It was beautiful, classic, and molded to her curves without losing its elegance. The dark midnight blue was elegant and tasteful. It had the appearance of being strapless with the blue satiny material clinging to her generous breasts in a sweetheart design, the sheer bodice flowing into snug fitting sheer sleeves that were covered with lace appliques down the top of her arms and ringing the top around her collar bones like a lace necklace. The lace helped cover her special forces tattoo. The A-line skirt hung straight to the floor after cinching at the waist with a jeweled clip. She asked the clerk to help her fasten it before looking at it in the 360-degree mirror. The guys were calling for her to come out, but she just stopped at stared for a long minute at her reflection. The dress was perfect. It didn't even need any alterations. It was as if it was custom made for her.

"You will need to pick up a bustier for underneath, dear." The clerk said.

"I don't know what that is."

"Oh, it's like a strapless bra that fits down your torso. I think a garter belt would be good too. Easier than pantyhose."

Kris paled at the idea of pantyhose and shopping for underwear with the guys. The clerk looked at her curiously. "You've never bought lingerie before, have you dear?"

"Is it that obvious?" Kris said dryly. The woman chuckled.

"I don't suppose you want those handsome brutes to help with that hmm?"

"Over my dead body," Kris said with all seriousness.

"Don't worry, we'll send them on their way and take you to this wonderful store down the block. I know they have just the right things for you. What size do you wear, I'll make a call."

Kris just stared ahead for a moment.

"I don't know my size. I've never bought a bra before."

The woman seemed a bit startled by that but took out her measuring tape and got to work after helping Kris out of the dress and hanging it up. When Kris came out in jeans and a t-shirt the guys all had something to say about not seeing the dress on. Kris ignored them. When the woman said she'd take Kris next door to pick out the lingerie Javier got up to start for the door with an eager grin and was swiftly shut down by Justin who slammed him back into his seat informing Kris they would take the van back and send it to pick her up later.

"Thank you, guys. I wouldn't have been able to do this without you."

Jeffries summed it up, "Hey we are a team. It's what we do!"

Kris went to pay for the dress and found it already boxed and bagged.

"It's all taken care of dearie."

Kris looked at the woman questioningly.

"That rather built dreamy one paid for it already."

"They are all built!"

"Oh, the dangerous Italian one with the bedroom eyes and quiet brooding stance."

Justin, it figured.

"I'd hold onto that one if I were you honey!"

"We are a unit, teammates. We aren't..."

"Well two good looking people like you, that won't last long! Come on dearie, let's get you fixed up next door."

Kris had feeling this was going to be more taxing than the dresses, but she was tough. A Marine can face down any dangerous situation; even a lingerie store.

Chapter Nine

When Kris returned the hotel, there were two messages on her room phone. One was from the hotel spa confirming her appointment for the next day. The second was from Justin; telling her that he arranged for the appointment and to enjoy it- that's an order. She chuckled. Now she only wondered was how she going to look presentable when she had no idea how-to put-on makeup or style her hair for a formal event. Mel had been teaching her. She didn't feel the need to slap on eyeliner and mascara just to leave her bedroom like some people. And lipstick was still a major challenge. It still boggled Mel's mind how her hands could be steady enough to disarm live ordinance but not to keep lipstick within her lip lines. She pithily replied that she's had a great deal more practice with ordinance than lipstick. She figured she'd keep it simple. Hopefully she wouldn't look like a clown.

Kris dialed down to order room service. She hung up the phone and heard the ping from her cell indicating an instant message. She opened it and saw it was Justin.

What are you wearing?

She laughed. He was very playful in text.

Just a little something I picked up.

At the lingerie store?

MC Surplus.

I am trying to imagine you in a flak jacket and nothing else. Hmmm. It has possibilities.

Kris snorted. *Not a flak jacket. M-16.*

Umm. One clip or two?

Pervert.

Did you get everything you need for the Ball? I wanted to go with you, but there was no way I was going to allow the rest of them to come. No way I could shake them either. Missed opportunity.

I got a little something. Very little...

Hmmm. Interesting. I can't wait to see it.

Who says I'll let you see it, Sir?

Oh, you'll let me see it. I can't wait to see you in that dress. As soon as I saw it, I could see you in it. I wonder if my imagination has done it justice. I want to see you in that dress almost as much as I want to see you out of it.

It's a beautiful dress. You have excellent taste.

Her blood heated with his next response.

Of course I do, I chose you didn't I? Tomorrow can't come soon enough.

You could come up now.

If I come up now, neither one of us will sleep and we both want to be good for tomorrow. It will also give you time to get used to the idea. Get some chow and rack time. The next time you get in that bed......you won't be alone.

Kris's body got all hot and tight with that response. Her breathing was rapid, and her pulse was fluttering.

Sleep is overrated.

Uughh. You tempt me. I don't want to rush this for you. I want you to want me as badly as I want you.

She didn't want to disappoint him. He had significantly more experience than she.

Oh, I definitely want you.

You should undressed and get comfy.

Kris looked up at the knock on the door.

I would, but I don't want the room service attendant to think he's getting a different kind of tip.

Excellent point. Save it for tomorrow. Eat. Get some rest. You won't get any tomorrow night...

Is that a threat or a promise, Sir?

BOTH!

Kris logged off and opened the door for the room service tray. She was suddenly very hungry. After eating and taking a warm shower she settled down to sleep. She was beginning to think of the Ball like any other op. It was going to take a clear head and a rested body to navigate the political minefield she would have to enter tomorrow. Game on.

***

A day of spa treatments would seem like a dream day to most women, but Kris was not most women. Although the massage was nice and relaxing, she could do without the wraps, skin treatments, and waxing. It was a good thing the massage was last. She needed to relax after what she considered a day just shy of torture. Why the hell did women do this to themselves? And how the hell was it relaxing and gratifying?

Kris volunteered her suite as the ready spot for the women. Mary Jeffries and Sue Reineke were shocked speechless at Kris's transformation. Their husbands were not very forthcoming regarding their earlier meeting with Kris. Not sure how to describe Kris's transformation they chose to say little other than Kris being fit. After Kris made some quick explanations the women were quick to take her under their wings and help her get ready; what Kris had been hoping for when they arrived. The undergarments that seemed pretty straight forward in the shop appeared much more intimidating when she had to put them on herself. She had a hard time maneuvering the hooks on the bustier but got them in the end. The garters where a bit harder. She bought three sets of stockings just in case she tore them. The women helped her hook the garters after several failed attempts and one set of stockings were pretty much destroyed.

A knock on the door had her looking at Mary and Sue with confusion. They shook their heads. Sue went to the door and let in Davis Gentry. He was carrying a black bag. He pushed right in and announced, "I am here to do your hair and makeup, so sit down and shut up and we'll get through this without bloodshed."

"Davis have you lost your mind?"

"No Gunny I have not! I am going to let you in on a little known secret. I am a professional stylist. Or I was before the Corps and will be again one day soon."

"You don't say."

"I do say. I am one of the most sought-after beauticians in all of Louisiana! I keep up with the styles and trends by 'volunteering' my services to the lovely ladies of our fare Camp both here and abroad for a modest donation to my Go Fund Me account. I have passed the North Carolina state examinations to practice in our fair state, but I refuse to work for anyone but myself. In just one more year I will have accumulated enough to finally open my own salon and pick up where I left off five years ago when I took my commission in the Corps."

Sue stepped up as Davis set up his portable station. It seemed he really wasn't kidding as he rolled out a kit of scissors, hairbrushes, combs, hair dryer, and various curling and flattening irons. Kris stood there in just her stockings and lingerie and heels trying not to laugh. Well hell. Why not? It couldn't be worse than her attempts and the women would help if need be.

Kris stepped up to the chair Davis indicated and sat down. He covered her with a plastic cape and grabbed a spray bottle that he filled up in the wet bar sink. He sprayed her hair and started combing it out. He grabbed the scissors and started circling her as he looked her over.

"Why does a stylist leave the salon and enter the Marine Corps? And how does he end up in MARSOC?"

"Well that is easy. My Granny owned the salon I learned my trade in. I spent every spare minute in there from the age of twelve on. Got in a spot of trouble that year with some rather dubious acquaintances. After Granny picked me up at the sheriff's station and was informed of my crimes (we vandalized a local hated teachers house) I was given 100 hours of community service which Granny decided would be at her salon so she could mind me. Sweeping and washing towels every day after school and on weekends instead of hanging out at the lake." He shook his head in mock dismay. "The week of prom Granny had two stylists out with the flu, one run off to Boca leaving just her and I for a full house. She had me washing hair and toweling up. Then the Mayor's wife Mrs. Mitzi Beauregard walks in."

Davis continually snipped Kris's hair while the other ladies looked on in amazement. She must not have looked too bad then.

"She demanded Granny do her hair as they were eating with the Governor that night and she needed a fresh do. Well Granny was eight deep in teenage girls needing to be done by 6pm and here it is 4pm and each one needing at least a half an hour to style. You can do the math. She told her I am sorry but not today. Well you can imagine the Mayor's wife was not used to hearing no. She says, 'Ms. Vivian (that was Granny) you and I have partnership. I could go to any number of salons in the Parish much more stylish and sophisticated than your humble shop, but we go way back and I do not forget my oldest dear friends. I know you can make an exception for an old dear friend.'

Now Mrs. Beauregard was stone bitch. And powerful. One bad word from her could make my Granny's financial prospects dim for the foreseeable future so she nodded to me to take her back to the sinks and get Ms. Mitzi started. The girls started shift and grumble, but one eagle eyed look from Granny stopped them in short order! I got her back to the chair and started toweling her off and grabbed the cart with the curlers and such in it. I watched Granny for weeks setting styles and rolling curls. Wasn't a thing to it. I grab the comb and start combing her out. She's running her mouth and doesn't notice a thing. She had a style that was at least 15 years too old for her. Feeling being the Mayor's wife she needed to look a bit more reserved. I grabbed a pair scissors and started snipping away. Granny was too

involved to notice but the girls waiting were absolutely
spellbound! The snickering was legion!

I trimmed her up and shaped her hair so it looked less like the
helmet worn by LSU football team and more like the young thirty
something she was. Then I set the curlers and put her under the
dryer. When she was done she sat back down, still running her
mouth, and I combed her out. I grabbed the curling iron and
tweaked a few of the curls and set it with the lacquer. I handed
her the mirror and she stopped flapping her mouth for the first
since she got in. She looked aghast. Her hair was beautiful and
much more flattering than the old-fashioned style she had
before. She realized Granny had not touched her and that a 12
year old boy had just cut and styled her hair! She walked up to
the desk in absolute silence and paid Ms. Joleen and without a
word she left."

Davis grabbed the hair dryer and dried Kris's hair. After he
picked up the irons and dove in barely pausing in his story.

"Granny looked at me and said, 'Boy get to the next one.' So the
girl stands up and hands me a magazine and says, 'I want this.'
So I sit her down and look over the picture and look at her. Nod
and get to it. 20 minutes later she matched that magazine-
exactly! The next girl was called by Granny and she looks to me
instead a little scared that Granny would mind. She just waved
her over and called the next. The style she wanted did not suit
her and I said so. So she says make me beautiful. I did. Between
us we got every one of them done by 6pm. When we locked the
door Ms. Joleen looked like she had swallowed a porcupine! She
handed me a twenty dollar bill. A tip from Ms. Mitzi. The richest
and cheapest woman in town! I think it was her first tip in the
history of her patronage.

The next day Granny set me to doing the church ladies. The next
week Ms. Mitzi comes back in for a set. Well we were fully
staffed by then and one of the girls brought her to a chair. She
looks at me and says, 'Boy? Are you going to do my hair or just
sit there like a lump?' I get up to their absolute shock and tend to
her as she just runs wildfire on dinner at the Governor's.
Dropping names and lording over everyone in there. And saying
how many compliments she received on her gorgeous new

hairdo. I grabbed the scissors and took a bit more off and reshaped it before setting it. The girls almost had a stroke. I finished up and she gave me my tip directly and paid and left."

Davis finished with her hair put down the hair tools and grabbed a box. In it was a large variety of makeup. He started applying it to her like an artist on a canvas.

"Granny told one of the girls to show me how to mix color. And walk me through a permanent wave. By the time summer vacation started I had four regular clients- one being Ms. Mitzi! Granny set me up for summer classes at the hair college. By the time I started high school I had passed the state exams for beauty and barbering. I went to college for a business degree. I was going to take over the salon. Granny wanted to retire. But she got sick. Her savings wouldn't pay for all the hospital and she was going to lose the shop. I paid the rest of the bill with all the money I had saved since I was twelve working at the salon. That left me with a little Miracle and no means! One of my regular customers was a Marine. Told me about the GI Bill. That sounded great to me. And lots of men in uniform!

I tell you Gunny I love it. Best thing I ever did. I love being a Marine. I joined Spec Ops to impress a gorgeous Captain who was trying out. He did not make it, but I did. I found somewhere I truly belong. It gives me that same rush I felt the first time I picked up a pair of scissors. The GI Bill paid for my education and I get to travel. Meet all sorts and expand my knowledge. I have been able to save up so by next year between all the investments I have made with my regular pay and the GFM account I not only can start my own salon; I have been able to take classes at night for massage therapy and nails so I can have a full-fledged spa. I have bought a building and hired three stylists so when my hitch is up this year I walk right in. That way my little Miracle will have her daddy home every night instead of halfway around the world in the sand box half the time. Boom!"

He stroked across her face with a final flourish and stepped back. He picked up a hand mirror as Sue and Mary gawked at how Kris looked.

The make-up and hair were amazing. There are only so many styles her short hair can accommodate and since this was a formal and classy event, the make-up was simple and stylish. She was terrified she'd end up looking like the women on Javier's Telenovelas or a drag queen knowing Davis's flamboyant ways. Her hair was trimmed and styled in an elegant pixie cut that flattered her heart shaped hollow cheeked face. Her eyes were slightly smoky making the golden-brown pop. The blush and highlighter made her high cheekbones more defined and the light gloss on her lips finished the effect. The women gushed that she looked like a runway model. Unfortunately, she did. Davis saluted Kris with a jaunty smirk and kissed Mary and Sue then left to get dressed. The women left to find their husbands and Kris went to her room and pulled out the gown she would wear. After donning her gown and shoes she looked powerful and elegant. Beautiful diamond drop earrings with a matching bracelet she found at the jewelry store down the street from the dress store completed the outfit. She wasn't completely clueless when it came to being a female. Watching Mel and shopping with her the last decade gave her a basic idea of how to put together an outfit with accessories. It just didn't mean she was going to do so every time she got dressed.

She stood for several moments in front of the full-length mirror in the bathroom. She liked what she saw. She didn't have any false modesty; she had always known her looks were striking. For a man they were a bit pretty, but for a woman they were stunning. She had no doubts when she walked into the room people would notice. She knew Justin liked what he saw when she was in jeans and a t-shirt, so he couldn't help but like her now. She remembered how he looked with Trina; two beautiful sleek sexy predators. She couldn't help but think of how they would look together. Powerful? Intimidating? Time to find out.

Chapter Ten

The team decided to enter the Ball as a Unit, so they were all waiting in the lobby at the bar for Kris to arrive. Javier couldn't sit still so he was pacing back and forth glancing at the stairs. Justin leaned against the bar and finally grabbed Javi by his shoulder and stuffed a drink in hand telling him to calm down. The rest of the team was talking amongst themselves.

"If any of these guys try to hit on Kris we'll have to kill them," Tomball remarked to Gentry and Juarez.

Justin caught movement out of the corner of his eye and looked to the stairs. Their eyes met and held. Kris had just started descending when the team finally took notice of her. Javier looked up and promptly dropped his glass, not even realizing when it shattered on the floor. Conversations came to a halt all over the lobby as she reached the bottom of the staircase. Justin walked over to her and offered her his arm. A couple of the men complained saying they should be the ones to escort her, but Justin pulled rank on them effectively shutting them down.

When they entered the ballroom, a similar phenomenon occurred, and many pairs of eyes turned their way and followed them to their table. Justin pulled out the chair for Kris, to which gave she him a hard look but sat anyway and took the one to her left. The rest of the team followed suit. Davis signaled for a tray of champagne to be brought to the table and the team toasted to the Corps and their unit before settling down to hear the Commandant's speech. The Marine Corps Birthday Ball Speech was broadcast to every ball worldwide and kicked off the event. Afterwards the dancing started. Justin claimed Kris for her first dance but did not get to keep her long as the Commandant cut in only after a few moments. They had only taken a few steps when he addressed her attire.

"Gunnery Sergeant Cole I am shocked to see you are out of uniform."

Kris just cocked her head to the side and gave the Commandant a measured stare.

"Sir! I am shocked you are making issue regarding my uniform considering the letter I received yesterday from your office telling me I was not fit to wear it."

The Commandant looked both confused and furious at this statement. Seeing the equal fury behind Kris's eyes he measured his words carefully.

"What exactly did this alleged letter say?"

"I was hoping for an explanation for it Sir, so I have it right here." Kris opened the small handbag she carried with the letter folded inside. "I have to say I almost did not come, personal invitation or not, I was so disgusted and insulted. To have my integrity so impugned did not sit well with me Sir."

The Commandant stopped dancing to read the letter, fury playing over his face. He looked at Kris with a hard-fierce look that would have quelled a lesser Marine. Kris knew the look was not for her, but on behalf of her.

"I would like to apologize to you Gunnery Sergeant Cole for the actions from my office. I deeply regret that someone in my ranks could treat a decorated Marine, a Medal of Honor winner, and a valuable asset to our Spec Ops program-hell to the entire Marine Corps in such a cowardly insulting way. I would like to hold on to this Gunny if you don't mind. I promise you; I will get to the bottom of this. Whoever abused my office in such a way is going to be dealt with harshly. I don't tolerate this kind of antics. No Marine has the right to treat another Marine in this manner."

"Thank you for that Commandant. I believe whoever is responsible for that letter is also responsible for my uniform turning up 'missing' from the hotel laundry. No doubt it will turn up in the morning like magic. Someone has a hard on for me and is trying to make a statement. I hope you find them before I do. I'd hate to ruin my first manicure beating them to a pulp." Kris said with heavy sarcasm and quite a bit of dark humor.

The Commandant threw back his head and laughed as he tucked the letter in the inside pocket of his dress jacket and moved back in to dance with Kris. They circled several more times until the

Commandant signaled to someone behind Kris and stopped dancing.

"I want you to know this will be handled. I didn't take this to make it disappear."

"I know Sir. But if you find it does wander off, I have several dozen copies." Kris said with a blinding grin.

The Commandant chuckled in response and handed Kris's hand to a Marine that had just come up behind her.

"Watch out for this one Colonel, she is tough and smart. Let me know if you do not see that uniform again Cole, I will see that it gets replaced."

"Thank you, Sir!" Kris raised her arm but let it drop to her side. It was hard for Kris not to salute the Commandant. It was reflex, but she was not permitted to out of uniform.

Colonel Stirling moved around and finished the Commandant's dance. He looked around the dance floor at the dozens of eyes cast on them.

"You have caused quite the sensation tonight Kris. If you hadn't been with the team, I doubt I would have recognized you." The Colonel looked at Kris like he'd never seen her before which made her a bit uncomfortable. She looked at him and realized he had some light bruising at his jaw and his knuckles were torn up.

"I hear from the scuttlebutt my reception was a knock down drag out success."

The Colonel smirked and pulled Kris a little closer, so she couldn't look in his face.

"It had its moments."

"I hear the highlight was a certain Army Major finally getting what he so richly deserved."

"You heard right." He muttered under his breath, 'that son of a bitch.'

Kris pulled away to look at the Colonel. Her eyes were full of pride. He was oozing smug satisfaction. Kris did something she may not have had the courage to do in uniform. She said something she'd always thought, but never shared with the man who was her hero. She leaned over and kissed the Colonel on the cheek and said, "Thank you, Dad." As she brushed his insignia at his collar with the lowered rank of Lieutenant Colonel. She was aware how much that comeuppance cost him.

The Colonel looked shocked at the endearment and looked into her nearly identically colored brown eyes with his own and said gruffly, "You don't have to thank me, it truly was my pleasure."

He motioned to someone behind her and the next thing Kris heard was a familiar voice asking to cut in. The Colonel moved back to allow Justin to step in. He nodded to the couple and walked off the dance floor.

"What did you say to the Colonel to make him so upset?"

"I thanked him for defending me to the Major."

Justin pulled her a little closer. Kris pulled back a bit. Justin raised an eyebrow in question.

"Need to watch the distance Sir. Everyone is watching us."

Justin took a look around. She was right, everyone was watching them. He'd have to be careful. Instead he just drank in how she looked. She took his breath away. Even his imagination wasn't so fantastic that he could have visualized how luscious she looked in the gown he chose for her. Just having her so close was wreaking havoc on his body but he couldn't stay away. Before the song ended Juarez showed up.

"Ok Sir, time to let us have a dance with Kris."

Knowing he needed some distance he grudgingly let her go and returned to the table. In order to keep anyone from getting to her the team stayed close. Over the next couple of hours each member of the team and a majority of the top brass at the event asked Kris to dance. She looked like she was quite ready to sit down. He walked over and asked a State Senator that seemed to be making her uncomfortable if he could cut in. He was not gracious about it but stepped aside.

"Thank you for saving me. He wouldn't take no for an answer about me being some sort of poster child for his Women's initiative. No way in hell, Sir."

Justin laughed and moved her off the floor to the doors at the far end looking over the garden.

"You look like you could use some air."

"Thank you, Sir. I can't believe the number of posturing peacocks here this evening. It almost makes me wish I was being shot at."

"So, you want to get out of here?" Justin's eyes got deeper with desire as Kris's breath hitched slightly in response. She didn't trust herself to speak so she just nodded. He placed his hand around her back and steered her around the edge of the ballroom floor and out into the corridor that lead to the lobby. They didn't say anything as they walked up the stairs to the elevators and got in. As they ascended to Kris's floor they looked at each other; each mirroring the other's desire. Kris had butterflies in her stomach as she anticipated what was to come when they got to the room. Justin tried not to think at all. They walked down the hall once they left the elevator and Kris keyed them into the room.

In the ballroom Tomball nudged Juarez as he caught sight of Kris heading out of the ballroom with a Marine.

"Hey, Gunny is leaving. Who is that guy she's with?"

Juarez looked over but couldn't make him out. "Don't know, he looks like everyone else here. Did you see who she was with last?"

"No, I lost her in the crowd when she was dancing with that Senator."

The two men got up from the table and followed the couple out.

"Stay back some, she would beat us bloody if she thought we were spying on her."

"We are not spying; we are protecting our Gunny. Did you see how some of these jerks were staring at her? Anyone messes with her; they mess with all of us. I don't want some jerk hitting on her or her having to protect herself."

They both smirked at each other over that statement. That was tantamount to saying they needed to protect a cobra from a kitten. They continued to follow her but were just far enough behind to lose them in the elevator. They took the stairs up to Kris's floor and got out of the door just as she and the guy she was with entered her suite.

"Man, we missed them."

Javier hit Mike on his arm, "C'mon, I got an idea!"

The two men went down one flight to Javier's room and he grabbed a device out of his bag. It looked like a modified MP3 player but had a folded flap that opened into a little dish on the top.

"What the hell is that?"

"Listening device of my own design. Has amazing range and can go through anything. It's more accurate and clearer then the crap we have in the field." Javier tuned it and pointed it in the general direction of Kris's room. They picked up several conversations until they heard Kris's voice. The device was very sensitive, they could hear every movement, every rustle of fabric.

***

Justin opened the door to the suite for Kris and gestured her inside then shut the door behind them. She walked into the dining room of the suite.

"Why is it a universal truth that dress shoes must break your feet? Whoever invented heels is a misogynist," she said as she lifted one foot up to remove the low-heeled shoe. Justin had the same idea and leaned down to remove his shoes as well.

"If it makes you feel better, it was a man. But they were invented for men not women. Over the centuries men gained stature in height and didn't need them so women appropriated them. Blame your kind!"

With his shoes in his right hand he reached his left out for Kris's shoes. She handed them to him and he set them neatly next to the chair of the dining table. She watched him bend over and marveled at the play of his muscles and the way the uniform looked on his body. She'd seen him in the uniform countless times, but never fully appreciated how amazing he looked in his finest. That uniform was lucky to have him.

Justin let his eyes roam over Kris. Seeing her in that dress coming down the stairs nearly did him in. After all the years they'd known each other, after all the months he suffered in confused silence imagining his best friend in various sexual scenarios, she blew his fantasies away. Every erotic thought, wet dream, and sexual desire seemed to be embodied in the woman right in front of him.

"I never told you how incredibly beautiful you look tonight."

She turned to look at him. "I had a lot of help." She smiled and ran her hands down the gown. He shook his head. She didn't see herself yet. Heaven help him when she did.

Kris moved further into the room and stopped. Several vases of roses rested on surfaces throughout the room with a bucket of chilled champagne in a stand next to the sofa. Soft flickering light came from the bedroom indicating candles were lit. She turned slightly and caught Justin's slow grin as he made his way to the entertainment center and turned on the stereo. Seductive music with a sultry voice played throughout the room. Justin walked to the bucket for the chilled champagne to open it.

"Are we celebrating?" She asked with a raised eyebrow and grin.

The sound of the cork filled the room as Justin turned to her with a filled glass.

"Yes. We are celebrating your first official night as a woman."

Kris let out a husky laugh. "I've been a woman for quite some time now." She sipped the champagne and enjoyed the coolness of the liquid down her dry throat.

"You've been *female* for quite some time now." He walked to her after taking a large drink from his glass and setting it down on the table. He took the glass from her hand and set it next to his as stepped up in front of her with barely a breath between them. He placed his hands on her hips and slowly moved them around to her back. Her hands rested on his arms briefly then began the journey up until they rested on his wide shoulders. Their eyes held. His dark brown almost black with the intensity of his desire; her golden-brown ones just as intense but holding a touch of wariness. "Tonight, you will know what it means to be a woman."

"Are you trying to seduce me, Justin?" Kris's heavy-lidded eyes grew sultry and sharp.

He leaned that miniscule bit forward to touch her lips with his own. He moved slowly and firmly as if he had all the time in the world. Kris's breath caught in her throat as a maelstrom of sensation poured through her. She opened her lips to his probing tongue as he stoked the fires to life only he seemed to spark in her. She moved her hands into his hair and moved in closer increasing the pressure of their kiss until they were devouring one another. His hands flowed up her back until he was skimming his thumb lightly up her neck, pausing to brush her sensitive earlobes, then thread into her hair. He pulled away and looked into her eager eyes. He didn't see any fear, only uncertainty.

"I don't know what to do."

The frank statement belied the intense purpose he read on her face. He brought her hands down to the collar of his uniform then moved his hands away giving her control. She set to work unfastening the hooks and buttons. Her sure fingers completing the task on him that she performed dozens of times on her own dress formals over the years. Once opened she pushed the coat off his shoulders all the while running her hands over his chest and arms. It took every bit of strength he had to hold still and

and give her time to adjust. Mindful, he caught the coat before it fell to the floor and hung it carefully over the back of the chair. Little by little they divested each other of clothing as they moved into the bedroom. Kris and Justin spent the next several hours exploring one another. The long friendship changing to an intimacy neither one expected, but one that filled all the empty spaces the two Marines had always acknowledged but rarely examined. The missing pieces of each now being filled by the other. Their calls of passion filled the night as they consummated the next phase of their relationship.

A floor below them Tomball and Juarez turned off the listening device. Both men seemed shaken by what they heard. Javier got up and went to the mini bar pulling out several of the small bottles and poured both Mike and him a drink. They drank in silence mulling over what they just heard and what it meant. The only sound in the room was the ice clinking in the glass. Javier let out a heavy sigh. They looked at each other grimly. Mike stood up to leave and turned to Javier.

"I would hate to have to kill him."

He set the glass down and left the room to head back to the ball. Javier sat on the bed heavily looking down into the glass dangling from his hand between his legs. He rubbed his hand harshly on the back of his neck. He hoped so too. He sat on the edge of the bed for a long time with the glass dangling from his fingers. He got up several times to leave the room and go back downstairs. He couldn't do it. He was too keyed up. There was no way he could go back to the team and pretend nothing was wrong. He didn't feel like mingling or dancing. He argued with himself for the better part of an hour. This was private. It was none of his business. These were his two best friends in the world. He would protect both with his own life if need be. Even if it meant protecting them from each other. He closed his eyes and sighed, then turned the device back on.

Chapter Eleven

Justin lay next to Kris not wanting to break their connection he reversed their positions, so she lay sprawled on top of him. He struggled to catch his breath and wrapped his arms around her. She snuggled her head into his chest and neck and let out a heavy sigh. He gently stroked his fingertips up and down her back with his eyes closed content in the moment. He tried to remember the last time he had passion had consumed him like that. He couldn't come up with a single time. He lay there holding Kris, listening to her breathe for quite a while before she stirred. He could feel her eyelashes flutter on his chest as she opened her eyes.

She lay on top of Justin's hard body trying to get her bearings and remember how she ended up on top of him. She moved her head to look at him and he captured her mouth in a tender passionate kiss. He tightened his arms around her as she snuggled down into his chest once more. He continued to run his fingers up and down her back. She lay contented and thoughtful.

"You alive up there?" he said teasingly.

"I think so. I am too relaxed to be sure though."

She lifted her head to look at him.

"Well at least now I understand why you all got so angry after having to go for so long without sex on deployments. I can't imagine having to spend six months without doing that now that I have. I am bound to be insatiable for a while."

"Hmmm" he uttered as he captured her mouth in a greedy kiss. "You are not the only one!" Their kiss deepened leading to another round of lovemaking.

"If we don't pace ourselves, we are going to kill each other!"

He chuckled thinking the same thing. She groaned as he got up and went to the wet bar to get them both a bottle of water.

He got off the bed and grabbed her hand pulling her after him.

"Where are we going?"

"Time for a bath."

"Like we are really going to bathe..."

The large bathroom was almost as large as the master bedroom in their house. The white marble against the dark contemporary wood tones of the cabinets was streamlined and was saved from being harsh by the modern chandelier over the tub with matching sconces above the sinks. The shower could fit several people comfortably with shower heads from every direction and a soaker head in the ceiling. The white freestanding egg shaped tub was built easily for two. On it was a bottle of bath salts with a French label.

"Where did these come from, they weren't here earlier."

"I took a detour to the PX in Germany. I remembered from past visits, there are duty free items from all over the world. It wasn't hard to convince the Colonel. He pretended it was his idea."

She looked at everything he had done to make tonight special and memorable. She felt humbled.

"You did all of this for me?"

"I did all of this for us."

"How long have you been planning this?"

"I plead the fifth!"

She smirked as he started the water and marveled at the lengths he'd gone to make tonight special. As the tub filled and Justin added the salts she suggested they get in while it was filling to avoid overflowing the tub as she cited the physics of water displacement.

"I have got to have it bad if hearing you say, 'water displacement' turns me on!"

She walked up running her hands up his chest and captured his lower lip in her teeth pulling lightly.

"Wa-ter dis-place-ment."

He grabbed Kris around the waist and put them both in the tub. They both nestled down and sighed at the feeling of the hot water. The scent of the bath salts wafting up around them steamy and sultry. Kris sighed and leaned her back into Justin's chest tipping her head back to rest on his shoulder.

"Ummm. This is amazing. I have never taken a bath with anyone before."

"Another first."

"Ummm. I seem to be experiencing a lot of firsts with you. First person I shared my secret with, first dance, first embrace, first kiss, first time making out, first time having sex, and first bath. That is a lot of firsts. You've done all this before."

"Well that is true. I don't have any firsts for you; I am hoping you'll help me experience some lasts."

"Lasts?"

"The last woman I share my secrets with, the last I will dance with, the last I will hold, the last one I will kiss, the last woman I make out with, the last I will have sex with, the last I will take a bath with, and the last I will ever love."

She turned and saw that same blazing look on his face he had in Germany. Now she saw it for what it was she was stunned.

"You're in love with me?" she asked in stunned disbelief.

"I can't remember a time when I didn't love you Kris."

She was too involved before to notice the addition to the black ink of the tattoo that ran over his ribs up his pec, shoulder and down his arm; the design had an open area right above his heart that had been empty. He said he meant to put a special tattoo there for the person he planned on spending his life with. He never filled it with one for Trina. It now had what appeared to be three pieces of coal on fire with flames rising above the rest of the design. The color flames were quite dramatic next to the black and grey tones of the rest. She ran her fingers over the flames on his heart and looked into his eyes.

He cradled her face as he drove his tongue deep in her mouth making her pant and writhe. He broke the kiss and settled her back down trailing his fingers up and down her arms as they rested on the sides of the tub. She had no words. It was taking a while for her brain to catch up with her heart which was trying to pound its way out of her chest.

"How long Justin, I really need to know."

"Kabul."

"Kabul!" she yelled as she turned to face him in shock. "I was still a man in Kabul Justin!"

"Yeah, trust me I know. Do you know how hard it is suddenly finding yourself attracted to someone who has been your best friend for nearly a decade, and oh by the way is supposed to be a guy? I thought I was losing my mind. As much as I hated to see my marriage with Trina end and how relieved I was to have it over I couldn't get my mind around the 'why'. Which just happened to be that I was lusting over and falling in love with my best friend. I was so pissed; I was so confused. I still found females attractive and sexy, so why was I dreaming about you every single night for months? Why couldn't I stay away from you? When I couldn't make sense of it, I figured it had to be your fault. You must have done something! When I finally couldn't take it any more I picked a fight with you to let out some of my frustrations."

"Picked a fight! You sucker punched me!"

"And you gave as good as you got. That fight is what finally brought it all together for me. When I grabbed you by the throat it all clicked; all those clues my subconscious kept trying to put together. The bizarre dreams of you with long hair, the constant sudden attraction, all the little things that didn't add up. You never grew a beard, you never made any sex jokes; then when I grabbed your throat-you had no Adam's apple. Women don't have an Adam's apple. I was so stunned; you got the drop on me."

She couldn't believe it. "How did you get past the fact I looked like a man?"

"I couldn't. That was the only thing I couldn't reason. Then I just decided it didn't matter. Whatever the reason, it was you. At that point I was done trying to reason it and just accepted it."

She could see the truth in his eyes.

"What would you have done if I hadn't been wounded? If the truth hadn't come out?"

"I don't know. But that is why I arranged that R & R we were supposed to take to Germany. I was going to tell you what I suspected. I don't know if I would have been able to tell you how I felt then. I guess it would have depended on your reaction. But you were wounded instead. I hated to see you all torn up and in so much pain, but I was glad to finally have a reason that made some sense! In the middle of all that craziness was the sanest I had felt in a long while."

She sank back down in the water and leaned back into him. He went back to running his fingertips up and down her arms. It felt incredible.

"Well I guess you did still have one first."

"What was that?"

"You were the first to know how you felt."

"What are you feeling right now?"

She turned and looked at him again with everything she felt in her eyes. "I feel like I have got a lot of catching up to do."

He knew the words were in there, but just like him she measured what she said very carefully. She wasn't ready to say it yet; she needed time to digest what she had just learned. She needed to understand the difference between what he was making her feel and what she herself was feeling. He knew she loved him. But she hadn't yet realized she was in love with him. She would tell him when she was ready. She leaned in and kissed him. She ran her hands up his chest and neck into his hair. She climbed up and straddled him changing the direction of the kiss. His arms came around her pulling her tightly into him and holding on as if he would never let go. She knew him. He would never let go. She knew it wasn't easy for him to speak of his feelings, especially considering the depth and scope of them. He wasn't a man who let his feelings rule him. He took time to think things out, to explore every possible outcome. That is one thing they had in common. Patience.

She pulled away gasping for air. The room had become charged. Oxygen seemed to be in short supply.

"I don't know what I feel just now because I feel too much."

"Then we'll table this discussion for now." He pushed the hair back from her face.

"Justin, you are my best friend."

"That isn't going to change Kris."

"You're wrong. This changes everything."

***

Chapter Twelve

The sun had barely come up when they both woke. After an impressive demonstration of Kris's flexibility and Justin's strength in the shower they both dressed in PT gear and headed down to breakfast. Some of the team had already arrived. Kris was hailed to the front desk, so Justin went inside to grab a table. Tomball and Juarez were there nursing coffee looking bleary eyed. Reineke and Jeffries arrived with their wives and sat down. The breakfast buffet was enormous and held enough food for a regiment. Kris told the group with a great deal of sarcasm that her uniform magically appeared in the hotel laundry this morning. They all smirked and made comments while waiting in line. Kris and Justin filled their plates and sat down with the team. Mary Jeffries was regaling the group with a play by play from last night. The group laughed at her comic portrayals of the attendees. Sue Reineke gushed over Kris's dress. That set the two off on a discussion of who wore what. Juarez was unusually subdued.

Justin commented, "Mike's snoring keep you up all night Javier? You look a bit beat."

"No Sir. It was a couple in a neighboring room. They had sex all night. She was a bit of a screamer."

The ladies oohed and laughed, "Too bad Rosie had to stay with the kids, Javi! You could have given them a run for their money!"

Javier laughed wryly and went back to his coffee. The muscle in his cheek twitching as it did when he was really pissed. He kept glancing furtively at Justin and Kris. Kris looked from Javier to Justin and quirked an eyebrow. Justin just shook his head minutely. When everyone was done eating the team got up to join the other members who'd just come down in the lobby. They had planned to have a morning run in Rock Creek Park. They assembled after they finished stretching and Kris and Justin took the back of the line.

They started the run and fell into a rhythm. Kris looked at Justin and flicked her head toward Javier.

"I don't know. Mike looks pissed too. Think they had words last night?"

"No, I don't think so. They don't seem to be mad at each other. Javier's jaw only clenches when he looks at you or me. Do you think they...?"

"No! No. No one saw us leave."

"Are you so sure of that?"

Justin wasn't so sure. They were trained observers. And Javier liked to carry equipment on him. Sometimes it was tracking equipment and sometimes listening equipment. Many of the pieces were his own design and only he knew what they did.

They had run just under five miles when Justin said, "Javier, your shoe is untied."

Javier pulled out of the line off to the side while the rest continued.

"If you have something to say, say it now."

"Nothing, Sir."

"Spill it Marine! You have been glaring at me all morning and I want to know why."

"Why?! Ok, I'll tell you why!" He pushed Justin's chest hard. "What the hell do you think you're doing, huh? You two screw each other up and you screw all of us up. You could have any woman you want. Girls practically drool when you come into the room, why'd you have to start messing around with Kris?!"

"Watch what you say. My personal life is not your concern Captain!" Javier bristled at Justin referring to him by rank; like they were coworkers instead of best friends.

"It is when it affects the team. And anything you start with Kris can and will affect all of us. You mess her up and it messes us all up, Major!" Javier said with a sneer.

Justin grabbed Javier by the front of his jacket and brought the man close to snarl in his face.

"I have no intention of messing Kris up. And anything between me and her, is between me and her-got it?"

"I don't want to get in your business, but this is Kris. She isn't like other chicks. She doesn't have the right training for this. She doesn't know how to be a girl. If things go bad between you I don't think she can just shrug that off. She doesn't have any defenses, man."

"You think I don't know that Javi? Huh? That woman has been my best friend for nearly ten years! You think I am going to do anything to mess that up, to hurt her?"

"I don't think you would hurt her on purpose Justin, but Kris isn't just some chick to cruise."

Justin's face took on a murderous look. Alario was as angry as Juarez had ever seen him. But behind the fury was something else.

"Oh, man! You're in love with her, aren't you?" Javier's face took on a mask of shock and he relaxed his hold on Justin.

Justin pushed Javier away from him roughly. "It's none of your damn business Javi!"

Justin started to walk away. Javier grabbed him by the shoulder. "Hey, man."

Justin ran his hand through his hair and crossed his arms glaring at Juarez.

"That's why. That's why you and Trina imploded. You started having feelings for Kris. All this makes sense now. Why you were having such a hard time being around her before. Why you kept picking fights and why you wouldn't give Trina an answer when she asked who the woman you were messing around with was. Because Kris wasn't a woman then. Oh, man. Oh, man. Did Kris know?"

"No. I told her last night. She's ...processing. It's complicated."

Justin turned to see the team pulling quite far ahead. They resumed running to catch up to the team. Javier fell in alongside him. "What are you going to do, Justin?"

"The best I can Javi."

"Madre de Dios! If Command finds out you two will be done. Your career will be over. You two better be sure about this because there is a lot at stake here."

Justin gave Javi a dark look.

"We have a great deal to work out and discuss. This isn't going to be solved overnight. And I am not going to rush her. She needs time, so she's going to get it. This is just one more thing on top of a ton of things she's had to deal with suddenly and with no warning. I'm not going press her."

Javier had to say one more thing. Justin was trying to fight off the fury he was feeling.

"You're my brother and I love you. I'd take a bullet for any one of you. I don't want to see you messed up either. I know how the situation with Trina screwed you up and how hard a time you've had since the divorce. We are more than a team; we are a family. You don't get any tighter. Kris is my brother too. Well, my sister now. Which means I will look out for her. I know she doesn't need protecting, but I can't just leave her be, man. I love her too."

Justin looked at Javier and saw the concern on his friend's face. He placed his hand on Javier's shoulder. The peace made, they continued to double time until they caught up with the team.

Justin rode back to North Carolina with Kris giving them the privacy to talk. To keep Kris from going crazy Mel towed up Kris's car for her to work on in the many hours of off time after therapy. Kris's mother gave her the car as a 16th birthday present; her grandfather's vintage 1968 Pontiac GTO. It had sat in a storage facility after Jenna's father died and when her mother passed she brought it home and placed it in storage for Kris. She never told the Major about it knowing he would take it over. She wanted to bond with Kris and felt restoring the car would give them a chance to work together as well as learn.

Armed with a Chilton's manual and a full set of her father's tools, Jenna and Kris, with Mel's sporadic help, slowly restored the vehicle to its original condition. The body was rough, and the engine had needed completely rebuilt as had the transmission. Kris spent the last twelve years lovingly bonding and sanding the body, re-chroming the bumpers and wheels, and fixing the electrical. As a surprise, Mel got it painted a beautiful gun metal gray that complimented all the chrome Kris had restored. The interior was original black and only needed minimal work. Knowing once the team saw her car up close they would fight to ride in it she had several boxes stacked in the back seat for all the new clothes Mel insisted on her buying. Only the boxes were empty; Mel had already taken everything home. She wanted to make sure she and Justin would be alone.

Justin briefed Kris over the discussion he had with Javier. Kris would have to make it a point to have a talk with Javier when she got settled in. She was more than a little pissed that he would dismiss her wants and needs as well as diminish her choices by suggesting she was unable to resist Justin just because she'd never had a sexual experience before as if he was the aggressor and she was just a deer in the headlights unable to flee and helpless to escape. It was insulting. Mostly because it cast her in the helpless damsel in distress role; a laughable place to put the deadliest person on their team. She had more hand to hand kills than the everyone else in the team put together and then some.

When they arrived home, they carried their bags up to the bedrooms. Kris hung up her uniform and dress and dumped the rest into the hamper to be washed. Justin came up behind her and wrapped his arms around her waist. He nuzzled her neck and slid his hands under her t-shirt. It quickly hit the floor as his t-shirt followed as did Kris's jeans. Just as they were getting hot and heavy the door opened and Mel came in.

"Whoa! As bad as I feel for interrupting, you two might want to put more clothes on-we have company."

With a steely glare Kris turned her head and said, "Define company."

"Rosie is here with the kids, and the rest of wives will be here any second."

Kris groaned and leaned her head to Justin's forehead.

Mel looked apologetic knowing how Kris must feel.

"They've missed you Luv. It's been months, they want to see for themselves you are ok."

Mel backed out of the room and headed downstairs while Kris and Justin redressed.

"Well, this should be fun."

Justin smirked. "They are family, and they love you."

"I know. You better hang here for a bit; don't want to wag their tongues more than they already are." As Kris looked down at the impressive bulge in Justin's pants. Grinning, kissed him passionately before heading downstairs. He laughed as he picked up his shirt and adjusted his pants. Damn her that was not going to help.

When Kris got downstairs Javier and Rosa's kids swarmed her.

"Tia Kris! Tia Kris! We missed you!"

Rosie concentrating on the dishes she was unwrapping at the counter chastised the boys without even turning around.

"Gabriel! Stop calling Kris Tia! It's not funny anymore."

The kids had started calling Kris 'Tia' Spanish for Aunt last year after a joke that got out of hand.

"But Mama! Kris is Tia! How come, Kris?" asked Ernesto as Kris picked him up.

Rosa turned, and her jaw hit the floor.

"Kristian?!"

"It's Kristin now Rosie."

Kris put Ernie down as Rosa walked over and threw her arms around Kris' neck. Kris hugged her back as the smaller Latino woman held on tightly. She pulled her arms away and clasped her hands in front of her mouth. Shaking her head, she muttered furiously in Spanish. Kris let her process as she looked her up and down several times. She kept pausing at her breasts. Kris was getting a little uncomfortable at how she kept staring at them.

"Kris?! Madre de Dios! How? What has happened? Talk to me!"

They sat down at the table with the coffee Rosa had just made.

Kris worked out a brief explanation that skipped over the details and told Rosa of her condition and how she found out she was female. Of course, Rosa was not satisfied with the short version and over the next half an hour peppered Kris with questions until she had told her everything. Rosa missed her calling. She should have been a professional interrogator. Kris worked with people that could take lessons from Rosa. She sat with her hand over her mouth shaking her head repeatedly closing her eyes and casting them to heaven. Then her gaze turned murderous.

"Javier has some serious explaining to do. He tells me nothing! I talk to him this morning and nothing! He just says the ball was fine and you are coming home! How can he keep this from me?"

"Honestly Rosa if he had told you, would you have believed him?"

"No, I probably would have thought he was screwing around like always."

They both started laughing.

"I wish I could have seen the look on his face when he saw you the first time! Oh, that might have made up for this."

"They were all pretty shook up about it."

"How did Justin take it?"

"Justin already knew. Justin told me. He'd figured it out awhile before I was injured. He couldn't understand how or why. He said he'd tried to talk to me a few times about it but then backed off. When I was wounded it was Justin who performed the surgery to remove the shrapnel. They had to open me up and..."

Justin came into the kitchen with Mel behind him.

"There were a few extra pieces in there we weren't expecting."

Rosa stood up to hug Justin. She grabbed his face in her hands and looked at him with sympathy.

"I cannot imagine how hard this has been for you! That puta Trina cheating on you and now this! No wonder you have been so distracted and angry. My heart broke for you but Javi said to leave it. You would talk when you were ready."

"Yeah, it's been hard. How do you tell a guy you've become brothers with you think he's a woman without sounding crazy? If I'd known about Kris's condition, we could have had this talk a long time ago. But I guess everything happened the way it was meant to. "

Justin grabbed a cup and poured himself some coffee while leaning against the kitchen counter.

"Melody, how are you holding up with all of this? I cannot imagine it was easy to hear your *marido* was a woman."

Mel came up behind Kris and wrapped her arms around Kris's neck; Kris reached back with her left arm to hold Mel's head.

"Well no. I certainly wasn't expecting that! It's ok though. Kris and I have been such good friends for so long; we are family. We'd been talking about getting a divorce forever. Once we realized we were more like brother and sister than husband and wife. It was hard since both of us have no other family to give up the only one we had left. We put it off a long time but there was no reason not to any longer."

"You got divorced?!" The horror on Rosa's face was sobering.

"Yeah, while Kris was in Germany. We kind of had to; I mean um. Our marriage kind of wasn't legal now anyway so...It was final the week after she got back to the states."

"But you are still living here?"

"Yeah, well where would I go? Kris is my family. Kris and I stopped sharing a bedroom a long time ago, so nothing has really changed."

Rosa was shocked to hear this. She believed that Kris and Mel were happy; the perfect couple. It was hard to hear they weren't as they seemed. Kris looked back at Mel and Mel kissed Kris on the cheek before taking the seat next to Rosa. She reached over and stole Kris's coffee. Kris got up to get another cup. A knock on the door announced the arrival of La Tanya and Taylor. La Tanya, a tall thin black woman with enough sass to back down a bear, was a DOD employee on the base and had been dating Mike Tomball for three years. Taylor, a tall heavily built woman with short blond hair and a tough demeanor, was a fellow Marine who was friends with Gentry. The shock was evident on their faces when they came in the room. Kris took advantage of the silence and gave an abbreviated version of her change that she'd been working out on the drive home knowing she'd need it sooner than later. After many questions and some heavy emotion everyone started talking normally and the mood in the room became less tense and more like old times.

A bit later more knocks brought Sue and Mary with their husbands bearing food. The rest of the team filed in shortly after. When Javier entered the room, Rosa smacked him over the head yelling at him in Spanish for not telling her about Kris's transformation. He quickly got out of the way heading to the counter to fill a plate for his wife hoping if she was occupied, she wouldn't come after him again. The women had brought an enormous amount of food; hot dishes and frozen meals to tide them over not knowing if Kris or Mel would be able to cook being unaware of the extent of Kris's injuries. The last to arrive was Colonel Stirling. Kris's mentor and surrogate father seemed more at ease with her today. She sat and talked to him while everyone mingled. The next couple of hours flew by as everyone talked and ate.

Rosa watched Kris and Justin. Nothing had seemed to change between them but there was something she couldn't put her finger on. The feeling in the room changed when they got near each other. Rosa watched Justin carefully. He didn't move out of the way when Kris reached around him to grab the coffee pot.

He handed her the creamer before she asked for it and took the spoon from his own cup to give to her to stir her own. Her eyes narrowed. Kris's face and Justin's face were impassive. Nothing in their expression gave away anything. But Rosa's mother was a skilled observer and taught her daughter that the true way to know what a person was thinking was to look at their eyes. They could school their features but could rarely keep emotion out of their eyes. While the group all talked and ate, she sat back and watched. The heat that entered Justin's eyes every time he looked at Kris was palpable. It wasn't just because Kris was muy bonito. When Kris relaxed and smiled her features were incredible. But it was more than passion that she saw in his eyes.

Mary brought out her tablet and showed the others the photos she took of the event last night. Rosa scrolled down and landed on the pictures of Kris and Justin on the dance floor. Mary had taken half a dozen of them dancing. One in particular grabbed her interest. The two stood a respectable distance apart, but she enlarged the photo with her fingers to look at their faces. The look they had for one another was penetrating. Not one of two friends dancing but of two people whose passions were running hot and swift. Rosa swiftly moved along through the pictures. She brushed the screen when she saw one of Javier. He always looked so *guapo* in his dress uniform. She had one of the team as they entered the room. The look of fierce possessiveness on Justin's face was impossible to miss. She gave Javier a look he knew well; one that meant she had a lot to say to him when they got home. He noticed that it did not come with the usual look that he'd done something to anger her, but one of concern. She kept looking at Kris and Justin as if she was trying to figure something out. She handed the tablet to someone else at the table and sipped her coffee. She was unusually quiet. He wondered what had upset her.

Rosa and Javier were the first to leave to get their kids home. Their littlest was getting over a bad cold which is why Rosa stayed home from the ball, so they departed after hugs and promises to get together later in the week. By the time the sun had set everyone had started to leave. Sunday night meant getting ready for the work and school week, so it was generally an early night. Rosa and Mel had cleaned up. Other than the dozen or so casserole dishes in the fridge and the dozen containers of meals in the freezer you'd never know anyone had been there.

Mel made herself scarce as Kris and Justin went upstairs. They curled up on the bed in Kris's room and lay down holding one another. Kris turned on her music app and they lay quietly listening to Classical Spanish Guitar.

"You know the guys all think you listen to nothing but thrash metal."

Kris smiled with her eyes closed, listening.

"That went better than I expected."

"How so?"

"I was dreading this. I was worried everyone would be awkward. That my gender change would be the elephant in the room that everyone just tiptoed around until it was convenient to leave. I didn't want them to treat me differently."

"You are still the same person you were before, Kris. And they are family. Family loves you for everything you are, good and bad."

"I know. But something like that is a shock. It's not like Davis coming out and telling us he's gay. I went from being a man to being a woman. My gender condition isn't a common one and nothing anyone knew about before. I could see if they knew and we all found out; it wouldn't be a big surprise. But no one was looking for this."

"Did you say Davis is gay?!"

Kris lifted her head to look at him, bemused. He was serious! He didn't know.

"Uh, you didn't know?"

"I guess I didn't think about it. What about all his girlfriends?"

"Girl friends. Probably gay themselves like Taylor and using each other for convenience. He's careful. I think he's afraid of what the guys would say. You know how people can get. I feel his pain. I've always been apprehensive of what would happen if my condition were known or if something like this happened and everyone found out. I have to say that so far, it's far less than I expected. But then I haven't been back to duty yet. I am sure there will be quite a bit of crap then. But I don't care about anyone else. If the team is good that is all I need."

Justin wrapped his arms around her and closed his eyes. This was nice. Just holding one another without worries and without pressure. He could stay just like that for a few centuries. As much as he wanted her this was almost as good. It felt right.

Kris loved listening to his heartbeat under her ear. She couldn't believe how quickly she became accustomed to the sound. The music felt like accompaniment to his heartbeat. She hadn't felt this relaxed and this secure in more time than she could remember. As frantic as they were earlier to get their hands on one another, each was as content as they were just now to just lay down and hold one another. The music played on as the two soaked up the quiet and just listened. They talked quietly. Justin leaned down and captured Kris's lips in a heated kiss. They necked on the bed for the better part of an hour. Soon their clothes slowly peeled away and ended up on the floor. They sank into one another and loved each other with a slow thoroughness. They reached their peak and melted into one another as their heartbeats slowed. They drifted off to sleep wrapped in each other.

Chapter Thirteen

Two days after getting home Kris cornered Javier. She was in the garage working on her 2003 Indian Roadmaster Classic motorcycle when he dropped in to see how she was doing. She took a moment to finish and grab a rag to wipe the grease off her hands before she faced him. He got water from the garage fridge and handed it to Kris while helping himself to one. He leaned up against the work bench while she stood next to the bike. She looked at him for a few minutes until he started to squirm.

"Ok man, say it! Geez, that stare. What did I do, huh?"

"How could you think for one second that I am some clueless helpless female? I believe the words were, 'She isn't like other chicks. She doesn't have the right training for this. She doesn't know how to be a girl. She doesn't have any defenses, man.' I think I got it all, right? Since when am I not able to handle unexpected situations when they arise?" Javier didn't say anything but looked abashed as Kris continued.

"Contrary to popular belief I don't think I know everything. What I don't know I find out! You think I'd let even a minute go by once they told me I was a woman before I started researching what I could expect? By the time my surgeries were done I had already spoken to three doctors who specialize in gender issues and read an entire medical journal's worth of information on the hormone therapy I would be getting so I'd know what I was in for. Then I spoke with other patients who have gone through this same situation to get their intel.

THEN.. I spoke with every woman at that hospital getting information not to mention what I talked over with Mel, so I'd have a clue on the basic everyday things women go through that no one thinks to cover. I asked questions. So many they'd run in the other direction when they saw me coming."

Javier leaned against the work bench drinking his water with a stern thoughtful expression. He was thinking over everything Kris said.

"Once I'd talked with Justin and he told me how he felt, and I realized that I FELT THE SAME WAY we talked about what the next step would mean. We spent weeks discussing things we'd never even thought of before. Many of the questions I felt too uncomfortable asking doctors and Mel I talked over with Justin. So he knew exactly what I was going through and where I was at. And then I did what I always do; I found books and manuals for everything else. I probably know more about sex right now than you do! My practical knowledge is still being built, but my academic knowledge is definitely greater than yours! Do honestly think I'd go into an unknown situation blind?"

Javier's face grew taught and harsh as anger overcame him.

"Oh you talked to Justin! But you couldn't talk to me?! When have we not been able to talk about stuff? You cut me out Kris, both of you! Why the hell could you tell him and not me?!" He slammed his empty water bottle down on the workbench.

"Javier he's the one that told me! I didn't know! But he knew for months. Months! All the tension down range and times he blew me off and picked fights were because he figured it out! He wouldn't talk to me about it. He didn't know how. The longer he dragged it out the harder it got for him to address. He put us in for leave because he meant to tell me what he suspected. He was sure it would end our friendship. That I would hate him for it. It was eating him alive and he wouldn't open up to me, you, or anyone. He needed to talk about it and I did too. I wanted to tell you guys but how do you say something like this in an email or over the phone?"

He stood there stone faced shaking his head angry. He wouldn't be placated.

"Javi, you were still on the mission. It was bad enough that I was wounded. You were all torn up and distracted about that, how much worse would it have been to hear it all with no context, no background, and no way to talk to me about it? Then you'd have a thousand questions that couldn't be answered easily over email. How would you have been able to think about what you needed to do to get home with all that in your head? Huh? Then there was the shit storm from the brass. They are trying to dishonorably discharge me! They were convinced I did this as some sort of feminist empowerment stunt. They wouldn't believe I didn't know.

"Think Javi! Think! I have been cleared by medical. I am five by five. Yet here I am still not cleared for duty. Why do you think that is? They are still trying to railroad me. It's not as if Command decided I needed a bit more of a rest before I head back after my difficult ordeal. Someone out there is trying to hamstring me!

"The Colonel ordered Justin and Lieutenant Commander Campbell not to say a damn thing. That week Justin disappeared he and the Colonel had to fly to Washington to testify in front of the Armed Services Committee in front of SECNAV, the Commandant, SECDEF, and group of Senators wanting to crucify me. They are trying to bring criminal charges against me for falsifying official documentation. They want me in Leavenworth! I couldn't say anything to anyone. Anyone who had knowledge of this was at risk. Keeping quiet and not telling you would give you plausible deniability if they decided to question any of you. But once you all got back there was no way to keep it from you or any reason to. If they were going after any of you, they would have done it before you got home; before you got the chance to connect with me."

"Justin could have said something, anything!"

"And disobey a direct order? I wanted to tell you guys. But there was no way I was going to do it differently. It had to be face to face. There is too much that can't be said in an email. Too many holes, too many gaps. I didn't want to leave it so you guys had too much to say and no way to get it out. That just leads to random thoughts and over thinking that would have jacked up everything. What wasn't said would fester and become more than it needed to be; you know that as well as I do man."

"Yeah. Yeah it would. Apart and thousands of miles away. It's easy to build up something in your mind that has no basis in reality."

"Yeah. I had a hard time keeping it together over the last few weeks imagining what you would say. How you would react. I was scared for the first time in my life. All I kept thinking was if you guys didn't accept this and accept me I couldn't do this anymore. If my family didn't support me..."

Kris turned her head away and took a long swig of water. She looked down and fiddled with the bottle hanging loosely from her fingers between her legs. Kris finished her water. She walked over and put the bottle on the workbench leaning up against it beside him. He looked over at her.

"You ok Jefe?"

She pulled him into a one-armed hug. He pulled her in tight for a closer one. They stood a few minutes holding on to one another tight. He slapped her hard on the back and squeezed her shoulder as he pulled away. She could see he wasn't mad, just concerned.

"Yeah. I'm sorry I didn't take into consideration you are all just now having to deal with all this and cut you some slack."

"Yeah and I'm sorry I went off before I really thought it through and remembered who I was dealing with. I didn't mean to insinuate you are weak or helpless and I can see how you would think that's what I meant. But it wasn't. The three of us have been *mejor amigos* for a long time. We do everything together and it made me angry that you both left me out. I know you had to, but it doesn't make it feel any less shitty that you've been working this out together for weeks without me. My best friends were going through some of the toughest stuff anyone could possibly deal with, and they didn't let me help. I'm playing catch up and trying to deal not knowing you were both already miles ahead of me."

Kris crossed her arms over her chest and stared hard at the ground. She never meant to hurt Javi. She was irritated he thought so little of her coping abilities, but she wasn't mad. But now hearing it from his perspective she was upset. She never meant to exclude him or deny him the ability to help. But she could see how both she and Justin had been so focused on themselves they forgot him.

"Hermano we never meant that to happen. Justin only told me everything he'd been going through in D.C. I'm not going to get into it, I think you need to ask him and have him tell you, but I don't think it was easy for him to acknowledge it. At least I know now he hadn't lost his mind when he kissed me on that operating table!"

"Oh yeah! I forgot about that! He snap or what?"

Justin walked into the garage carrying his go bag. He dropped it next to the bench and went to the fridge for water.

"I thought I was going to lose her, and I wasn't about to let her go without a fight."

Javier looked bemused when Justin walked over to Kris and placed a kiss on her lips.

"Damn man give me some time before you start that stuff. I'm still trying to get used to Kris having tits."

They both laughed at his mortification. Kris walked back over to her bike and squatted down replacing the oil filter she'd removed. She got up and headed into the house.

"Mel has a late class so I have to start dinner. You two stay and talk. We good now Javi?"

He walked over and pulled her into a one-armed guy hug and clapped her hard on the back.

"Yeah man, we're good."

Kris walked into the house and left them to clear the air.

"Are they really trying to charge her with a crime and dishonorably discharge her?"

"They are trying. They won't succeed. They don't have a leg to stand on. If they persist my Uncle Tony has already offered his services to Kris as a lawyer to fight for her."

"That the uncle who takes down the Mob bosses on a regular basis?"

Justin laughed. "Yeah." He took a long drink from his water.

"Wow. I almost hope they do so we can see him slam them down!"

"Bite your tongue. No way we are going to let it get that far. They are not going to put so much as an ink smudge on her record."

"Kris said you knew. Before she was wounded. When did you know, huh? That Kris was a woman?"

"Shortly before Kabul. I'd started putting clues together weeks before. Things I'd seen before but didn't think much of. My subconscious started piecing them together at night with these messed up dreams. It got to the point I didn't want to sleep. I was confused. Then I got angry and blamed it on Kris. When I realized I was falling for Kris I panicked. I didn't know what to do. No one including her knew she was female. I didn't know how to deal with what I was feeling. But what if I was wrong and she wasn't? How could I be falling for a guy? After Trina and I ended it I struggled. Then I just didn't care. I wasn't going to pass off happiness with someone because of anatomy. That last fight you had to pull us apart," He looked to Javier as he nodded in remembrance. "That's when I figured it out. It all came crashing down on me. I was so stunned I couldn't fight back. She beat the hell outta me!" He said with a wry laugh. Javier busted up.

"Yeah she did. Don't ever make her mad man! Is that why things went south with Trina? You never answered me before."

"I'd been thinking for a while that things with Trina weren't going to last but I didn't want face it. I hated thinking I'd made a mistake there. But we didn't want the same things. We never did and I didn't want to face it. I figured I'd bring her around. But she didn't want a family. She wanted to party and be the 'it' couple. She wanted to travel and be seen. She only wanted that with me because of how we looked together. She didn't love me. Or if she did it wasn't enough. I loved her but I was never *in love* with her. Now that I know what that means I know I did the right thing. But her getting pregnant was like a knife to my throat. She didn't want a family or kids. Now she's having one and Kris and I want one and will never have one. Ironic huh?"

"What the hell do you mean you'll never have one?"

"Javier I removed her uterus when she was wounded. That's how we found out she was a woman. All that was left was meat; didn't have a choice."

All Javier could say was a stunned "Man!"

Justin looked out of the garage and drank down the rest of his water.

"We good here Javi? I know you had to be angry to be kept out of it, but I wasn't about to disobey when the colonel made that order. We're bros man and ordinarily I'd find a to get around it, but not this time. Not when her head was on the chopping block. I couldn't risk it."

"She told me some. You will tell me the rest! Later. Rosa's texted ten times since I came over and I'd better get home before my woman kicks *my* but!"

They hugged and slapped each other on the back.

"I don't envy you right now man. You two are going to have to watch your six good. With all the controversy around her right now if anyone catches you two together your careers are over."

Javier headed out and Justin closed the garage door before heading inside.

Chapter Fourteen

Over the next week as Kris settled in, neighbors dropped by and several curious acquaintances that had heard the rumors made it a point to come by and see for themselves. Kris just grinned and bared it knowing they would move on to something else soon enough.

What wasn't easy to handle was hearing her orders to return to duty still had not been cleared. She was still on medical leave. Getting tired of the inactivity she got up after Justin had left for the base and decided to get on with things. She dressed in her utilities with a full pack, helmet, and the weighted training M4 mockup and enjoyed the run to gate. The ten-mile trek would help her get back into condition. She was slightly winded. That made her mad. She'd never gotten winded from running before. Arriving at the gate she showed her ID and spoke briefly with the guards; most of which she knew by name. It didn't take long for the looks and whispers to start.

She talked with a Sergeant she had become friends with through martial arts; who mentored in the same youth programs as she and Justin who was currently on gate duty. He was a bit shocked that the rumors he heard were actually true. After a few minutes of talking he realized Kris was the same old wise guy he had always known and just fell back into their old rhythm. Several others joined in the conversation. She told a darkly humorous story about having to adjust her firing hold on her rifle; breasts were great for a bikini, not so much for a M4. They joked about her changes and laughed at the story she told about the first few times she got up in the night and forgot she couldn't pee standing up anymore. They all laughed as she described having to clean the bathroom floor and the sign she placed above the toilet as a warning to remind her *before* she made a mess; 'no stick now you sit'. As she resumed her run, she heard a loud wolf whistle from the Sergeant as she ran off. Laughing she turned around to flip him off. She entered the base and continued her run to the Special Operations division building. It felt good getting back into it.

Justin was leading the men in a circuit of the obstacle course in the training area adjacent to the division building checking on times for the new men and making sure the old ones were maintaining when he saw a familiar figure running up the road. Kris came abreast of the obstacle course and stopped by Justin who was overseeing the newer men running their times. She took off her pack and laid down her practice weapon. Justin handed her the clipboard with all of the times for the men. She watched as several ran through the finish. Three of the four looked up to the time board to verify their time against the time posted. The Marine Corps record for the course was 15:58. They shook their heads with disappointment and went around. Kris shook her head and sighed roughly. They needed an attitude adjustment. Justin tilted his head and looked at her questioningly.

"The Colonel release you for duty?"

Kris looked over at Justin. "Not yet. I need to go see him. I told him I was coming on base today."

"When he does get back here. These new men are good but need work."

Kris nodded and walked away. She went to Colonel Stirling's office and had a conversation. She brought her medical files which cleared her for duty, but division was stalling. They wanted to evaluate her prior to releasing her for full field duty. So she was granted a conditional return, but to admin tasks only. She was to meet with a Lieutenant Shelly Cook who was to evaluate her. Division wanted a full psychological work up before allowing her to return to combat. Kris knew it was just bullshit politics, but it still galled her she had to prove herself again. She returned to the training area just as Javier came up with the men he was leading on the other course.

"What did the Colonel say?"

Kris looked at Justin and repeated their conversation adding that her orders were emailed to Lieutenant Colonel Anderson approving her for limited duty. She took back the clipboard looking at all the runs from that day and the previous. Man were they green.

"These scores are crap. They should be much better than this. Why are they not progressing?"

"Good question. Javi and I were just discussing that."

Kris shook her head. "I was watching, and I think I have a theory. Get them over here. Let's have a talk."

Javier called over the men and they all gathered around the three Alpha leaders. Kris looked them up and down. While Justin introduced her to the group.

"This is Gunnery Sergeant Kris Cole. The Gunny will be overseeing your training from here on out. Listen and learn. There is not a finer Marine in all of SOC and you will benefit greatly from this education."

Many of the guys started muttering and looking at one another. Cole was a legend in SOC. Every one of them learned combat tactics from the manuals she wrote and all of them studied her missions. As the only team leader to ever have a 100% mission success rate. She was the first major casualty from a mission; previously just a handful of wounds with no men lost, she had earned every bit of awe and respect the men gave her. Most Generals didn't command the level of reverence the men spoke in with regards to Cole.

Kris thanked Justin and stepped up in front of the men. She looked at them for several moments evaluating. They were all trying to look suitably impressive. She stood with her arms crossed and addressed them.

"I have been watching today's run. I have also looked over your scores. None of you are consistent. None of you are progressing. So I have to ask; what exactly is your motivation on this course?"

She looked at the men waiting for an answer. Finally Captain Russell stepped forward and responded.

"My motivation is to be the best on this course Gunny."

She walked over to where the Captain stood and faced him.

"And how do you determine who is the best on this course Captain?"

"By beating that number Gunny." He tossed his head to indicate the board on the edge of the course that held a card at the top indicating the rank, name, and unit of the man who held the best time for the course. Kris addressed the rest of the men.

"How many of you are looking at the number and using it as a measure of success on this course?"

More than half raised their hands. Kris laughed humorlessly.

"Then you have already failed the objective of this exercise."

The men looked a little uneasy. Kris continued.

"This course is designed for you to have to move from one type of movement into another so you can be prepared in the field to change tactics, movements, and methods with little or no warning. You never know what you will face in the field. Your enemy will not attack with a prescribed set of actions. This course is to enable you to have to adjust quickly and seamlessly. It teaches you how to adjust. The speed and efficiency in which you maneuver each obstacle will allow you to make similar adjustments in the field."

Kris looked over the men. They were engaged and watching with rapt attention.

"The only reason we time these runs, is so you can see where your strengths and weaknesses lie. Each obstacle individually and the course as a whole is timed so you can find which areas you are stronger so you can play to your strengths and where you are weak so you can shore up those inadequacies. And for no other reason. That number up there? It's meaningless. It means nothing to you unless it's your last run on this course. Everyone has different body types, mass, muscle tone, mental prowess, and psychological toughness. It takes every one of them to make it in SOC. Teams are built with this in mind. Not everyone has the same capabilities. You should not be trying to beat some faceless Marine for the number that Marine put on a board. Your goal should be only to beat the last score you made. For only you have an unbiased and equal competition to yourself. You are the only Marine who you can honestly measure yourself against if you truly need to pit yourself against someone else. For you are the only one whose strengths and weaknesses can be measured against your skill exactly."

Kris pointed to a group of three Marines on the end.

"You will never beat him at the barbed wire; he's more compact and can move more efficiently under it. You will never outrun him; his legs are longer. And with your reach, he'll never take you on the bars. You see what I'm getting at? If you want a fair race, a fair competition; you are your only perfect competition. You should only be concerned with your last score. Was it higher? If so, why? Which obstacles slowed down this time? Are you struggling with one or two in particular? If the answer is yes then you need to work on those until they are no longer an issue. Are your scores all over the place? Inconsistent times across the board are not a physical issue, but a mental issue. Your head is not focused. When you are in this course you cannot have your head somewhere else. Everything outside of here needs to be put away. You let your mind wander in the field and you go home in box. Every time you enter this course you should be thinking on what you need to do succeed right here right now. Nothing more, nothing less. It is the same in the field if you want to get your team out alive."

Kris handed the clipboard back to Justin.

"Now I want you to start again. Remember what I have just told you. Put everything else out of your mind and work on you."

The Captain that spoke with before spoke again. "What is your score on this course Gunny?"

The men started nodding and muttering to one another. All of them looking at her expectantly.

"Well I can tell you it's nowhere close to that!" As she indicated the board with the Marine Corps high score.

The men were all smirking and laughing. Kris smiled, but it was a feral smile. She knew something they did not.

"Why don't you show the men how it's done Gunny. I think that will illustrate your point better than anything." Kris looked over to Javi with a knowing smile. Yeah that would do it. Nothing hammered a point home better than a quick and bloodless smackdown. Kris nodded.

. Javier set up the electronic scoreboard that fed into the computer which recorded their times and showed on the display at the end. She removed her lid and unbuttoned her fatigues top and laid it over the bench at the end of the course. Justin came over.

"Are you ready to show them something?"

She gave him that famous grin and turned to the group.

They all stared in amazement. Not one of them knew Kris was a woman. The muttering started again in earnest as they all commented on this new information. Kris didn't give them time to dwell.

"Everyone in the center viewing area. Captain, call the time, Sir."

Kris set herself as Javi set up the timers that would record the run. He set up the official timer that used infrared beams across the obstacles. The clock stopped when the final stream was crossed. Each obstacle had to be taken for the clock to stop. If anyone skipped an obstacle the clock would continue until it was run. Kris burst onto the course at Javi's mark flying over the equipment. She took the monkey bars like a rocket. The second was a log climb that had thick logs staggered several feet apart twenty feet high. She amazed those looking on by leaping up to the first log and rising up like lightning using nothing but her legs to propel her. Usually, the men used a two-handed grip on each log to be individually climbed. Kris used the strength in her legs from martial arts and Parkour to climb them like stairs; something the men had never considered before.

She kept going hitting each one and shredding it. Her only pause came when she reached the barbed wire. She hadn't run this since becoming a woman and forgot to compensate for the additional five inches around her chest. She caught her shirt at the beginning and just tore out of it as she plowed through the length. She rose out of the end with her t-shirt in shreds in the wire behind her wearing only her sports bra and fatigue pants. She reached the salmon ladder and propelled herself up the ten rungs to reach the top and grab the bar for the zip line. It had a brake to slow down for the drop. She never touched it.

"What the hell! She isn't braking!"

Javier commented to the group with great pride. "The Gunny doesn't brake."

She used the momentum from the speed and swung her legs back to gain distance. She let go of the bar and flew through the air to grab the rope for the water cross with only her feet. She swung upside down holding on only by her feet trailing her fingertips though the dirt. She swung her body up to flip off the rope and with a powerful lunge vaulted up to grab the handle of the next obstacle with both hands hanging in a perfect 'L' keeping her body tight along the slide.

One of the Sergeants turned to Juarez. "I heard a story about her getting operated on awake; that was the truth wasn't it, Sir?"

"Yes Sergeant Schmidt, it was. I was one of the four men holding her down. She watched them cut into her and continued to watch until the Major Alario told her to stand down."

The men close enough to hear stood with impassive faces and hard looks. They all hoped in the same situation they could do the same. Most of them knew they couldn't. They turned back to watch Cole.

She dropped off and continued to the beam. She decided to show off a little by handspringing down the length and dismounting with a backflip with a half twist landing in a crouch at the bottom. She hit the tires without a pause and worked her way through the dozen more additional pieces. She loved the burn of finally using her muscles at full tilt. She hadn't taken it easy since her release but hadn't pushed herself either not wanting to reinjure herself. She finally made it near the end as she climbed the rope. She got to the top and looped the rope so she could roll down instead of descending normally. She headed to the final obstacle and tore through the forty yards to reach the finish. She was winded but didn't show it. As badly as she wanted to lean over and rest her hands on her knees to gulp her next breath, she stood straight and tall controlling her breathing, so it appeared that the run took her no effort. This was a lesson in endurance, and she didn't want to lessen it by looking beat. She looked to the board as it put up her score-13:14. The men's voices exploded. The cheering and yelling was deafening. She looked at them and waved at them to calm down. When they silenced she turned to Javi.

"Captain Juarez Sir, will you please fill out the rest of the board, Sir?"

There were slots for the last time run and the best previous score. Kris's last time was 13:28 and her best previous was 13:15. The men looked at her silently in awe.

"And that gentlemen, is why that," she pointed at the Corps top score, "is meaningless."

They looked at Kris with new eyes. Standing in just her sport bra and trousers the men saw all the scaring on her abdomen and the scar running all the way across her waist right at her belt line. Her muscles were highlighted by a layer of sweat. Anyone looking at her would see raw strength and unbridled power. Kris stood and drank from the water bottle Justin handed her. He moved behind her with a towel.

"Hold still a second Gunny." Justin pressed the towel against her back.

"What is it?"

"You tore up your back on that barbed wire. You're bleeding all over the place."

"I didn't even feel it! How bad?"

"Bad enough to ask when your last tetanus shot was."

"You should know Sir; you gave it to me!" She looked over her shoulder laughing. He shook his head and finished cleaning her up. "Thank you, Sir." The men were always getting hurt on the course, so he had plenty of bandages. She grabbed another tshirt out of her pack and her blouse and redressed, replacing her lid.

Kris addressed the men.

"Alright everyone, now that you have a better understanding of what is expected of you-do it again! Captain Juarez Sir, can you clear the time please, Sir?"

Javi went over to clear as the men moved away from the board. He looked up and shook his head.

"What?"

"I can't clear it Kris. Someone sent it up."

"Hold! Who sent up that score?"

None of the men responded. Then Sergeant Schmidt stepped forward. "I did Gunny."

"Sergeant did you hear nothing I said?"

He stood straight as Kris walked up and got in his face.

"I heard every word Gunny."

"Then explain that."

The Sergeant was huge, much bigger than Kris physically, but her presence made him feel half her size. He looked her dead in the eye as he replied.

"Gunny I sent that time because I won't have some slacker in the First MRB thinking that they have the baddest son of bitch in the Raiders in their ranks when we all know the baddest son of bitch in the entire Marine Corps is right here Gunny!"

"What did you call my mother Sergeant?!"

"I meant no disrespect to the Gunny's mother, just to say that you are the toughest Raider to ever wear a Marine uniform and everyone should know that Gunny."

All of the men were nodding in agreement. Oorah was said from all sides. Kris stared down the Sergeant until sweat started to bead up on his brow. She narrowed her eyes and nodded at him.

"Humph. Well played Sergeant. Get out of here." She nodded her head toward the front of the course. He took off running.

"That should give them something to think about for a while."

Kris looked over to Javier's stone-faced expression, but she saw the twinkle in his eyes. She clapped him on the back and went back to watching the men as they retook the course. She could already see improvement. They wouldn't stay green long.

From the window overlooking the course General Hammond turned to the young blonde Lieutenant next to him. She was pretty in a wholesome girl next doorway. Not too tall, not too thin with wide blue eyes that left her looking a little overwhelmed but hid a sharp and intelligent mind. She stood smiling with incredulousness.

"Well Lieutenant, what did you think of Cole?"

She turned to the General.

"She is very impressive General. That level of skill and focus is always impressive. Gunnery Sergeant Cole's skills as a Raider are not in question, however. Division is concerned with her emotional and psychological wellbeing. The kind of injury she sustained in combination with the psychological trauma of finding out she is a woman was not something easily absorbed. Then I read the medical report on her extensive hormone therapy. Her condition means she hasn't really had any emotional highs or lows in her life. After the therapy she will have a more normal emotional and hormonal reaction. This is what concerns division. That she is able to handle the mood swings she will now be subject to in a combat position. That is what I am here to determine."

"Well I can tell you one thing. Cole is determined to get back into combat post haste. That fricken spider monkey has become my achilleas heel! Every time I pull up an email or a stack of paperwork her name is on it with a request to return to duty. I want her back where she belongs and soon. I have been the brunt of Cole's ire before when she is passionate about something and I'm not going to go another round with her. She's the best for a reason and I'm sick of coming out on the losing end with her. It's bad for my ego and my reputation!" He said with a great deal of humor and pride.

"What do you mean Sir? Why do you refer to her as a spider monkey, Sir?"

"Cole is trained in Counter Surveillance and as a sniper. She also trains in martial arts and Parkour. Because of that she literally climbs the walls-without gear. She's like one of those spider monkeys on Animal Planet. She's the damn best there is if you'll pardon my language." She nodded in ascent.

"The last time she decided she wanted something that was not forthcoming she drove me crazy. Requests, requisitions, emails; you name it she sent it. I finally blocked her from my email address and refused to take anything sent by her. But she got around that. Paperwork and files started showing up in my car, on my desk when nothing had been there the night before when I locked up the office, and at my home on my kitchen counter for heaven's sake! She got through every obstacle until she got her way."

"What did she want Sir?"

"She performed an analysis of security for high target buildings on base that were not in her opinion secure enough. Tactically each of the buildings housed a major base infrastructure or command that could become a target and had too great of accessibility. Several bases had incidents of attack that year and she assessed a vulnerability of attack here to protect the men. The base commander took her report under advisement but it was only lip service. He felt his people had the right of it and Cole was just looking for glory. Humph. The man didn't know her very well. Cole will never accept glory. I was surprised they got her to her own medal ceremony last month. She isn't in this for the glory. That is why she is the best."

"What did she do?"

"She repeatedly circumvented security at every building multiple times. Sometimes during the day during office hours and sometimes at night when the buildings were closed. Every time she got in and out completely undetected."

"So how did you know it was Cole Sir?"

"In every case the section of her report that illustrated the weakness for that building or area was left in view for someone to find. Security Forces performed an investigation but could never point the finger on her. A Captain taking his dog out for a walk at 4 A.M. reported a dark figure scaling the building to the roof and a dim light shining in an office just after.

When they arrived no one was around and another copy of the report was on the table. They set up a sting to catch the culprit. For four months they watched and waited. Increased security and more cameras. She got through them all. She was never once ever caught on surveillance camera. And they were never hacked or blocked. No one knows how she did it."

"Her last entry was this." He pulled up a piece of paper showing a several scenarios of infiltration at different points of the day on different days of the week. The analysis of loss of intel, loss of men, loss of readiness if a terrorist or enemy of the state ever exploited the weaknesses she was using to make her point.

"The cost in man hours and property if any one of the buildings were attacked physically or virtually spelled out in black and white. The Commander's report wasn't anywhere near that comprehensive. I think that is what finally changed his mind on the matter and he set his people into the problem. By the end of that month changes were made and upgraded security measures were put in place.

Her coup de grace was after the new measures were in place and the buildings were secure to her satisfaction. The morning after they all came online security discovered on the Commander's desk was a vase of flowers with a thank you note. Signed by Cole. No one knows how they got there. They weren't there at midnight when the patrol went through but they were when the next patrol came in an hour later."

Cook laughed at Cole's audacity. She knew the Gunny was smart and tough, but also very canny and cagy as well. Good to know.

"Well the sooner I get started the sooner we can get that monkey off your back. It will take time, however. So I hope she is patient."

"I do too Lieutenant. If she starts up again I may forgo the investigation and just ring her neck myself!"

A knock on the door had them both turning as the door opening with Corporal Smith the General's admin.

"Colonel Stirling to see you Sir."

Colonel Nathan Stirling returned the Lieutenant's salute as he gave one to the General.

"Come on in Nate. Meet Lieutenant Cook. She will be evaluating Cole."

"Kris just came to see me and I informed her of the conditions of her return. She wasn't thrilled but eager to get started so she can get back to duty. I put her on admin only until you make your recommendation. Keeping her idle I feel is counterproductive." Stirling helped himself to a cup of coffee and sat down.

The General snorted into his cup of coffee.

"Now General it was never proven Kris was behind that incident."

"If you will pardon me again Lieutenant, BS!"

Stirling sat back in the chair and grinned as he drank.

"Colonel I will be shadowing Cole while on duty, watching how she interacts with the men then I will be speaking with her ex-wife Melody and her friends as to how she has been coping with the emotional and physical changes she has gone through. I have addresses and phone numbers for friends and acquaintances I will be interviewing over the next few weeks. I'll also question her team."

"Let me know if you need anything from me. If it's alright with you General I think I should take Cook over and introduce her to Cole. The sooner this is completed the faster I can get Alpha team back up and running. Luckily we are in a down rotation for them. They will be in Camp for several weeks but are slated to redeploy in a few months. I want Cole with them!"

"As long as Cook's report is favorable I don't see a problem with that." The two saluted and left to head out to meet Cole.

Once they finished on the course the men returned indoors to the weight room. Kris had gone inside to change into PT gear. She watched the men for a bit and then turned to Justin to team up for lifting. She spotted him as he bench pressed, performed squats, and dead lift as he did for her. Justin favored a workout to maintain his enormous physique. He was big, but he was also quick and flexible. Necessary in the field. She favored a circuit that lent to the agility and flexibility she needed in martial arts and parkour. They split off as he went to the hand weights and she moved to the bar. She started with pull ups after adding 25-pound weights to each ankle. She removed them and swung up to a handstand preferring to do her pushups on the bar. She descended and rose 50 times then swung down using her momentum to flip her body back over the bar. She twisted in the air to catch it as she swung down and completed the maneuver again. Kris ensued the standard weights for a tough street workout that used all of her own body weight. She flew over the bar a dozen more times before dropping the ground.

Using her agility and strength she cantilevered her body from one side to the other supporting all of her body weight on one hand or one arm while her body moved sinuously back and forth stopping and holding just inches from the ground. At one point she supported all of her body parallel to the ground a few inches off the floor on nothing but her fingertips. Then just her thumbs. She slipped into pushups where she pushed her entire body off the mat bringing her arms back to clap her hands behind her back. Then swung her legs under to catch herself on her hands holding her body off the mat like a gymnast. She swung her legs around in a circle lifting her arms one by one as her body completed the turn. She continued to circuit through these exercises until she completed her count.

Javier was sitting next to Justin curling 35-pound weights on the bench. Sergeant Schmidt stopped his workout to stare at Kris. He stood there for several minutes not moving. Javier looked up.

"Is there a problem Schmidt?"

"Ah, no Sir Captain. Can you do that Sir?"

He looked at Javier and Javier looked over to where Kris had her arms stretched almost fully extended while she slowly lifted her weight off the ground and pulled her arms closer together then went into a series of moves that required her to lie on her back and kick to propel her body until she landed on her feet and flipped into a forward flip landing in the push up position where kicked her feet around until she was on her back and repeated the maneuver.

"Hell no Sergeant! Only Gunny over there can do that."

Kris continued to move until she finally started to feel her arms shake and stopped grabbing her towel. Many of the men were staring. Most with respect or awe. Some with lust. She just ignored it knowing it would probably happen. They'd need to get over it. She moved over to the mat and hooked Justin with a look. He rose from the bench and came over. She nodded to the sparring mats in the corner and he went to his bag to grab his kickboxing gloves. She donned hers and they both put on head gear. Gentry whooped and ran over to grab the board that was on the floor and put it up on the stool against the wall. Cole and Alario's names were on the top with a line drawn below and a series of hash marks under each name. For the last three years once a month they fought hard hand to hand combat. The men started keeping a record after an argument broke out as to who had beaten who more. Right now it was tied at 14 each. A busy schedule and Kris's injury had stopped the fights for a while.

Alpha team gathered around while the new ASPOC guys questioned what was going on. Colonel Stirling entered the weight room with Lieutenant Cook. They walked over to the mats where the fight had just begun.

Justin learned long ago the only way to beat Kris was to strike hard and fast taking her off guard. He hit her hard in the gut and tried to knock her feet out from under her. She was ready for it and used the momentum to swing her body over his back and elbow him to the ground. He stood and got several blows to the head that bounced off the head gear as she swung around and kicked him in the chest. He went to the ground and jumped up to grab her about the shoulders throwing her to the ground. The fight was brutal and harsh. The Lieutenant was shocked. Justin wasn't giving her any quarter.

"Isn't someone going to put a stop to this?!" She winced as Justin's elbow connected with Kris's nose. She pulled back, but not fast enough which had her nose bleeding profusely. Kris dove under Justin coming up on the far side of the mat. He struck out a few more times connecting with her abdomen. She performed a swinging kick that knocked him to the ground and placed several short jabs to his sides. He reached back and connected with her side dislodging her and allowing him to gain his feet. They circled a few more times.

Javier answered her, "Don't worry Lieutenant. We won't let the Gunny hurt the Major." Lieutenant Cook looked at Javier nonplussed. He could tell she was just playing with Justin. Wearing him out so she could take him down. Suggestions began to fly from all around as the men shouted encouragement to one or the other of the fighters. At first glance no one would have figured Kris stood a chance against Justin considering their size difference. Their height was nearly the same, Justin only two inches taller, but he outweighed her by a seventy-five pounds and it was all hard muscle. She was just as ripped but her lean physique gave her speed and agility which balanced the scales. She went on the offensive using martial arts to back him into the corner as he deflected kick after kick. He sent a few jabs connecting with her ribs as she jumped back out of his reach. They danced around one another a few times as Justin swung out and Kris blocked the blows. She jabbed connecting with his ribs.

"You need to bring your arm up, Sir. You're dropping your left."

"No I'm not."

She reached out a jabbed him twice in the jaw snapping his head back.

"Sure about that, Sir?" she said mockingly.

He reached out again and connected with her gut as she turned and kicked him back.

"Something wrong with your hands Sir?"

"Why would you think that Kris?"

"Because you're hitting like a girl Sir!"

The men all groaned, catcalled, and laughed making predictions for her demise.

He connected with her head twice more.

"Really Kris, because I'm not the one who's nose is bleeding." He flashed a cocky grin as they continued to circle. She grinned back as he jumped forward pinning her to the ground with an arm around her neck. He held her in a sleeper hold as she fought to break his grip. It looked as though Justin was going to take this round with Kris pinned on her stomach to the mat with him on top of her holding her down.

Just then Kris bucked and applied pressure to a pressure point on his arm breaking his hold and brought her knees up to fling him off and through the air to the other side of the mat. He landed hard losing his breath as she flipped up and swung around connecting with his chest. Three more kicks and he was down the last snapping his head around and dropping him to his knees. He got up and she flew through the air grabbing him by the neck with her feet flipping him so hard he bounced. In a move that defied gravity she flipped around and regained her feet so quickly most of the men never saw the move. Justin stayed down and after a moment lifted his hand conceding the match. Kris helped him up. He staggered a bit a little off balance from the last blow and shook his head to clear it. She brought him in for a one-armed hug while clapping her hand on his shoulder. Javier brought them both water while Tomball threw them both towels. Kris used hers to wipe the blood off her face.

Colonel Stirling stepped up and introduced the Lieutenant.

"Gunnery Sergeant Cole, this is Lieutenant Shelly Cook. She is a psychologist from Division who has been sent to evaluate your readiness. She will be shadowing you while she determines your fitness to return to full duty. Her report will determine your ability to return to combat missions. Show her every courtesy."

Kris saluted the Lieutenant and the Colonel. Cook reached out to shake Kris's hand.

"I look forward to working with you Gunny. That was an impressive fight. Are you ok?"

"Of course ma'am. Nothing I haven't done before." She turned to Justin who had just cut a tampon in half and stuck each piece up her nose to stop the bleeding.

Cook looked bemused and asked Kris to walk with her outside. Kris grabbed her water bottle and slung her towel over her shoulder as they left the building.

"I have never seen tampons used quite that way."

Kris laughed. "We love these in the field. Ironically most of the men don't realize we use them for their original purpose-field triage."

"I just wanted to talk to you about what I will be doing over the next few weeks. I am sure you know that there has been some concern from up the chain regarding your gender change from male to female. Command wants to make sure that your process has not affected your ability to continue in a combat role. They also want me to monitor your team and the unit in regard to how well the rest of the MSOT and MSOC are handling a woman in the unit."

"And as I am officially the first woman to make it into a MARSOT and Command wouldn't be Command if they didn't have some concerns."

Cook smiled at Kris's understanding of the situation. "Exactly. I will be not only observing you individually, but I will also be observing you working with your team and with the other teams and SOC. Command is concerned that the sudden introduction of a women into SOC will create issues."

"Lieutenant, permission to speak freely?"

"Of course."

"I have been in SOC for eight years. My gender may have changed but I have not. I am exactly the same person I was six months ago. Other's perception of me may change based on their own prejudices and opinions but that is their problem, not mine."

"Well I'd have to disagree with you on one point Kris. You have changed. The experience you went through being wounded and having your world turned upside down changes you. You may not think it does, but trust me it has. Maybe in ways you never expected or subtly enough you don't see the changes yet, but you will. It's my job to make sure that you can deal with these changes before you are allowed back into the field."

"If you've read my file, I assume you have?" Cook nodded her ascent. "Then you are aware that I have known about my gender issue since I was ten years old. I have had a long time to acknowledge and accept the fact that I may not be male. But circumstances determined that I would live my live as male and identify as male regardless of the truth. I did not decline to find out my true gender because I was afraid to know. I chose to leave it because I knew I would have to live my life out as a male as long as I could not remove the prosthetic device that identified me as male. I refused to live a lie. If I didn't know the truth then I wouldn't be lying to myself or anyone else about who or what I was.

But the gist of the matter is it truly doesn't matter to me one way or the other. I don't care. I was raised by a mother who understood the challenges I faced as I grew older and she met them head on by raising me to be a well-rounded person. Someone who could handle anything and everything. Someone who was able to take care of anything that needed doing. Not a woman or a man, but a person. She did not prescribe gender roles to me or my sister growing up. We were expected to learn how to cook and sew with the same skill and effort as we were expected to change the oil in the car or fix a flat tire. She didn't believe that we were predestined for specific chores suited to our gender. We were expected to learn everything to be self-sufficient. If you think that I am going through some sort of identity crisis or that I am ignoring what I am in some sort of denial you are way off the mark. I am a woman. Apparently I have been one all along. So my skills, knowledge, and training are all as much a part of me as my breasts now are. Will I have to adjust to becoming a woman? Yes. Found out that the hard way on the course today when I forgot to compensate for the added chest measurement before I entered the barbed wire obstacle. I tore up my back on the wire because I forgot my chest is larger than the last time I ran it. I had adjustments to make in not being a man too. Can't pee standing up anymore. But I am really good at cleaning the floor around the toilet now." Kris said with that engaging grin. Cook laughed.

"It will be a learning curve. I will have to learn along the way. I won't know what or when I will need to adjust until it happens. Good thing is with my training that is my forte; adjusting in the moment as needed."

Chapter Fifteen

Just after Kris returned to limited duty a break took the team of the roster for a couple of days. Brittney Lewis was on base to shoot the Men of MARSOC calendar photos. The calendar was a major fund raising tool for the GenZ foundation and split the profits with the Marine Corps Toys for Tots program. Brittney was a professional photographer who volunteered her time to shoot projects for charity organizations. It was a charity organization that put her on the path to photography when she was ten and put in foster care. Photography was the one thing that made her transient new life bearable. It was a constant during a turbulent time. Now it helped ease the pain of loss. She was on year two as a Marine widow. Her husband Staff Sergeant Mike Lewis was KIA in Afghanistan by an IED on a routine patrol. She was also Bobby B's press photographer.

She arrived in early afternoon and drove her pickup and trailer to the outdoor obstacle area to set up. She took a variety of photos in different lights from dusk to dawn. They were sexy and paid tribute to the intensity and skill of the subjects. Showing them in several scenarios that were consistent with Special Operations; only with limited clothing and attention to their cut bodies rather than their hard core tactical skills.

Justin, Davis, Javier, Mike, and Dan had already arrived. When Kris got there the guys were already in their 'gear'. Tight camo pants with boots and ammo belts over bare oiled chests, Marine Corps standard PT shorts and no shirt or shoes, and other combinations of standard equipment with bare muscle. Kris went into the trailer and Brittney was in the back office area on the computer with her back to Kris.

"Hey Britt!"

"Hey Kris. Just a second. Your outfit is on the rack. Go ahead and get changed."

Kris grabbed the cut off camo pants with the mockup M4 rifle and cartridge belt and snorted.

"Uh Britt. We have a bit of an issue with this outfit. I don't think this is going to work."

"It's the same as last year. You a different size now?" She continued to fiddle with the computer not turning around.

"Um yeah. When I was wounded some of my measurements changed."

She jumped away from the computer and spun around coming forward quickly. Kris was partially behind the rack so she didn't get a full look until she got closer.

"Oh Jeez! I am so sorry Kris! I didn't even think about your wounds and how you might be a bit sensitive about wearing...."

She stopped dead and stared. Her mouth falling open. Which meant Bobby didn't tell her about Kris's gender change. She'd find a way to pay that little punk back later.

She looked Kris up and down her eyes wide and unblinking as they went from her face to her feet and back up again pausing at her breasts before jerking up to her face.

"Not so much about my wounds as about something else we discovered." Kris stated ending with her famous shit eating grin.

"What in the....!" She ran and gave Kris a tight hug and pulled back laughing.

"So you got blown up so bad it made you a woman?"

They both laughed as Kris propped a hip on the truck that held props.

"Not exactly. Apparently I always was one, and just didn't know it."

"Oh man. You could have said just about anything else and I wouldn't be shocked. But this. Talk about out of nowhere! Wow. Does Bobby know? Is this a GenZ thing?"

"Yeah. To both. He came to see me in Germany. Brought me some really cute 'it's a girl' balloons and a little pink bear."

"Awwwwww!!"

"So this outfit, is going to need a little um *more*. Or we will only be selling these in adult bookstores. Which will lower our potential demographic. And porn really isn't my aim at this point."

"Ok. Let me think. I know. I have an outfit I had designed for a female fitness model using Marine Corps camo that might fit you."

She rummaged through the hanging rack until she pulled out an outfit that barely had enough material to qualify as underwear. The bra top was cut low in the designed to show generous cleavage and the bottoms were practically floss. Kris looked at the bottoms with an arch look that clearly said, 'no way in hell' and handed it back to her.

"I know. The bottoms are too much. But it is the same camo as your pants. If we cut those down a bit shorter and with the bra top that would be sexy as hell. Let me grab my scissors."

She went to work on the pants until they barely covered butt. Kris pulled the curtain to block off the entrance and stripped. Brittney held out the clothes for her.

"Wow Kris. I can't believe you are a woman. How are you doing with that?"

"No different than before. I am the same person."

"Well yeah, but...."

"But what? Nothing has changed but how people see me. And my chest measurement."

"But damn how'd you get so lucky to get the body of a super supermodel? I would kill to look like that."

"Just hard work and dedication. You could get cut in no time."

"Yeah but my pecs would be bigger than my boobs."

She placed her hands like a shelf under modest B cup breasts to bring attention to their small size.

"Yeah well you have no idea how lucky you are. When these things started growing I thought they were going to keep me out of the field. They are always in the way. I had to special order body armor." Kris shook her head as she pulled on the skimpy outfit. "Then I had to put up with my guys forgetting their own names once they got a look at them. Javier still drops whatever he's holding anytime he sees me in anything that makes me look like a woman. The rest of them are getting better but, what are you gonna do?"

"Do you like being a woman?"

"I don't really examine it. I am who I am and always have been. I am starting to like my body now that I have gotten used to it. I don't like that so many people take one look and assume whatever. Mel has helped. I've always been a sexy beast, I guess now I'm a sexy bitch."

"And still just as modest!" Brittney laughed along with Kris.

"Hey Britt, do you happen to have a long blond wig?"

"Um yeah. Let me grab it."

Brittney went to the back and came back with a beautiful blonde wig a little lighter than Kris's natural hair color. Brittney had Kris sit down while she put a stocking cap over Kris's hair and affixed the wig. It was long, past her shoulder blades, and slightly curled with a natural look. It was made of real hair so once she got it on and glued you'd never be able to tell it wasn't Kris's natural hair. Kris grabbed a bandana and tied it around her forehead. Then she grabbed the face paint to start disguising her features. Since they were all actively in the field they didn't shoot photos that could allow them to be recognized by the enemy. All of the men wore face paint camouflage or used shots that only partial exposed their features.

By the time Kris was done applying, her eyes were highlighted and smoky with black liner. The pattern which is usually rough to blend better with the natural environment was carefully applied in a smoother less random pattern to accentuate her high cheek bones, full lips and intense eyes. Her lips were lightly lined and shaded to blend into the camo but still show the sexy shape to its best advantage. It disguised her features while it ramped up her sexy looks to a new level. Gentry was a good teacher.

The bra top barely fit. She was obviously more endowed than the model it was created for. But since it was stretchy it worked as long as she didn't bend over. It had a scoop in the front designed to accent the model's cleavage but barely contained Kris's. The bottom had a little belt that fastened just below her breasts to help support them. The short shorts hugged Kris's hips and butt. They rode lower on her waist than last year due to her weight loss from the injury but that just added to the sexiness of the outfit. She put on her boots and started looking through the prop trunk. She grabbed a thigh strap knife holder and put it on her left leg and a handgun thigh holster and prop gun and put it on her right leg. Then grabbed a cartridge belt around her waist.

The look was amazing. She looked dangerous and sexy as hell. Brittney was smiling so big that Kris didn't even look in the mirror to see how it pulled together.

"So this is good?"

"Oh yeah. I..." She stopped and just stared at Kris.

"You..."

"I am sorry Kris. This is probably making you uncomfortable. But hot damn are we going to sell a ton of calendars this year. All I see when I look at you is what I want to look like when I grow up and major dollar signs."

Kris laughed and threw an arm around Brittney's shoulders as they walked out to join the men. Brittney pulled away as she realized she walked off without her camera. The five guys from SOC that were chosen to be in this year's calendar had arrived and were talking to the team. When Kris walked up every one of them stopped talking. Javier dropped his prop M4 with a "Madre de Dios!" Gentry whistled long and low shaking his head and smiling. Mike just said, 'Oh Hell!' and suddenly was very interested in the trees behind them. Dan stood and stared saying nothing. Kris was mostly interested in Justin's reaction.

He was standing a bit apart from the rest having moved away to take a phone call. His eyes had turned almost jet black with desire. They slowly walked toward one another stopping with just inches between them. He was wearing tight pants with no shirt and just an ammo belt crossbody. He had a backwards camo ball cap on. He'd left off shaving over the weekend to have a good start on a beard to disguise his features and the rest of his face was artfully covered with paint. She could see Gentry's fine hand. He usually applied all the paint to be more photogenic then concealing. The sun had come down into the trees behind them and they were so focused on one another they didn't notice the rapid clicking of the camera as Brittney crouched to capture the moment.

They pulled apart to provide some distance so as not to give the men anything to talk about. Brittney was looking at the shots she just took and called them all to get going. Over the next three hours they took hundreds of shots. Kris at one point laid down to set up a sniper shot that Brittney shot once from the front with Kris's intense gaze and several from the back showcasing Kris's amazing body. Gentry performed some maneuvers on the course for some action shots; the best was one in a tight t-shirt hanging from the chin up bar by one arm flexed. He looked amazing. Mike had a great one on the rope climb that was sexy and strong. Javier set up some field equipment for a mock command post and had a shot of him looking darkly over the top while leaning on the table showing his strong arms and chest. Rosa would love that photo. Dan made a great one with a Mr. Universe pose holding up his M4 and sighting a shot downrange.

The winner for Justin was at dusk when they went down to the water and she got a shot of him coming out of the water wet and glistening with the sun going down behind him. Brittney got some of all of them in night shots using a night vision lens. They broke for the evening and made plans to meet up two hours before dawn. They dragged Brittney out of her trailer knowing she'd be there half the night going over the shots and made her go with them to dinner. They went to a popular steak house and had a great time. The night was full of good humor, affectionate teasing, and great conversation.

The next morning they met up and got back into costume and took one at sunrise of the group in a zodiac coming up to the beach. A team shot at dawn with them in various tactical poses in the pearly light won for the December pick. They finished up and Kris arranged for Brittney to email her the shots she selected for the calendar. Kris, as project leader, always had final say. Since the object of the photos was sex, Kris looked them over for any potential security issues. If any shots showed anything that could be used to identify them they had to be scrapped. Brittney used photoshop to change or erase tattoos or any identifiers that could compromise the men's identities. Kris just had one thing to add.

Brittney,

I only ask that when you photoshop the pics, not to erase any of my scars. I've earned them.

Kris

Of the photos selected by Brittney in the preliminary choices two worried her. The first was the pictures she took of her and Justin. They were very intimate. The second was one of her on the beach at dawn. She was laying down in the surf crawling onto the shore. It was erotic and dangerous. And she feared trouble. She didn't want any of the men to see her as a sex object but as a Marine. She also didn't want Command getting it and using it as a reason to keep her out of the field. But it was a powerful picture. She had no doubt Justin would want a copy. Now that play was done, time to get to work.

Over the next several weeks Kris's days consisted of monitoring drills and training as well as performing classroom lectures and paperwork but was still not able to join the team in field training. Paperwork was endless as every member of the team gladly dumped all the monotonous drudge onto her, at her request, to keep her busy. Stirling sent several sitreps to Division regarding

Kris's fitness to return to full duty but was getting only b.s. responses. The whole team was getting angry. If they were called up for a mission they'd have to carry on without their leader and none of them were down for that. That was ok while she was recuperating, but out of the question now that she was back.

 In the evenings she added online courses to complete her master's degree. She'd been steadily taking courses for the last four years online, as she had time, to complete her Bachelor of Science in Homeland Security. She was only 15 credit hours away from her Master's Degree in Security and Resilience. She had been steadfast in refusing Officer's Candidate School so as not to be separated from her team, but she wanted to be ready to go when the time came. If the DoD or the Corps decided she couldn't rejoin her unit she needed to be ready to explore her options. Not that she was giving up. She had no intention of going quietly. This at least gave her some options. If she had to disengage, she could complete OCS and get her commission. Then screw it, she'd reenroll in MARSOC if she had to and start over again. She had no problem going through the training again. It would be a walk in the park.

Her nights were spent with Justin. He kept up appearances by leaving his clothes and things in his room; but every night he slept with Kris. Every day they maintained the same working relationship they had always enjoyed; challenging one another physically and mentally. At night they lay wrapped in each other's arms. Mel spent a lot of time out, so they took advantage of the alone time. There wasn't an area of each other's bodies they hadn't explored. There wasn't a boundary they didn't push. They challenged each other in bed the same way they did in the field-by pushing each other to do more and reach further. They tested each other's stamina with lingering caresses and slow deep kisses then switched to hard heavy and punishing. They started going up earlier and earlier to make up for the time they spent intimately. They were reporting for duty with only a handful of hours of sleep. It was hard to stay away from each other. They actually started setting an alarm at night to keep from losing control and track of time. Being overtired during training could be deadly.

One day five weeks after her return, just as she was completing last week's PER for the teams active training scenarios Justin came in.

"Hey Asshole, gear up."

Kris looked up sharply. He was smiling, but not joking.

"I am not cleared for field training. Or do you know something I don't?"

"If we wait for those bureaucrats in Division you'll be retired before your cleared. Gear up. Full field pack and camouflage. You just became Kristensen. None of these new guys know you, so you get to field the work ups without the politics. And they won't recognize you through the war paint even if they do know you."

Kris thought about it for a second, "Is that an order, Sir?" she asked with a grin.

"Yeah, that's an order."

Sweet. Time to get dirty.

Chapter Sixteen

Kris arrived at the field training center in full gear and camouflage. She was one of the last to arrive and stayed in the back. Justin as the team leader assigned groups to run through scenarios. Many of the exercises were from prior missions. The training center was a rabbit warren of rooms and buildings that could be reconfigured to meet the mission specs. They allowed the teams to work in real life conditions that are close to what can be expected in the field. This enables the teams to work in a real time atmosphere and build cohesive units working through obstacles prior to the mission. Each person learns their own part and the part of the person above them so if anyone goes down the mission can still be completed. The roles are run through several times with different outcomes allowing the team members to adjust for issues and compensate for losses. That way they are prepared for anything.

The teams were paired in eight person units. Each practice team had four experienced Raiders and four new recruits. This was so the new guys can learn from the experience of those that had been in the field. Kris was put with two guys from Delta, one from Bravo and four from the last ASPOC. The team leader was Captain Max Nunez. He was a hell of a Special Operations Officer. He was currently on Bravo but would be coming to Alpha as Kris's Executive Officer once she was reinstated.

She'd already talked it over with Justin and he accepted that they needed to be on separate teams. Kris would not bend on this. Their personal relationship put themselves and the team at risk. She would not allow anything that would distract them in the field. Justin had been team leader while she was out, and if any of the men asked they would be told he was taking the team lead spot to replace the vacancy in Bravo due to attrition.

Several teams had lost members from attrition. Most teams acquired at least one new member a year or were loose configurations that constantly rotated as members went from team to team depending on the needs of their MOS. Alpha team was an exception to the rule. The team dynamic stayed the same for the last five years. It was unheard of in SOC. Rotation was the rule of thumb because it kept the men focused and allowed them to develop skills and experience. Also with injuries and battle rotation not all of the men were able to redeploy together as needed. Because of Alpha team's skill and unique unity they were given dispensation.

Kris assembled with her team and waited for Nunez to outline the mission. Ironically it was a replay of a mission she and Alpha ran last year. She was given the role of rear point. Good. She wanted to stay in the background so that the newer guys could get in and gain experience. Nunez ran them through their roles and had them all run their part. He looked at Kris a little strangely as if trying to figure out what she was up to. She didn't pay it any mind. Her lead was a Sergeant Lewis. He had been in a year and run three previous missions.

They got in formation and ran the drill. The objective was a group that was selling weapons and intel. The mission was to capture as many as possible and get any and all equipment. The group used the dark web to arrange meets and buyers which had made them hard to locate. Finding their contacts and getting their URL would shut them down. Surprise was the key here. The Sergeant was chatty and kept trying to talk to Kris. Kris didn't want to give herself away so she said little. Kris knew the lead was going to be jumped and the team would be attacked from the rear. She held herself ready without giving away her advance knowledge.

The drill went well. Two of the newer men jumped out of formation when attacked putting the rear at risk. Nunez ran the drill three more times in order to complete the objective. The team stood aside to allow the other units to go in and complete the drill. Each team watched the drill through cameras in the drill area to see how each group performed. After completion it was back to the classroom where the teams would watch their own drill and discuss strengths and weaknesses in order to shore up their performance. By the end of the week the groups had rotated several times to allow everyone to work with one another and learn each other's skills. No matter where Kris rotated,

Lewis was there. Kris couldn't shake Lewis. That guy stuck to her like glue.

"How do you think we did Gunny?"

Kris looked over at him. He was as eager as a puppy.

"Fine."

"The new guys seem to be holding up well. Not too many errors."

"Yup."

"I'm surprised you are not up there leading. I'd really like to hear your take on the drills. With your experience I'm sure we'd learn a lot more."

Kris looked at him sternly. He gulped and sat back in his chair waiting for the assessment to start.

"Why would you think I'd have anything more to offer than your group leader Sergeant?"

"C'mon Gunny! No one is better than you. Everyone knows that!"

"Sergeant I think you are confusing me with someone else."

Lewis looked a little confused. Just then Justin came in and glanced around the room.

"Kristensen! You're needed in the Comm."

Kris got up and left with Lewis sitting there more than a little confused.

"Thanks man, you saved me. Lewis knows who I am. The guy is like a dog with a bone and won't let go."

Justin laughed. "The myth, the legend! Your fame precedes you. Suck it up Marine you're famous!"

Kris punched him in the arm.

"Lieutenant Cook is looking for you. Better wash your face."

Kris didn't have time to duck into the restroom before Cook spotted her.

"Nice makeup Kris. Little heavy on the concealer though."

Kris shook her head. "It's a learning process. Lip stick is a serious business."

Cook liked Kris's dry wit. They moved into the offices to Kris's desk and sat down.

"I was just going over my conversations with the team. I was curious as you are not training with them, but with the newer recruits. Why?"

"I have not been cleared for full duty Lieutenant. Admin only. I don't want to get stale, so I arranged it to observe and run drills with the new guys."

"And I wasn't supposed to know?"

"It's your eval that is determining my status Ma'am. But every minute you evaluate you are taking me out of run. Those runs are an important part of field work. Until you ok it I can't perform the runs with my team. The Major didn't know I've been running with the recruits. I took it upon myself to review and make sure I am back to full before requesting my status update."

"Wow. You are good. I actually believed that. Like you I am a trained observer. I like your loyalty to your team. I know Major Alario ok'd you to go incognito. I am actually here to tell you that you are ok to rejoin your team. I am giving you the green to go back into full status. I can't really evaluate you on partial duty can I? You are cleared for training, but not yet for combat. I have to judge the team dynamic before I can authorize that."

"You will do what you feel is best Lieutenant. As will I."

Cook smiled and stood up. Kris saluted her as she turned to leave the room. Justin came over.

"We in trouble?"

"No. She cleared me to return to the team. But not to combat. She wants to observe our dynamic before she does. I hate this moving forward by inches. It's politics, but what are you gonna do?"

Chapter Seventeen

Over the next couple of weeks Kris felt more like herself. The team fell back into their old rhythms. The only hitch was having Justin on Bravo. Kris felt as if something was missing. Nunez was a good choice as he fit the team very well. He seemed to have no problem working under Kris. The drills went smoothly and everyone seemed to be working well together. She couldn't complain, it was her decision to move him. But she didn't have to like it.

They worked hard and developed a good team flow. The days were moving fast now. Then the word came down they were up for a mission. Five weeks and they would return to Afghanistan. Kris routinely stopped into Colonel Stirling's office looking for her paperwork returning her to combat until he finally ordered her out. He'd summon her when it came through. She was getting pissed and impatient. Which wasn't like her. She usually just let things happen, but she wasn't content to do that. She was used to making things happen.

Two days later when the team was in the gym General Hammond came in looking furious.

"Where the hell is Cole?!"

Kris stepped away from where she was spotting Justin and stood at attention before the general.

"Sir!"

"Cole what the hell is this doing on my desk?" He asked waving a folder in front of her.

"Sir?"

"It's a fitness evaluation and a form to return you to combat status. Filled in-all but my signature. I did not requisition this Cole. Nor was it on my desk when I left last night. Can you explain how it got on my desk Gunnery Sergeant?"

"No Sir!"

"I find that hard to believe. I believe we have had a discussion previously about what would happen if I discovered you in my offices without official purpose of being there."

"Yes Sir!"

"Your case is under review Gunny. Until I say otherwise. Dismissed!"

Kris saluted the General and turned back to the weights. Justin got up from the bench and approached her.

"What are you doing Kris?"

"I don't know what you mean Sir."

"Don't do this. Don't antagonize him and jeopardize everything. We're too close."

"The team leaves for Afghanistan in five weeks. If it hasn't escaped your notice; I'm not on the roster."

"This isn't going to make that happen any faster. If you piss him off, he could pull you for good."

"I don't think he'll pull me just to spite me. He won't scuttle the mission just to put me in my place."

"You don't know that. After everything you've worked for and fought for I would hate to see you lose it all now over an emotional response that is completely not like you. Let Cook give her eval and let them come around on their own. Don't start a fight you may not win."

"Don't worry Sir. I don't intend to lose."

Kris picked up her towel and headed to the mats to stretch. Javier came over to Justin with a concerned look on his face.

"What's going on?"

"The Gunny is getting impatient and that is not a good thing."

"You don't think she'll do anything rash?"

"I think she already has and has no intention of stopping until she is on that transport with us."

Later that afternoon, just prior to leaving for the day, Justin and Javier were called into Colonel Stirling's office. He motioned for them to sit while he finished up some paperwork. He filed the papers and addressed the two.

"General Hammond called earlier and just about chewed my ear off. Something about a 'Friggen Spider Monkey' getting into his office again. What do you know about this?"

Justin leaned forward. "Nothing Sir. But I have my suspicions. We are getting ready to deploy and we are one man short on Alpha. We all know who should be in that slot Sir."

"Just what in the hell is she doing? Bating the General is not going to end well for her or for us. You two have got to keep her in line until it's time to go."

Javier smirked. "If you have an idea of how to go about that Sir I would accept any suggestions. I don't even know how or when she could have managed it considering we've been with her practically every moment of the day for a week now."

"Colonel is she going with us? Do you have any news?"

"I don't Major. As soon as I do you all will be the first to know. Just as I've told Cole. This is something they could use to yank her and decide she is not fit! What does she think she is going to accomplish by this?!"

"Sir you know as well as the Major and I that Kris is more than ready and able to return to combat status. You can't expect to put a combat trained mission specialist on lockdown without repercussions. That's like hooking a thoroughbred up to a pony bar and giving five-year olds rides. It's not going to be happy or not put up a fight to be restrained."

Justin agreed with Javier. "Can you talk to the General Sir?"

"I have Alario. He's not budging. I have told him all this and more. He's still stalling. I don't know what he is waiting for.

And I don't know what more we can do to expedite the process. But I do know if she is behind this and he catches her at it, this could mean the end of her career. You two are her best friends. Reason with her. Get her to talk to you. Don't let her do something stupid. I'll keep you updated but keep her busy so she doesn't have time to harass the General."

Over the next week the General was kept on full boil. His personal diary was removed from his locked desk drawer with the pen his grandfather gave him and found in his safe. His decanter on the shelf in his office was moved from one side to the other. The password to his desktop was changed. He blew up and summoned Stirling to his office.

When Stirling arrived, the General looked mad enough to chew glass.

"Sit down Colonel."

Stirling took a seat and waited for the General to speak. He had a really good idea as to what was on his mind.

"Colonel Stirling over the last week my office has been under siege. Personal items removed or moved. Computer hacked. Paperwork missing or refiled. I want it to stop! We both know who is behind it."

"Who do you suspect is behind it General?"

"You know as well as I do it is Cole! You need to get that woman under control!"

"Sir, do you have any proof that Cole has accessed this office? Surveillance or witnesses that can put her in here?"

"You know I don't! She's too good. Dammit!" He threw a book down on his desk.

"General I am not saying it is Cole. But if it is you know as well as I do she is not going to quit until she gets what she wants. She's not asking for the impossible here. You can't expect a fully trained Team Commander and Combat Specialist to be content to ride a desk filling out forms when she should be out there doing what she was trained to do. All she wants to do is her job. The job she was trained for. Hell, the job she was born to do!"

The General walked over to the shelf and picked up his coffee pot and poured them both a cup. He handed one to Stirling and sat down.

"Nate I agree with you. But this is over my head. Division is calling the shots on this one."

"Yes Sir, but your say would carry a lot of weight on getting her back to where she needs to be."

The General sat and mused as he drank his coffee.

"Just think of her a thousand miles away harassing a terrorist cell or an insurgent's hideout and how peaceful your life could be."

Hammond barked out a laugh. "Are you trying to bribe a superior officer Colonel? Because that just might work. I'll consider it. But if I find one more thing out of place in here or find my computer hacked again, I am coming after her-with or without proof!"

"I will relay the message Sir."

"Do that! Dismissed!"

Stirling looked around for Kris, but it appeared everyone had already left for the day. He gathered up his briefcase and left. On the drive to Kris's house, he thought about the person he'd mentored since high school. Kris was brilliant and dedicated. And didn't have a malicious bone in her body. He wondered if he would be able to get through to her. He arrived and didn't see her truck in the drive. He went up to the door just as Melody was coming out of it.

"Oh Colonel. Hi! What are you doing here?"

"I came to talk to Kris. Is she here?"

"Oh no Sir. Everyone is over at the Officer's Pool. It's Ernesto's birthday party. I forgot to grab the presents."

"Damn, that's today? I guess I will see you over there."

He walked her back to her car and pulled out to swing by his house and pick up the gift he bought for the boy. He didn't change, just went in his uniform.

When he pulled in he could hear the music and the laughter. The kids were cheering on two in the pool who were racing. Javier and Rosa were at the big table covered by the awning setting up refreshments.

"Colonel so glad you could make it." Rosa took the bag and embraced him handing him a beer. He sat down and watched the race as the kids yelling reached a fever pitch as the combatants reached the final lap. They reached the side and hit. The kids were yelling and jumping. It was hard to tell who won but the kids declared it a tie.

Javier came out from the bathroom holding two-year-old Sebastian. He put him on the seat next to the Colonel as he smiled and shook the older man's hand. He picked up a can of soda and went to drink right as Kris and Justin exited the pool. He took one look at her in her bikini and promptly dropped the can.

"Ah! Javi! Watch it! What are you doing?"

"Dammit! Will someone please tell Kris to stop doing that! Madre de Dios!"

"Doing what? She got out of the pool. Stop being ridiculous."

Stirling looked over to see Kris drying off. She had on an OD green two piece that left nothing to the imagination. The boy shorts covered most of the scarring on her lower abdomen. The bra top covered her but the sheer size of her breasts left a great deal exposed. The bathing suit wasn't provocative but on Kris's body it looked sexy as hell. Patches on it mimicked a uniform. Seeing Javier's jaw twitch and realizing why, she grabbed a tank to pull on over it before she came over to join the group.

Rosa was muttering under her breath in Spanish about Javier's puritan ideals when Kris muttered something in a low voice to her that had her laughing out loud. Kris sat down next to the

Colonel. Over the next hour the kids played and then in a boisterous jumble came over to have cake and open presents. Rosa had been working with the kids on signing the birthday song. The whole team joined in. Sebastian grinned and laughed his face covered in cake. Kris noticed the Colonel wasn't eating but just pushing his cake on the plate.

"Something on your mind Sir?"

"Yeah. Had a little meeting with Hammond today. He's pretty pissed."

"At what Sir?"

"You know at what Kris. Do us all a favor and stop. You won't get an answer faster because it truly is not up to him. Cook is calling the shots here. Just do the job and show her the outstanding Marine I have become so proud of and stop baiting the General. I don't want him to make an example of you and he doesn't want that either. He wants you in the field. He knows what it's like having to ride a desk when you want to be in the action. Just let the system work please."

Kris didn't say anything; just ate her cake. She gave him the nod and he relaxed some. He took a bite and stood up. He hugged Sebastian and then Rosa. Shook Javier's hand and waved to the rest before leaving. Justin came over and took his place.

"What was that?"

"A warning."

Justin just raised his eyebrows and cocked his head.

"Yeah, yeah. I'll stop. At least Hammond is on my side this time."

"Yeah I bet he is. Anything to get you thousands of miles away and out of his hair."

Kris laughed and picked up a piece of her cake and smashed it into Justin's face. She rubbed it in so that the icing covered him from nose to chin. He licked off what he could as he laughed with the rest of the crew. He leaned over and whispered in Kris's ear.

"I'll get you for that when we get home."

She kept smiling but her gut was churning. She wanted him bad.
How long were kids birthday parties supposed to last?

***

The last Thursday of the month when the team was home was
always exciting on base. That was the day that Bobby Ranson
came to Lejeune to train with the team. In the last year the team
had been deployed more than home and Kris's injury kept her
out of the ring. Now that she was healed it was time to rattle the
cage. This was the first time Kris was going to see Bobby's crew
since her change in gender. If she knew Bobby, he didn't tell
them a thing about it just so he could see the look on their faces.
Bobby had come to visit Kris in Germany when she first got there
and they Skyped quite a bit but they hadn't been face to face
since Bobby's schedule had him on the fight circuit in Europe
and Kris had been recovering then training for the field.

A crowd had already gathered outside the Camp Johnson Fitness
Center where the fights usually took place. Because of past
issues with crowding only the team and a handful of senior
leadership would be allowed in the fight area. This included the
base commander, the public relations officer who brought a local
news reporter to catch the story, Kris's commanding officer, the
unit commander, and several officers and senior enlisted from a
variety of commands on base.   For everyone else they watched
on the screens outside. Bobby's crew had already set up the
screens for the crowd. Right now they just showed the warmup
area and the boxing ring. Kris and Bobby always warmed up
with a HIIT workout and some limbering exercises. Neither one
of them could afford an injury.

The team was inside when Bobby's van pulled up with him and
his manager and trainer. The cheers outside announced their
arrival. Bobby always stopped to sign autographs and take
pictures with the Marines. He knew a lot of them by name
having come to the base for so long. He knew what it meant to
the men to say they met him and he was able to express how
much it meant to him that they laid it on the line for freedom.
Bobby considered serving but Kris talked him out of it. She told

him he is doing what he was meant to do. Everyone had their destiny and he was following his.

After talking with the men and taking some good-hearted teasing as to whether or not he'd win today's fight Bobby and the crew went inside. They greeted the team and hugged, slapping backs and giving out headlocks. Bobby's manager Lou Russo was a former fighter. He was smaller and more compact than the six-foot two-inch Ransom. He was tough and fierce, turning to management after an injury took him permanently out of the ring. He followed Bobby all along the youth circuit. He moved to North Carolina to train him once Bobby announced he wouldn't leave his brothers stationed here. With him were his trainer Andrew and publicist Nadine.

The crew that worked the cameras and ran the website were friends of Bobby's from school. The Chandler Brothers came to LeJeune the year they all started high school and became immediate friends with Bobby. Ryan, Jake, and Brad took Bobby out his shell. They thought it was cool he didn't know he was a boy until just a few years ago. The twins Ryan and Jake were 20 years old like Bobby and Brad was a year older. They were computer nerds and tech geeks. Not at all like the super athletic boy who would rather fight or train than anything else. But they were tight and completely loyal to one another. Through Bobby they realized their lifelong dreams of owning a web design company and a production company.

Bobby stopped just inside the door to perform his pre-fight monologue. He spoke about Kris, being wounded, and reconditioning. Kris lost the rest with the escalating noise as they all filed in. Ryan walked over with the camera on his shoulder getting the crew and Kris in the shot. Once they got past the team to where Kris was doing pull ups on the bar she dropped and turned to address them with a "You're late kid- hit the mats."

Everyone stopped talking at once and just stared. The brothers stood frozen in shock and if Nadine's eyebrows got any higher they'd be lost in her hair. Lou let out a string of Italian that Kris knew from Justin as mostly swear words. Andrew just smiled and whistled. Bobby broke the ice.

"Damn Gunny. You really believe in go big or go home! Whew!"

Kris just pinned him with a withering stare. She had taken off her shirt and was only in her PT shorts and a sports bra. Sweat already glistening on her muscles from her warmup. Her ripped body was impressive, but added to that her significant curves and she looked like a warrior goddess. She'd taken off her shoes and taped her ankles waiting to tape her wrists until after they warmed up. She let them just stare and get it out of their systems. Jake started gaping like a fish unable to get anything out. Andrew finally was able to articulate.

"What the hell Gunny? How....."

Kris pulled down the right side of her shorts to show a new tattoo she had on her hip. The GenZ foundation symbol. She had the image trademarked for the foundation so it could only be reproduced with permission from the foundation. And only to people with GenZ. Since all of the crew volunteered with Bobby for the Foundation they all knew what it meant. It only took a few seconds for them all to start yelling and cheering for Kris. They all began talking at once. The exclamations and comments kept coming until Kris waved them off and shut down the gossip session.

"Those Marines outside didn't come to watch you six titter like a pack of high school girls, they came to watch a fight. So you girls take a seat and let us warm up." To Bobby. "You get going. You spent too long signing autographs and we are behind. Catch up kid."

Kris and Bobby started by doing burpees. They went into a series of stretches and lunges to make sure neither of them pulled any muscles. Then they worked through a quick HIIT workout that worked their whole bodies. They went to the bar and completed single arm pull ups for each arm then two arm pull ups until they could no longer meet the bar. Once they completed their stretching and headed into the ring the crowd outside started to yell and clap.

The Marines inside the fitness center all gathered around the ring with the team taking up point on the back side of the ropes to lend a hand to the fighters if need be and stay out of the camera's range. Kris let Justin tape up her wrists while Lou taped Bobby's. They pulled on their gloves. Kris flexed her fingers to make sure her gloves weren't too tight and moved her wrists in circles first clockwise and then counterclockwise. Both fighters put in mouth guards and moved into the center of the ring and squared up. They formed a fist bump routine that started every match then danced back from one another and moved into fighting stances.

Bobby struck out first. He charged Kris taking a low swing at Kris's ribs. Kris moved quickly away and swept her leg out catching Bobby and taking him down to a knee. He bounded back up and circled while Kris moved to counter him. Bobby charged again attacking Kris with several punishing blows to the head. Bobby darted in and danced back several times taking aim at Kris's head, chest and gut. Each time he landed a hard blow. None of them seemed to phase Kris, however. She continued to counter him.

She struck out with a right and while he was distracted by that she swung her body through the air and landed a hard blow high on his ribs and across his back which sent him staggering. She swung around and connected her foot to his chest and gut several more times before he grabbed her foot in both hands and used it to flip her away. She used the momentum to arc through the air in a spin which put her on her feet facing him. He kicked out again connecting with her gut knocking her back against the ropes. Three more kicks and he kept her pinned to the ropes. He reached out to connect with her head and she grabbed him in a head lock and flung him across the mat to land hard on his back on the far side. When he got up his eyes, which should have been looking at hers to judge her next move were focused on her breasts. It was just a flicker but he was distracted. That wouldn't do.

Justin stood and watched Kris. This was her first fight in a while against a skilled opponent. Unlike their fights where they were just exercising and not trying to really take one another down, Kris and Bobby gave each other no quarter. Justin just stood with his arms crossed smiling. Kris had a look on her face that threw him for a second. It was a relatively recent scowl. It usually accompanied someone looking a shade too far south of her face during conversation. Bobby was getting distracted. Kris wouldn't allow that.

Kris flew through the air in a complicated flip that brought her down on top of Bobby before he could recover, she plowed several hits to his kidneys. He brought his legs up and pushed Kris off him twisting around to regain his feet. He aimed several kicks with his legs that a less skilled opponent would have connected but not with Kris. She anticipated his moves and was able to move to avoid contact over and over again. They squared off and the swings started in earnest.

Bobby swung his left leg up connecting with Kris's side and his right came up to parry. Kris grabbed his leg and Bobby struck out with his right leg to connect with Kris's ribs on the other side. Bobby fell to the mat as Kris was knocked to the mat. Bobby got up quicker than Kris and launched another attack at her. He picked her up by the waist and slammed her into mat. Bobby rolled over her and gained his feet as Kris leaped in a 360 degree turn and plowed both feet one by one into Bobby's chest. Bobby continued to swing at Kris connecting twice with her jaw and kicking up missing her head as she parried and connected a knee to his chest.

The fast pace of the fight kept everyone on their toes. Ryan had his hands full with the camera keeping close into the action while following the fighters around the ring. The platform had him overlooking the scene from slightly above the fighters. The sounds of pummeled flesh rang through the room.

Kris performed a jump looking like she was going to connect with Bobby's face but at the last minute he moved; her foot just glancing off his cheek. He wasn't getting off that easy, however. She brought her other foot up bracketing his head so that with the momentum his head ended up between her thighs and used her momentum to flip his body onto the canvas. He landed hard on his back and used the thrust to gain his feet and swung around to face her. She went on the attack.

She ran up on him and kicked which he blocked with his hand the first kick, but she connected with the second as he went back against the ropes. He held back and she decided to teach him a lesson. She landed a solid right to his cheek and spun to complete a back spin kick which went wide of his head as his fist connected with her chest. He pulled the punch and his gaze flickered down again giving Kris the second she needed to through him on the defensive. Kris spun again and swung her arm straight and back bending at the last minute to connect with his stomach sending him toward the ropes. A right hook to the jaw and a left leg swing into his hip sent Bobby flying.

Kris took advantage of his moment of being off balance to continue her offensive advantage and spin in another 360 degree kick connecting with his head and flipping him across the ring. He bounced hard and was slower to rise. Kris got in several hits to the gut and he grabbed her by the head bringing his knee up into her ribs. He brought his knee up several times impacting her abs over and over as she reached around to grab his head in a head lock with her right arm. He pulled free and reached around her waist to bind her from behind with both arms locked around her middle. She swung back with an elbow to connect with his face staggering him back and grabbed his arm flipping him over her shoulder. He hit the mat hard. She advanced on him and he rolled several times to gain distance.

He got to his feet and she met him at the ropes on the other side as she lashed out again. He took blows to the head and stomach doubling him over and she brought her knee up to connect with his head. He fell to his knees on the canvas. She moved in again as a fought to gain his footing and grabbed him in another head lock. He grabbed her around the waist and used his bent posture flip her backwards into the ring. He advanced again as she gained her feet and his head was whipped around as she landed a spin kick to his head. He staggered and fell to the mat. Shaking his head he tried to get up but realized he couldn't. He lifted a hand indicating defeat. Kris grabbed his hand bringing him to his feet and pulling him into a hug. She pulled back and looked in his eyes. He was dazed, but ok. Just got his bell rung.

Both combatants moved the ropes where the team met them with water bottles and towels. They were both dripping sweat. Kris slicked her hair back from her brow. Her hair had grown out some in the last few weeks which made it hard for her to see a couple of times during the fight when it got into her eyes. She threw her arm around the younger man as she used her towel to wipe the sweat off her face. Ryan climbed down from the tower and brought the camera into the ring to catch the after match debrief.

"Ok Bobby. Why did you lose?"

After every fight they discussed what happened. This helped him understand what he could have done to change the outcome. It also showed whether his loss was from a physical issue or a mental issue. Sometimes it was failure to follow through on an advance or because he underestimated his opponent.

"I held back."

"Why?"

"Because I let my opponent's physical appearance" as his gaze drifted to her breasts, "get in the way and instead of remembering I was fighting a skilled fighter I let it get in my head that I was fighting a woman."

"And the result?"

"I got my ass handed to me by a woman." He said with a grin shaking his head.

"Wrong. You allowed yourself to fall back on outdated stereotypes that overruled your knowledge of your opponent. Does my having breasts suddenly change my abilities or skill?"

"No Sensei."

"Does my having breasts suddenly make you forget every other fight we've had in the past and the outcome of those fights?"

Jake leaned over to Ryan and said, "I think her breasts made him forget his own name."

Ryan choked as he tried not to laugh not wanting to get in the line of fire.

"Is that a trick question?"

She pinned him with a glare as he chuckled and the Marines in the room catcalled and whistled.

"I'm sorry Gunny. I know this is serious, but damn. I know we have always strived to see more of people than their anatomy. We don't prescribe gender stereotypes or roles because we know they are meaningless in regard to ability. Some is physiology, but most is mental strength. But I'm a guy and it's really hard for me to ignore that impressive display of greatness so beautifully in view in front of me. You suddenly having breasts is a miracle of nature I'm having a hard time not going on my knees and giving thanks to God for his bounty."

The Marines in the room lost it at that comment as did the ones outside. In the deafening din Kris just threw up her hands stepped out of the ring. Laughing Bobby followed her out. He ran up behind her and jumped on her back piggyback.

"Oh, c'mon Gunny don't be mad!"

She flipped him over her shoulder to the floor mat and climbed on top of him pinning his arms to the ground with her knees; this time aiming her fingers at his sensitive sides. He'd always been horribly ticklish and she gave him no mercy. The camera followed them and witnessed his final defeat at the hands of his mentor as she made him laugh so hard he cried. She got off him and grabbed his hand pulling him to his feet since he was as limp as a noodle from laughing so hard. They hugged in a one armed hug used by guys when they relented enough to show each other emotion and walked him over to the table set up with drinks and food for the group. Bobby moved off to the side with Ryan to do his post-match monologue.

Kris walked over and saw Cook by the table with Bobby's publicist. Kris grabbed a sandwich starving after the 28 minutes of brutal exercise. Nadine moved to the side now talking on her phone, briefly abandoning the conversation with Lieutenant Cook.

"I have never seen an MMA fight before. That was something."

Kris laughed. "Something as in 'violent but cool' or more like 'crossed that off and never want to see that again'?"

Cook laughed. "Somewhere in between I think. I didn't think it would be so uh brutal. I figured there would be head gear and pads or something. He was really hitting you hard."

"That would be why they call it a fight. He got in some good ones. I admit, I'll be a bit sore tomorrow. But I haven't had a good workout like that in a while so it will be worth every sore muscle. I've been looking forward to getting back in the ring for some time."

"Do you ever miss fighting for the Corps?"

Kris was the Marine Corps top Male MMA fighter and had an undefeated record in the Armed Forces. She had 26 wins to her name. It became a source of pride that a Marine held the title. Kris loved fighting. It allowed her to use all her skills and keep them honed. In her last fight she was pitted against Army Captain Joe Huggins who was touted to be as good or better than her. When she got in the ring with him she realized they had overstated his skill. She tried to end the match when she realized he had no prayer of making it. Not only that, he was in danger of getting seriously hurt and that was not the intent of those matches. She was in this to pit her skill against opponents of equal skill, not beat the crap out of someone that shouldn't even be in a ring. She attempted to reason with the Captain and he kept coming at her. He was good for an amateur, but Kris was a 10 degree black belt in Aikido, a five degree black belt in Jiu Jitsu, and a six degree black belt in Tae Kwando at that time. She'd since attained ten degree belts in each discipline. But six years ago she was still acquiring skill which far out matched the Captain.

She tried to give him an out and allow him to save face, but he wouldn't take it. He felt the younger Marine was just trying to show him up. Kris looked to his wife for help. The hugely pregnant woman pleaded with him to stop. When Kris realized the man would not give up or give in Kris decided to end it by sending blow right to his sternum that would take his breath away and make him black out thus ending the match. It did end the match, but not as Kris would have liked. The Captain fell to the mat dead. An undiagnosed heart issue caused his heart to stop when Kris hit him. He was dead before he hit the floor. Joe

Huggins Jr would never know his father. He was born a month later.

Kris said in a formal statement that every member of the Military accepted that fact that they may go down in battle. That is why they trained and they all accepted the risk. To lose a valuable member of the Military community in such a senseless way was inconsolable. Kris quit right then and there. When Joe Jr. went for his first day of kindergarten Kris was there to walk him to school. She stood for his father as did several men from his command. Huggins' widow never blamed Kris for her husband's death. It was a tragic accident. She talked with Kris about others she spoke with reaching milestones without their loved ones and it spurred Kris to set up the Huggins foundation. It was charity that had volunteers from each service stand in for deployed or fallen warriors. Children missing a parent for school events, birthdays, dances, or any milestone could contact the foundation and they would find a member of the parent's service to come and be there for them during their time of need. It had grown all over CONUS and within the second year went OCONUS.

Over the years Kris had stood in for mothers and fathers for first days of school, birthdays, and several times for a driver's test. As well as a dozen other events. Over time the whole team signed up to volunteer. Kris hated the reason for its conception, but was overjoyed by the results.

"No I don't miss fighting in the ring. I'll leave that to Bobby."

"I was talking to Nadine about the foundation that Bobby supports, the GenZ Foundation. I asked her if you were involved and was I surprised to hear you founded it."

"Yeah. When I was 18."

"That is impressive. I was looking it up online and the scope of work the foundation does is amazing. I didn't realize you were that knowledgeable about your condition before you were wounded."

"Yeah, I just don't dwell on it."

"Understandable."

Cook continued to look at Kris with a measured look. Kris wondered what was going through the Lieutenant's head.

"Well you will be happy to know I am going to complete my report and I am recommending Command place you back on full combat status. Now before you get too excited I plan on joining you in Afghanistan to continue to observe you in the combat arena. I won't get in your way, but I have to know that you will be able to handle the pressure of combat by seeing you in action."

"No problem Lieutenant. The sooner you have your data, the sooner you can write me off and go after someone who actually needs your valuable services."

"Somewhere in there is a compliment I think. Congratulations Gunny. On this fight and the other one."

Cook stuck out her hand to shake Kris's. Kris's smile was warm and genuine. She was getting used to the Lieutenant and she actually wasn't as big a pain in the butt as Kris feared she would be. As Cook left Justin and Javi came over.

"She looked a little green, the fight gross her out?"

"A little. But not enough to keep her from signing me off for combat. Let's get cleaned up and celebrate. First round is on you two!"

Chapter Eighteen

The Action Zone was a bar just outside the base. A retired Marine everyone called Cuffy owned and operated the establishment which catered to a largely Marine clientele but saw its fair share of members of the other branches. It was a good-sized place with several pool tables, a large bar with a better than average selection of draught beers and imports, a stage and dance floor, and plenty of tables to hang out at. During the week it did brisk business, turning into a madhouse on the weekends.

Alpha team tended to steer clear of the weekend crowds to enjoy a relaxing night out. In the last three days before a deployment they had a gathering at night for just the adults, one with the whole team and the families during the day, with the last day just for immediate family. They were due to deploy in three days and activities as a team with their families helped keep the unit tight and close. They were a large party with 15 men and women including wives and girlfriends. Or in Kris's case, ex-wives. They comfortably took control of the corner pool table and several of the high tops around it. Kris and Justin teamed up against Javier and John in a round of pool while Davis, Mike, and Dan threw darts at the adjacent board. Mel sat with Rosa, Sue, and Mary; the wives gravitating to one table. Gentry's friend Taylor, Tomball's girlfriend LaTonya, Jenkins girlfriend Lori all sitting at the next high-top chatting about various topics and commenting on the snarky comments the men were making regarding each other's shots.

As Kris leaned over to take a shot she noticed a man at the bar giving her the eye. She ignored him and took her shot moving around the table. Something about him was familiar. It kept nagging at her. She leaned over for another shot and he shot her a killer grin. She looked away and kept playing. Justin came up to her and handed her a glass of beer.

"You know that guy?"

Kris's brow furrowed. "I'm not sure. Something about him is familiar, but I can't place it." Kris finished the glass and went to the pitcher and found it empty. She took the two pitchers up to the bar as it was her turn to buy, and felt someone move up behind her.

She turned and looked at the well-built handsome man who had been staring her down for the last half hour. He had longish brown hair and blue eyes. Darker stubble on his cheeks and chin made him look sexy and dangerous. He had a scar that ran across his eyebrow and another on his forearm.

"Looking good, Cole."

She cocked her head to the side and stared at him hard. Then it came to her. Chambers. Lance Corporal. Injured in Fallujah. She carried him out after her team went in to retrieve a platoon trapped after a botched raid. He didn't make it; died in surgery.

"Chambers. You're looking good for a dead man. I don't often get to speak to ghosts. Or should I say Spook?"

Chambers laughed. He sat on the bar stool next to where she was standing and leaned on the bar to place his head out of the line of sight of her men.

"I always liked that about you Cole. Smart as hell and no nonsense. Just cut to the business."

"What brings you back from the dead?"

"I've been working with a particular counterterrorism task force. We get a lot of intel on cells and collaborators. Funny thing. During a routine sweep, your name came up in a missive."

"What kind of missive?"

"One with lots of numbers attached to it. Numbers that make smart people do stupid things. Makes stupid people do stupider things. Like lure a Spec Ops team into a village to blow them up."

Kris's eyes went sharp.

"Know anyone who would want to attack an entire MSOT just to take you out?"

"I can think of a few people I've pissed off who'd like revenge, but none of them know me by name."

"I have intel for you, but not here. We need to meet. Midnight. There is a park about a click from your residence. Meet me there alone."

"Why should I trust you?"

"Because I owe you for pulling me out of that shit hole. I figured I would die there. Tell no one. Officially, I am not here. We did not speak. If anyone finds out about this, I won't have to fake death. Technically just being here is an act of treason. What I have to tell you will take away the technicality and make that a certainty. A lot of good men have died, and more will follow." He brushed his finger down her cheek. She grabbed the offending digit in her hand.

"I am not going to agree to a meet without knowing what it's about."

"El Moufas knows his daughter is alive and you know where she is."

Kris's body went rigid at the name. Behind her, her whole team took notice and was moving to help her.

"Midnight. I will see you there."

"If I let you touch me and walk away my team will know something is up. So sorry for this, but it's the only way you get out of here in one piece."

Kris twisted his finger until he staggered and then placed a knee to his gut and a right hook to his jaw. As he lay on all fours on the barroom floor she grabbed his hair and yanked his head back.

She whispered, "I'll be there." Then in a louder voice, "No means no asshole. Learn some manners." As she pushed him away and he fell to the ground.

She signaled Cuffy who was busy at the opposite end of the bar that she was reaching over to fill their pitchers. He gave her the nod while glaring down Chambers who was slowing crawling across the floor toward a table near the end of the bar to drag himself to his feet. He coughed a couple of times as he staggered holding his stomach out the door. Kris took the filled pitchers back to the pool table. Justin took them from her and gave her a look.

"Later." She took the glass he just filled and took a long drink and handed back to him. She picked up her pool cue and took the next shot. He took a long drink from the glass and looked at the guys shaking his head. They all went back to their conversations.

"Hey Mel. What's going on between Justin and Kris?" Mel turned to answer LaTonya at the adjacent table.

"What are you talking about?"

"Oh, c'mon girl! Those two have been orbiting around one another all night. No one here notice they been sharing the same glass all night?"

Mel turned to look at them. Huh. Kris took a drink from the glass then set it down. A couple of minutes later Justin picked it up and drank from it then handed it to Kris when it was his shot. She leaned against the wall and took a drink.

Mel turned to LaTonya and shrugged. "Maybe they're short a glass?" Several glasses were on the tray the pitcher was brought over on.

"I don't think so, girl. The way their eyes follow one another. Major sparks." LaTonya added with a smirk.

Justin came up behind Kris and said something low enough only for her to hear that had her nodding. They didn't touch, but they couldn't get any closer without touching. Rosa, Sue and Mary were all leering at one another.

"Kris left the ball early and no one saw Justin again either." Sue remarked. Mary nodded.

"You should have seen them together. The steam coming off them was enough cook broccoli!"

Mel shook her head. "I think you are imagining things. They're just friends." She was trying desperately to steer them to another subject, but the women wouldn't budge.

"Javier has been moody since he got back from Washington and said it was work stuff but won't tell me what. He keeps saying he can't talk about it and he tells me everything."

"Well if they get together isn't that against the rules or something? You can't date someone you work with."

"It's not just that," Mary said, "it's their rank. If they were dating it would be fraternization. Kris is enlisted, and Justin is an officer."

"Kristian would never break a regulation. She is muy estricto regarding regs. She would never jeopardize her career or Justin's like that."

"They are just friends, like I said. Everyone forgets they were like brothers. That hasn't changed."

"Well I for one think their relationship is going to take a drastic sharp turn and soon if it hasn't happened already. Maybe they won't admit it to themselves, or each other, but those two are going to end up horizontal sooner rather than later you mark my words."

Everyone took in Sue's words and looked over at the two who were standing within a hair's breadth of each other, but not touching. Mel poured another beer and drank it quickly. Then another. Then she went to the bar and ordered up three shots of tequila and a shot of seltzer water. She took it back to the table and passed them out keeping the water. They drank, and Rosie signaled the bar for another round of shots and Cuffy brought them over making sure to serve Mel the water. She smiled at him and thanked him with her eyes. After her second 'shot' she got up and walked a little crooked to Kris and Justin.

"Time to let the girls play!" She reached for Kris's cue and fell a little forward then snorted and giggled. Kris looked concerned.

Mel could drink the 7th fleet under the table. She couldn't imagine what she was up to. Justin racked the balls while giving Kris a measured look. Mel lined up the cue ball and aimed missing the ball and falling over laughing. She stepped back and tried again sending the ball into the side rail and missing all the balls in the process.

"OK Rosie, your shot!"

Mel went to the bar for another round. Kris intercepted her halfway back.

"What the hell are you doing?"

"Hey, if I want a shot I can have one! You are not my husband anymore; you can't tell me what to do!"

She shook off Kris's hand and weaved to the table taking her 'shot' and giving out the others. She threw it back and huffed, "Whew!"

She went back to the pool table and tried to aim and hit the balls but sunk the cue. Kris picked up her glass and sniffed the contents. Her face hardened as she grabbed Mel's wrist.

"I think it's time to take you home Mel. You've had a little too much to drink."

"I am fine. I don't need a babysitter!"

Kris looked at Justin and walked behind Mel scooping her up and carrying her out.

"Sir, you have the keys-you drove." Justin handed his cue to Javier and said his goodbyes for them. Mel complained loudly that she wanted to stay, and they can't treat her like this as they walked out of the door. She continued to loudly voice her opinion until they left the parking lot. Kris turned to her in the back seat with a pointed look.

"Sorry guys. I didn't know how to get us out of there without wagging any more tongues. You guys have to be careful. Everyone there was remarking at the sparks flying between you two."

"What the hell are you talking about? We didn't behave any different then we always do."

"Except for sharing a glass all night long!"

Kris and Justin looked at each other. "The wives were commenting on how you kept looking at one another and someone mentioned you both missing from the ball at the same time. I tried to change the subject, but they kept coming back to it. Besides, something is up. That guy. I saw you hit him and you barely touched him. I've seen you hit a thousand times Kris;

you barely tapped that guy. He looked hurt, but you couldn't have hurt him pulling punches, what gives?"

"Not here. At home."

They continued the drive in silence each lost in their own thoughts. When they pulled into the driveway they got out and went inside. Kris immediately locked the door behind them and went around pulling the blinds and shades. She asked Justin to go through the house and check all the doors and windows and search the rooms. She went into her briefcase and pulled out several devices and placed them around the room turning them on. When he came back in and nodded Kris turned to Mel and said, "It's time."

Mel's face turned ashen. She looked at Justin and shook her head violently. She said, "No!"

"Something has happened."

Justin said, "What has happened?"

Mel stared at him in terror. Kris said, "I have a meet in an hour and I'll get more information. Mel-he knows it was me. That IED was not an accident."

Justin's face grew tight and Mel started to shake. She wrapped her arms around her waist like she was trying to keep herself from breaking apart.

"He can't know. She is dead! He can't trace her to you or me! You swore to me!"

"Who?! Who is dead. What are you two talking about?!"

"Mel, we have to tell him."

"NO! You can't! That psychopath will torture or kill anyone to get to his daughter. I will not allow another person I love to be hurt! No one can know! He can't know! Oh please!" She fell to the floor sobbing. Kris picked her up and held her on the couch. She rocked Mel back and forth while sobs tore from Mel's body.

"We can trust Justin. We need him right now Mel. He can help me get us through this." She sat shaking her head crying. Justin brought over a box of tissues. Mel blew her nose and wiped her eyes. She shook for a couple of minutes and defeated, nodded.

Kris looked to Justin whose face was a combination between being concerned and furious. Kris pulled in a deep breath.

"When I was a kid I had a best friend. In truth she was my only real friend. She lived in a strict Middle Eastern area and her parents were very traditional. Her dad ruled absolutely.

I knew things were bad at home for her. I talked my mom into becoming an emergency foster care provider so if she needed a place to go they would allow her to stay. That day came. Her father sold her virginity to gain influence with a government official. He arranged for several young virgins to be there for his guest's pleasure. She was raped half the night and escaped out a window. She ran almost naked and barefoot two miles to our house. My mom and I took her to the hospital and stayed with her while the police arrested her parents. She was placed in protective custody and testified against them. Her father went to prison for 10 years for trafficking minors for sex and drug charges. After the trial she was taken to protective custody, but she never made it. Her family's men attacked the Marshalls and she disappeared. A mole in the Justice department was suspected but never found. The man in charge of her case made it so she could disappear. He had forged papers giving her a new identity and placed her with our family to keep her safe off the grid. Her name was Amalia El Moufas."

Justin's head snapped up. They all knew the name El Moufas. The family had recently made the FBI's top ten terror watch list for ties to Isis, the Taliban, and weapons trafficking.

"Ten years ago, I killed Amalia El Moufas. Her body was found in a single car wreck. The fire had burned away all DNA, fingerprints, and she was only identifiable through dental records. The authorities confirmed the body in the car was Amalia El Moufas. Her father never accepted her death. He knew somehow, she wasn't dead. He found out about her having a special friend at school and our sudden departure after the trial. He tried for years to find us. But we moved around a lot. When Mom was killed we at first suspected him. I hacked into the state records of her death. It was ruled an accident, but there were several things that didn't add up. It took me years to piece it all out, but we believe El Moufas must have discovered a hospital record with mom's name on them and tracked her down to see if Mom knew where to find his daughter, but they ended up killing her. We think he got to Mom and tortured her to find his daughter and when she wouldn't break, they arranged the accident to cover the crime. She had far too many superficial injuries for the details of the accident. Most were indicative to torture, not a traffic accident. The ME just didn't have the background to recognize it. I've seen too many victims of torture in our work not to recognize the signs when I relooked at Mom's autopsy years later. "

"You killed El Moufas' daughter?!"

"No, I arranged for it to appear she was dead. He never truly believed it even with all the evidence. With no fingerprints or DNA, he was sure it was a trick. That the government conspired to hide her and fake her death. He gave up for a long time. She was safe. I made sure that she could disappear. I figured he accepted it. Guess he was just biding his time.

The guy in the bar tonight. His name is Chambers. I pulled him out of a bad situation in Fallujah. Supposedly he died in surgery. Apparently, he was recruited instead. He came here to give me a warning. He wants a meet. Says he had intel. He said the team was lured to that building for that family for the express purpose of taking me out. He says it was a hit."

"Can you trust him?"

"Wherever he got this information, he's taking a risk. I can circle around and verify it's not a trap. He claims he owes me. By coming here like this he's committing treason. Whatever hole he's been in- to come out now- he must be taking a risk. Especially to someone who knows him or could recognize him. The CIA doesn't like when their dead Marines reveal themselves as a live Spook."

"I don't like this."

"Neither do I, but if there is even a chance that this is on the up and up, I have to meet him. No one knows about her and my connection to them. The only way he could would be if this intel is for real. I will not put her or any of us in jeopardy."

"Why are you doing this for someone who's been dead to you for a decade? Where the hell is this woman? Why are you sticking your neck out for her?"

Kris said nothing. She just met Justin's hard gaze with a steely eyed one of her own. She gathered Mel a bit tighter in her arms and it came together for Justin in a flash.

"Oh my Lord."

He looked at Mel and saw for the first time her features without the back story of her coming from South Texas and being Tejano and realized her features and coloring was wrong. The light hair and makeup distracted from it, but it was clear Mel was Middle Eastern, not Mexican.

"The childhood friend that taught you Pashtu. Of course."

Kris said nothing, just continued to hold Mel.

"That's why you always got on base housing. Why you never have any personal items laying around; photos or anything that could be used to identify you. And why Mel has been getting proficient in weapons and martial arts. Why when I walked through the house to check the doors and windows I just noticed all the glass is bulletproof and the door is reinforced steel, not wood. You two have been preparing for a war your whole lives."

"I still keep in touch with my contact from Justice. He makes sure we always have housing on every base we go to and arranges for some... modifications. He also keeps us updated to any intel he discovers so we can keep on top of the situation. Luckily my clearance also allows me to access a great deal as well."

Justin took this in with a pit growing in the base of his stomach. When he thought of the danger Kris was in and how badly this could end fast.

"I'm going with you."

Kris looked up sharply. "You can't. I need you here to keep her safe. I can't risk leaving her alone and unprotected."

"Let me call in Javi. He can stay with her and I can watch your six and cover."

"No! I don't want to leave him out again, but I absolutely will not risk his family. He stays out."

Kris set Mel down on the couch and went upstairs into the bedroom. She opened the safe in the closet and took out her 9 mm, a K-Bar knife, and her nun chucks. She checked the chamber and loaded a clip in the gun. She grabbed a harness she had made a couple of years ago securing all her weapons under her jacket but giving them easy accessibility.

"I'm going early to scout the area. Make sure it isn't a trap. When I get back we'll decide what to do."

Justin stood in the doorway with his arms crossed over his massive chest. Kris took two phones out of the safe. "These are untraceable and only programed with each other's number." She handed one to Justin. "I will text you when I recon the area and when I leave. I'm going in on foot; cutting through housing. "

"Watch your six."

Kris grabbed Justin by the back of his neck and moved in for a fierce deep kiss. He ran his hand down the back of her head, down her back, and ended cupping her backside hard against him. She pulled back and looked into his eyes.

"I will take every precaution. I have too much to lose."

Justin nodded curtly and stepped out of her way. She made her way back into the living room where Mel was curled up on the couch biting her nails. She jumped up and ran to Kris.

"Come back to me."

"Justin will watch over you. I will be back." She kissed Mel on the forehead and held her tightly before setting her aside and briskly walking out the door. Mel sat back on the couch and stared blindly at the wall.

"I hate this part. The waiting. It eats at your soul."

Justin sat next to her on the couch and pulled her close wrapping his arms around her. She shuddered violently and heaved out a harsh breath.

"It's going to be ok little sister."

She smiled at his attempt to calm and reassure her. It would only be ok when El Moufas was dead.

■■

Chapter Nineteen

Kris cut back a block and circled the blind area at the back of the park. She walked up around the houses checking for unfamiliar vehicles and anyone on foot. The park seemed deserted. She doubled back to the east and waited crouched near a row of bushes that concealed her from the park and the road but gave her an unobstructed view of the area. Twenty minutes later a car pulled up and parked dousing its lights. A man got out with a small dog on a leash. He walked the dog around the park once. He then walked across to the playground equipment and sat on a bench near the swings. Kris then heard the clickers they use in combat to signal a friendly. She circled around and whispered "Flash." The response "Thunder" came from the man with the dog. She walked over to Chambers.

"Cute dog. Looks like the one in the house on the corner."

"It is. Wanted to look inconspicuous to anyone watching so I borrowed it."

Kris snorted. She faced Chambers and waited.

"I am part of a special force inside the CIA who works deep cover in Afghanistan. We infiltrate civilian contractors, relief agencies, terror cells, just about anything to get intel. We find the little bits of information that can change everything. We are called the Lynch Mob; a kind of reference to a lynch pin. That one domino that tumbles the rest.

Last year I infiltrated an arms supplier that worked with terrorists supplying weapons and ammo. We came back stateside, Miami, to finalize a deal. I was muscle on a meet to discuss a deal with a buyer. The buyer was El Moufas. Aziz El Moufas was there with a tall thin man he referred to as 'Doctor.' He and El Moufas were discussing a charity benefit that was actually a front for a smuggling operation we were trying to get intel on. He and this 'doctor' seemed very chummy. They sat around the pool sipping drinks and talking and when I walked by and I heard the doctor say 'Kristian Cole.' I came back around behind them and listened. Then they started talking about a woman he had performed plastic surgery on who El Moufas seemed overly eager to get information on.

El Moufas looked thoughtful and asked if he could describe her features to someone who could do a composite of her. He said it was a long time ago and his memory wasn't what it was. But for the right price his memory could be jogged. A million dollars would go far to improve his memory.

I'd seen that look on El Moufas' face before and it did not bode well for the recipient. He put his arm around the doctor like a close friend and walked with him into the house. I left shortly after. A week later the body of that doctor was pulled out of the Everglades by a hunter. Dr. Anthony Standish. I believe you know him. It was clear he was tortured. There was almost nothing left of him.

Several weeks later we heard chatter. El Moufas went back to Afghanistan. He put a hit on a United States Marine. The Marine lived. 12 of his people were executed for that mistake. They said he's become obsessed with finding and executing this Marine. He was trolling for information and paying ridiculous amounts of money to find out everything about this Marine. Last week Aziz fell off the radar and was spotted in D.C. three days ago."

Kris listened rigid as stone. She carefully scanned the area for threats and her mind raced. Mel was in danger if El Moufas knew where Kris was.

"Last missive said he's still there. Why does an international terrorist want the location of a United States Marine? Why does he want that Marine dead? What the hell do you know that he would spend millions to get the information on?"

"Maybe my team took out his village."

Chambers laughed. "No way man, this is personal. He wants you in tiny pieces. What did you do to him?"

"The less you know, the better off for both of us. Let's just leave it at that."

Chamber's looked thoughtful. "Well whatever you have to do, do it fast. I can stall this information for about a day or two, but no longer. I can tell my people I had to corroborate my information and justify not telling them now."

"I appreciate that, man."

"I owe you that much, but I can't not report this."

"I don't expect you to. He is a terrorist on American soil. You can't not report it. Probably shouldn't wait. Do it now."

"What are you going to do?"

"We deploy in a couple of days. I will stay on base until we leave. He can't touch me there. It'll take at least that long before your people can gather intel and touch base with the Corps. I'll have everything I need tied up done long before."

"Whatever you did, I hope you don't get dead-he probably deserved it. Watch your six."

"Watch yours. The company you keep might end up finishing what I pulled you out of."

Kris watched Chambers walk the dog around the park again and get back in the car. Kris took the opposite way out of the park and headed several blocks in the wrong direction seeing if she could pick up a tail. When it was clear she wasn't being followed she headed toward home. Time to make a plan.

***

Justin sat in the dark in a chair he pulled up in the corner of the room with a good tactical position and waited to hear from Kris. He got a text about a half an hour after Kris left confirming the site was good and clear. Nothing since. He was struggling to digest the information he had heard. Kris harboring a terrorist's daughter for 17 years. Her mother tortured and killed. Everything he thought he knew about Kris was half-truths. He knew she had a foster sister, a childhood friend who taught her languages and Middle Eastern culture, and a high school sweetheart who became her wife. Only it was all a lie and the absolute truth. They were all the same person. He looked as the phone pinged. Kris was on her way back.

He tried to reconcile what he learned with the woman he called friend and lover. The woman he loved more than his next breath. She had kept this from him. He knew it wasn't because she didn't trust him, but to protect him and them. She stayed out of relationships and kept most people at arm's length because she knew one day she may have to disappear or risk them getting killed. But when the sticking point came, she didn't hesitate to let him in knowing he'd have her back. She trusted him where she didn't trust another living soul. He planned on talking to her about their relationship; on taking the next step. He couldn't imagine living his life without her. This changed things. Would she consider forever with him? Could he consider it knowing that at any moment they could be targeted? Taking on Kris now meant taking Mel too. Did he love her enough to take all this on? He was pretty sure he knew the answer to that.

When Kris got back the house it was dark. She pulled her weapon and slipped from the back onto the porch and went inside. Justin sat in the dark with a gun trained on the door. He clicked on the safety and lowered his weapon as Kris lowered hers. Kris went into the living room and looked up to the ceiling.

"She fell asleep. I just took her up."

Kris nodded and silently mounted the steps. She opened Mel's door and saw her curled up in a ball in the bed with a blanket over her. She walked in and smoothed the hair off her face and kissed her forehead before heading back down.

Justin sat on the couch waiting for Kris to update him.

"It's what I thought. That bastard just won't give up. He's here in the states. The CIA has him in DC. That is just too close for me. We have to get Mel to safety. We deploy in 96 hours; I can't leave her here undefended. If I have to go UA I will but I have to get her away from here where no one would think to look for her."

"I'm not going to let you go UA. And if you do then El Moufas will know you either went to her or took her somewhere and will trace your path to her. Something else. Let me think."

Justin got up and started pacing the room. Kris sat on the couch and watched him move. She could see him working it out. She needed fresh eyes on this. She was too close, and she knew it.

Justin reached in his pocket for his phone. Kris sat up wondering who he was going to call.

"Colonel? It's Alario. I need a 48-hour leave approved for me and Kris. There's a family emergency. Mel was offered an internship in Elizabeth City and we need to get her there or she loses the slot. Yes, Sir. Within the hour, yes Sir. Thank you, Sir." Justin disconnected his phone and dialed another number.

"You still wanna pay me back for that favor? Still have the Cessna? Can it hold three passengers? Yeah. Can you leave in an hour? How soon? That is the earliest? Ok. That will work. We'll be at the field at 0600. Chicago. Tell no one. No nothing illegal. Totally above board. Family emergency. Yeah. Thanks, man. We'll discuss more on the flight. Yeah. Roger, out."

Kris stood and faced Justin.

"I know a guy who owes me a favor. Solid guy, trustworthy. Doesn't ask questions. Pilot. Has his own plane. He will fly us to Chicago and we hide Mel with my parents. They have a large house, excellent security. If she stays put, no one will even know she is there. If she colors her hair she could pass for my cousin Carol. Right height, weight, and build. Similar features. No one will question it. My mom could hook her up."

"Justin if they find her, your parents could get killed. This guy wouldn't hesitate. I can't ask you or your parents to put themselves in that kind of danger."

"My parents can take care of themselves. They have an amazing security setup. This will keep her out of harm's way until we can get more intel. How fast can you pack? We have to be at the airfield at 0600. The flight can take off at 0630."

"Mel and I have packs ready to go always. We have always known this could and would happen and we may have to run. We'll let her sleep. Get your bag packed and I'll bring ours down."

Kris and Justin headed upstairs, and Kris grabbed their bags out of the top of her closet. She opened both of them to make sure they were good to go and remembered hers was packed last year. A few things had changed for her since then. She removed the clothes and repacked with new under garments and different pants. The ones she had still fit, but wearing masculine clothing looking so feminine would bring unwanted notice. Better to blend if you don't stand out. She repacked, put away her old clothes, and headed downstairs.

Justin came down a couple of minutes later.

"All set?"

"Yeah. Are you going to tell your parents or are we just going to show up on their doorstep?"

"Just showing up. The less our movements can be tracked the better. As a private plane he doesn't have to register his passengers, just his flight plan. So, he has to have a destination. Think we should get some shut eye?" Justin said to Kris.

It was just after 0230. Kris knew she'd never be able to sleep. She looked at Justin. He could have and should have said and done a number of things. They need to take this to command. Call the Colonel. Contact the FBI. Assembled the team. He could have raged at her, argued with her about sticking her neck out. He did none of those things. In the couple of hours since this came to his attention his mind had to be racing with all this information and the unexpected nature of it. He had to be questioning whether he knew her at all and what he'd gotten pulled in to. The trust and devotion in his eyes just about leveled her. He never wavered.

Instead she moved into Justin and wrapped her arms around his neck. She brushed her lips gently over his rubbing them back and forth. They passed the night until just before dawn slowly making love. Kris rolled on top of Justin trying to catch her breath.

Kris's head fell forward to have her rest her forehead against his. She sat with her eyes closed breathing in his scent. She slowly opened her eyes to look into his.

"I love you, Justin."

He wrapped his hands around her head as he looked into her eyes.

"I know that baby. I love you."

"I just put it together, what are you-psychic?"

Justin laughed gently smiling. "Kris. You would never risk our friendship over sex. And you wouldn't continue to have sex with me knowing I am in love with you if you didn't feel the same. You just needed time to figure out the difference between what your body is feeling and what your heart is feeling. To make sure it wasn't just lust. We are too good of friends for me not to understand you inside and out. We are too much alike in that way."

Justin lifted Kris up and stood leading her from the room to upstairs. Kris really hoped Mel would not wake up and see them walking through the house naked; she didn't need the payback she knew was coming from the woman after years of ragging on her for either dressing scantily or not at all.

He pulled her into the bathroom and into the shower soaping them both up while they sank into one another again. They dried one another and redressed. Kris walked into Mel's room to wake her and begin their journey.

Chapter Twenty

They grabbed their packs and silently left the house. The airfield Justin lead them to was on the far side of the base. Kris wasn't even aware this field was in use or that private planes could come hanger here. The four-seater plane was partially out of the hanger, the pilot making checks. He nodded to Justin and barely glanced at the other passengers.

Kris and Mel gave Justin their packs as he spoke with the pilot. They stayed off to the side in the shadow of the hanger, so he didn't get a good look at their faces and so any surveillance in the area would not see them clearly. Justin spoke in low tones to the man while stowing their gear inside the cockpit.

"Thank you, man, for this. I owe you one."

"No man, we are square. You saved me. Glad I can return the favor."

"I just want you to know you won't get jammed up over this. It's all above board. But should anyone ask you about this flight or the passengers you don't know anything."

"Yeah. No problem since, hey, I *don't* know anything. Don't use names and stay off the comm and we got no problems. The mics record everything so if you don't say nothing, they got nothing."

One good thing is thanks to Javier and Rosie's youngest child Sebastian being born deaf; they all knew sign language. The team learned to make things easier for him and Rosie. Justin relayed the conversation to the other two and they agreed during the flight to talk with sign only. The four-hour flight was smooth with little turbulence yet felt like longer due to the stretched nerves of the passengers. When they landed at the private terminal at Chicago Midway International Airport there was a car waiting for them. Since they were a domestic flight and a private charter, they didn't have to go through the main terminal which allowed them to exit immediately. Justin drove the 45 minutes to his parent's house easily through the congested streets of Chicago. They pulled into a suburban neighborhood with mature trees and long winding driveways. Toward end of the lane the houses were further between several had fences and gates surrounding the property. They turned right and pulled up to one with a large wrought iron fence with beautiful landscaping which blocked the sight of the house from the gate. When they pulled up to the gate Justin put his finger on the biometric scanner and keyed in a ten-digit code to open the gate. He was right, they had great security. They drove up the private drive to a beautiful white stone house. The beautiful two-story structure with arched windows and gabled front looked a hundred years old but was built in the eighties. The circular drive curved in front of the house and continued through an arch that lead to the garages and a guest house. Kris had always loved the Alario house. It always felt so warm and welcoming. Just like the people that inhabited it. She and Mel spent many holidays and vacations there as part of the family. It was home to her. Justin stopped the car and got out as the front door opened.

Dr. Salvatore Alario was a large man with thick grey streaked hair brushed straight back from his brow. Justin favored him strongly. He was powerfully built but not to the extent of his greatly muscled son. He stayed active and kept in excellent shape which let him handle 10- and 12-hour surgeries that he still performed several times a year. His intelligent brown eyes were both joyous and concerned at their unannounced arrival. He stepped out to welcome them with warm embraces and booming laugh. Connie Alario hearing the noise came bustling out of the kitchen and exclaimed as she ran to hug her youngest son and the two women she also considered hers. Justin's mother was medium height and slender with shoulder length dark hair. Her face lit up at the trio delighted at the surprise making her look much younger than her 60 years. After bringing them all inside and to the kitchen table where they had all spent many happy nights over dinners over the years. She insisted they all sit while she made them breakfast as Sal addressed their sudden and unannounced arrival.

"So, what brings our children home without a word of warning just days before they are supposed to deploy? I see in your eyes it is trouble. How can we help?"

That is the one thing Kris always loved about Justin's family. They never wavered. Always ready and willing to help no matter what the situation.

"Sir, I need to ask a favor that won't be easy. I don't want you to agree until you know all the facts. Agreeing to this will put your family in grave danger. I don't ask lightly, nor do I take it for granted you will agree even once you have the information. I don't want you to think you have to, but I couldn't think of anyone else I would trust," Kris wanted them to be very aware of the dangers.

"Kris, you are family. Mel is family. If you need our help, it is yours. Say what you need to say."

Kris was struck with how much is kind, brilliant man with his quiet strength and sharp mind reminded her of the Godfather. Must be the Italian. Or possibly that Sal was one of the black-sheep of the family who used his brains for science and medicine instead of loan sharking, racketeering and protection. Sal and his brother Antonio, who was the Attorney General for the State of Illinois, were the only ones to escape the long family history that went back to the 1920's with ties to organized crime. Sal's grandfather was a Battaglia; his mother the only daughter. Sofia Battaglia hated growing up in such a notorious family. She made sure to keep her distance and raise her family away from their influence. For all of Chicago's size, in the Mob world it's a small town and by staying in the city it wasn't easy to keep her family out of the rackets. Of her five children only her two youngest sons were able to escape into the straight world. Her oldest son Angelo was sentenced to prison on a ten year stretch for loan sharking by age 25. Since his release he kept himself out of prison but not off the radar of the police or the FBI. He just learned to keep ahead of them and beat the system. He was a person of interest in two mob connected slayings and suspected of dozens of crimes but was never again indicted. Her two daughters married into the Andriacchi and Cataudella families seduced by the money and power. It was a miracle Justin was even able to get a security clearance in the Corps. Kris suspected that money changed hands to ensure it. Not that it needed to. Salvatore was very vocal in his schism with his family as was his brother Antonio. Antonio was responsible for some of the most publicized arrests in the Chicago area families. He used the knowledge he had growing up in the families with his skill with the law to ferret out the heavy hitters and current players. His conviction rate and shrewd legal prowess propelled his career quickly to becoming the youngest attorney general the state ever had.

Kris didn't want to give them too many details for their own protection. She had been working on what to say on the trip up.

"You have known me and Mel for many years and you have kindly taken us into your family. But there is a lot about us you do not know. You know Mel as my ex-wife. Before that she was my sister. My mom and I took Mel in when she was twelve; when her family tried to assassinate her after she testified against her father and he was indicted.

She and I were friends in school. She came to us in the middle of the night beaten and raped. We took her to the hospital and she stayed with us until the trial when they put her in witness protection. She never made it. Her guard was slaughtered, and no one knew what happened to her. She got away and the next week she contacted us. Mom and I left everything behind and got her. We created a new identity for her.

When my mom was killed we feared they had found us, so I convinced a plastic surgeon to alter her appearance, so they couldn't recognize her. He did. I didn't trust him, so Mel had a couple of more surgeries over the next couple of weeks to alter her more so even he wouldn't recognize her. Good thing. Her family got to him and they tortured him for information and dumped his body in the Everglades. Over the years I used my clearance and position in the Corps to keep tabs on them. I found out they did kill mom. Someone put her name down as a contact on one of Mel's hospital records and it got missed when all information regarding us was redacted.

Mel's family is bad. As bad as they get. And dangerous. I know from Justin about your extended family. Her family is similar. They have a similar code. Similar means. But much different politics and methods. They use religion as a spear head, but it's about the money and power. Allah is a convenient crutch and gets those thinking they fight for a higher cause to be manipulated and used to sate their lust for what they really want. More power, more wealth, more fear, for more business. They have no fear, no conscience, and no qualms about getting their hands dirty. They will stop at nothing to get what they want. Right now, what they want is Mel.

 I arranged her death almost ten years ago, but recently they found out it was a ruse. They have traced her to me. They don't know where she is. They are trying to get her through me. They tracked me to North Carolina and as of three days ago her father was in DC. That is too close for me. They have a price on my head. They tried to take me out in Afghanistan; that mission I was wounded in was orchestrated to get my team there to take me out. They will take out anyone in their way. We have to deploy in three days. I can't leave her unprotected, but I can't ask your family to help without you knowing the risks. I have kept her safe for the last 17 years because only two people knew her real identity. I brought someone else in and put her at risk. That was a mistake. I know by telling you what I have I am not making another mistake, but I cannot put people I love and respect in harm's way by not giving them all the facts. I will not give you her family's name; both for your protection and hers. But you have to know what you are getting into."

Connie sat white-faced clutching her apron as Sal sat still and thoughtful. Kris could see he was working it out and weighing the information carefully. He sat forward resting his forearms on the table and addressed them.

"I understand dangerous men. I understand the kind of bloodlust that comes with this greed and power. I understand the lack of morals that allows them to do the terrible crimes they commit in the name of something good. You are our family. You both have been since the day Justin brought you home. Mel will be safe with us. I will personally guarantee it. I will call my brother and see what I can find out. In the meantime, Mel will stay here, and we will keep her safe."

By saying 'my brother' instead of 'your uncle' Justin knew he was not referring to Antonio.

"Dad, is calling Uncle Angelo a good idea? He has connections, but what makes you think he won't use them to his advantage? He could use this information to barter guns or money or build a relationship with Mel's family to grow his own power base here."

Sal sat quietly for a moment. "I know my brother. He is greedy and power hungry, but he would never align himself with terrorists. I happen to know for a fact he used his power to root out several terrorist cells in Chicago after 09/11 and gave the information through several of his shills to Antonio. He may be a criminal, but he is also quite patriotic in his own way. He plays the Italian card, but he is American to his core. He isn't a patriot; he just knows that terror hurts his business and how he conducts business. I have known him to brag about his nephew the Marine. When it suits him. I can speak to him without giving him any information we don't want him to have. He can get us what we need to know."

"I don't want you to do anything that will harm your family, Sal. I know you deliberately distanced yourself from them."

"Don't you worry about that. I keep just close enough to keep my ear to the ground. I know how to use my brother for my own needs just as he uses me and Tony for his. We know where each other stands. Don't think for one moment you are putting me in a difficult position. You are not. You are important to Justin therefore you are important to me and Connie."

Kris looked at Connie as she regained her color and by the expression on her face, her resolve.

"You are the daughters of my heart. You always have been. Well not you Kris, you were my son just as Brian, Justin, and Michael are. But you know what I mean." Connie said with a smirk and laughing eyes. "I wouldn't hesitate to open my home to either of you for as long as you need it." She reached across and grabbed Mel's hand. "We will keep you safe." Then she reached for Kris's hand.

Kris squeezed hers in response and visibly relaxed. With that she realized how tired she was. She stood and hugged Mel who got up and went into her arms. Mel then turned to hug Justin.

"Justin you and I should get some shut eye. Neither of us have slept in more than 24 hours."

Justin let go of Mel and went to Kris pulling her into his arms. Connie and Sal exchanged a look when the two sank into one another holding on tight. Kris closed her eyes and laid her cheek against Justin's. She pulled back and he moved in and laid his lips on hers. They stayed that way a moment, foreheads touching. Then Kris pulled away and headed upstairs. Justin looked at his parents. Sal looked thoughtful while Connie looked concerned. Mel followed Kris out with a look from Justin and he held onto the back of the chair and looked at his parents. He knew how lucky he was. He also knew they would take every precaution. Sal looked at his son a moment before he spoke.

"So, you and Kris now."

"Yeah. Is that going to be a problem for you?"

"No. No son not at all. But I worry for you. Not just with this trouble, but with everything she has gone through becoming involved so quickly after your divorce."

"There's something about my divorce I never told you. I didn't know how. Trina and I, well Mom you saw it. We liked the idea of how we were together more than the reality. She hated being alone and you always worried she'd get into trouble when I was gone. You worried she'd break my heart."

"I wish she had that power. You loved each other; this I know. But you were never in love with one another. Not all the way. I could see it. I just hoped you could make each other happy; which you did but not for long. You wanted different things. She wasn't the one for you. Not someone you could make a family with."

"When things started going bad she accused me of being unfaithful. She wasn't wrong. I never broke my vows, I never cheated on her. But I had developed feelings for someone else. I fell in love, really in love and I knew I would have to end it. I just didn't know how or what to do about how I felt. I knew what I was feeling was wrong, but I couldn't will it away and, in the end, I didn't want to."

"You were in love with Kris."

"Yes. Long before it was wise. Long before I knew what to do about it. Long before I could accept it or even understand it. Before I knew she was a woman. When I did realize it, I didn't understand how it was possible. Or how to tell her what I suspected. I never knew about her condition. She never even told Mel. She asked what I would have done if she hadn't been wounded, if it hadn't been discovered. The truth is it wouldn't have changed what I felt. I may have resisted for a while, but I would have eventually told her how I felt. I had arranged for some leave for the both of us in Germany for a couple of days after our mission was completed. I was going to tell her what I felt and what I suspected. Never got the chance. She was hit, and everything changed. I hated seeing her in so much pain, but it finally made sense. She is everything. I see my life in five years, ten years, fifty years; and she is there. Every step of the way."

"What about a family son? Her injuries-she can't have children."

"I was going to ask you about that. We could conceive with a surrogate. That's if..."

"If she has any viable eggs that have developed. Have you talked with her about this?"

"Not yet. I wanted to ask you to examine her, if she will consent, and see if the possibility is there. If not well, that's fine. We can adopt or take in foster kids. She's already proven she's a fantastic parent with Bobby. He's grown to become a fine man thanks to her mentoring. I know she wants children too, but she's never let herself even think it because of her condition and her situation. But if we knew for sure I think it would make a big difference to her. Give her hope. She's given up so much in her life. She won't even look at this because she doesn't want to have to give up something else. But what if I can finally show her something she won't have to compromise on? Something she never thought she could have, a real relationship and a family. Something I know she wants more than anything."

234

"Talk with her and then we can discuss this more. I have to get to the hospital for afternoon rounds. We'll talk more when I get home. You leave tonight, yes?"

"Yeah, we have to get back."

"Go now and rest. We'll talk more later." He left and they heard him jog upstairs.

Sal sat with Connie and finished his coffee before rising.

"Our son never does things simply does he?"

Connie chuckled as she picked up the dishes and loaded them into the dishwasher. No, he never took the easy path her youngest. She kissed Sal goodbye and went to check on Mel. They sat in the study for a half an hour looking at clothes online. Since she was staying she'd need more to wear and didn't want to be seen in public or with the Alarios for their protection. Nothing Connie said would change her mind. If she was staying, it would be out of sight as not to ruin all the subterfuge used to get her here. Connie left Mel finalizing her purchases and went up to put more towels in the guest bath and ran into Kris leaving Justin's room. She stopped when she saw Connie in the hall; looking a bit awkward for coming out of Justin's room. Connie took pity on her.

"Can't sleep honey? You need your rest."

"Yeah I know, I just can't turn my head off."

"Come downstairs with me and we'll have some coffee and talk."

Connie left the towels in the bathroom and turned to go back downstairs as Kris followed. Kris went to the cabinet and pulled out two coffee cups while Connie turned on the coffee machine. Kris pulled the creamer out of the fridge and started fixing her cup. They leaned up against the island.

"What's on your mind, honey?"

"Everything. Worrying about Mel, about you and Sal. Getting my head straight for the mission."

Connie could see she wasn't done and was having a hard time saying what she wanted to say so she just stayed quiet and let Kris set the pace.

"I think the biggest thing is being here. I have always felt like a part of the family here. I always considered this home. I can feel the love and the depth of emotion these walls hold. It's palpable. I see how you all are together, and it just hit me that I'll never be able to give Justin that. If we stay together like he wants he'd be giving up the thing he wants most; a family of his own. Kids. And everything that goes with them. If I love him, how can I do that to him?"

"Honey I think you are forgetting it's his choice too. He knows better than anyone what you have been through and what you can have together. He's made his choice. You are it. I can't say I'm terribly surprised. You two have always had a special bond. You look good together and better, yet you'll be good together. But you are just starting. You have time to discuss these things. And more I think you both need to discuss these things, so you know where you stand and what you want. You two, more than anyone I have ever known, find a way to make things happen. You are so strong. I have to ask you; do you want kids?"

"I never much thought of the reality of kids. In the abstract, yes, I have always wanted a family and felt I would make a great parent, but I never thought it would be possible."

Score one for Justin.

"Have you talked to the doctors about your options? I know you can't carry a child after your partial hysterectomy, but have you checked to see if maybe your eggs are ok so in the future you could-I don't know- work with a surrogate?"

"The doctors at Bethesda weren't sure when I was undergoing treatment what was going to happen. They were more concerned with getting me balanced out physically and hormonally. Since I've been back to duty I haven't looked into it. I've been putting it off, afraid to know for sure."

"Well. The only thing to fear is fear itself. C'mon, grab your coat we are going to the hospital."

"Connie we can't just show up and find out! There are tests and things..."

"Then Sal will set them up. I have to bring him his lunch. He thinks if he 'forgets' it I'll just accept he'll eat at the cafeteria or the diner across the street. He's putting on weight and I'm not going to let him eat all that unhealthy stuff! He has some pull in the hospital. If he asks it will be done. Let's go."

Kris knew once Connie got it in her mind she wasn't going to let it go. Justin was the same way. She grabbed her coat from the hall closet and followed Connie out to the car. Time to find out.

Chapter Twenty One

Northwestern Memorial Hospital was an impressive place. Since Kris was ten she hated hospitals but this one had the feel of a modern office building. She'd been here many times in the past visiting Sal with Justin, but this time she was nervous. What if she found out she couldn't have children? What if she found out she could? Her relationship with Justin was already fraught due to their difference in rank. She almost wished Justin was here. It didn't feel right doing this without him.

They took the elevator up to the surgery level where Sal had his office. Connie fussed over him forgetting his lunch and made a lame excuse to go downstairs to get something. Sal waited for Kris to say what was on her mind.

"Sal I was wondering. I never had the OBGYN examine my ovaries after my treatments ended. They did tests to make sure hormones were producing properly, but they never did any tests to see if they were functional. Since the hysterectomy was prior to the therapy I guess I didn't see the point, so I let it go. But I think I need to know if they are functioning. I need to know if I can have children."

"Did Connie put this bug in your ear, Kris?"

Kris laughed. "No Sir. Ever since I got involved with Justin it's been on my mind. Even more since we arrived. Seeing him with his family makes me realize what I would be denying him. I set it aside before because I didn't see how it was possible and considering how I was wounded I didn't let myself go too far down that path. But I can't not explore other options now. For Justin's sake. And for our future. If we are going to, by some miracle, be together I need to know. I was looking online how eggs are harvested and what must be done. My hormone therapy included ovarian hyperstimulation to jump start my hormone production. I am still taking supplements to maintain it so now's the time."

"Well then let us find out." Sal picked up the phone and dialed. He spoke with a doctor in the fertility clinic. He expressed the urgency with Kris deploying in just days and called in a few favors to have the doctor see Kris immediately. When he hung up he stood and led Kris to the elevators.

In the fertility clinic Kris was introduced to Dr. Sharon Wright. She was the leading fertility specialist in the state. Kris was taken into an exam room where she changed into a paper gown. This was the first time she was in an OBGYN exam room. Everything she'd had done previously was in the lab or a regular hospital room. The doctor was very thorough and explained everything to Kris as they went along.

Using the vaginal ultrasound outfitted with a needle the doctors extracted eggs from her ovaries. These would be stored and examined. Dr. Wright was concerned with the low count of eggs in her ovaries. It was not surprising however since her ovaries had been developed late and only been producing for six months.

Kris had Dr. Wright explain how invitro fertilization could be used to impregnate a surrogate if she decided to go that route. She was informed of the process and any issues that could arise. Two hours later Kris was in a taxi headed back to the Alario house. She had filled out a medical power of attorney to Sal for him to be able to monitor and maintain her eggs in storage. The good thing is if she were to get wounded again she knew she could still potentially have children with the eggs they harvested; if after study they were determined viable. Sal informed her that Justin had done something similar several years before and had his sperm stored in case he was injured so he could still have children. It gave Kris a lot to think about. It also set her mind at ease that she wouldn't be depriving Justin of a family since the doctor's initial look indicated the eggs should be sound and appeared to have developed correctly.

When she got back to the Alario house, Connie was still out, and Mel was on the phone with one of her professors speaking about a homework assignment. Kris slipped into Justin's room and undressed. She climbed in bed with him and went into his embrace as he reached for her in his sleep. She settled in and for the first time in weeks her mind was calm, and she turned everything off and drifted into sleep.

The day went quickly. Justin's brothers came to the house to visit and marveled over Kris's transformation. They'd heard of her change but seeing her was a shock. They teased her and made snarky comments which added to the joviality of the day. They played basketball on the court in the backyard and she and Justin took them down in several games of 21. Kris, Justin, and Mel helped Connie cook a large lunch for the group and they sat around the table for several hours talking and laughing.

At five they informed the group they needed to head to the airport to catch a flight. The mood got somber as Mel clutched onto both of them hard, not wanting to let go. They all embraced with Justin's brothers not fully understanding the abrupt change in mood everyone underwent with their departure. Sal drove them to the terminal and assured them he would watch the family and Mel. To just concentrate on the missions and leave this all behind. His mind would be more at ease knowing they were focusing on the task at hand. They assured him it would be done. Inattention in the field could be deadly. You had to lock it down and leave it all behind.

Kris and Justin boarded the plane and like the previous trip communicated in sign so as not to leave any evidence of their presence. When they arrived at the landing field they worked to clean down the interior of the plane to eliminate any fingerprints or hair that was left behind. Kris and Justin walked back to housing. They had quite a bit of work to get fully packed. Kris had nearly completed her packing before, so she helped Justin and arranged with Rosie to watch the house while they were gone. When asked where they'd been they told everyone that Mel had taken an internship in Elizabeth City for her degree program and they'd driven up with her to settle her in an apartment there. The last candidate had dropped out, so she had to move fast to take the slot or she'd be passed on. No one questioned it which made it easier. Kris and Justin missed the team gathering the day before. The team always got together with the families at one of the houses and had a big dinner together. Team bonding and farewell was important to the team letting everyone say goodbye to one another. Saving the last night just for immediate family. Everyone knew that every time they deployed there was a possibility that someone may not come back. They didn't dwell on the danger, but they did acknowledge it.

Justin and Kris spent the last night preparing the house for being vacant by straightening up and unplugging all unnecessary electronics and putting the thermostat and the lights on a timer. Javier and Rosie's oldest Ernesto would collect the mail and mow the grass. After dinner Kris lead Justin upstairs.

She held his hand in hers as she preceded him down the hall and into their room. They moved in closer every inch of skin in contact. They kissed as if they wouldn't be allowed to again. Which in all honesty, they wouldn't be. Not as long as they were deployed. They slowly circled toward the bed both climbing on while maintaining contact. They slowly sank into the mattress with Justin covering Kris as they continued to make out. They were in no rush. This would be the last time they were going to be together for months, so they had to make it count.

"I am going to memorize every curve of your body. So, when we are over there I can lay in bed at night and feel every inch of you."

 "I already have. I can feel your body every time I close my eyes.

They sat for several minutes wrapped around each other until Justin lay back and pulled Kris down to his chest.

Kris tried not to look at the clock but knew they needed to get some sleep before they had to meet the rest of the team at 0500. She didn't want to think about not being with him for the next several months.

"The next few months are going to be hard not being able to touch you."

Justin always was able to say what she was thinking.

"I was just thinking the same thing. We have to lock it down or we could end up in a world of trouble. Anyone finds out we can both kiss our careers goodbye."

"I've been thinking about that. I never ever regretted leaving medicine. I loved every minute I've spent in SOC and the Corps. But after you were wounded, I've thought more and more about going back to it. Taking the medical boards here and doing it for real."

"You'd leave SOC?"

"Yeah. I wanted to make a difference. And I know I have. I am not getting any younger. I am about to age out anyway. It's rare for anyone to continue downrange on the teams at 40. I am up for the Lieutenant Colonel's test in a couple of months, that means admin. I don't want to work a desk. I can still fight, but now I'd like to fight for someone who may not be able to fight for themselves. I think I want to go back into surgery. It can be exciting and dangerous; but the battle is life not death. My skill against the body in front of me. Same thrill, less chances of being blown up or shot." Justin ended with a laugh.

"Would you stay in the Corps or go civilian?"

"I don't know. It depends. I'll have to do some checking and see what I could do."

Kris pondered this new information.

"Working in the teams wouldn't be the same without you."

"No, but at least we wouldn't be in danger of court marital."

Kris lifted her head to look into his face.

"You aren't doing this just to protect my career are you?"

He looked back at her with a determined and strong look.

"No. Not that I wouldn't, but I have been thinking of this for a while. I just didn't want to say anything until I'd taken time to really think it out. I have. I think after this tour, or maybe during it, I am going to explore my options. I know they need surgeons on Lejeune. Campbell, the Lieutenant Commander who operated on you with me, emailed me not too long-ago inquiring. They want a combat surgeon for a permanent duty station. Someone who can deploy if needed with the teams."

"You would be amazing in that role. I would fully support you if that is what you decided to do."

Justin pulled Kris back down and dragged the covers up over their bodies. Kris double checked the alarm and settled into his arms. They lay listening to each other's breathing as they drifted off into sleep.

Chapter Twenty Two

The team landed back in Camp Delta and hit boots on the ground in the early afternoon. The dust and sand kicked up from the choppers limited their sight as they deplaned the gear. Several young Afghani boys ran up to help grab smaller bags from them to help carry. Alongside the camp was an orphanage that housed two dozen children. They ranged from three to fourteen years old. They were taken in by relief workers from several nearby villages. None of them had family that would take them in and several had been living on the streets eating out of garbage cans and stealing to survive. Kris saw many familiar faces. Several of the younger boys ran up to her and hugged her around the waist. She spent a lot of her free time at the orphanage helping the aid workers with talking to the children and helping them learn English.

"Gunny Kris! Gunny Kris!"

Kris looked up to see a dark-haired teenage boy in a white perahan tunban running to her. Fazil. He was the oldest at the orphanage. Once he turned 15, he would have to leave, but that was months off. Kris was planning on working with him to find a job and somewhere to live. Fazil had hero worshipped Kris from the day they met five years ago. He was separated from his family during an insurgent attack when he was nine. Nothing could be found on his family. His parents, younger sister and brother were among the missing and presumed dead. Fazil probably knew this but spoke of them as if he saw them daily. He latched onto Kris and adopted Kris as a big brother. He kept going on about how Kris could be his brother as his sister was old enough to marry and she would be thrilled to have him. Kris always shook her head and laughed reminding Fazil she was already married.

Fazil ran up to Kris and threw his arms around her waist placing his head on her chest. Something the kid had done dozens of times in the past. He hugged her tightly for a moment then pulled away with a shocked look on his face. He looked at Kris in the face then at her chest. He put both of his hands on her bosom, then pulled Kris's utilities shirt away and looked down it. He quickly pulled them back at an arch look from Kris and stood there with his mouth open. Kris spoke to him in Pashtu.

"Yeah kid. That's right."

"Oh, Gunny Kris. My sister is going to be so disappointed." He shook his head and looked at the ground. When he raised it, he was smiling and laughing. "But my brother is going to be thrilled!"

Kris let out a loud gut laugh and grabbed the kid in a head lock mussing up his hair.

"Get outta here kid!"

Gentry walked by carrying a small girl over his left shoulder and his gear over his right.

"Gunny did that kid just feel you up?!" Kris flipped him off as she grabbed her pack.

Everyone headed toward the Raider berthing to stow their gear then over to the Special Operations Command building to check in. Kris held onto her gear and headed straight to SOC since regulations dictated, she would no longer be able to berth with her team. She sought out Lieutenant Colonel Steven Anderson the division XO to find out where to go. No one had thought to verify prior to their arrival. Now that they were heading back into combat they fell into the same old rhythms. Anderson checked with several other division heads and found that the Female Single Officers Quarters had an area that Kris could occupy. As an NCO she should have been in the Senior Enlisted Quarters, but no space was available so because of her MOS she was placed with the medical division single officers. That way her comings and goings were not going to stand out and she'd have a bit more privacy. Base Command was concerned that Kris's change in gender would make her a target within the Enlisted ranks. The one barracks that had space was mostly lower rank enlisted; younger and less mature. SOC was not wanting their top team leader to be harassed by junior enlisted. The enlisted female barracks were a constant source of trouble.

Fights and petty harassment were common as the women fought more in there then they did in field. Discipline was a problem.

When Kris arrived at the building that was to be her home for the next little while she expected an issue. She opened the door and stepped inside to find two of her four bunkmates inside. Both in a state of undress. They jumped when they saw Kris. One grabbed a shirt to cover herself as the other stood up in just her underwear to block Kris from going any further.

"What the hell do you think you are doing in here?! Get out before I call the MP's."

Kris looked at both. "Is one of you Lieutenant Andrea Stohler?"

"No Stohler is not here."

"I am supposed to check in with her. Which bunk is available?"

The women looked at Kris with incredulous expressions.

"Are you crazy? You can't stay in here. This is female berthing."

"I am aware of that....?"

"Second Lieutenant Maria Tomas."

"Lieutenant Tomas this is where I am billeted. If you can't tell me which bunk is available can you tell me where Lieutenant Stohler is, so I can get this resolved and unpack? I am due back at my Command in half an hour for briefing."

Tomas continued to block Kris's way as the second woman in the room quickly dressed and said she'd go get Stohler. Almost a half an hour later she returned with another woman. She was small boned, about thirty with ash blonde hair, and seemed to be pretty no nonsense. She looked Kris up and down.

"You Cole?"

"Yes Ma'am."

"They just dropped your paperwork on my desk about 15 minutes ago, so I didn't have time to warn the others we're getting a roommate. You've met Tomas, this is Second Lieutenant Keri

Simms. The other bunk belongs to First Lieutenant Tasha White. Yours is this one here, closest to the door."

"Lieutenant, you can't be serious!" Simms's eyes were about to pop out of her head.

"The Gunny is berthed here. End of discussion."

"But this is *female* officer's quarters."

"Get off your high horse Simms. We have a Gunny in here. Get over it."

"But Stohler..." Simms was shut down by a sharp look from Stohler.

Stohler turned to Kris.

"You been here before Gunny?"

"Yes Ma'am, but I will need some assistance with a few things."

"Such as?"

"Where the female showers and head are. I never had occasion to need to know before."

Stohler looked at her with a bit of puzzlement but explained where they were. Kris set down her gear and grabbed her cover.

"I am due at Special Operations Command for a briefing, I'll stow my gear after if that ok with you Ma'am?"

"Yeah, no problem. Just keep it neat. There isn't room to swing a cat in here and if you leave a bunch of crap out I can't and won't be responsible if it comes up missing."

"Yes Ma'am. It'll just be my uniforms and undergarments, everything else will be stowed at SOC."

Kris turned and replaced her lid exiting the room taking her tactical gear. She could hear the hue and cry but paid no heed to it. She did smile though when she realized that Simms main objection was thinking Kris was male. Well she'd see soon enough when she dressed down for bed that is not the case.

Kris entered Special Operations Command and slid in the back of the briefing room as to not distract Anderson who'd already begun the briefing. He outlined the training for each team for the next few days and confirmed team structure. The Bravo team leader Captain Max Nunez was coming over as XO and Special Operations Officer for Alpha. Justin would be taking over as Bravo team leader. That discussion with Anderson was interesting as to why they wanted to break up the dream team but he didn't question it much and made the adjustments. He dismissed the group and called Kris forward.

"You are late Kris. Problem with your berthing?"

"A small one Sir. The Lieutenant in charge of quarters only got the paperwork 15 minutes ago and when I showed up the other women in the quarters were up in arms."

"Do they have a problem with you Kris? I am not going to have you distracted when we have a mission in 96 hours."

"No Sir. No problem." Kris replied with a smirk. "I think they are under the impression a man just got quartered with them. I recognized Simms, the one who was the most alarmed at my being there, and I am sure she recognized me; only I don't think they know yet I am not a man, Sir." Kris explained trying to hold in laughter. "Lieutenant Stohler seemed to the think the issue was my being a Gunny. I don't think she knows I used to be a man Sir."

Kris's grin was contagious. Anderson snorted trying not to laugh.

"Nip that quickly Kris. I don't want an incident getting out of hand."

"Yes Sir! I am headed back to unpack. I think once they see me dressed down, they'll figure it out Sir."

Kris saluted Anderson and left the Command building to head back to her quarters. Anderson went over to speak with Juarez. She stopped outside to put on her lid and saw her bags sitting in the dirt right outside the door. Shaking her head, she picked them up and went back to FSOQ. She went in to see three women in a heated debate.

When the door closed behind her, it got quiet fast. The third women was unfamiliar so must have been White. Kris took her bags over to the bunk Stohler said was hers and started to unpack. The women just stared at her and mouthed words to one another. Kris turned her back and kept unpacking. At the bottom of her bag was something shiny. Kris recognized it at once; the gold dress Justin had bought her in D.C. Mel placed a note on it. *Remember you are a woman and a Marine.* Kris shook her head and tucked it into the bottom of the footlocker. Once all of her gear was in the footlocker, she stowed her bag under her bunk and grabbed her PT sweats out. She started to disrobe, and the others started sputtering right up until Kris's utilities top was removed. They all stopped talking at once and stared. She ignored them. Their eyes were glued to her breasts as she stripped out of her pants and boots. She removed her t-shirt and stood in her panties and bra for a moment looking in the footlocker for her toiletry bag. She placed it on the bed and pulled on her Marine Corps issue sweatshirt and sweatpants. Then slipped on her shower shoes. Grabbing her towel and kit she addressed the women in the room for the first time.

"Female showers are opposite the chow hall, correct Ma'am?"

White shook her head minutely and answered in the affirmative. Kris nodded in thanks and left to hit the showers. When the door closed, she heard an exclamation from Simms.

"Holy crap! I don't believe it!"

Kris chuckled all the way to the showers.

Training commenced immediately for the coming mission. Alpha team was primary with Bravo running through as a back-up. Bravo was not slated for the mission, but only prepping just in case. The team performed several run throughs based on the intel. Practice worked out any issues before the mission and everyone was clear of their parts before getting into action. There was only one problem.

"Jenkins, get over here."

Daniel Jenkins stepped forward and faced Kris and Justin.

"What are you doing? You keep lagging at the door. How are you supposed to cover the team on the south end of the room if you are last through the door?"

Jenkins stood jaws clenched with a pained expression. He looked down for a couple of moments before addressing Justin and Kris.

"I can't do this man. I can't be on Alpha team anymore." They both looked at him with confusion and concern.

"I'm sorry but I can't go in there as long as Kris is heading the mission."

Kris's face didn't betray any emotion. The rest of the team stood stock still shocked at his words.

Justin stepped forward, "You want to explain that Sergeant?"

"I'm sorry I just can't. I can't follow her in." He turned and walked a few steps away. Out of range of the others. Kris and Justin followed.

"I'm sorry man. Coming through that door? I keep expecting... every time I keep seeing her on the ground bleeding. I can't make myself go in there. I can't do it man."

Everyone had their breaking point. Jenkins had reached his. Justin had worked with the Marine on several missions after Kris had been wounded with no issue. There had been no issue during work ups at Lejeune. But here, back in combat the Sergeant was having an issue.

Kris inhaled and exhaled long and slow. She hadn't figured this but considering the last mission they were on together and the trauma he had to face getting to her and bringing her back, that was not a surprise.

The Sergeant's eyes began to fill as his face grew red. They weren't just teammates; they were good friends. They all faced the possibility of losing a friend, but they had been more than just lucky. Kris's attention to detail and the team's ability to work so closely together enabled them to get in and out of tight situations that ordinarily would have resulted in some sort of loss without harm. It was unprecedented. And it made it hard when something bad happened to get over it. Kris got it.

She broke her cardinal rule and grabbed the Sergeant and pulled him into a hug. He grabbed her and held on as she could feel his shoulders shaking. She held on for a minute and he pulled back dashing his hand across his eyes wiping away tears.

"I get it man. It's ok. We'll talk to Anderson."

Jenkins just sat there looking at the ground away from them.

"Hey, Dan. There is no shame in this. That was rough. Coming back from that isn't easy. I know you can do the job. I have no doubts, neither does the Major. I don't want you in a situation that's going to put you or anyone else at risk. We'll get you on Charlie or Delta for now. You good with that?"

He sighed heavily and nodded resigned.

Kris walked over the teams as Jenkins walked away back toward SOC.

"Everybody gear down. Get some chow and back in the ready room in 30."

There was a great deal of muttering and talking among the men as they headed off.

Justin looked at Kris. "Did you see that coming?"

"Yeah, I saw it but hoped once we got going it'd be ok. He should be fine over in Charlie. But we need to get someone over here to fill his slot. Now. Any recommendations?"

"Let's get Anderson and go over the personnel files. There's a couple of newer EODs but I'm not familiar with all of them. We could do this without him, but I think we need a full team."

"I agree. We need a full complement for this to be successful. Let's grab some chow and get to work."

Kris and Justin hit the chow hall and were discussing possibilities while they were filling their plates. Kris looked down at her plate confused. She looked up to the Private serving the chow with a borderline hostile glare. On her plate was salad, fruit, and cottage cheese.

"Private what the hell is on my plate?"

The man looked a little nervous but answered.

"Uh Ma'am, that is what all the women order, Ma'am."

Kris raised an eyebrow and stared down at the Private.

"Get this straight Private, I am not a woman. I am a Marine. I am a Raider. If I tried to fight with just this....rabbit food in my gullet I wouldn't make it ten minutes in the field. For your sake there better be a steak under that lettuce."

He gulped audibly and suddenly exclaimed, "Oh look Sirs, General Thomas!"

Both turned looking for the Assistant Commandant of the Marine Corps when Kris felt her plate lurch and they heard an audible clank of the utensil hitting it. She turned back to see a large piece of mystery meat on the lettuce and a hunk of bread next to it. Kris looked up at the Private with a smirk.

"Oh, he was just there Sirs, you must have missed him."

Kris turned from the line and went down for a cup of coffee while Justin chuckled at the Private.

"Smooth son, very smooth." He walked away laughing out loud as Kris shook her head and found a table. Kris didn't bother to wonder what was on her plate but ate everything quickly. One hard and fast truth is when you had chow you ate it. You didn't wonder what it was or linger over the taste, the point was to fuel the engine because you never knew if you would be suddenly called out and it could be hours or days before you'd get regular chow again. MRE's were good in a pinch, but you didn't want them to be your primary form of nutrition. They got old fast. She and Justin ate and went over to SOC to confer with Unit XO Lieutenant Colonel Steven Anderson.

Anderson was a great Executive Officer. He was young for the position at 39, but he earned it. He fought in MSOT for three years and went to MSOC four years ago taking a desk after being wounded. He worked in every position in Special Operations at some point, so he had a working knowledge of the jobs of everyone under him. Which meant he was invested in knowing the skills of everyone on the teams and in the command.

Kris, Justin, Nunez and Anderson looked over all the personnel files to find the best options to fill the hole quickly. They had to get someone in today so they could train with the team for the mission in 72 hours. Kris had a stack of files of six she was whittling down to her top two; one was a Lieutenant and the other a Staff Sergeant. They went back and forth, and she was leaning toward a Lieutenant Matthew Perea. He was an outstanding EOD Specialist. His record was impressive. But both Nunez and Justin had severe reservations.

"Gunny it is your team, but I don't recommend Perea. His skills are impressive, but I don't think he would fit well with your team."

"What's wrong with him, Captain?" Nunez looked at Justin.

"It's his attitude Kris. He is arrogant and can be belligerent. He tends to have an opinion on everything and thinks his is the only one that matters." Justin said with some concern in this voice.

"Geez a Raider that is arrogant. Say it isn't so." Kris said deadpan with a touch of sarcasm.

Anderson laughed. "The Major is right Gunny. A little arrogance is good but only when it's tempered with brains and skill. When it's backed with bragging and bravado it can be dangerous. We've run him in the teams for several missions and they all went well but there was some serious grumbling from his team mates afterward. He was dressed down in simulations twice, once by me, for failing to follow the parameters set. He's a wild card. He will be good, but he is green."

"Well this is a good way to shake that green off him. Everyone on the short list is green. But he has the most promise."

"Well Kris I'll back you, but with reservations." The Captain still looked uneasy.

"If that is decided I'll call him in for a sit down. You're sure Gunny?"

"Yeah, Colonel I am. Let's give him a shot."

Kris and Justin stood and returned to the ready room. Nunez went back to the Communications area to get the latest intel on the area. They worked for several hours when Perea came into the room. The Marine was broad and solidly built. He was a couple inches shy of Kris's 5 foot 10 inches and walked with a bit of swagger. He saluted Justin and nodded to Kris. Kris returned his salute.

"Lieutenant welcome to the team. Major Alario and I were just going over some of points of the Op. Let's get you filled in."

Kris gave him a run down on the operation. They were headed about 12 kilometers north into a village that was on the edge of the main supply route through the region. Insurgents had taken up point there and were targeting the supply chain between Feyzabad and PRT Kunduz. Kunduz had long been a source of trouble for the military with constant attacks by insurgents putting the 1400 Marines and civilian Provincial Reconstruction Teams at risk. The teams had gone in four separate times to take out the insurgents, but they never stayed gone long. For every one they killed it seemed two more took their place. It was a constant frustration for the teams who worked to stabilize the area to see their efforts upended time and time again. Kris explained how the op was formulated and walked him through the motions that he would be taking in the training the next morning.

Perea had some good questions and seemed to be knowledgeable regarding the EOD needs for the team. Kris dismissed him after informing him of the mission training schedule and telling him they'd see him tomorrow. She and Justin cleared out the mission intel and filed the mission stats away until the following day and went to grab some dinner. They stopped by the MSOT barracks so Justin could grab his cover and Kris B.S.'d with several of the guys. She caught up with a couple of guys she hadn't seen much of since returning to duty and talked briefly with Gentry. He was on his way out to hook up with a 'hot lieutenant over in purchasing' and left with a wink and a cocky grin. They left to head out for chow. They didn't see Perea watching them.

"Hey what's the story with those two?"

Ostrowski, a Communication Specialist on Delta, looked at Perea with a puzzled expression.

"What do you mean? Cole is the Alpha Team leader and Alario used to be the Alpha XO but took Bravo team lead when Nunez went to Alpha. Why?"

"I'm just curious. It seems every time I see them, they're together.

"They're friends. Apparently, they were before joining the Raiders. They joined up together and requested the same duty station. That team is close. More so than the others. Rumor has it that is why they are so successful."

"Successful?"

"Yeah, the only SOC team in the military with a 100 percent success rate. Never been done before. You just got called up to the big show man!"

Perea smiled and looked over Ostrowski with a superior look and a cool stare. Yeah, he knew it was only a matter of time before everyone noticed he was the best EOD in the Command. He figured it wouldn't be long until he was the one calling the shots. Everyone would see then-Perea was the shit. He followed Cole and Alario over to the mess hall and got in line for chow. He could see them further up talking and laughing. They filled their trays and went over to a table near the door filled with others from the command. The unit Colonel Stirling and XO as well as Division Commander Bell. The conversation there was lively, and everyone was listening to Cole. She had the attention of everyone at the table. Probably sleeping with them. He sneered. He sat down with a group of guys he liked to hang out with. They were all impressed with his rise to Alpha team. He watched the other table with growing rancor that he was excluded from the comradery. He'd be there soon enough, and everyone would be talking to him with the same respect they gave to Cole.

The next two mornings at 0500 Alpha team assembled to run through training for the mission. Everyone took up their point and followed through the motions. They ran through five times before quitting at 0630.

"Everyone break for chow. Be back in the ready room at 0730."

Kris turned from the group and gathered up her gear. Juarez and Gentry came over as the rest disbanded and headed off to the Mess Hall.

"Kris- a word?"

Juarez looked uncharacteristically serious. Gentry had a similar grim expression.

"What's up guys?"

"Kris it's about this guy Perea."

Kris looked at Gentry as Javier stood with his arms crossed over his chest and his face stony.

"There has been some talk. I've overheard some guys in the barracks and it's not good."

"What kind of talk?"

"The kind that means serious trouble. This guy Perea? He's been on only four missions and the word is that he doesn't take to following orders. He thinks his shit doesn't stink."

"C'mon Davis; most guys in MSOT think that. Arrogance is almost a requirement to serve here."

"Yeah Kris, but not like this. He talks shit about everyone he works with behind their backs to anyone who'll listen. Anytime something goes down it's never his fault; always someone else's screw up."

"He's been saying stuff about you too Kris."

Kris looked at Javier with a steely expression.

"What kind of stuff?"

"The usual stuff morons like to spread. How everyone panders to you because you are a woman. How you probably got to team leader on your back. Shuff like that."

"You heard him say this?"

"No. A couple of the guys from Delta came to me when he was talking to them. I tell you Kris this *gilipollas* is bad news. Anyone who'd talk that way about a teammate is no team player and will not stand."

Kris took a deep breath and exhaled slowly. She hated this kind of nonsense. You couldn't get a diverse group of people together without having someone spreading hate.

"I have heard a variation of that crap everyday we've been here. Seems to me too many people forget up until just a couple of months ago I had a penis. He's young and apparently stupid with it. Right now, we have a mission in 24 hours. We don't have the luxury of time to weed out the malcontents. Regardless he's going. We'll see how he does. His performance will determine whether he stays. Keep your eyes and ears open for anything else. I want to know everything you find out. Keep close, but at a distance."

Kris saluted the two officers and turned to take her gear to MSOC. She met Justin there.

"What's going on with Javier and Dave?"

"They've heard chatter. Some slander they thought I should know."

"Humph, don't tell me-Perea?"

"Yeah."

"Well this doesn't surprise me. This one of the reasons I didn't like him for the team or for this mission. You can still pull him."

"No, it's too late. We go in 24 hours. I don't want to rush someone else through just to fill a hole. He'll stay and I'll evaluate him and his future on the team when we return."

"As long as you're sure Kris."

"Yeah. He talks big off the field but in the field, it looks like he'll be ok. He's just one of those that wants the glory and is too impatient to earn it. He'll chill out once he's got some time under his belt."

Justin and Kris walked over to the chow hall and met up with the team. He looked over at the Lieutenant. There was something in that guy's eyes he didn't trust. I hope you know what you're doing Kris. Justin sat down and ate keeping his thoughts to himself.

The training simulations continued throughout the day. The next day consisted of briefings and verifying intel. Kris typed up the five paragraph warning letter for the team and Command. It outlined all of the mission parameters in detail. The team had gone up against this bunch of insurgents several times before. They understood their fighting style and their tactics. One thing Kris reminded them is the tendency of these insurgents to use guerrilla tactics to confuse and engage. The one calling card of the group was their tendency to come up on a Marine's six and use that person as a shield while getting their own men to fire upon them. That way their enemy did their work for them. Most losses in the field against this group were from friendly fire; the five to get hit were all shot by their own team. They figured this out quickly and armed their weapons with light rounds so no one had yet been seriously injured or killed, but it was enough to take someone out of the action for a mission cycle. No one wanted that.

Kris addressed the teams.

"Alright, everyone listen up. Read your mission brief to the letter. I want everyone to know this directive inside and out. We've run through our route but be prepared. Changes may be made in the field depending on conditions. We've faced them before and beat them. We can do it again. Any questions speak now. There won't be time in the morning. Make sure if you have anything to say you do it now. Has everyone read the brief? Has everyone said everything they need to say?"

Everyone answered in the affirmative.

"Good. Hit the rack and assemble at 0400."

Everyone disbursed and hit the rack. Kris had already let her roommates know she had an early mission and they made sure to stay quiet and let her sleep. 0300 came before she knew it and she got up and headed over to MSOC. She got in and rounded up her gear. There was a box on top of her body armor. She lifted the lid and there was a note on top.

So you don't lose another fine pair.

She pulled back the paper to show a military issue nude colored sports bra. But it wasn't thin and flimsy, but hard and heavy. The cups were unyielding. She turned it a couple of times examining it then busted up laughing. The bra was lined in layers of Kevlar. She held it up over her breasts and found it was an exact fit. She recognized Reineke's handwriting. That guy could really scrounge anything! She didn't even want to guess how the guy knew her cup size that exactly. She almost set it aside. Even though she knew it was given as a joke, she decided to wear it. She chuckled as she put it on. Who the hell thought of getting a Kevlar bra? She put on her new vest and found it was too big. She had to get a larger vest to fit over her breasts. The Rambo bra flattened her breasts quite a bit which made her regular vest fit better and hurt her chest less. Luckily, she still had her old one. She set the new one aside and put her regular vest on. It also gave her better movement as the larger vest tended to restrict her movements and limit her range of motion.

She went over to the briefing room to confirm with the mission commander and set up their call signs. The team started filling in. Her XO Nunez handed out the mission specs to everyone. Everyone was checking their weapons and gear. Kris addressed the team.

"For this run we use .223 three rounds. Everyone have one full clip in play and two in the vest. Also have a knife handy. We tend to grapple with these pricks more than we get to shoot at them."

Perea glanced over the specs. .223 rounds? He sneered. She was pussying out. Everyone he'd talked to said these guys were brutal. No way he was going in there with light rounds. The bitch didn't know what she was doing. He grabbed three clips of .556 rounds and loaded them up. He wasn't going to let this bitch get him killed because she was too scared to go in hot. He grabbed his gear and met up with the rest of the team outside. They could hear the choppers coming in-show time.

Chapter Twenty Three

The team landed one mile outside of Feyzabad to the south moving with the brush and the terrain for cover. The hilly terrain gave them plenty of cover, but it also gave the insurgents cover as well. Everyone was primed for attack. You never knew where they were going to pop out. The team stayed in formation winding through brush keeping the hill to their left circling around to the mountain road. They followed the road staying as far off it as possible to remain concealed. Kris signaled the team to hold. She crouched down and motioned for the team to do the same. She used her night vision to scan the area looking into the juts and the outcroppings. She stayed quiet, still listening for any sounds of movement.

The attack came from the rear. Two insurgents popped out from the scrub on the ridge and opened fire on the team who dove for cover. Kris started barking orders moving the team out of harm's way. They climbed up the outcropping they were using for cover and circled back around to engage their attackers. Jeffries climbed up the side of the rock face to gain the high ground to provide fire support for the team. Kris jumped over a boulder and surprised one of them and took him out. She moved steadily over and across covering Tomball and Perea who were setting up charges to send into the ravine. Juarez was under fire moving up on her six when he was engaged by two who jumped out of the brush to his right. He fired on one but missed as the other grabbed him around the neck and maneuvered him around to use him as a shield. The two pulled him back toward the ravine as he fought to get free. He grabbed his knife from his leg holster on his right leg and swung it back behind him impaling the guy and loosening his hold. Kris took aim and took the second one out before he could aid his buddy. They moved up and around as Perea signaled fire in the hole. Kris switched off her night vision and took cover as the explosion shook the hill and showered them with dirt and sand. She and Juarez came back around to cover Perea and Tomball who were engaging with those flushed out of the ravine. Jeffries continued to lay cover fire from above.

Reineke and Gentry weren't in sight but could be heard on the opposite side of the ravine. Kris and Javier were moving in to give them back up. Two more jumped out but gained cover before either could be targeted. Kris and Javier moved in to get Reineke and Gentry in view. Two were moving in behind them and Javier took one out, but Kris had no shot. The second grabbed Gentry and used him to maneuver into the gulch. Kris took a knee and grabbed her M4 and sighted them. Gentry was so much larger than the insurgent he was completely covering the man. Kris waited patiently for her opportunity. Javier was deflecting fire to give Kris an opportunity to take her target out. She had it when for a brief second the man's head came out from around Gentry's neck. Kris held her breath and took the shot. The man fell behind Gentry and he grabbed his neck. There was no blood, but the bullet had hit so close it left a burn along the side. Gentry kept moving and caught up with Reineke who took him and Juarez to aid Tomball. Jeffries no longer had a sight line and moved down to assemble the rest of the team.

A movement behind Kris caused her to engage. Perea had come up after taking out two on his flank and moved up to cover Kris. She lowered her weapon and made to turn when she was jumped from above. The surgent had grabbed on around her neck and was pulling her backward into the brush looking to escape over the ridge. They could hear a truck just over the hill. They couldn't tell if it was for the insurgents leaving and abandoning the fight or if it was reinforcements coming to aid them. Kris flipped the man over her shoulder and Perea took him out just as a second came up and tackled Kris to the ground. Her weapon flew from her hands and the man grabbed her knife from the sheath and held it to her throat. They rolled and he pulled her up with the knife on her jugular as he pulled her into the ravine. It was too uneven and narrow for her to use any martial arts or tactical maneuvers. She could hear Juarez's report through her earpiece but was not paying it any mind as all of her focus was on breaking free of the hold and keeping that knife from cutting her throat.

Perea was two hundred feet away. Kris quickly calculated his distance with the velocity of the .223 round fired from an M4 and determined the decreased velocity after it struck the body would keep the round from penetrating her body armor. She grabbed her attacker by the pressure point on his wrist making him lose his grip on the knife then spun them around quickly ordering Perea to fire. Perea brought up his weapon and fired. The insurgent's body jerked hard as the bullet cut through him and the force of the round hitting her vest knocked Kris backward off her feet. Perea ran over as Kris was rolling on the ground robbed of breath. Juarez and Reineke saw Kris take the hit and came up from the side and pulled Kris from the ground moving them quickly out. They could hear the truck pulling away which meant the remaining insurgents were bugging out. Small sporadic pops could be heard as Jeffries back up on the rise fired upon them covering the team. Juarez called into Command and they could hear the chopper moving in to evac the team. Kris was still fighting to breathe as they made their way to the chopper and headed back to camp.

When they arrived at camp and disembarked, Justin and several Bravo team members came over to grab their gear and congratulate them on their mission. Kris pushed Perea into Command with the wrath of the Gods on her face. Everyone was talking and discussing the mission when Kris grabbed Perea and slammed him up against the wall.

"Captain Juarez relieve Lieutenant Perea of his weapon!"

Perea had gotten over his surprise and went after Kris; Justin stepped in to defuse the situation.

"Are you crazy? Bitch you just attacked a superior officer! I'll have your stripes for that!"

Justin held Perea back looking at Kris for an explanation. Juarez gave his weapon to Gentry and took Perea's weapon.

"Captain Juarez verify the rounds in that weapon."

Javier looked at Kris then removed the clip and unloaded the rounds from the chamber. He held them up and verified what she already knew.

"They're NATO rounds Gunny."

"And Captain Juarez what was the directive for this mission?"

"All ammo was to be .223 rounds."

By this time the whole room was silent, and Stirling and Anderson had come out of the Comm to see what was going on.

Justin addressed Perea. "Lieutenant did you read the mission directive you were provided yesterday?"

The Lieutenant gave the Major an insolent look, "Yeah I looked at it."

"I asked you Lieutenant Perea, did you read the mission directive?"

"I said I looked at it. It was a just the usual crap."

"Lieutenant were you or were you not told in the pre-mission brief that the rounds to be used in this mission were .223 rounds?"

"Listen I talked with a lot of guys who have gone up against these guys and they said how brutal they were. I'm not going to load light rounds because some female is too chicken to go in hard."

The atmosphere in the room suddenly changed. There was a dramatic shift as every person who was muttering about Kris's uncharacteristic attack suddenly grew still and rigid at Perea's words. Most of these people had worked with Kris for years and knew there wasn't one person in the room who was more fearless or more knowledgeable in combat.

Perea was too stupid and too arrogant to realize that he just made a fatal error. No one in that room had any doubt that whatever had set Kris off was most likely justified.

"Lieutenant those mission directives are set for a reason. People a hell of a lot smarter and more experienced and skilled than you created those directives in order to make sure that the team would be safe in the field. Had you read that full directive instead of just 'looking at it' you would have known prior to engaging with that particular enemy that they like to use our men as human shields. They don't have body armor, so they use ours by using our guys as defense. Because of this .223 rounds were directed in order to protect our men from harm if we had to fire at our own people to kill the enemy."

Kris moved to intersect him, "Defying a mission directive is tantamount to disobeying a direct order."

Perea sneered at her and addressed Alario.

"I don't know what you are getting so twisted up for. She told me to take the shot, and I did. The enemy was down, and none of our team got hurt ."

Kris stepped up and got in his face. "That is where you are wrong."

Justin swung his head around to face Kris shoving Perea away as he watched Kris take off her vest which had a hole all the way through it. Javier and Davis stood with identical looks of horror as they took in the round hole in her uniform tinged with red. Justin stepped forward and pulled the zipper down on her top opening to show a hole in her t-shirt just above her heart. His eyes connected with hers briefly as he reached up and pulled her t-shirt up to see the bullet hole in her bra. He looked at Perea and ordered him be taken out of the room. Stirling and Anderson came forward as Justin grabbed the top of her t-shirt and bra and ripped it down the center exposing her breasts to the room.

"Damn it Major!"

"Shut up Cole. I need to assess the damage."

Reineke handed Justin the medical kit from his pack as Justin assessed the wound. The bullet had hit the fleshy part of her left breast where her cleavage met. It wasn't bleeding much as most of the bullet fragment had been deflected by the vest and the Kevlar in the bra. If she hadn't been wearing it, it would most likely have been a kill shot going right into her heart. As it was the bullet only just impacted the surface. The velocity was substantially decreased by passing through the insurgent's body and her body armor. She'd be in some pain as the rib that stopped its progression was going to be severely bruised, if it wasn't cracked, and the wound would need some stitches.

Justin started cleaning up the wound rinsing the area. Feeling around for any soft tissue damage. Kris stood impassive as he felt around her breast. The rest of the team was watching to make sure she was ok while trying not to look at her breasts. A good many people in the room were trying to look anywhere but at what was happening between Justin and Kris. Most were in small groups talking in low concerned voices. Justin grabbed the gauze and butterfly sutures and placed four stitches to hold the wound closed and cleaned the area. Then he placed a bandage over the spot. Kris would have to go to medical to get a round of tetanus shots and several rounds of antibiotics since the bullet passed through another person, but she would be ok.

Perea could be heard shouting and yelling down the corridor as he was forced from the room. He maligned just about everyone on the team except for Reineke regarding his treatment and training. They heard him shout Kris's name and several words that shocked the room with several other unintelligible things as one Sergeant and a Captain ran down the corridor and slammed the door to the mission briefing room he had been shoved into with raised voices of their own. A few muffled thumps and a crash could be heard before they came back, uniforms slightly rumpled and the Captain had a satisfied smirk on his face and bloody bruised knuckles.

Justin's jaw was clenched so tight it was lucky he didn't break a tooth. Anderson and Stirling watched while trying not to stare at Kris's breasts. Justin pulled the ragged pieces of her clothing back over her breasts and refastened her top. He kept his hand fisted on her collar for a moment before letting go and backing off.

"Cole get to medical. Then get back here for a full report. I want to know exactly what happened out there."

Kris saluted the Colonel and turned to do just that. The muttering grew louder as she left once the guys all realized how this mission could have ended.

Anderson took a long look at Alario. Alario didn't realize it, but his hands were shaking. His face was taut, and his eyes looked like the wrath of hell. Anderson stepped over to the Alpha XO and quietly told him to go and keep Perea out of sight and make sure he was writing up his mission report.

Justin turned to Anderson. "That bastard could have gotten her killed."

"I was hoping that she would be the one to turn this guy around. He showed so much promise and is very skilled. There isn't anyone Kris can't teach. She didn't really have any time to work with him, but he just can't seem to get it. His scores were high and he's smart as hell but he has a problem with the command structure and won't hear anything but his own voice. He ignores more experienced enlisted in lieu of the fact that he is an officer. The only MSOTs that make it are the ones who learn and grow. He won't do either. So, he is out. I am not going to put any other team at risk by having that prick watching someone's back. Colonel, considering his previous insubordination and his disobeying of a mission directive I am going to recommend that we submit Lieutenant Perea to a general court martial. I cannot allow this to go undisciplined."

"I agree Anderson. We knew when we accepted him to the program, he had issues with following orders and figured we would be able to shore that up within the command. Yet over the last year he has slipped a little bit more each time he's gone out. I have been listening to the men. Not only is he not well liked he tends to be a bit of a braggart. One day he is going to say too much to the wrong person, and someone is going to get killed. And it won't be one of my Marines. So, I am going to take this one step further. I am going to rescind his acceptance into SOC. Just because you can make the cut into Special Operations, does not mean you are cut out for it."

Justin nodded. "I agree Colonel. The men have been coming to me for a while with bits about him. It didn't paint a pretty picture. I only wish I'd informed Kris before the mission. She would have been more diligent and better prepared. I take full responsibility for this."

Anderson shook his head. "This isn't on you Major. Or on Kris. Perea just finally showed his true colors and that color is yellow. Let's get to the team debrief. See what happened out there. After

Kris is done getting checked out, we'll pull those files and relook at the other EODs. This will not happen again."

Kris went to medical and got checked out. An x-ray showed no broken or fractured ribs so the throbbing in her chest was merely a bruise. Worse was the round of shots. She had five shots in her backside to combat any biohazards that she may have been exposed to from the bullet. The good thing is that medics could not detect anything in the wound and the material of the vest cleaned off the bullet before it impacted her, so her exposure was minimal. She'd still go for a blood test once a week for the next six weeks, but it could have been worse. She was out of rotation due to her wound, so she spent that time looking for a replacement for Perea. She kept coming back to the same guy. Noah Miller. He was a Sergeant and was in the same ASPOC as Perea. While Perea's record shouted, Miller's whispered. On paper and on the surface Miller seemed average. In some areas, below average. But something about the Marine impressed Kris. He was quiet and he watched everything. The men in Delta razzed him something fierce, but he never got riled. He never got mad. Many said it was because he was too stupid to know he was being insulted. Kris knew that was not the case. He wasn't stupid. He was.... basic. He didn't complicate anything. He simply took things as they came.

She read through his mission reports and they were brief and to the point. Sometimes too brief. He reacted well in the field. He never explained why he did what he did or when he was forced to adjust what his rationale was. It was as if he reacted off instinct or some long buried animal sense that humans forgot as they evolved. Many of the men talked of him as if he was retarded, but Kris could see the intelligence in his eyes. He just didn't need to talk everything to death. His demeanor was simple and to the point. Homespun common sense with Midwestern know-how and ethics. The more she read on him the surer she was he would be the right fit. She asked around to those who have worked with him before. They all had good things to say. Even those who razzed him the most said when it came down to it, he was the one they wanted to go through the door with them.

She had a sit down with Justin one evening to discuss it with him. In the four days since the mission a great deal had happened. Perea was put on barracks restriction awaiting paperwork for his transfer. He blamed everyone on the team and several in the Command for targeting him. He had some rather nasty things to say regarding Kris and her sexual activities with several ranking officers in the Command, including Anderson and Stirling, and Javier got put on 48-hour barracks restriction for beating the crap out of him for it. Gentry would have joined him if several of the MSOC communications guys hadn't grabbed him and held him down. Perea filed several motions himself claiming that Kris wasn't fit to lead, and 14 team members in three separate teams filed even more that he wasn't fit to serve as a Marine at all. That had been a hard day. Perea had left earlier and it was ugly. He was in medical overnight then was put on a transport to Germany to await his JAG review of his Article 92 rights. Everyone breathed a sigh of relief once he was gone.

She'd already spoke with Nunez and he was all for giving Miller a go. He'd worked with the Marine several times and found him to be knowledgeable and steady. Justin was not ready to jump in after Perea. He and Kris talked for several hours about Miller's record and his style and how it would fit in the team. They conferred with others in the team and brought Miller over on a run through to see how he worked with everyone. The guys all seemed to like him. Though he seemed to be at a slight disadvantage as everyone on the team was a strong personality with the mouth and attitude to back it up. His quiet demeanor almost made him seem overwhelmed by them all. But he handled it with a steady quiet strength that Kris admired. Over the next several days he seemed to mesh well with Jeffries and Gentry taking the young Sergeant under their wing. He seemed to be excellent with electronics which made Javier warm to him and they could be seen often working on some device or another. They ran training for the next op, and everything seemed to click. The op itself went off without a hitch and Miller proved himself to be invaluable to the team. He was able to recognize weaknesses in the enemy to exploit that made the next two ops not only successful but gained intel that allowed two other teams to succeed as well. Miller was welcomed as a permanent member of Alpha team.

Kris expected some issues with the Marines in camp having issues with her gender change. But she figured it would be from the men. Guys she previously had joked and laughed with, played pickup basketball games with, and sparred with on occasion would most likely not handle her being woman well. Some had issues; mostly just not knowing how to react or act around her. They were used to treating her like one of the guys. Once they realized she pretty much still was one of the guys, just with breasts, they calmed down and got back to normal. Some couldn't and stayed away. Kris considered it their loss. The surprise was the women.

Kris noticed it after her first time in the showers. She became a subject of first fascination, then ridicule. The enlisted women had a reputation in camp; and that reputation was bad. They were largely rude, undisciplined, and combative. But mostly with each other. She knew from experience with the men some men just couldn't help getting in a pissing contest with others to prove who was the toughest. The women weren't any different, but their tactics were. She was used to throwing punches or verbal slurs. The women did this as well, but they added vindictive little insults to the mix. It was not uncommon for Kris to open her eyes after scrubbing her face to find her change of clothes on the floor in the water. Or items in her toiletry bag missing. With the open showers it was impossible to tell who was doing it. There were 15 stalls with three times that many women milling about waiting their turn or taking their time getting ready once they were done.

It came to a head on day after about month after her arrival. She had gone to the showers after a brutal day of training. Alpha and Charlie were working on a mission due to go out in one week. Nothing was meshing. The Charlie team guys kept clashing with her men. They weren't used to tactics Kris used nor did they understand the communication structure. Alpha team used a great deal of ASL along with their standard nonverbal communication signals that tripped up the guys on the other team. Charlie had a huge turn over in the last rotation home and the newer men were still learning. The previous team adapted to the communication quickly and easily. Not so this one. They were hesitant to respond, and signals kept getting confused so that changes were not being communicated effectively. Reineke punched a Master Sergeant on Charlie for saying some off-color remarks about being deaf and dumb.

She wore her utilities in and brought her sweats to change into. She'd had issues before with women sabotaging her uniforms; one had ripped the insignia off tearing the sleeve. Another had slashed the leg of her pants almost from waist to ankle. So, she stopped wearing anything hard to replace to the showers. Today she was just too tired and sore to care. All she wanted was a hot shower and a full tray of chow. The showers were packed, and she had to wait to get a stall. She took the time to undress and put all of her clothes and boots on the shelf behind the stall with her towel. She turned the water on and sat for a minute absorbing the heat. She took her bar of soap and lathered her head and body. The klaxon sounded and the showers emptied with only one or two voices left behind with her. After a minute even those were gone.

The sudden silence made her wary so once the soap cleared her eyes, she opened them and looked around. The showers were deserted. One look at the shelf behind her an she let out an explosive explanative. She reached over and turned off the water to see all of her clothing gone. Her utilities, boots, sweats, and towel were nowhere to be found. A search of the facility showed this time they hadn't dumped them in a puddle or shredded them but removed them entirely. Someone was going to die. Son of a bitch! She stood there and breathed in and out trying to calm down. A quick look outside showed no one near the showers to hail. She wasn't going to stand there cowering in the shower waiting for someone to rescue her. What these women were doing was emotional terrorism and she was trained never to give into terrorist demands.

She shook her head and slicked most of the water off of her body. It was cool outside, and in a uniform you would be comfortable, but wet and naked would be cold. She wasn't going to be out there long. She opened the door to the showers with her head held high and shoulders back and walked buck naked out into the camp. Several men outside the divisional building smoking were staring in shock and open admiration. She just continued to walk calmly in no great rush to her quarters. Unfortunately, before she reached it the division Colonel Gerald Matthews came out of the building and walked to intercept her.

"Gunnery Sergeant Cole! You are out of uniform!"

Kris met his glare with a steely eyed one of her own. "Yes, Sir. That I am."

"Explain yourself."

"I think that conversation would be better suited in your office after I am clothed Sir."

"You seem to be comfortable enough to walk around the camp stark naked, so talk!"

"Very well Sir! Your enlisted women are out of control Sir. They are at large a petty undisciplined group of malcontents and need to be taken in hand. I have put up with nothing but vindictiveness since I got here. Uniforms torn or missing. Personal items stolen or destroyed. Tonight, they emptied the showers, but not before taking both the uniform I wore in and the change of clothing I brought with me, my towel, and my toiletries and doing heaven knows what with them! I have let my command know of the minor issues I have dealt with just as a matter of course but now I plan on issuing a formal complaint. I have been subjected to taunts, threats, and slurs. All of which I can and have ignored as the Junior High school locker room antics it is.

 They stand in groups talking behind me while I shower, as if I couldn't hear them, that they fantasized about me sexually when I was a man and if they stand behind me long enough while I shower they could take that fantasy to the next level-as long as I didn't ruin it by turning around. I have even warned several of them that they are dangerously close to violating UCMJ article 120 and Marine Corps regulation MCO 1000.9A with their actions regarding speaking of and staring at my person in showers."

The Colonel earned her respect by looking at her dead in the eye. Though his eyes flickered slightly at the mention of her breasts, he fought the urge to glance down at them so magnificently on display right in front of him. She never raised her voice and she never lost control.

"I am no longer willing to let this go. I am a Marine. I am a Raider. We are not in Junior High School here and I am no longer going to tolerate this. If I may be excused Sir, I would like to get back in uniform, get some very long overdue chow and then I have every intention of reporting this formally through my command. As was my intention as I left the showers."

"Did it never occur to you Cole to flag someone down to bring you cover?"

"Yes, Sir it did. But there was no one about. I am not going to stand there wringing my hands like a damsel in distress waiting for someone to rescue me Sir. I'll damn well rescue myself! I am not about to give in or negotiate with these emotional terrorists. But I'll be damned if I am going to stand here another second Sir and provide a peep show to the whole camp Sir!"

"Report to my office once you are suitably attired and fed. I'll make sure your division commander is present. You are dismissed Cole."

Kris nodded to the Colonel and kept her pace to her quarters. Once she got inside she let herself show the emotion she kept off her face outside. Simms looked up and blanched. Kris stood just heaving trying to control her temper. Anyone got in her face right now and they were going to be put down. Hard. Simms's eyes were nearly popping out of her head as she tried to formulate a sentence.

"Um Kris? You ok?" She looked as hesitant as she sounded.

Kris was still calming the blood roaring in her ears and didn't hear her. A few deep breaths later and she realized she was not alone in the room. Simms was reading a book but kept looking up at her every couple of seconds.

"You have a nice shower then Gunny?"

Kris moved her head slightly and gave Simms a dark look.

"They stole your stuff again huh?"

"You could say that, Lieutenant."

Kris turned and reached into her footlocker for a towel and her underclothes. She pulled them on while she looked for a uniform. She only had one whole set of utilities left. She meant to take time to hit the MCS trailer and pick up several new uniforms. With training there hadn't been time. She'd make the time tomorrow even if that meant delaying training. She couldn't get by on one uniform.

"Listen I've heard some of the women talking. About messing with you. I know most of their names. If you want I can write them down for you."

Kris looked up at Simms. "Thank you, Lieutenant. That would be helpful. I am going to Colonel Matthew's office as soon as I'm dressed to address this. I know all their faces, but I don't know most of their names."

"They really took everything, so you'd have to walk naked across the camp?"

"Yeah."

"That's not right. You could have gotten hurt. Some of the men, well, they don't....that is they could have tried to..." She ducked her head as her face grew red. Kris knew what she meant.

"Any man who tries to take what I have not offered to give is going to find himself in a shallow grave. And they'll know it was me because the last thing I'd do is spit in his eye before shoveling the first shovel full of dirt."

Simms smiled at Kris. She knew Kris meant exactly that. Kris didn't talk big. She didn't act tough. She was tough. She didn't need to get in anyone's face. And anyone that got in hers was in for a surprise. Simms wrote down all the names of the women she knew for a fact had been giving Kris a hard time. She wrote down a couple in a different column she heard others saying they heard talking about her. She wasn't sure of Kris when she first got there but she'd grown to like the older woman a lot. She wasn't anything like she thought. A lot of the women talked tough about Kris because they wanted to be thought of as tough. Kris didn't care what other people thought of her. She did her job and kept out of other people's business. She didn't pry and she showed everyone respect. She also never backed down from a fight. That was tough. She handed the list to Kris.

"Thank you, Lieutenant."

"Kris? I hope you nail them to the wall. It's hard enough being a Marine and a woman without a bunch of morons acting like they are gang bangers trying to prove they have bigger balls then the men or worse those that whine and cry that someone treats them unfairly because they are a woman. I joined the military to serve my country. Not be a female in camo."

Kris looked over at Simms. She'd never given the Lieutenant a lot of thought since Simms seemed to avoid her whenever possible. It seemed she was ok. Kris was just about to leave when a knock sounded on the door. She opened it to find Colonel Stirling on the other side. She nodded to Simms and walked out pulling on her lid. The Colonel was not amused.

"Why in the hell am I getting reports of one of my people walking naked across the camp?"

"I'll fill you in on the way to Colonel Matthew's office Sir."

Kris walked with the Colonel and filled him in on all of the shenanigans she'd been subject to. She informed him of the emails she'd sent to Anderson, keeping him in the loop. She finished with what happened today.

"Damnit Kris why didn't you come to me with this?"

"Because it's ridiculous Sir. Stupid kid stuff. Lieutenant Colonel Anderson has addressed this several times informing the command of this nonsense. They did nothing. Well they will do something now! If they don't I know a ghost ninja who damn well will stop it and they won't like how it ends. The upside is the stupid morons in charge of this parade won't try anything else ever again. But if I Code Red them I risk disciplinary action.

And I am not about to get a mark on my spotless record over a bunch of wanna-be banger chicks! They wanna play ball? I will cram it down their throats, Sir!"

Stirling listened. When they got to Matthew's office Stirling picked up the phone on his Corpsmen's desk.

"Anderson? I'm at Matthew's office with Cole regarding the harassment issue. Forward every email you have regarding the harassment of Gunnery Sergeant Cole to me right now. Good!" He hung up and knocked on the Colonel's door. Kris and Stirling entered. Kris spent the next hour giving the other Colonel chapter and verse of what had been going on. Anderson also included the paperwork he sent asking for action to be taken against Kris's antagonists. Matthews read through all of it. He was quite mollified when he finished.

"Gunny I want to offer you a personal apology for my behavior earlier. I had no right to address you in such a way and no right to further subject you to ridicule by making you explain while you were vulnerable. I humiliated you further and that was not my intent."

"Permission to speak Sir?"

"Granted."

"You did nothing wrong Sir. You addressed the situation in front of you. And I was not humiliated Sir. Not by a long shot. Not that I make a habit of, nor do I feel the need to, parade naked across camp Sir, but I wasn't about to let that bunch of sniping junior enlisted think for even one second they can or will get to me. I don't have any false modesty Sir. I could care less about a bunch of Marines I don't know seeing me naked. I really don't care. I just want this crap to stop. This is my last uniform because those little shits have destroyed all of the others. I only hope they have my size left over in MCS. I have my ex-wife sending three more, but it'll take a while for them to get here. I will be satisfied to have this situation dealt with once and for all. I don't want to have to handle this myself and trust me, my antagonists definitely don't want me to either. But if the command can't or won't get them under control I will! But I do not think you will like the tactics in which I will achieve my aims."

"No Kris you will not handle this yourself, and that is an order. Let us deal with this."

"I only ask you work quickly Sir. If they try that again I will not hesitate to retaliate."

"Dismissed Cole."

Matthews turned to Stirling.

"Will she?"

"She will. But in such a way they won't see it coming, they won't see it happen, and no one will know who was behind it. One day when we have a minute I'll tell you how Kris got General Hammond to sign her release papers to return to full duty."

"Wait...is she the Friggin Spider Monkey?!" Matthews laughed so hard his chair moved several feet.

"You know Hammond?"

"Yeah, we play golf when I rotate through LeJeune."

"Well then. I won't say anything further, but you get my meaning. Kris makes things happen. Don't give her the chance to make anything happen here." Stirling shook Matthew's hand as he departed.

It didn't take long for what happened to Kris to spread through camp. After the incident in the showers it was not uncommon to routinely see members of Alpha or Bravo company lurking outside the women's shower area. They were all pretty ticked off about what was happening to Kris. More so that she wasn't telling them this was going on so they could be there to watch her six. Justin was particularly mad that she had downplayed the hazing to him. She told them to back off, but of course they ignored her. It finally came to a head when she and Juarez got into it in a very heated argument about needing a babysitter. So the teams decided to put Miller and Gentry on it. Gentry was popular at the women's showers anyway and it never seemed to be an issue with him hanging out; it wasn't uncommon for several of the women to be hanging out there with him. Miller seemed quite out of place as Gentry seemed to make it his mission to show Noah how-to pick-up chicks. The shy Staff Sergeant didn't seem to want the instruction which of course made Gentry try harder.

Over the next week all of the culprits to Kris's uniform thefts and property destruction were rounded up and put on restrictive duty. Every one of them was forced to make restitution for the loss of Kris's uniforms. She had already purchased new ones, so she gave the money to the orphanage for the kids. Some of the women still gave her dark looks and talked tough, but it was very subdued after Kris's last use of the women's showers. Kris was raised to never hit a woman. But that was set aside for Littleman.

Her main tormenter, a Master Sergeant Littleman, got in her face after being told to go away. She grabbed Kris and Kris put her on the ground. She grabbed her field knife and went after Kris again. Kris disarmed her easily but decided to teach her a lesson. For every three hits Littleman got in, Kris put one hammer down on her. Littleman fought like a gutter rat. No discipline, just wild throws. She connected a lot but did no great damage. Every one of Kris's blows hit a vital area. Kidneys, gut, solar plexus. She was going down. She wouldn't shut up, so Kris shut her up. A hard blow to the jaw broke it in two places requiring it to be wired shut. Kris's parting words were to tell her she'd do more than shut her up the next time. So there had better not be a next time. All of this was done without Kris raising her voice or even working up a sweat. When she left that time, she decided to take her chances in the Raider showers for the duration. The MP's questioned Littleman regarding her injuries. She told them she slipped in the shower. No one said otherwise.

 After a particularly grueling training Kris ordered all the men to the showers. The men tended to linger in the ready room, so she went in and took advantage of the idle. They waited until she came out then went in to shower themselves. Everyone but Miller. He was only two years younger than Kris in age, but in demeanor they were decades apart. When she ordered them in, he went. She was a little nonplused the first time he entered. She had stripped down and had her head under the water full of shampoo when she heard the unmistakable sounds of someone across from her. At first, she thought it was Justin but was surprised to see it was Miller.

"Miller what are you doing in here?"

"You ordered us to shower Ma'am."

She raised her eyebrows and looked at him with an arched expression.

"It's either Gunny or Cole, Miller. Not Ma'am. I am not an officer."

"Sorry Ma'am-uh Gunny. I was raised to address all women as Ma'am; it's for respect."

"I am not a woman Sergeant; I am a Marine."

"Yes Gunny."

"Miller you are either the bravest man in that room or the craziest."

"Gunny?"

"Not one of them would try to come in here while I'm in here."

"Well you said to hit the showers Gunny. So, I hit the showers."

Kris shook her head and continued showering. Miller kept talking.

"It's not that the men aren't brave Gunny. They just don't know how to not look at you. They don't want to be caught staring. They just don't know how to shower with you in here. They tend to take care of their 'men needs' in the shower. They are afraid if they get a woody with you in here, you'll think it's because of you."

"I was a man long enough to know how it works Sergeant."

"Yes Ma'am, I mean Gunny. At least most of them are. Major Alario isn't. I think he'd like to get a woody in here with you and he wouldn't be worried at all if you knew it was because of you. He wouldn't mind showing you what he'd like to do with it."

Her head snapped up and she pinned Miller with a stern glare.

"You need to watch that kind of talk Sergeant. Talk like that could get the Major into serious trouble."

Miller grew red in the face and his expression turned sheepish.

"Sorry Gunny. My sisters always said never to say everything I see. That sometimes I see more because I keep my mouth shut and my eyes open but that didn't mean I always had to talk about it."

"They sound like smart women." Kris continued to clean up as Miller did the same. She sighed as she realized she should shave her legs. Since she was there, she set about the task.

"They are smart Gunny, much smarter than me. They raised me when my mom died. They taught me all kinds of things that I wouldn't have learned otherwise."

She finished up and stepped out of the shower the same time Miller did. She grabbed her towel and started drying off.

"What kind of things Miller?"

"Oh, so we only had one bathroom and lots of times we had to be in there together getting ready. They taught me that it's ok for a guy to get a woody around a girl, because it was a natural biological reaction. And being naked wasn't a bad thing. But when you are in the bathroom with a sister sometimes you couldn't help but see, but you didn't look. Things like that. Things no one thinks to teach."

She looked over at him and he was concentrating on drying off and gathering his kit. He didn't spare her a glance. He just did what he had to do. She got dressed and gathered her stuff. He looked at her. His boyish expression was nearly comical in his large muscled body. It almost didn't fit. But his simple kindness wasn't an act or a mask; it just simply was. She smiled at him.

"That is excellent advice. It sounds like they did a good job raising you."

"Yes, they did Gunny. They are smart and strong like you. Well not like you exactly but..."

"I get what you mean Sergeant.

"Sergeant? How do you know that the Major would like to..."

"Oh, when he gets around you, he's red. You get red around him too. When you get close to one another you both turn gold."

Kris stood there confused and wary until something she once read came to her.

"Miller are you reading our auras?!"

Miller looked surprised then masked his expression with a schooled blank look. He liked the Gunny and she was the one person on the team he could talk to about anything; like his sisters. He thought of her like his sister, but sometimes he forgot she wasn't his sister. His sisters always told him not to talk about things that would make other people think he was crazy. They didn't always understand him, but they accepted it. Not everyone would.

"I don't know what you mean Gunny."

Kris had enough experience in shutting down people who got too close not to recognize someone else doing the same thing. Kris stood and knowingly looked over him. "Yeah. I guess that would be impossible. We'll just not talk about that either."

Miller smiled at Kris and stared at her a minute. Then with a blinding grin and left with his towel slung around his waist. Justin walked in. Kris stopped in front of him.

"We are going to have to watch out for Miller."

"Why? What did he do? Did he try something..." His face grew darker with suspicion.

Kris shook her head and laughed, "No-no. Nothing like that. He is just a little too perceptive for his own good. He sees a little too much."

"How so?"

She relayed their conversation to him quickly as she could hear the men heading that way.

"Everyone thinks he's dumb, but he has to be the smartest guy I have ever met."

Justin looked at her with a dubious expression.

"I'm serious. He doesn't see things the way everyone else does. He cuts out the nonsense and gets straight to the heart. He's simple in the best sense of the word. He doesn't clutter his thoughts or feelings with a bunch of crap. He is cut and dried and that's how he sees the world. It's amazing and it's scary. We are going to have to be very careful around him."

Kris left as the rest of the team filed in. A couple of them made comments about her staying and washing backs or anywhere else she'd like, and she gave them the one finger salute on her way out amongst the cat calls and whistles laughing her way down the hall.

Chapter Twenty Four

In the last couple of weeks, a subtle change could be detected in the teams. Kris's wound shook many of them up. Everyone on the teams worked hard to find things to blow off steam. Captain Javier Juarez sat on a pile of crates watching the battle in front of him. The area was ringed with stacks of crates ranging from three feet tall to six feet tall all arranged in a semi-circle like theater seating. The twelve-foot square area was used by many people on the base for a sports area. Someone had mounted a woven basket to one of the higher crates and cut the bottom out for a makeshift basketball hoop. The dirt was pounded flat from constant use. Currently the combatants were circling each other and occasionally flinging out a hand or a foot to make contact. The grunts and sounds of skin striking skin echoed through the area. The two in the ring were only focused on each other. They circled like wary adversaries knowing the other's skills and strengths. Looking for weaknesses to exploit.

Both combatants were skilled hand to hand fighters. A mix of MMA and boxing moves combined with the usual holds and jabs common in hand to hand combat made for a good show. Usually this kind of thing drew a large crowd as watching two skilled opponents fight was a great way to break up the routine and the boredom that is inevitable between missions. But this fight happened so often now people found other areas in which to entertain themselves.

Both Kris and Justin were dressed in their PT gear of a Marine Corps t-shirt and shorts. Kris had removed her shoes and was barefoot; her preferred fighting style. Justin retained his issued tennis shoes preferring not to get a rock in his foot. Both were dirty and sweaty in the cool January afternoon air. Both were covered with marks and bruising from this battle and all the previous matches they'd had pretty much daily since Kris was shot. Kris advanced quickly taking advantage of Justin leaving his right down and moved in to strike. Justin was prepared and countered. Obviously, he left his guard down on purpose to draw

Kris in. He now had her in a sleeper hold which she tried to break by taking his feet out from under him. They fell hard to the ground, Kris still trying to break the hold around her neck. She may be a more skilled fighter than Justin, but he had considerably more strength in his arms which he used to his advantage. Her wiry build helped her move quicker and avoid capture, but his massive arms formed an unbreakable hold across her chest and around her neck. The grappled while Kris tried to get the advantage back.

Colonel Nathan Stirling approached the area watching the battle and addressed Juarez who jumped to his feet, saluted, and leaned back against the crate. Stirling watched the battle for several minutes as Kris was able to flip Justin and break his hold.

"How long have they been at this?" Stirling inquired of Juarez.

"Today? Just started. A little over an hour."

"How long do they usually keep this up?"

Javier flashed the Colonel a smart assed grin and crossed his arms over his chest.

"Well, that depends. When we first got here, they met up once or twice a week for a couple of hours. After a few weeks that became three or four times a week. Once Kris was shot that went up to five times. But now it's every day."

Stirling watched the fight as Justin went back on the offensive.

"Every day? If Alario is concerned about her fitness to fight, why isn't he saying anything to command?"

Javier laughed, his shoulders quaking as he cracked up.

"Oh, the Major isn't concerned about her abilities, Sir. She's 5 by 5. I could be wrong, but I doubt it, but I think this little sparing match is about something else entirely Sir."

"And what the hell is this about then Juarez? I have my team leaders beating the hell out of each other daily. It's setting a bad example for the men. You can't tell me there isn't something going on between those two. What is their problem with one another? They're best friends."

"Yeah. Well, I think the best way to say it Sir, is that they have found this is the only way they are able to get their hands on one another without breaking regulations Sir."

Stirling stared hard at Juarez's grinning face as he turned smirking to watch the fight.

"Good thing the camp doesn't have to worry about running out of cold water or those two would be in real trouble."

Stirling's face sobered with awareness as he caught on to Juarez's meaning. Oh for the love of all that's holy! This was the last thing he needed.

"How long Juarez? And don't lie to me. How long have they been together?"

"Since we returned stateside is my guess Sir. But I think something was brewing before that when Kris was still in Germany. Justin spent an awful lot of time online emailing. He said it was a woman he met in Germany when you stopped there, but it doesn't take a rocket scientist to add that up. He'd been acting off for months, even before he and Trina imploded. I have a feeling this is why. They don't talk about it, at least not to me, but Justin wasn't surprised when Kris turned out to be a woman. He knew but didn't know how to process it or tell her. It'd be pretty easy for them to keep it on the DL since they are still living together."

"What do you mean they're *still* living together?"

"When Justin left his wife, he moved in with Kris and Mel. He's still there. He was looking for a place before we shipped out, but Mel convinced him to stay until after the deployment. It was a waste of time and money to move only to leave the place vacant for the duration. So, he stayed. When we got back, he talked about looking for a new place, but I think that was just for form. He and Kris are besties. It never raised any flags for them to share a place. Especially with Mel still there too. They've been too tight for too long. I saw this coming. I've tried to get them to focus on other things outside of missions. Keep them entertained but I haven't been able to stop them from coming back here."

Stirling watched as Justin got Kris back into a hold she couldn't break. They were both soaked in sweat and showed the tolls of battle. He took in the bruises on the two of them. Kris had a cut over her eye and Justin had the beginning of a shiner. He watched with this new information and saw that Kris wasn't trying to break the hold with any aggression. He knew she could. They were wrapped around one another tightly. He shook his head and looked down rubbing the back of his neck. Armed with this information he made up his mind on a course of action.

"Well I can. I ought to beat them senseless, but I think I have a solution to this." Stirling marched forward and snapped.

"Alario, Cole!"

Justin's eyes darted over to the Colonel and his hold loosened a bit giving Kris the in she needed swinging back her elbow and connecting with his mouth before she realized the Colonel's presence. She pulled away and swung around to face Justin who now had a split lip.

They pulled apart and snapped to attention. Stirling marched up to the pair shaking his head.

"As of right now this is going to stop. Look at you two! What the hell kind of example are you setting for the men coming out here every day beating the hell out of one another? How are you supposed to have the energy to command after brawling every day?! Both of you clean up, get back in uniform, and report to my office in one hour. That is an order!"

They all saluted the Colonel as he left to head back to his office. Javier chuckled and left shaking his head wondering what the Colonel had in mind.

"Shit, Sir I'm sorry!" She grabbed the towel on the near crate and held it to his bleeding lip.

Justin grabbed the other towel and held it to her bleeding eyebrow.

"Well he was pissed."

"Yeah. I don't think I've ever seen him that mad. Well I guess it's time to face the music."

Kris and Justin walked back to the SOC where Justin used butterfly bandages to patch up the cut over Kris's eye.

"Thank you, Sir."

Kris and Justin looked at each other for a moment before Justin grabbed his gear and headed off to the showers. Kris went back to her berthing and grabbed her gear and did the same. Fifteen minutes later they met up outside dressed in full utilities and headed over to the mess hall to grab some chow. They still had more than a half an hour before they were due to report. If they were going to get their asses handed to them it might as well be on a full stomach. They intercepted a few comments about inquiries to who won the round today and a few smart-ass comments from the Marines having lunch. They filled their trays and sat down bolting the food down. They were both starving from their grueling workout. Both had undergone a change from the constant exercise. Even though both trained at home they had been working each other over much more brutally then their ordinary regimen did. Justin had lost weight. While Kris had added on more with the extra muscles she'd developed. She had been playing catch up from her injury, but now had surpassed her previous physique being harder than before.

They cleared their trays and left the mess hall walking over to the Colonel's office. The base was a Hodge podge of a handful of Eastern village buildings and ready to assemble prefab units and tent structures. The Colonel's office was a prefab the size of a single wide trailer with a wall a third of the way in separating the admin space from the office/living quarters. Justin knocked and received an affirmative to enter.

Justin opened the door and let Kris go in ahead of him. They walked up to the desk of the Colonel's admin Corporal Palo Fujikawa. The older man was from Guam; in the way as with many people of Asian descent with the smooth skin and ageless features he could have been anywhere from twenty years old to fifty. The grey around his temples indicated he was on the higher end of the age bracket. His small stature and slight build belied

his strength as Fujikawa had served in a Raider team for six
years before taking a job as the Colonel's admin 6 years earlier.
His face was impassive and gave nothing away as he sat at his
post and gestured to the chairs outside the Colonel's door.

He was legendary for his blank expression; never giving anything
away. He was privy to everything that happened in the office,
but he was as closed mouthed as a sphinx. No one was sure why
the man who had once held the rank of Gunnery Sergeant was
now a Corporal, but he was completely loyal to the Colonel. They
sat straight and silent waiting for the Colonel to call them inside.
They watched Fujikawa maneuver the files on the desk and
compile data in the computer. Kris was impressed with his
efficiency. Not one move was wasted. She got caught up
watching the older man and did not hear the door to the
Colonel's office open. He called them inside and shut the door
behind him. Fujikawa smiled at the closed door chuckling to
himself. The afternoon was going to be very interesting.

Kris and Justin saluted the Colonel and the other officer in the
room not recognizing him. He was partially turned away from
them drinking a cup of coffee. The Colonel moved behind his
desk and sat down. On the near wall a cot was flush with the side
wall using the side of the metal cabinet wardrobe as a headboard.
The Colonel's desk was centered in the room with a file cabinet
and a small bookshelf behind it holding books and manuals. A
table on the opposite wall held a coffee maker and several cups as
well as a five-gallon dispensable cooler with drinking water.
Two metal chairs in front of the desk completed the room. It was
spartan but clean and neat. Kris and Justin continued to stand
at attention in front of the Colonel's desk.

"I shouldn't have to tell the pair of you that your behavior is not
becoming of Team Leaders. You are both supposed to be setting
the example for the men to follow. How in the hell are we
supposed to implement a command structure and maintain
discipline if my two team leaders are beating the hell out of each
other every damn afternoon?!"

Kris and Justin continued to stand without saying anything
letting the Colonel have his say.

"I am not going to let this continue. As of right now you two will find another outlet for your passions."

The Colonel walked around the desk to the file cabinet and pulled out a file and a small box.

"Last year when you were wounded Gunnery Sergeant Cole, I put you in for a battlefield commission. I figured we were never going to get you to OCS unless we knocked you out and shipped you there in a box. The paperwork naturally got stuck in channels and was bogged down. I re-sent it last month and finally got a response. Apparently, the Commandant flagged anything to do with you Cole in case anyone tried to mess with you again. So, I received a packet yesterday and was mildly surprised to see my recommendation to have you commissioned as a Second Lieutenant was denied. "

He paused and walked in front of the desk to stand in front of Kris.

"The Commandant did not feel that the rank of Second Lieutenant was appropriate. So, he instead changed the paperwork to the rank of Captain effective immediately. Congratulations Captain Cole."

The Colonel handed Kris the box with her new silver Captain's bars. The Colonel saluted Kris and she returned the salute with more than a little pride and a great deal of awe stuck in a bit of surrealism.

"The Commandant back dated the promotion to coincide with the original submission date, so you will be receiving the back pay over the next four pay periods. However, it will take about a week to complete the paper trail and filter into the command, so you won't be official until then."

Justin grinned and saluted Kris who returned his salute then sat looking at the bars in the box in her hands wondering which angel to thank for watching over her.

"Now in regard to your afore mentioned behavior," the Colonel pressed a button on his intercom. The door opened admitting

Fujikawa with two file folders that he handed to the Colonel and stood aside next to the Colonel's desk.

"In these folders are two sets of papers. The pair of you will sign one of them and we will put this behind us."

The Colonel laid the folders on the desk and stepped back to let the Captain and Major look. On the left was a written disciplinary form documenting the pair for fighting and conduct unbecoming. On the right was a marriage license. Both sets of forms had Kris and Justin's names on them. Just then the officer in the room who had stayed in the background with his coffee during the Colonel's talk turned toward them and they saw for the first time his chaplain's insignia on his uniform.

Kris and Justin just sat staring at the forms both with a thousand thoughts running through their heads. Kris's hands shook as she lifted the marriage license from the folder to read it through. She looked at Justin stunned at the turn of events and for the first time ever had no idea of what to say. He took the form from her and signed it without hesitation handing it back to her. She stared into his eyes.

"We've never even spoke of this Justin. It wasn't something we could have seriously considered before."

Justin took her hands in his and said, "Kris I can't think of anything I have ever wanted more than to have you as my spouse. I told you before, this is it for me. You are the last person I am ever going to love. And I know you feel the same."

"But if we get married regulations stipulate, we cannot serve in the same unit. One of us will have to either leave or change duty assignments. The teams we have worked so hard to maintain and hold together through all of this will be taken from us and make all this sacrifice we've made be for nothing."

"Answer me this, do you want to marry me?"

Kris didn't need to think about it. With a firm look she turned to Justin, "More than I want to continue breathing."

Justin walked into her and took the paper and lay it on the desk grabbing the pen and placing it in Kris's hand.

"Then we will work through the rest and figure it out. They won't yank us out this second. Paperwork takes time. In the meantime, we continue as we have. We are on separate teams and the Colonel can schedule it, so we don't work directly with one another so as not to be violating regulations. Besides this won't change how we work together. We have managed for the last six months to keep our private lives and duty separate. We will continue to do so. We have options, like we discussed before we deployed, that we can explore." Justin smirked. "It's almost as if the universe was preparing for this."

Kris looked wistfully at the paper and realized her whole life had been leading up to this moment. She could either reason it to death or she could for once in her life go with what she wanted rather than what was expected. She put the pen to the paper and signed.

The Chaplain moved forward with a smile and grabbed the Bible opening it up and addressing the couple.

"Major I know you are Catholic and Captain you have nondenominational on your records. Am I correct that you are both divorced?" They nodded in the affirmative. "That means you would have to get special dispensation to wed in a Catholic ceremony. I can officiate in a civil ceremony or a nondenominational ceremony if you want to marry today as you have approval from your Commanding Officer."

"That would be fine, Sir. I was raised Catholic, but in my family, we are not as strict about how we pray as long as we do pray." Justin turned to Kris, "Besides I'm not letting her get away even if I have to defy the Pope himself!"

"Well luckily it won't come to that! Colonel and Corporal if you will stand by the couple as witnesses."

The Chaplain performed the ceremony with a warm and competent manner. Neither of them felt slighted at the hurried hasty wedding. The end justified the means as far as they were concerned. They repeated the words after the Chaplain surely and with great purpose. Someone had provided the Chaplain with two Qalo rings. He gave them to Kris and Justin to place on one another's finger. At the ceremony's conclusion the brief kiss they both intended dissolved under weeks of pent-up longing and lust that drew it out long minute after long minute until the Colonel had to clear his throat a third time to get their attention. The usually staid Corporal had a huge smile on his ageless face.

"Thank you, Sirs." Kris and Justin shook the hands of the Chaplain and the Colonel then the Colonel showed the Chaplain out.

The Corporal handed the Colonel a file and mentioned the time.

"I have a meeting over at division that will last about two hours. Finish signing that paperwork and lock the door behind you." He turned to the Corporal who followed the Colonel out of the office. Once the door closed an audible click of the lock could be heard.

"Did he just lock us in here?" Kris asked with eyebrows raised.

Justin walked over to the door and found it had been locked. Locked with the Colonel not returning for two hours.

Kris walked over to the paperwork on the desk. "What paperwork? We filled everything out already. What more is there?"

Justin grinned. "That was the Colonel's subtle way of saying we have two hours of privacy before he returns. I think it's the only honeymoon we are going to get, babe."

"But it's the Colonel's office; it's like trying to score in your parent's bed. We can't do anything in here!"

Justin moved Kris up against the wall and quickly started unbuttoning her utilities top. He brought his mouth to the spot just under ear that he knew drove her crazy and started teasing it with his lips and tongue. She leaned her head back against the wall and felt her pulse scrambling under his lips.

"That is not fair!"

He smiled against her neck as he continued lower following the line of her neck. They gave in to their emotions and put all of their longing, fear, and passion into a frantic coupling that left the office looking like it was hit by a tornado. Files were all over the floor and the desk was several feet from where it started.

Once their blood cooled and their breathing went back to near normal they realized how much time had passed and set to getting dressed and cleaning up the mess they made of the Colonel's office.

Kris moved the desk back to where it started and picked up the papers they knocked to the floor. As she arranged them back into the files and placed the piles back on the desk she felt a small square shape in between several pages. It was a picture in a leather frame. The picture was laminated to preserve it. The frame was worn on the sides. The picture was of a younger Colonel Stirling and a woman with a small boy. The blonde woman and boy were beaming as the he held up a black martial arts belt. Kris sat stunned as she looked at photo of herself and her mom at Kris's first martial arts competition. The one where Kris won her first black belt.

Justin noticed her stillness and the shock on her face and came over to inspect the picture. It wasn't hard to see Kris in the young boy's features. He'd seen pictures of Jenna Cole once when helping Kris dig through some old boxes. What struck him was the young Nathan Stirling. He was about 29, the same age Kris was now. He looked from the picture to Kris several times.

"I've never seen this picture before. But I remember this. My first competition. I won my black belt. I was eight. The youngest in the dojo to ever get a black belt in Aikido. I don't remember the Colonel though. I couldn't see anything past that belt. How did he get this picture? And why? Why does he have it? And why didn't he tell me we'd met before?"

"Kris is it possible the Major wasn't your dad?"

"Where did that question come from?!"

"I am looking at a man roughly the same age you are now and, I mean look at it Kris, you are his spitting image!"

Kris studied the features on the picture and compared them to her own. She walked over to the cabinet in the corner which had a mirror on the front. She looked at her reflection and saw what Justin had noticed. The same shape face and eyes, same jawline, same ears with the little fold at the top of the right one. His grin. That same grin Kris saw every time she let go and really laughed.

"I got an email from Mel this morning that said she was reading our Mom's diaries and to call her at a decent hour, she found something unexpected. How much you want to bet somewhere in them it says that Major Cole isn't my father?"

"I don't take sucker bets. Boot up the computer and get ahold of her. We don't want to do this in the common room computer bank. Too many ears and eyes."

Kris's trepidation at using the Colonel's computer without his permission or knowledge paled against the ramifications of this if this were true. She pulled up Skype and put in Mel's contact information. The connection stuttered a moment and then went through. Mel answered in the dark. Kris wasn't concerned about the time difference.

"Sorry to wake you, but I got your email and needed to talk to you."

"Hmm. Uh yeah. Um give me a sec. It's like five AM here and I didn't go to bed until after 2 AM."

Mel stirred and reached for the bedside light.

"Ahhh. That is bright. Ugh. Um. Yeah, I was reading your mom's diary from when you got hospitalized. It was brutal. She mentioned how you needed blood and she was going to donate some, but they couldn't give it to you because you didn't have the same blood type. She was A positive. She thought you should be able to take it because you were O negative and could receive any blood type. The nurse corrected her that O negative is a universal donor, not a universal receiver, but at any rate you were B positive."

"The Major was O negative; I remember reading that on his dog tags."

Justin piped in, "There is no way an A positive mother and an O negative father can have a B positive child. It's biologically impossible."

"That's what Jenna wrote too. She looked it up. Then she added when the divorce was final, and Kris was healed enough she was going to look for the man that should have raised Kris. And this doesn't surprise you."

"Did she mention any names?"

"Yes, she said she was going to find Nate or die trying."

Justin and Kris looked at one another. Colonel Stirling's first name was Nathan.

"Did she write anything else?"

"I found a diary from the first year she and the Major were married. She talked about how he changed once they were married and how he became verbally abusive and controlling. She was going to leave him. She met someone. A guy going to the University of Northern California who was in Washington officiating a youth martial arts competition. She didn't put in his name in case the Major found the diary. They went out to dinner and talked. When he got back to California he invited her to visit him. She came down every weekend for several weeks. Then he drove up to see her and they became lovers. She went back with him to California. She stayed with him for almost a month. She drove back to pack up some things she wouldn't leave without and while she was there a base Chaplain and counselor showed up and informed her of the Major being wounded. She called Nate and said she couldn't come that her husband had been injured badly, she wouldn't leave him so cruelly like that, and she would call him soon. Two days after the Major came home, he was drinking heavily, and he raped Mom. She writes she wished she'd stayed in California; that she'd never come back. She realized he wasn't going to change and if anything, he was worse. She was going to go back to this Nate guy. She was scared and he wouldn't let her leave. She bided her time and made plans. She was going to leave.

After a few weeks, she called him back and she told him she couldn't come. That it was over. She was staying with her husband. She was devastated. She said how Nate was crushed and didn't understand why she changed her mind. She was pregnant. She wouldn't go to Nate carrying another man's child. She loved him too much to do that to him. She didn't tell him why, just that she was staying. She said it was the hardest thing she'd ever done."

"Does she say anything else about this guy Nate?"

"I skipped around looking for any mention of the guy. The reason we kept moving east was because she found he was stationed on the east coast. So, it sounds like the guy joined the military after college. When you decided to become a Marine and insisted we move close to a Marine Corps base so you could join JROTC she literally 'ran into him' 2005 when we moved to Georgia. Literally. She turned the corner in the Commissary and their carts collided. He wasn't wearing a ring and she told him she was divorced. He wanted to get together with her, but he was deploying. So, they reconnected over email while he was in Iraq. When he came home he accepted a post in North Carolina; administrative so he wouldn't be deploying so much. We moved there that summer. They started dating right after we got there. He asked her to marry him several times, but she wouldn't answer him until we'd gotten to know him. By 2006 he had to deploy again. He wanted to meet us, and mom kept trying to arrange it, but he'd have to travel, or we'd be at camp when he got home so never happened. Right before she died the last entry was that she finally was getting us all together and she had some big news to tell us that would change everything. She'd give him his answer once he knew. Only she didn't mention what that was. That was the last thing she wrote."

"She was going to tell us and Nate that I was his child and that she wanted to marry him. Remember how nervous she was and how excited?"

"Yeah. I do. So how are we going to find this Nate?"

"I think we already did." Kris held up the picture to the screen. "Colonel Stirling's first name is Nathan Mel." She sat there with her mouth open rapidly looking back and forth between Kris and the picture.

"Oh crap! Do you think he knows?!"

"If he knew he would have told me. I don't think he knows. Mom's diary implies she didn't tell him. I think he had this picture because he wanted a something of her. Before it was laminated the area around her face is faded, probably from holding it or rubbing it. It's all he had left of her."

"You're going to make me cry! He still loves her!"

"I'll keep you updated. Go back to sleep. I'll let you know what I find out."

"Wait, where are you and what is that on your finger?!"

Mel pointed to the ring on Kris's finger. Kris rubbed it and grabbed Justin's hand in hers showing Mel his ring as well.

"We are in the Colonel's office. Where the ceremony took place."

"OH ARE YOU KIDDING!!! Married?! YESSSS!!!!!"

"Shut up Mel, you are going to wake up my parents."

"They are going to flip when they hear this!"

Behind Mel the bedroom door opened and in stepped Connie Alario.

"Mel honey are you ok? What happened?"

"Connie, come here!"

"What is it... Justin, Kris? Oh, look at you! They aren't feeding you. And you are all beat up! Are you alright?"

"Better than alright Mama." Justin grabbed Kris's hand and kissed her palm and Connie zeroed in on their rings.

"Are you about to tell me something that's going to make me very happy?"

"Only if you want another daughter-in-law."

"Oh! Kris honey! Oh, welcome to the family! I mean you have always been family but now you really are! Oh, I am so happy."

"Don't cry Mama. This time I have found my forever."

"Don't cry. Pssh. A woman has a right to cry when her baby gets married! And to a woman his Mama loves and respects!"

Kris was staggered by Connie's warm acceptance. "Thank you, Connie. I feel the same."

"I'm not waking your father- he has surgery, but oh I can't wait to tell him when he gets home!"

Kris and Justin spoke a few minutes more to Mel and Connie before disconnecting the call.

"I am going to wait until the Colonel comes back and talk to him."

"I'll stay with you."

"I should have you check on the teams, but I want you to stay."

Justin stood up from where he had been squatted down behind the desk on the Skype call and started laughing.

"What's so funny."

"I just thought about it. This is really funny. You didn't want to stay in here because it was too much like scoring in your parent's bed; only for it to really be your parent's bed!" He continued to laugh as she leaned her head back and groaned.

Justin took advantage of her position and kissed her upside down as the door to the office opened. Corporal Fujikawa stepped in followed by the Colonel. They seemed genuinely surprised to see them there.

"Why are you two still here? If you tell me you want leave time I am going to have to disappoint you. And if you didn't take advantage of the time you had, too bad! And why the hell are you behind my desk and on my computer?!"

"Sir, I need to ask you to close the door and sit down."

Corporal Fujikawa reached in and closed the door as the Colonel walked behind the desk Kris had just vacated. Just then he noticed the picture Kris was holding in her hand. He sat down, and Kris handed it to him.

The Colonel looked at that picture and rubbed his finger gently over Jenna.

"I suppose you have some questions."

"Actually, Sir I don't have as many now. I contacted Mel using your computer. She's been reading Mom's diaries. She sent me an email this morning saying she had something important to tell me, but to wait until a decent hour. I was going to wait until tonight, but after I found that picture, I called her anyway."

Kris sat down in the chair opposite the desk.

"Did Mom ever tell you why she stayed with the Major?"

"No. She didn't. I think she didn't like to think she could leave him wounded. The way he treated her it's what he deserved. Bastard. When I saw her at that competition my heart stopped. I almost didn't hear her when she said she was there with her child. I did the math. It didn't take a genius to realize she got pregnant and that is why she stayed."

"When we met at school, why didn't you tell me you were dating my mother?"

"Jenna was adamant that she tell you she was dating. She was afraid of upsetting you and your sister. Mostly Emily I think. I knew she'd been raped and how strange men still sent her into a panic. She was so afraid my being a Marine would be an issue for you after your dad. So, I felt if you got to know me outside of your mom and realized I'm a decent guy it wouldn't be so hard to accept. She didn't know at first, I was mentoring you through ROTC at school. I think you must have mentioned my name, because she went off on me when she next saw me, and I explained why I did it. She was actually very happy in the end since she could see how much I liked you and how proud I was of you and what you achieved in ROTC. She told me that when you mentioned me she could tell that you liked and respected me as a person. In the end she was glad and the night before she died she said she was pleased on how everything worked out and how it was all going to be alright. She couldn't wait until the next day and how much she loved me and how everything she had done for the last eight years was to get back to me and how it was going to be perfect now."

The Colonel paused, and his face got unbearably sad as he looked at her picture.

"But it wasn't perfect. She was gone, and nothing was the same. I wanted to tell you at the funeral, but I couldn't find the words. You were both so devastated. Then your sister took off and you suddenly got married and left for basic training I knew I had to watch out for you. It's what your mother would have wanted."

"Well, in that you are more right than you know. That is what she wanted. Only I don't think this is what she had in mind." Kris got up and started pacing the room. "Mel read in my mom's diary that after my surgery she realized there was no way the Major could be my father. That left only one person."

The Colonel's head snapped up from where he was looking at the picture and looked at the woman standing across from him. He explored Kris's face for an explanation when the truth slammed into him. He started looking at the younger Marine's features and realized why Kris always seemed so familiar to him. He thought it was because of the features that reminded him of Jenna; the blonde hair, the high cheekbones, her chin. But what he saw this time was everything else; the shape of her face, the color of her eyes-the exact same color as his eyes. That unusual golden whiskey brown. He looked back at the picture than up at Kris. Kris was familiar because he saw that face every time he looked in the mirror. Only he never saw it before now.

He stood up and walked over to Kris and stood in front of her trying to gauge what she was thinking. Her face was completely blank, so he went with his gut. He reached out and grabbed her into a tight embrace. She didn't hesitate to return it. They held on to one another for several long minutes.

"If you both consent, there are blood tests we can run that will confirm paternity. A true test takes several days but I can run a basic one that will answer that question."

The two embracing did not give any indication they heard him, but after a couple more moments they did break apart. Stirling wiped his eyes. He didn't need to say anything. Kris knew how he felt. She had always considered Stirling a father to her. She knew he regarded her as a daughter. Now it looked as if they both got their wish.

"Do it! Not that we really need it, but it's better to be sure." Kris looked at the man she thought of as her father for so long. He nodded to Justin. The three set off to the infirmary. Justin was all set to perform a blood test until he looked in one of the cabinets.

"Huh. Well that makes things easier."

"What does?" The Colonel walked over to the cabinet where Justin was looking. He held up a pharmacy home paternity test kit.

"Hmmm. I don't know whether I should be dismayed or not that that is in there. If the Corps requires the medical units to have them then we need to step up on our fraternization talks. There is a problem here!"

Kris laughed at the Colonel's wry indignation. He gave the box back as Justin pulled on gloves and opened the packaging. He pulled out the buccal swabs and stepped up to the pair. He swabbed first Kris' mouth then the Colonel's. He stepped up to the analyzation equipment and cut the head off of each one and placed them into an individual tube. He closed the machine and went to the computer and ran the test by clicking on the list of quick run programs. Paternity test was number 8. It was good they were programed in as it would have taken considerably longer if he had to input the parameters himself. In ten minutes, they had the results on the screen.

"Congratulations Sir, it's a girl."

Kris and Stirling looked at each other and flashed identical grins. He wrapped his arm around Kris's shoulders and pulled her close and surprised her by kissing her square on the mouth. Justin printed off the results and deleted the run making sure to delete all the history. He took the swabs out of the machine and put them in a bag which he placed in his pocket with the gloves he used and the box for the test. He cleaned up the area and they departed. The Colonel walked with them back to the SOC.

"Well this day took a hell of a turn. I got up this morning ready to run training for the team's next op and instead got a daughter and gave her away at her wedding and set up a honeymoon. And just so you two don't forget we are in a war zone here-the honeymoon is over. For now. You can pick that up stateside. Right now, we have to have our heads in the game. Don't let this distract you. I have a shit ton of paperwork now thanks to all this and you two need to figure out how keep this on the DL."

Kris and Justin looked at each other for a long moment then took off their rings and hooked them on their dog tags then placed them down their shirts.

"Don't worry Sir, we've got this." Kris saluted the Colonel. He returned the salute.

"I have no doubt of that at all Captain. I never did." He turned heel and went back to his office and Kris and Justin went inside to check on their men. Javier was sitting at the communications console. He looked up when they came in.

"Well neither of you are walking with a limp. So, I guess the Colonel didn't beat you both senseless like he threatened."

Kris just shook her head and headed into the command module while Justin checked on the team readiness with Javier. They went over the plans and drills fine tuning the mission parameters falling into a familiar routine. He left and went into the command module to check communications with the rest of the team. Kris stood over the communications tech John Farmer listening to transmissions from the other team.

Chapter Twenty Five

The next couple of weeks routine and training took over Kris and Justin so free time was practically nonexistent. Since the teams didn't wear rank or identifying markings on their uniforms no one that knew that Kris had been promoted. She didn't mention it. They also had not informed anyone of their marriage. They didn't want that to be a distraction for the men. It was hard on Kris and Justin keeping apart now that they didn't have to. Nor did they sneak off to the supply closet as so many others did for a little relief. As much as they wanted to be together they felt it would not be fair to the men who had to leave their spouses and significant others behind for them to be indulging while they did without. It was a testament to the bond and respect they had for the team that they denied themselves when they didn't have to.

About two weeks after their wedding Kris received a package from home. Mel sent them a wedding gift. The note on the box said to open it when Kris and Justin were together. One afternoon when her quarters were empty she called Justin over to unwrap it. Inside was a bullet shaped plastic device about the size of her thumb and a remote control. There were no directions or instructions with it so at first, she didn't know what she was looking at. Justin's wide smile and barking laugh gave her an inkling that it was probably sex related.

"Your sister is very naughty."

"What is it?" Kris picked it up and examined it.

"It's called a bullet. A remote-control vibrator that is inserted vaginally and controlled by the remote. Couples use them for role play and titillation. You can use it alone or your partner can control the remote." Justin talked Kris into trying it out.

"I guess I don't get it. How is it supposed to be naughty?"

"It adds spice since the person with the bullet never knows when the person with the remote is going to activate it or what level they will put it on." Justin clicked the remote turning it higher and higher; alternating between steady vibration and alternating pulses. Kris lay panting on the cot fighting the surge of desire the device generated. She grabbed the pillow to keep from yelling out loud afraid someone passing by would hear her.

She lay on the cot getting her breathing back to normal looking at Justin with heavily lidded eyes. She was about to suggest they take advantage of their privacy when an alert klaxon blared from outside. That was the tone for Special Operations to report for a mission. Kris quickly redressed. Justin stuffed the box under her cot and grabbed her gear pack on the opposite side of her bunk. Justin was at the door holding it for her as she grabbed her bag and exited the room. He started after her when he saw the remote on her cot. She was already out the door on the run, so he went back in to grab it. The bullet was nowhere in sight. He looked around quickly but couldn't see where Kris had put it. So, he grabbed the remote and put in his utilities pocket. He knew it bothered Kris when the younger women talked suggestively with her limited sexual experience. She'd taken enough bullying from the women on this base. If they saw the remote they'd immediately know what it was for. He'd give it back to her when they got back.

Justin rushed to the Raider HQ and grabbed his gear. All the others were already geared up. He quickly put on all his gear and activated his comm. Kris was giving out the mission parameters.

"This op will be on full radio silence. Signal only. We need a quick quiet on this one. In, hit, out; no mistakes and no screw ups. Everyone has their part so stick to the plan and we will get through this easy."

Justin tried to get Kris's attention, but she held him off while she spoke with the chopper commander. With the final prep and gearing up Justin never got to talk to Kris. They double timed it to the chopper with Kris and Alpha team in the near chopper and Justin and Bravo team in the far chopper. They got settled in the for the ride each one looking intently for snipers and insurgents in the hills. It was not uncommon for them to have RPGs, rocket propelled grenades, to try to knock out enemy transports. They got to the LZ and leapt from the Huey to the ground. The teams separated and took opposite routes into the town.

Kris felt jittery and wired. She didn't understand it; she never had a problem being keyed up on missions. She crouched down in an alley looking for activity when it hit her. She wasn't jittery, she was vibrating. The bullet was on! Kris's eyes widened with the realization. Which means Justin had the remote. It was small and only had a range of a few yards. No way it could have been triggered from camp. Holy Shit! What was he thinking! They were on a mission! Was he out of his mind?!

Kris took a deep breath as the first orgasm overtook her and her breathing grew harsh. Javier at point looked at her oddly trying to figure out what was going on with her. She shook him off and concentrated on ignoring the sensations inside her and focusing on the mission. It was damn near impossible. The thing was on high, the last setting Justin had demonstrated. She felt like her legs were made of jelly. She had a hard time walking in a crouch down the alley to the area where they would launch their attack. They entered the side of the building and engaged the enemy. Kris let off two rounds taking out the sentry inside the door. Kris followed the plan going through the dark corridors with Juarez and Miller on her six. They got through the building and into the heart where Miller set up the device to blow the door hiding the six insurgents their intel said were inside. The door blew and the three went into the room under heavy fire.

Kris paused infinitesimally as another orgasm hit her hard. She fired at the men taking them out. They secured the room and gathered up the cell phones and laptops. After placing them in Juarez's pack they exited the room and met up with the rest of the team who were under fire. Kris had sweat beading up on her brown and her lip. She swung around and dropped onto a knee and took aim taking out a man coming up on Gentry's six.

Kris signaled the others they achieved their objective and they pulled back to the hall that lead down to their entry point. As they were headed down the hallway Kris's legs almost gave out as another huge orgasm swept over her. She paused a moment as more sweat broke out on her forehead and she heaved a harsh breath trying to fight the black spots over her eyes. Half a dozen bullets hit the wall just over her shoulder near her head. Juarez grabbed her arm and pulled her down the corridor.

They burst out of the building and ran around the far side of the building getting cover. Bravo team was coming out of the other side heading down the opposite street toward the exfiltration point. Kris tapped Juarez on his helmet and he turned to signal the rest of the team to follow. They could hear the choppers approaching. They skirted out from the cover of the building into fire. They returned fire and covered Bravo team who were boarding their ride. Bravo took up cover fire to let Kris and the rest of Alpha get on board their ride. The two birds lifted off and headed back to camp. Three hours after the klaxon sounded their mission was over.

The team was relaxed and calm now that the mission was over, but Kris was doubled over trying to calm the spasming muscles in her pussy that were working on overdrive. The sensations were so intense they were starting to hurt.

The Huey's touched down in camp and Kris launched out of hers before it touched the ground and ran over to the other chopper grabbing Justin by the front of his gear and dragging him out of the chopper and slamming him on his back on the ground. The rest of the team couldn't deplane. They held with varying degrees of shock and confusion. Her face was a mask of fury.

"You son of a bitch. Where is it?! Where the hell is it!" She tore at his pockets while he lay there stunned at the furious women attacking him. What could have gotten into her?

She patted him down furiously while the other members of the teams all spoke at once trying to figure out what was going on. Javier grabbed Kris by the shoulders trying to drag her off the Major, but she threw him off. She kept slapping a Justin until she felt something in his pants pocket and reached in to yank it out.

"Kris, what are you doing? What the hell has gotten into you?!"

Kris held up the thing she ripped out of his pocket. Looking for the off button. His eyes got wide as he realized. She dropped it on the ground and crushed it under her boot finally turning the device off for the first time in three hours.

She gulped air as she heaved in and out trying to catch her breath.

"I can't believe you-during a mission! You could have gotten me killed. You could have gotten my men killed. I...." she stopped talking horrified as the stress of the situation caught up with her and tears filled her eyes when she turned and walked off toward her quarters.

Justin felt sick. Javier picked up what was left of the remote and examined it realizing very quickly what it was and what it was for. Justin got up off the ground and met Javier's hostile glare.

"Man. I had no idea!"

"Madre de Dios man! What the hell you playing at? Huh?"

"Mel sent it. I was showing Kris how it worked when the klaxon sounded. She bolted so fast I didn't know man, I didn't know. I thought she took it out! I saw the remote and knew she wouldn't want the others in her bunk to see it, so I put it in my pocket. It must have gone off when I got in the chopper. Shit. I can't imagine how she got through that. I need to go talk to her."

Javier grabbed his arm and held him back. "Man, you try to talk to her now she will kill you. You need to give her a bit to cool off."

Javier wasn't far wrong. Kris limped into her quarters dumping her equipment on her cot trying like hell to keep it together. Grabbing a towel and her toilet kit, she left the building heading to the showers. Lieutenant Cook saw the incident at the chopper and hurried over to find out what happened. She fell in step with Kris. Kris kept walking needing all her concentration to get to the women's showers. She couldn't trust herself to go into the SOC showers in case she ran into Justin or the team. She needed to get it together before she faced any of them again. She peeled out of her utilities and got under the hot spray. Only then did she let the tears go. Her body was racked with sobs as she let out the tension that had built up over the last few hours drain away. She cried for several minutes cussing out Justin along the way. Several other women in the facility looked over curiously. Trying not to be caught staring.

"You want to talk about it, Captain?" The young blonde Lieutenant stood outside the stall where Kris was leaning with her head hanging down under the spray. Kris didn't want to say anything. She wasn't in the habit of sharing her personal business. But right now she needed another women to confide in. Kris told the whole story to the Lieutenant who was stunned by the events. The other women weren't even trying to pretend they weren't listening.

"How could he do that? How could he put the mission at risk that way? How could he put me a risk that way?"

"Kris if it makes you feel better I genuinely feel he didn't know. I think it was an accident. His face when you walked away was horrified. I don't think he knew that you still had the device in you. Was it going off the whole time you were on the mission?" Kris nodded. Whew. "Three hours?! That vibrator was on and going for three hours? How the hell were you able to walk much less fight? I had one on for ten minutes and couldn't even get out of bed much less lead a combat mission. Damn!"

Cook knew she had to tread carefully here.

"One thing I know after observing you and your team the last few weeks is that man loves you beyond reason, he would never do anything to put you in harm's way. He'd also never do anything to deliberately upset you. Are you ok?"

"No. I. Um. I don't know how to get it out." Kris met the eyes of the psychologist squarely. There was no shame or chagrin on her face, just angry resolve. Cook knew it was from feeling inadequate. Kris really was a know-it-all asshole. Anytime she came up against anything she didn't know it rubbed her raw.

"Oh! You just reach your finger up there and push it down."

Kris tried and couldn't get it to release. She shook her head. Cook looked uncomfortable.

"I'll go get Major Alario."

"No! I don't want to see him right now. Can you help me?"

Cook was a little off put, but she knew how hard it was for the other woman to ask for help or to appear at a disadvantage. Just as hard for her to ask someone else for help. Kris turned off the water and Cook stepped into the stall and crouched down in front of Kris. She used the stool in the shower that the women used for their toiletries and to shave their legs to hold her balance. The other women gave up the pretense of not intruding and avidly watched.

"Can you lift your leg and prop your foot on the stool?" Kris did as she asked, and the younger woman reached a finger inside her vagina and felt around for the device. It was really far up there. She hooked a finger around it and after several tries it pulled down and she was able to remove it. Kris took it from her and balled it up in her fist.

"Thank you." Kris sat down on the shower stool and sat with her head in her hands. There was still moisture on her face hiding her tears. Cook washed her hands and looked back at Kris. Kris sat for several minutes with her shoulders shaking. Cook's heart went out to her. She squeezed Kris's shoulder before walking out.

"Any time you need to talk I want you to know you can come to me. All you have to do is knock."

Kris nodded but otherwise did not acknowledge her. Just sat there with her head in her hands. Cook left and went outside.

A couple of yards away she saw Major Alario and started toward him. He stood up as she saluted him, he returned the salute.

"Is she alright?"

Cook's eyes twinkled as she replied, "I don't think you want to know what she thinks of you right now. She is more than a little upset."

"I need to talk with her, is she in there alone?"

"No, she isn't and no you aren't going to talk to her right now. She is in there crying her eyes out."

Justin paled hearing that, but the Lieutenant was smiling a huge smile. Justin's face was a mask of fury looking at the mirth on her face.

"You think that is funny, Lieutenant. Does knowing that my wife is in there crying give you some perverse thrill?!" Cook was the only one in camp notified of their marriage outside of the Colonel.

"As a matter of fact, Major, it does. Seeing her in there crying and cussing you out makes me very happy. Do you want to know why? Because it is normal. It is a normal female reaction. I have been so worried that her lack of emotional response was due to an emotional retardation from her condition. I was afraid that she wasn't capable of a normal reaction. I was afraid that I would have to put down that she wasn't able to remain in a combat arena because she wouldn't be able to handle the emotional upheaval from the stresses of the job. She never had to deal with strong emotion and up until now I haven't seen her exhibit a single typical emotional response. I was beginning to think she wasn't capable of one. Or that she hadn't yet learned how to demonstrate emotion in a healthy productive way. What I just saw was all of the above and it makes me happy to say that she is not only able to handle the emotional response, but knowing what she just went through and the physical and psychological stresses that she had to endure, that it is my opinion that Captain Cole is assimilating normally and is more than able to continue in her present position. I think as difficult as this was, it was the best thing that could have happened. It showed me she knows how to physically, emotionally, and mentally handle the rigors of being female. It showed me she can emotionally handle the burdens of her position with the new emotional stressors she is being subjected to. Not only can she handle it, she is killing it! So yeah, I am very pleased. More so because after I file this report, I can go home knowing that Captain Cole will be fine. You Sir may walk with a limp the rest of your life once she gets done with you, but Kris will be fine."

Justin gave the Lieutenant's words time to sink in. He wanted nothing more than to go in there and reassure himself that she was ok; that they were ok. But the Lieutenant was right. Kris would hate having him see her like that. So, he waited outside for her to come out. Colonel Stirling looked around for both Kris and Justin after being regaled with several conflicting stories. Gentry left and came back after tapping one of his sources who was in the showers and got the story from Kris's own mouth. He was furious at both of them. He saw Justin leaning against a pallet of gear that had been offloaded from the supply trucks earlier that had a clear view of the showers. He was just about to dress down Justin when Kris came out of the door. She stopped dead in her tracks and as Justin moved to intercept her, she signaled for him to remain where he was as she moved with great anger and purpose to her quarters a few yards away. Two minutes later she emerged, and Justin's eyes nearly popped out of his head.

She came out in a familiar slinky gold dress that barely covered her backside. It had long sleeves and was cut in a low V that ended halfway between her high full breasts and navel. It molded tightly to her hips with the sleeves ending at her elbows. The shimmering sinuous fabric draped over her curves like loving hands and flowed around her like water. Her hair had been towel dried and flowed gently around her face. The high color in her cheeks and the redness of her lips after the hot shower were a deadly combination. A truck driving by her suddenly veered from the path and connected with a spectacular crash into the building adjacent as the driver was so focused on Kris, he forgot to watch the road. Kris ignored it and kept coming. Her pace was hard and focused as was her face.

She strode right up to Justin and looked him straight in the eye. She stood for moment before she pulled her arm back and slugged him straight in the gut. He fell to his knees from the force of the blow.

"Just so you know that was from your wife and not your mission commander. I didn't want you to be confused by the uniform. That is a reminder for the next time you think to handle me."

She nodded to the Colonel and turned on her heel to march back the way she came. Several people had come out to see what caused the truck to crash and the air was thick with whistles and cat calls. Just as she came abreast of the truck a Humvee coming from the opposite direction crashed into a post while the driver's eyes were glued to Kris as she marched to her quarters.

"I'm going to take the cost of the repair for those vehicles out of your pay Major."

Justin gingerly picked himself off the ground and chuckled at the rye tone from his father-in-law.

"It will be worth every single penny Sir. Damn. Just look at her! She is magnificent." Justin exclaimed with a great deal of pride in his voice. She stomped off in high dungeon entering her quarters the door slamming behind her like a gunshot. Justin just sat back and grinned like a fool holding his gut.

Colonel Stirling shook his head and stood with his arms crossed over his chest.

"I'd wipe that grin off your face if I was you Major. If she sees it, you are liable to find your privates tied in a knot and your butt in a sling. Right now, I need your mission reports. Then you better find a way to fix this with your wife. Before I give into the urge to beat the hell out of you for putting my daughter in danger. You damn near got her killed."

Justin's head snapped quickly to look at Nathan in the eye. The man was furious.

"Watch the mission footage. I want to see that report in one hour." Nathan left to head back to SOC.

Justin followed and got to work so he and Kris could talk later and iron this out.

The tale of Kris's extreme ride had spread like wildfire through the camp. Within the hour everyone in camp was telling some version of the tale. She could see everyone looking at her and rushing to gossip as she passed on her way back to the Command Building. The men looked at her with a new-found respect. Most were more than a little intimidated by the Marine, but they all admired her strength and will. The women were less catty and were more tolerant of her. Many of them had known her as a man longer than as a woman so they were unsure of how to treat her. This incident enabled them to commiserate with her and gave them common ground. They didn't know how to relate to her before. Now they could see her as one of them.

When Kris came back into the SOC building there was a minute pause in the conversations but everyone there was busy finishing out mission reports or following Charlie and Delta on their active missions to spare any time for her. Kris sat down at her desk and filled out the mission reports detailing her actions on the mission. Then writing an overview of the team's efforts.

Each member of the team wrote their own version of the battle from their vantage point detailing their actions and reactions to the events. That way a comprehensive look at the battle from each person could fill in details that the others may have missed; it also made sure that no one left anything out of their report. In past missions' some actions that were less than honorable would be left out to avoid reflecting themselves in a bad light. This led to inquiries and tribunals of war crimes and other unpleasant and time-consuming investigations. Kris started this new way of reporting when she became team leader to make sure everyone on her team acted above board. It was not only the best way to keep everyone honest, it also provided a 360-degree view of the battle. Command adopted this practice and it became the SOP with all the teams in the division.

Over the next hour Kris finished her reports and read over the team's. Then she read the overview from the controller who wrote a report off the helmet cam footage. She stopped on the part that said while she was nearly blacking out against the wall in the building several bullets were just inches from her head. She let out a heavy breath and sat with her eyes closed. She owed Javier for pulling her free. She was so overwhelmed she had no idea she'd taken fire. This pissed her off at Justin all over again. She finished up and shut down her computer and stood up to leave. Justin had just come in from the office area into the ready room. He hesitated a second and then headed straight to Kris. She stood with her arms crossed over her chest and a hard look on her face.

"Are you ok?" Justin's face was strained and looked harsh in the shadowy room, but she could see the concern in his eyes.

"Yeah. I'm good."

Justin closed his eyes and put his hands on her shoulders. Several people in the room were watching. Miller walked in right behind them with Juarez and they were looking for anywhere to go to get away from this private moment. He opened his eyes and spoke candidly to Kris.

"Kris I am so sorry. I had no idea you still had it on you. I saw the remote there and I grabbed it. I just wanted to protect you; not to mess with you."

Kris stood without moving looking at him square in the eye. Her blood was boiling.

"Protect me?"

Miller blanched and made to push Juarez back through the door.

"Oh, shit. We need to move-move now Captain. Clear the area," Miller was grabbing Juarez by the arm attempting to drag the other man from the room.

"What the hell, Miller?"

"Captain, I am trained to know when something is set to explode and if we don't get out of here right now I can't be responsible for our safety. She's going to blow." He was looking directly at Kris as if they only had seconds to live. She met his terrified look with steel which froze him to the spot. He and Juarez didn't move. She turned her attention back to Justin.

"Protect me?"

"Oh c'mon. I've seen how vicious those women can be. How they just can't wait to say stuff about you behind your back. They don't hesitate to start talking about you under normal circumstances and finding something like that on your bunk they would go to town."

"Am I a capable Marine Major?" The ice in that question set Justin's jaw to lock down.

"Yes, more than."

"Am I tough? Can I handle difficult situations as they arise?"

Justin knew he'd better just weather this by answering with straight answers and not try to reason with her.

"Yes."

"I am a good person to have around in a fight when everything goes wrong?"

"Yes."

"So, let me get this straight. You picked up the remote to protect me? Do I look like someone that needs protecting?"

"No."

"Do you honestly think I am going to wither from a couple of young women talking about me?"

"No."

"No. I would think not. I do not need protecting. From anyone. Remember that the next time you think to act on my behalf without consulting me first. Remember that I have been trained to kill with my bare hands and I have ten times the kill ratio than you do. I am not afraid of what a couple of twenty-something junior officers might say about anything."

Justin lowered his voice, "I don't ever doubt your skills or your abilities. You are my wife. I vowed to love, honor, and protect. Just because you don't need protection in the standard sense doesn't mean I can just turn that off. I will never not have your back no matter how little or how big; here or at home. I can't tell you how much it kills me to know that I put you in harm's way. I never meant to do that. I only wanted to help."

"This is why they say the road to hell is paved with good intentions."

"Yeah. I understand that a lot better now." Justin tried to pull her closer. Kris pulled back more conscious of all the eyes on them in the room.

"Hey. Don't pull away. They need to know we are ok. We are ok?"

"Yeah. We are ok." She let him pull her into his arms and returned his embrace. She hated being mad at him. It wasn't a comfortable feeling. She kept the hug brief against her desire to hold onto him in lieu of all the eyes on them.

"Oh, look Miller; Mom and Dad aren't fighting anymore!" Juarez quipped with a smart-ass grin.

Kris and Justin each slapped him upside his head as they passed by him on the way to Lieutenant Colonel Anderson's office for the after-mission briefing.

Over the next several days both Alpha and Bravo Team were a little on edge. Rumors were flying fast and thick about Justin and Kris. A couple of people speculated over whether the pair would be facing disciplinary action over fraternization. Anyone caught openly talking was told to button their lips. Everyone was uncertain if the teams would be broken up or if Kris and Justin would be court-martialed. Kris and Justin talked and worked out the issue between them. Like any new couple they were still feeling their way. They may have been friends and confidants for the better part of a decade, but marriage changed things. They talked out what marriage meant to each of them and set some guidelines. They both had a better idea of what the other expected in their relationship which smoothed the road some. They remained very professional and did not appear overly familiar either in front of anyone or behind closed doors. They gave no one any other reason to gossip.

By the end of the week a general order was issued by the base command banning vibrating "personal massagers" on the base. It seems several other women trying to prove they were as tough as Kris tried to duplicate the incident and two of them ended up in medical. Six days after the 'Bullet Incident', as the rest of camp referred to it, Kris was summoned into Stirling's office. Everyone on Alpha and Bravo made an excuse to hang in the ready room. She was gone the better part of two hours. As time dragged out everyone found other places to be. Soon, just Justin was left. When Kris came in, Justin stood up and was surprised to see the elation on her face. She handed him the file she was holding, and he read over the contents. His smile grew broader as he finished looking over the paperwork inside.

"I think I might have to kiss your father, Kris." He said laughing.

"Try it and he'll kick your butt. However, I feel very confident to do this," Kris said as she grabbed Justin's head and pulled him into a very passionate and heated kiss. They were as close as they could get without climbing into each other's uniform. Voices came down the hall and grew louder as they got closer but neither of them broke apart.

Lt. Colonel Steven Anderson and Juarez came into the room but didn't see the two right off. The Lt. Colonel was still speaking to Juarez about the briefing he was reading over as Javier looked up and panicked.

"Colonel, I think we left some papers in your office let's go grab them." As he made to exit the room back down the hall.

"Nonsense Juarez they are all here. What we need is to..." He looked up and saw the couple making out as if they were alone a world away. He was momentarily shocked to silence. The last two people in the world he would imagine blatantly break a regulation were in front of him doing just that.

"Alario! Cole! What the hell are you doing!?"

They did not stop or even acknowledge the Colonel other than Kris holding out the file she took from Justin to hand to him. He came over and snatched it out of her hand. Kris renewed her grip on Justin by driving her fingers through his hair and deepening their kiss.

He stared in shock a second longer then opened the file and started to read. Juarez came up behind him trying to get a look.

"Well congratulations Captain Alario!"

"Wait, what! They demoted Justin?!"

"No Juarez, I wasn't talking to him." He handed over the file with a huge grin on his face as Javier read the forms with his eyes getting wider by the second. Several more people entered the room and stopped dead at the sight before them. Gentry was one of them. He laughed as he returned down the hall to call to the rest of the teams who were in the back to get to the ready room. They had to see this.

Kris and Justin were so wrapped in each other they never heard the rest of them come in. Which was surprising as the noise was huge because they were all talking at once. Kris and Justin slowly pulled apart, the joy evident on their faces, as several wolf whistles and cat calls reached their ears and they realized they were no longer alone. They were laughing as they held on to one another looking at their men. Javier looked up from the file and addressed the room.

"Ladies and Gentlemen! May I be the first to present Mr. and Mrs. Alario!"

Everyone was more than a little shocked by the news, but the pair were so popular with their teams there was nothing but joy and best wishes as the pair were passed around for hugs and back slaps.

"Correction may I present Major and Captain Alario!"

The din grew deafening as the men cheered Kris's promotion to Captain. Soon Javier was relieved of the file he was reading as the other members of the team passed it around reading it for themselves.

"How the hell did you get promoted for fraternizing?"

"These two have been married for three weeks and never told us!"

Their scrounger Reineke left the room quietly as the team started peppering the pair with questions.

"Sir? How could you not tell us?"

Justin and Kris let them fire away and get it off their chests as they waited for the group to settle down and let them talk.

"We weren't trying to exclude you, any of you, we were told to keep it on the DL until paperwork was filed. The Colonel wasn't sure what was going to happen once it made it back to division and didn't want any wild rumors or panic to ensue over the teams' fate. He didn't want this to be a distraction for anyone. We just got the word earlier today," Justin explained.

Tomball raised the file high and with his deep voice and addressed the group, "If I may quote here for everyone, 'From the office of the Commandant of the Marine Corps to Commanding Officer Nathan Stirling regarding the marriage of Major Justin Alario and *Captain* Kristin Cole. Ahem. The exemplary records of both Alario and Cole speak for themselves. There is no question in my mind that they will continue to work in an exemplary manner with the dedication to duty that they are known for and uphold the standard of conduct becoming officers of the United States Marine Corps. I have no doubts that the working relationship that they have endeavored to build as team leaders over the last several years will continue regarding their recent marriage. Therefore, it is the decision of this office to grant permission for Major Alario and Captain Cole to continue in their roles as team leaders while deployed in the same unit under the watchful eye of Colonel Nathan Stirling who will ensure that they uphold the level of professionalism and character that each have shown individually to date. Breaking up or changing the command of a well-structured team in the field can be detrimental to the mission. So, it is this office's wish to keep them in their present roles at this time. If at any time they are seen to be unable to uphold their duties due to their personal relationship it will be the decision of their Commanding Officer as to any reassignment necessary. It is with my hardiest wishes that I congratulate the new couple on their nuptials and offer my best wishes for the future.' Signed the Commandant of the Marine Corps. How in the hell did you two pull this off?"

Kris chuckled, "Don't look at us this is just as much as surprise to us as it is to you!"

Reineke came in as quietly as he left carrying two unmarked boxes. He quickly opened the top of the first one and started passing out the amber bottles inside to everyone in the room.

Everyone's eyebrows raised as they received a bottle of beer and Reineke raised his calling for a toast.

"To the happy couple. Even though we weren't there for the wedding we can throw them a hell of a reception! We wish them both a hearty Oorah!" The teams loudly echoed the toast around the room and drank up. Before he could drink from his bottle he saw Colonel Stirling enter the room. He turned and handed his bottle to the Colonel who looked on sternly at the beer everyone was holding.

"Reineke I don't want to know where you got this or how you managed it. But I better not hear anything about it from anyone higher up." Reineke grabbed a new bottle for himself and nodded to Stirling. "Make sure you account for every bottle and get rid of the evidence."

Stirling turned to the couple still in each other's arms.

"To Justin and Kris! If they are half as good a team off the field of battle as they are on the field of battle, they will have a long and happy marriage. Take care of my little girl. Oorah!" Kris moved away from Justin and walked to Stirling and hugged the Colonel. "Thanks Dad." He flushed with pleasure and returned the hug.

The last several weeks Kris and Nathan spent as much time as their duties allowed together. They spent a great deal of time really getting to know one another. Mel had emailed Nathan dozens of pictures of Kris from when she was little and she and Nathan spent hours looking over them and talking. Kris learned of Nathan's family and found she had a Grandmother and two aunts in California who were dying to meet her. She told Nathan of her childhood and her time in Texas that influenced her to join the Marines. He looked up Gunnery Sergeant Arlon Buckley, Buck to Kris and all the hands on the ranch, and looked into the man who had become an honorary uncle to Kris and Emily. Last year he had passed and left his land, home, and possessions to Kris. With everything that happened she hadn't been able to get to Texas to check it out. Mostly she had been keeping it a secret in case she and Mel needed to hide out. The bunker was fortified and would be an excellent place to lay low. Marrying Justin and finding Nathan changed that a bit. She wouldn't cut and run now that she had them. But she still hadn't told either of them of the bunker. Just in case.

She remained with Stirling's arm around her waist as they clinked bottles and drank to the toast. They sat and grinned at each other as the men in the room took in what they never noticed previously. The startling resemblance between the two. The din rose in the room again as more question flews to this startling news. Kris gave an abbreviated explanation of how they found out when everyone started talking at once trying to get answers. Everyone got a kick out of the Colonel 'ordering' them to marry only to find out after the fact Kris was his daughter. Justin got teased a lot about having a shotgun wedding.

"Shotgun my ass. The only one who had to be shoved to the alter was Kris!" Justin said with humor.

"Ha! Gotta be within regulations! Where she have that manual tattooed now Major?!"

"Plenty new territory!" Several guys miming her breasts in exaggerated poses.

The laughter grew raucous. Ridiculous comments flew from all sides.

"Don't ever piss off your wife dude, her dad will break you in half with his Kung-Fu!"

"If it comes to that Kris will break him in too small of pieces for the Colonel to have anything left to Kung-Fu!"

"Hey, if you spar now, is it domestic abuse?"

"Uh oh! Who the hell is gonna cook at your house?"

Ten people yelled out, "Justin!"

"Kris will kill it and skin it and Justin will cook it!"

"Which one of you gets to be the husband?"

"Kris was a husband longer than you Justin, better let her do it- she has more experience!"

"You'll have to get lessons from Mel on how to be a wife Kris!"

"You think she'll let him call her 'the little woman'?"

"There is nothing little about Kris!" Every guy in the room laughed and either stared straight at her chest again or mimed endowment with their hands half a foot out from their chests like massive boobs as she laughed, shook her head and looked skyward.

Over the next half an hour the ribald comments and ribbing continued with the toasts and well wishes.

"All right," Kris said laughing, "that's enough. Everyone put their bottle back into the box, so we can dispose of them."

Lt. Colonel Anderson stepped up. "Kris gather up your gear and bring it back over here. You are longer eligible for FSOQ."

"Sir? You want me to move back into the barracks?"

"Report to my quarters in 30 minutes, Captain to collect your new billeting assignment."

Kris looked at Justin and he shook his head just as confused as she was. There was no extra room in the barracks for another person. They barely had enough room now. But Kris followed orders. With Justin's help they gathered up all her gear from the Female Single Officer's Quarters. Lt. Stohler came in the room while Kris was packing up.

"Going somewhere Cole?"

"Yeah, I've been ordered to pack up and report to Raider barracks."

"Command figure you're getting into too much trouble over here?"

Kris chuckled. "I guess. You haven't been introduced; this is Major Justin Alario."

Stohler's eyebrows shot straight up into her hairline. These two had been on everyone's lips lately. The talk from all the women was that they would give just about anything to be in Kris's shoes. She didn't see what the fuss was about. Until now; she'd only seen him briefly from afar. It was late afternoon, so his face was starting to get five o'clock shadow that turned his action hero good looks to dangerous and sexy.

"Uh. Major." She reached out a hand to shake his. He smiled at Stohler and returned the greeting while she stared dazed. Kris chuckled more while Justin shot Stohler a sexy grin. Stohler pretty much forgot how to breathe. Justin turning on the charm was enough to render any female speechless. This was the first time she has seen the Major up close. She had to take several gulps of air to regain her senses.

Kris finished loading up her gear and zipped her bag shut. Justin picked up the footlocker and slung it over his shoulder like it weighed nothing. Stohler just gawked as how his muscles bulged in his uniform and tried not to let her mouth water. She reached out to shake Kris's hand.

"Well it's been good having you as a roommate. You are alright Kris. For a Gunny."

"Well it's Captain Cole now I'll have you know."

"Oh Captain! Well then." She snapped a sharp salute as she started to laugh at Kris's smart-ass tone.

They both laughed as Stohler gave Kris a quick hug.

"I guess I'll see you around camp then Captain!"

Kris and Justin carried all her things out of the room. As the door closed behind them the Lieutenant spoke into the empty room fanning herself.

"Damn! That is one sexy man. Whew."

Justin and Kris carried her things across the camp to the barracks and stopped outside of Lt. Colonel Anderson's quarters. Justin knocked on the door and it swung open. The ten-foot square room was utilitarian. The door was dead center. They walked inside and there were two beds side by side centered against the wall. To the left, Justin's footlocker was on the floor next to the metal cabinet with room on the opposite side for Kris's. A desk was shoved into the far-right corner with just enough room to slide the chair out before hitting the bed. A paper banner taped on the wall above the bed said *"The Honeymoon Suite"* in black sharpie. They hadn't quite taken it all in when Anderson stepped into the doorway.

"Oh good, the guys got your trunk in."

"Ah, Colonel where are you going to sleep?"

"In the main barracks with the men. There wasn't room for another bed, so you two will just have to cram in here; I took Justin's old space."

Justin walked over to Anderson and clapped him on the back. "That is above and beyond, Steve. I can't tell you what it means to have you do this."

"Consider it my wedding gift to you both. And try not to get carried away in here. You both know how hard it is to be away from home."

Kris answered for them both, "Not to worry sir. We won't take advantage."

"We won't?!" Justin seemed a bit panicked by her admission. She just sent him a withering look as she arranged her gear in the cabinet with his. Anderson was laughing his head off as he left.

Justin and Kris made short work of putting away their things. Kris took two thick zip ties from her field pack that they used to secure hostages and combatants and lashed the legs of the two beds together in the middle. They used one of the blankets to cover both mattresses and keep them from separating then used the sheets over top to secure them. With the bed finally made and all their personal items put away the room felt less cramped and cozier. How cozy it would feel in over the next few weeks remained to be seen. On the desk someone had put a black and white printed copy of a picture of them dancing at the Marine Corps Ball. A makeshift frame out of cardboard colored in black marker held the photo. It looked like a bad version of a Kindergarten art project. Next to it another cardboard frame held a picture of the team from just before deployment. Kris stood there and looked at the homey touches and felt a catch in her chest. She was greatly touched the men would do this for them. It really measured how much they cared about her and Justin to go to all this effort. Justin came up behind Kris and wrapped his arms around her waist resting his chin on her shoulder. She leaned her head against his and held onto his arms. They stood that way for a while just enjoying the closeness of the moment and the small oasis of peace they'd found in a not so peaceful place.

Chapter Twenty Six

The peace was short lived. Just when Kris and Justin finally developed a working rhythm a wrench was thrown in the works. Charlie team had just come back from a raid on an insurgent nest bringing intel. El Moufas had a base of operations in country. They had hired local talent for escort service for a shipment of weapons they were running across Afghanistan and they were intercepted. The group was not as experienced as they let on and got caught. Kris spent the next several days compiling the intel she'd been hording with the new information developing a plan. She and Justin sat up late every evening working on piecing together the intel until Kris could see the whole picture. With the information she had on the weapons trafficking and the lines she knew regarding how they funneled their money, she figured how to hit them where it would hurt and most likely bring down the organization. She wasn't ready to go to command with it yet as she still needed to find out the structure of the command and how they disseminated the organizational operations. It wouldn't do to cut off the head if the body could still function.

Kris spent a great deal of time in communications listening to chatter and working with intelligence trying to locate the terrorist's main base of operations. With that they could watch and determine how best to strike. The teams were on alert and it was all hands on deck. They were all focused on one thing; find El Moufas.

Kris and Justin spent a great deal of time in their quarters talking over plans and options for a strike. Kris brought out all of the information she had on El Moufas. Information she had been gathering since she was 12 years old. Justin was amazed at what she had gathered and a little dismayed. He had no idea that Kris's obsession with Aziz El Moufas ran that deep or that she had been effectively been training to kill him since she was a child. She shared with him everything she had been doing her whole life to prepare for taking out the terrorist.

She told him everything she'd kept to herself about herself and Mel. He was shocked. He was also proud and a little in awe of everything she'd done to bring herself to this moment. He'd always known she was strong and focused but he had no idea how deep it ran. He saw a whole new side of her and it only made him love her more. She really was the perfect woman for him. She was what he'd been missing his whole life. She confessed to him during the long nights they lay together that he was what had been missing in her life as well. How much loving him and building a family with him meant to her. They talked about children and what the future would hold. Kris was adamant that she finish this war with El Moufas before they make any concrete plans. The sooner the better. She was planning on going to Command in the morning and making a full disclosure of what she knew and how she gathered it in order to get them to sign on to a plan she had been concocting since she arrived. If they couldn't find El Moufas, they would get El Moufas to find them. All it would take was a leaked communication with Kris's name in it and she had no doubt they would coming running to hunt her down. A knock at the door changed the plan.

Javier stood outside the closed door pacing back and forth. He really didn't want to disturb them. When Lt. Colonel Anderson walked into the ready room and asked the room at large to go back and get Kris no one moved. Everyone assumed when that door was closed it was for a reason and no one was going to disturb them. Though a bit jealous, they all were living a little vicariously through the newly married couple and didn't begrudge them their alone time. Everyone there knew that every time they went out it could all go south. No one blamed them for the time they eked out in their off hours. All of them agreed they would never want their spouses here; they wouldn't be able to shut down and focus. Cole and Alario seemed to have no problem compartmentalizing their relationship. So when they were 'being married' no one wanted to horn in on their time. He listened for a moment trying to gauge whether he was interrupting anything when he heard the bed springs squeak and Kris's husky laugh. He squeezed his eyes shut hanging his head and rapped on the door before he lost his nerve. Kris called out to come in.

Javier opened the door and was shocked to see Kris sitting cross legged on the bed and Justin kicked back with his feet on the desk, his lap covered with folders. Kris looked up and motioned Javier inside and to close the door. He took a look at the folders on the bed.

"Seriously? Quarterly evals? You two have a room to yourselves with a locking door and it is your off time and you are going over team evals. I don't know whether to be horribly disappointed in you or extremely impressed."

Kris smirked and threw a pillow at his head.

"Thought you'd bust in and get a sitrep for the team on our love life? Sorry to disappoint you man."

"No uh actually Anderson came in and said you have been ordered over to Division Command. Like now. They had a group come in earlier and the General's office has been like a revolving door for hours. Now they want you there."

"Gotta be about El Moufas. Finally. Well I have some stuff for them too."

Kris got up and put on her utilities top and grabbed her lid. Justin did the same intending to walk her over. They cleaned up the files and put them on the desk before leaving. Kris and Justin talked companionly as they walked across the camp. They were laughing and joking as they kidded one another. At one point Justin grabbed Kris in a head lock as she teased him about a misspeak earlier in the week that had everyone in the ready room rolling on the floor. They got the division offices and straightened their uniforms. Then went in. Colonel Stirling was there with a very hard look on his face. The room got very quiet when Kris entered. Kris looked around and saw varying degrees of dismay, shock, and anger displayed on the faces of the men and women in that room. And they seemed to all be directed at her. Justin squeezed her on the shoulder and made to leave when Stirling stopped him.

"You might as well stay for this too Alario. Close the door."

"Colonel this is a need to know..." Stirling cut off the older man in the khaki pants with the kerchief around his neck and the bad sunburn across the top of his face.

"This concerns the Major as well. And he is cleared for this."

The looks in the room got more heated and the pair was unsure of what they had just walked into.

"This is CIA chief Tom Briggs. And this is CIA officer Kyle Chambers. You know Colonel Matthews and General Adams. This is NCIS director Anna Booker and Special Agent Tamara Jackson."

Kris saluted the Marines and shook the hand of the civilians in the room. She deliberately did not engage Chambers. Justin held him with a long look before returning to the General who began to speak.

"A few weeks ago we intercepted a missive that implicated a United States Marine with ties to a terrorist organization. NCIS was asked to investigate which they did. What they uncovered was shocking to say the least. That a Marine in this division was determined to have been harboring a terrorist. That for the last ten years that Marine has been steadily maneuvering into position in order to subvert and undermine the mission of the United States Military in the hunt and capture of El Moufas. That same Marine has been secretly gathering intel to allow El Moufas to have inside knowledge of the military's actions in order to stay one step ahead of us and allude any attempts to detain."

Stirling stood arms crossed and rigid with his face set in mutinous lines. He slowly shook his head as the General continued. Clearly not believing a word of it.

"We have information that shows that Captain Kristin Cole is guilty of treason."

Justin's head whipped up and he glared at the General.

"What kind of bullshit is this....!" Kris put a hand on his chest to forestall anything he might say that could get him a reprimand. Kris addressed the room.

"I am not a traitor and any information you have is bogus! Your conclusions are wrong. I have worked my whole life to get where I am and it is not to subvert our mission to bring El Moufas down but to ensure it! I have been working every day since I was little more than a child to do one thing. Bring down Aziz El Moufas and his entire family with the organization they built. Period. If you have proof otherwise I demand to see it."

Director Booker stood and faced Kris. "We are under no obligation to provide you with that information."

"Director, I happen to know that the rights of the accused and one of those rights is discovery. Kris has the right to see any and all information that implicates her in order to be able to perform a rebuttal." Justin challenged.

"That Major is true in a trial, but we are not in a trial and you are not a lawyer; that is not necessarily admissible when the charge is treason. DHS and the FBI have the ability to detain and question anyone regarding the charge of treason and discovery is not required. Needless to say my office has determined that Captain Cole is guilty of harboring a terrorist and falsifying information in order to deceive the US Government."

Kris snorted. "I did not falsify a thing, and any papers I do have were provided by the US Government Director. I have at no time attempted to deceive the US Government but have been working with the help of the Department of Justice in order to protect the life of a woman that the US Government failed to do. She was not a terrorist but the victim of a terrorist who if left unprotected would have been tortured and murdered by the very person who was supposed to be protecting her. Her father. She was no more a terrorist than the General is Ma'am. She was a woman who just happened to have a piece of shit for a father. A piece of shit who has made it his life's mission to find her just so he can end her for betraying him. Just as I had made my life's mission to make sure that would never happen."

"Where is Amalia El Moufas?"

Kris smiled a feral smile. "Dead Ma'am. Died in a car crash at the age of 20."

"We all know that is not true Captain. She is alive and you know where she is."

"Amalia died in a single vehicle accident. Dental records proved it was her in the vehicle."

Kris's face was stone. She did not betray anything in her expression that indicated that she was lying.

"That body was burned beyond recognition and there was no DNA left to match."

"Damn shame that." Kris said with a barely concealed smirk.

Briggs stepped in. "This is pointless. Cole isn't going to give up El Moufas' daughter. We have enough evidence for a nice long stay in Leavenworth. However. If Cole cooperates I can see to it that she doesn't have to spend the rest of her life there."

Justin asked, "Cooperates how?"

"Chambers here has managed to infiltrate El Moufas. He has gotten close to Aziz but he hasn't been able to get in with the other brothers. They are careful and very suspicious. We need someone else in there. I think we have that perfect someone."

"You want Kris to infiltrate a terrorist organization?"

"Oh I think Cole has proven without a shadow of a doubt she's capable of playing any role she sets her mind to. After all she's had a great deal of experience doing just that."

Justin almost didn't wait for Briggs to finish his sneering comment before he went for him. It took the General, Kris and Stirling to pull him off. Kris pushed him back keeping her hands on his chest as he glared daggers at Briggs.

"Major that will not help. What did you have in mind for me to do? El Moufas will recognize me."

At this point Chambers entered the conversation.

"He's never seen you close up and they are looking for a male Marine. Not a female. If we get her into his household or the compound as a woman he would never catch on. "

"That is possible. Aziz is a misogynistic bastard who constantly dismisses women as inferior. However he may know by now I am a woman. The Corps did make rather a pointed effort to announce that fact when I was awarded the Medal of Honor. Considering how long Aziz has been gunning for me and how determined he is to get the truth, there is little doubt he is in possession of that fact."

"In every conversation I have overheard he refers to Cole as 'he'. I don't think he's picked up on that."

"Chambers I'm not ready to place Kris's life on the line for a probable. He could simply be carrying on with the male reference out of habit. Half of the Marines in this division still refer to Cole as 'he' and they work with her every day!"

"I am certain he doesn't know."

Kris remained thoughtful and said nothing. She agreed with Justin. Aziz believed in research as did his whole family. It's how they managed to stay successful for so long and under everyone's radar. As much as she wasn't going to be blackmailed into this, she couldn't help but think this was the chance she had been waiting for. But somehow she needed to get the upper hand.

Director Booker spoke up. "Our plan is to use Jackson. She looks enough like Cole to get in and has enough experience to get what we need."

"We need Cole's information so we can finalize our plan. We know she has accessed countless databases over the years and has significant intel. I don't doubt that she has been able to extrapolate locals and networks that they are using. I also know that she has accessed suspected shell companies that we've been unable to significantly link to El Moufas which I assume she's been able to do. We need everything you have to make sure we aren't missing anything when we go in. We won't get another chance at this."

Kris nodded thinking about the next move.

"If I agree to this I am not going to do it with an ax over my head. I have not broken any laws; I have also not committed treason. Everything you think you have is wrong. If I do this I will have assurances both in this room and in writing that when this is over I will not be facing any further judgement. Or this stops here and you will have a nightmare when the District Attorney for Illinois takes my case and files defamation charges against the United States Government. And with all the intel and information I have in my possession I can guarantee you I will win and you will look like fools. Your careers will be over. And you will be no closer to stopping El Moufas that you ever were. But with my willing help I can assure you we have enough to finish their organization. For good."

Briggs looked thoughtful. He was careful and clever. And he wasn't about to lose his leverage. He knew he had Cole by the short and curlies and wasn't about to let up. The key was to get her to give up what she knew. He had no doubt she knew quite a lot more than what she was saying.

"You give us what you have and we will consider that."

"No deal Briggs. Justin contact your uncle." Kris turned to Booker and Jackson. "Do we leave now or do I pack a bag before you take me to Leavenworth?"

"Wait a minute! Damn it Kris stop being so bullheaded and let's talk about this!" Colonel Stirling wasn't about to let his daughter be accused of treason.

"Sorry Sir. I am not going to let these CIA tools railroad me. I have not fought all this time to give in now. I would rather spend time in prison than allow them to destroy my career or destroy our only good chance to end El Moufas. NCIS won't be able to hold me. No doubt everything they have is circumstantial. Once DA Alario gets ahold of it he'll be able to dismiss it and I'll be right back here. I am not afraid to fight. Especially when I know I will win." Kris said with a lethal grin. It was apparent to everyone in the room she was in possession of a great deal more information than they were. Briggs was recognizing his advantage was gone.

Kris asked Jackson in Pashtu how she planned to get close. Jackson answered with several scenarios in flawless diction. Kris nodded to her and looked at Justin.

"How much Farsi do you understand?"

"I don't understand any."

Kris turned back to Booker and Briggs with a resigned look.

"Then this plan is done. If you don't speak Farsi then you are useless to this op."

"What the hell are you talking about? All of El Moufas speaks Pashtu."

"You have obviously not done very diligent research. Or you may not know simply because you have not gotten close to them. The El Moufas brothers only speak Farsi at home or when they are together and want privacy. They make sure to hire only men who don't speak it so they can speak freely. They will only discuss the intricacies of the business in Farsi."

Briggs looked at her with a sneer, "How do you know that?"

"Because unlike you I have gotten close. As close as you can get. If you send her in there she will be useless. She may get in and get close but she'll never be able to get anything useful because everything sensitive will be spoken of in Farsi-mark my words. If you don't know that then you know nothing about the people you are looking to infiltrate and you have already given them the advantage because I can guarantee they know plenty about you."

"There is no way a United States Marine got close enough to El Moufas to know all of this and got away with it. If you got that close why are they still operating? Why didn't you take them out?"

"I was hardly in the position at the time to do anything. I watched and I waited. I gathered intel until I could piece it all together."

Stirling looked at Kris. "When was this?"

Kris looked at her father and replied, "When I was 11."
Stirling straightened and looked at Kris with a hard look. She
could see that he was starting to put everything together. It
didn't take him long. She could tell the minute he figured it all
out and had answers to a great many questions that he'd had for
a long time. She figured her mom stuck enough to the truth
without giving away everything for him to have more than
enough information now that the key piece was presented to
him.

Stirling looked at Kris and with an impassive face betraying
nothing nodded curtly to let her know he understood.

"The only way this is going to work is I am the one to go in."

"No way Captain. I am still not convinced you're not in league
with those terrorists! I let you go in and we never see you again.
Not a chance."

"Briggs you are as short sighted stupid as I suspected. I am not
going to run off with my husband here and my father left holding
the bag." As she indicated Justin and Nathan. Briggs eyes
widened. He obviously was not in possession of that
information. Which surprised Kris. It was a part of her record
now. It had only been a few weeks but the letter from Command
indicated it was all documented as a part of her official record.
That being said, how could he not have the information? Yet
every time the man opened his mouth Kris's dick twitched.
Something was off with Briggs. She made a conscious effort to
give no further information if he was a part of the conversation.
She didn't trust him. She signaled to both Justin and Nathan in
sign that something was off. She wanted them to be on alert.

Stirling stepped up and addressed the General.

"Let's take this back to MSOC. We need to go over Kris's intel
and see what new intel communications has gathered in the last
couple of hours."

The group left Stirling's office and headed to MSOC. Jackson
went with Chambers to Communications to get intel, Briggs
moved to a corner to use his SAT phone while Justin, Nathan,

Booker and Kris huddled around the war table to confer. They were soon joined by Colonel Matthews and General Adams.

"What it is Kris?" Justin always knew when she was feeling something off.

"Briggs. How much do you know about him? How'd you hook up?" Kris addressed Booker.

"He contacted our office and asked for a joint investigation."

"Why? CIA has more capability than NCIS to verify and gather intel. Why bring in NCIS? Do me a favor. Contact his field office and verify this investigation. He is either operating outside of the lines or without sanction."

"What makes you think that?"

"Every time he opened his mouth my dick twitched."

Booker looked shocked and a little put off by the comment. But everyone else understanding the significance of the statement eyes went sharp and cautious. All of them looked at each other with concern and a hint of mistrust.

"What exactly is that supposed to mean?"

Colonel Matthews answered, "I'll fill you in later Director. But I will say that this changes things. Limit the intel you give to Briggs. And I agree with Cole. Check him out. Cole's dick is never wrong," he finished with an evil smile.

"Someone in the US government has been feeding intel to El Moufas for years. They were able to stay one step ahead on all efforts to tie them to any wrongdoing. Every time anyone got close they would pack up and move on. Aziz's arrest was a mild inconvenience to them as it put attention on the family but it gave them more contacts as Aziz used his prison time wisely. Considering the information they were able to access it points to someone quite high up. Someone with access and who would not be questioned for the information they had access to.

Only three people were supposed to know how and where Amalia was being transferred after the trial. They massacred the Marshalls. They knew the size of the force, the route, and

firepower needed. The only reason Amalia got away is because I
had been training her for months on evasion. I taught her how to
hide. We discussed protocol if she needed to contact us for help.
How to do it in code without giving anything away and how to
give information so that it could not be flagged as code by anyone
else. She used it and we left California and moved slowly across
the country.

We stayed off the grid, mom home schooled us, and she worked
in places that either paid cash or in trade for rent and utilities.
The case worker for Justice redacted everything about our
involvement. Find him. He ran his own off the books
investigation and made sure we had the proper documentation
for Amalia. We have not been in contact with him for years.
Once I graduated and married there was no need to. I have kept
him appraised of my intel through a secure channel. He retired
several years ago, but he keeps in toe in."

"What's his name, I'll run a search."

"No, you search it here and Briggs will tail gate. What until you
get stateside. Be careful. I will not pay him back for all he's done
for us to get him killed now."

Booker nodded and shut down as Briggs joined the table.

"I have updated my people on the current plan. We execute in
the morning. General I want a guard on Cole. I won't have her
sneaking off in the night."

"That won't be necessary. Cole I am ordering you to remain in
camp and present yourself to Briggs at 0700 for JSOC with NCIS
and CIA." General Adams was having a hard time biting the
words out as it was clear he wanted to tear Briggs apart. She
nodded to the General.

Kris walked up to Briggs and got right in his face. Her face was
pure stone. She looked down her nose at him which pissed him
off as he was several inches shorter than her.

"Briggs don't make me do something I won't regret. You impugn
my integrity again and I will end you. You have my word as an
officer and a Marine that I will not disobey any direct order by

my superiors. You on the other hand had better watch what you say and how you say it. I will do my duty but I will not stand for any bullshit from you. You may be the operational leader, but never forget I am the operation. You have nothing without me. And I am willing spend the rest of my life in Leavenworth if it means screwing you over. So don't mess with me."

Briggs seemed visibly shaken. He took two steps back from Kris and wiped his upper lip with his neckerchief. He swallowed several times before answering.

"Cole you are hardly key to this operation. Chambers is already in. I don't need you. But I will use every asset available to me because bringing this cell down is the priority. I will see you in the morning. Don't be late." He motioned to Chambers and they left the building.

He left and the remaining men and women looked thoughtfully at one another.

"Kris, go gather your gear, give control of the team to Nunez. Justin go with her."

Both saluted Stirling and the other officers and left the room.

Booker spoke up. "Anyone else notice he didn't even look over or confer with anyone regarding the intel communications has gathered on El Moufas' recent movements?"

The General's eyes narrowed. "That doesn't mean anything. He may have been briefed on the phone by his people. But I agree with Cole. Something is off. Find out what."

The General nodded to the other officers and NCIS and left. Matthews went to Communications to consolidate the intel for an AM briefing for Kris before they left. He wanted her to have everything she needed.

Stirling stayed with Booker and Jackson.

"Briggs seemed shocked to hear Kris is my daughter and Justin is her husband."

Jackson answered, "I noticed that. It is part of her record. He should know that. He said he has been gathering intel on her for months and was only just able to confirm her involvement which is why he contacted us."

"I just found my daughter; I don't want to lose her now. Find out."

"Colonel, can you arrange transport for us stateside? We can leave now if necessary. I will tell Briggs we have a lead on Amalia's location and are going to investigate. I bet we find a tail."

"I will arrange for transport. I will let you know what the ETA for departure is. Oh, and Booker-I don't take sucker bets." Stirling said with a smirk.

Kris met with Nunez and gave him the news of her JSOC mission without any of the details. Mission NTK and immediate for an indeterminate length of time. He went to make some changes and get with Anderson about replacing Kris on the team. She and Justin went back to the team equipment area and pulled what equipment she thought she'd need.

Kris went to a locked cabinet and removed several devices from a box on the top shelf. She secreted them in the pocket of her utilities. They were small and nondescript. One looked like an MP3 player. But it was a great deal more. She hid them before Justin realized it. Chances are Javier would notice his toys were missing. But she wasn't going in without backup. She couldn't depend on her team or that she'd even be able to contact them. She definitely couldn't depend on the men she was operating with. Chambers maybe, but he was held by Briggs and she wouldn't count on his help. He'd proven himself with her before but he may not do so again now that they were square.

She and Justin returned to their quarters where she packed a small go bag. She wouldn't need her uniforms but she would need personal items. She'd change into black ops gear that had no colors or ranking. More than likely she'd have to jettison those once they got to wherever their staging was. But she didn't pack any civilian clothing this trip; except the gold dress Mel snuck into her bag and she wasn't going in that!

Justin came up behind her once she zipped her bag with the gear and spun her around suddenly pulling her hard against him and claiming her mouth. He held her down dominating her. She realized he needed to have control and let him take it.

He continued to ravage her moving downward confining her to the mattress. He wrapped her hands around the top of the headboard squeezing them enough to let her know he wanted her to keep them there. They savagely took one another knowing this wasn't just another mission. This could be it for them. It made their passion all the more volatile and explosive.

They lay tightly holding onto one another loathe to let go until the sounds from out in the hall brought them back to reality and they realized where they were.

He rose up on his forearms and looked into her intense gaze. They stay for several moments just absorbing each other's presence before slowly pulling apart. Kris unwrapped her hands from the metal bedframe and flexed her fingers which were tingling from her white knuckled grip. Justin pulled Kris up from the bed and held her gently to him in a full body embrace. Neither of them wanted to say anything. Nothing would be enough and anything would be too much. They both knew the stakes. They both knew the dangers. Someone knocked on the door and announced they were needed in the Comm so they pulled apart and redressed.

Only an idiot would have missed the signs of their recent activity but no one said anything when the pair entered into the ready room. Kris dropped her go bag next to the table entered the discussion where Stirling and two communications officers were discussing the latest intel. Kris memorized the locations of the recent movements as well as the suspected locations of hideouts and meeting areas. She filed this away with everything she already had on them.

Briggs and Chambers joined the group and shared more information that they had gathered. Kris started formulating a plan as to how she would infiltrate the El Moufas compound. Her height and manner could get her in as a man but her breasts would be nearly impossible to disguise. As a woman it is. Her dark eyes would be an asset, but her blonde hair would stand out. She'd have to see about getting a good wig. Long dark hair would go a long way to disguising her. She turned to Briggs.

"Do you have an entry plan for me?" Chambers spoke up.

"They are always going through cleaning girls. The men are rough and tend to corner them so they never last long. It wouldn't be hard to introduce you in. Faces change so often a new girl wouldn't raise any alarm."

"Well the Corps did ensure I could spit shine and polish," Kris said with a smirk. "And cleaning girls are in every room without suspicion so that works. I need a wig. Blonde hair is unusual and mine is too short."

Briggs looked her over for a second and replied, "We have a complete wardrobe we set for Jackson. She is smaller but they are loose so they should fit you. You are close in height. In it are wigs and colored contacts. As well as several traditional garments. Chambers will take you to change." He tossed his head to the door indicating that Chambers take her now.

They walked out of the ready room to an office that was being used as a holding area for the CIA's gear. Chambers opened several suitcases which had skirts and blouses in the regional traditional style. Luckily they were loose, Kris had such a well-defined physique that they were nearly snug across her back and shoulders. Once the hijab was on it would cover her shoulders and back enough to disguise her muscular frame. She rummaged through to find the largest garments. She disrobed and started to pull them on when Chambers spoke up.

"Hey, Marine." He was standing with his arms crossed and legs crossed leaning against the wall clearly enjoying the show. He nodded to her underwear with a smirk. They were Marine issue undergarments. Damn. She looked in the trunks and found several pairs of underwear and a couple of bras. She stripped down and replaced the underwear. The bras were tight. Jackson was not as broad nor nearly as well-endowed as Kris was. Kris dug some more and found some bra extenders in one of the pockets. The band no longer dug in, but the cups were still at least a size too small, but they would have to do.

"Not to speak out of turn, but Alario is one lucky son of a bitch."

Kris gave him a hard look and continued to dress. She and Jackson luckily had the same size feet. She was not looking forward to wearing too small of shoes. Once she had the clothing on she selected a wig out of the second suitcase. It was made of real hair and was nearly the same color as her dark brows. It took her two tries to get it on. Once it was secure she put on the hijab. The effect was amazing. Other than her height she looked like most Afghan women. At least until you looked her dead in the face. The dark hair didn't detract from her beauty. If anything it made her look exotic and more alluring.

"This won't work. You won't blend. You are too beautiful. Make sure you keep your head down and don't look anyone in the eye. I hope you can act shy and unassuming or you are going to be in a world of hurt."

"Don't worry about me Marine. I've got this."

They left the room and returned to the ready room and an unnatural hush fell over the room when everyone got a look a Kris dressed like a woman. Most of them had never seen her out of uniform or even in civilian clothes since her change. Javier snapped a picture of her with his camera but didn't get a really good look at her until he looked directly at her. Then he dropped the camera with a 'Madre de Dios!' The rest of the team had come in to speak with Kris before she left. They had just been informed of her mission. Reineke looked her over for a minute then stepped out of the room. Gentry walked over to adjust her wig a bit and show her where to glue it down. Tomball whistled and shook his head.

"Man Captain. You look like a woman. Not used to that!" He chuckled.

The rest of the men looked on thoughtfully. Miller stood with his arms crossed and an inscrutable expression next to Jeffries. Kris looked at each one of them. It was strange going off without her team. Reineke came back in after a few minutes with a wrapped parcel. Kris raised an eyebrow and then opened it up. Some make up and two bras inside in her cup size. They even looked new. She looked at them with a strange choking feeling in her chest before she looked at him again. Screw protocol. She grabbed the older man and pulled him into a hard hug. He hugged her back just as hard. Next thing every member of the team came up and pulled Kris into a hug. Javier was near the last and held on the longest. When he pulled away there were tears in his eyes. He turned to Chambers.

"You let anything happen to her and what we pulled you out of two years ago will look like a holiday at the beach. That is our team leader and we want her back exactly like you took her."

Chambers nodded in sober acknowledgement of the feeling in the room. Justin held back and tossed his head unperceptively toward Stirling. Kris walked over to him and he held her close. One hand against the back of her head and the other firmly on her middle back cradling her. He rocked back and forth looking up at the ceiling trying to hold it together. He never had a problem sending Kris into the field before, but he shared her gut feeling that something was off here. They pulled away and Kris faced Justin. She walked right into his arms, and he pulled her in for a long thorough kiss. It went on forever. Some of the guys started shifting feet and looking around. She pulled back and he let her go.

"Watch your six."

Miller who was still looking at her from his spot on the wall walked up. The quiet Marine hadn't said anything or tried to interfere with the goodbyes. He pulled Kris into a hug which surprised her. Then he put his mouth to her ear. He whispered so lightly she almost couldn't hear with the ambient noise in the room.

"Don't trust them. They are dirty. The older guy hates you and wants you dead. The younger is only out for himself. They are not team players." He pulled back and said louder. "Take care of my sister. You promised to teach me how to evade an unbreakable hold."

Kris smiled at him fondly. She was really starting to like this kid.

"As soon as I get back we'll work on that."

Miller didn't look at her while she was speaking but at Briggs. His look darkened with what he saw in the older man. He took a step forward and Kris forestalled him.

"I already got this Marine. Stand down."

Miller immediately backed off and went to stand next to Justin. Kris picked up the bag.

"Nunez take care of my men. I want a full eval of their missions when I get back."

"You got it Kris." He reached out for her hand not feeling close enough to offer her a hug. Kris pulled him into a one armed guy hug and slapped him on the back. Kris walked to the door followed by Chambers and Briggs and exited. The room grew loud as everyone began to speak to one another and Justin and Nathan followed the others out. They watched them enter the Humvee and close the doors. It pulled away and they watched until it disappeared from view.

Chapter Twenty Seven

Kris walked around the marketplace looking at various items. She had purchased a hairbrush, toothbrush, and toothpaste. She also purchased several toiletry items that were traditional items for women to have. She inquired at several stalls asking if they knew of anyone looking for a cleaning woman or someone to attend to children as she needed work. Everyone turned her away. She had been coming to the market twice a week for the last two weeks establishing her cover. She was posing as a widow with two children looking for work. Her back story was that she was staying with her sister and her sister's family. She continued shopping. She stopped at a food vendor and bought a kabab and a cup of strong coffee. Then bought several fruits. As she rounded a corner several large men caught sight of her. She paused wary and continued looking pretending to ignore them but keeping them in her periphery. They made their way toward her and cornered her next to the stall.

"You are looking for work, yes?"

"No. I am shopping for my family."

The man who spoke looked back at a stall out of her vision and confirmed with the owner she was the woman looking for work that had inquired.

"You asked for work at several stalls."

"I am a respectable woman. I am a widow with two small children. I do not work for men."

"Our employer is looking for a cleaning woman to tend to his family's home. It is a respectable job. You will come with us and he will give you work."

"If he is respectable why are his men finding his family cleaning women?"

Kris kept just enough reticence and timidity in her voice to lend credence to her fearful demeanor.

"The family is wealthy and very private. They do not come into the market. We bring workers to them and they hire or not."

"Where is this place? Do they live in town?"

"No. It is in the mountains."

"I cannot work that far. I have to care for my children. Thank you. Excuse me."

She tried to move past them and they impeded her progress. They crowded her in and she looked around as if for help. All of the market vendors moved away and disappeared. They knew better than to interfere. One of the men grabbed her forearm and pulled her toward a waiting truck.

"It is a good job with a respectable family. They will pay you well and whoever has your children now can watch them until we can return you next week. You will make enough to support them. Get in the truck."

The one doing all the talking she recognized from her files as a low level El Moufas enforcer. He was used on household security. He wasn't particularly smart but he was very observant and knew how to keep the men in line. He'd been with the group over five years. A record for them. They changed men often to keep anyone from gaining too much information or power. Wouldn't do to have someone think they could take over. He knew how to do his job and stay out of the way. Valuable in an errand boy. She lucked out. One risk of her blind entry was getting noticed by someone else and ending up having to maneuver her way out of a situation and avoid detection. Luck was with her that El Moufas was here looking and not some other warlord or chieftain.

She kept her face impassive but still fearful as she resisted them pulling her into the truck. She let them overpower her and push her inside. Two men got in beside her and pressed her tightly up against the driver while the others got in the back. The truck sped off out of town. Kris watched the roads and memorized her location so she could lead her team back but then the man next to the door pulled a black hood from the floor and slammed it over her head. She cried out as if in fright and struggled. They told her to keep quiet. It was only a precaution. The family preferred their privacy. She would be able to take the hood off once they got to the compound as long as she didn't struggle.

She stayed still and shook slightly as if she were terrified. She continued to monitor the turns and lengths of time to pinpoint the location. After about two hours they arrived at their destination. She memorized the maps of the region, and she had a pretty good idea of exactly where they were. She knew that Amir had a house in the mountains but no idea where. This must be it. The hood came off right as the truck came to a halt. Her hair was mussed but luckily she had glued down the wig and it was still tight to her head. She pulled her hajib to cover her hair fully and adjusted it to cover her forehead and ears like a proper Muslim women of good family.

She was instructed to follow the men into the house as she took note of all the windows and exits. She noted the corridors and the doorways to memorize the layout. It was a traditional house. The compound had high walls surrounding and two doors; one on the west side and one on the south with the main gate to the east. It was a good set up with no blind areas and the main egress points not inhibited by the rising or setting sun. Only one road in or out and the mountains to the back. It was heavily fortified with men on the walls, in the compound and in the courtyard; all heavily armed.

She continued into the house until she was ushered into a large room with comfortable furniture and a large desk. She stood in front of the desk with her head down in supplication and pretended to be fearful. A handsome trim man in his mid-fifties with dark neat hair and a nicely barbered beard came in. Aziz El Moufas always took care of himself. No grey to mar his hair and no wrinkles to indicate his age. He walked around her several times looking her up and down as she kept her eyes on the floor. It was hard to keep emotion out of them.

For the first time in twenty years, she was in the same room with the monster she had vowed to kill. It took all her training and patience to stand there and not snap his neck. She had to remember the end game. She needed him alive. For now.

"You are a cleaning woman."

She glanced up very quickly at his face then back to the floor. "Yes."

"Good we need a cleaning woman. Ours keep having problems with the work."

She stood still as he continued to circle her.

"You have experience?"

"Yes."

"What are you called?"

"Fatima."

"Good. We are a simple household. We do not entertain as my family prefers our privacy. You will be expected to see to your duties quickly and quietly. Do not go anywhere but where you are told. Stay away from the men. Use your manners and we will get along fine. The wage is 500 Afghani for the week. Do well and you may be kept on for longer. If you disobey you will be punished by having to work for the men. They do not need a cleaning woman-just a woman will do. Do you understand?"

"Yes Seydi."

"Good." He addressed a young man at the door. "Take her to the kitchen and get her started. The cook will show her where she is to sleep." He watched her as the man took her away with a measured look. He had a small smile turning up the sides of his mouth as if he was amused. He signaled to the remaining men to exit as he sat behind his desk. His smile grew wider as he sat with his elbows on the chair's arm rests and his hands steepled in front of him.

Kris's days took on the same basic routine. She got up before dawn, ate, cleaned, helped with laundry, ate again, and slept. She was never left alone in a room, so she had to work quickly and efficiently. After the first week she was informed she would be kept on another week. She acted grateful and kept her head down. She was paid at the end of each week. The wages were less than half of the minimum wage. She hid the wages in her belongings. She might need it to bribe someone later.

Chambers cornered her one day to check on her progress. She angrily informed him to stay away from her before he blew her cover. He told her he didn't trust Briggs so he brought someone local in. Someone who could give them a hand if everything went sideways. He didn't give her a name or description. He was nervous and jumpy. Something was off with him. He said he couldn't reach Briggs. He was out of contact. He didn't like it. He was going to scout on his own. For her to be alert and keep watch. He would try to signal her if he got any intel. She didn't feel confident that he or whoever he pulled in was going to be of any help.

Four more weeks passed. She kept her eyes open and her mouth shut. No intel was left out where she could get to it, and she wasn't allowed in areas where it was likely to be. She listened to the gossip of the men. Nothing out of the ordinary. A break came while she was cleaning the office one afternoon and Aziz was on a phone call. It was in Farsi which meant he was speaking with one of his brothers. It appeared one or more of them was planning a trip to visit. She listened intently for the dates and any other information she could gather. She started to leave the room after cleaning when Aziz called her over. He spoke in Farsi. She stayed still with her eyes on the ground. He spoke to her further. She didn't respond. He came up behind her and right in her ear raised his voice and said, "Well?"

She jumped as if startled and stood silently.

"Are you going to answer me Fatima?"

"Za pe poe na shum Seydi."

"Do you not?"

"No Seydi. I do not understand."

"I asked you if you are happy in my employ?"

"Yes Seydi. It is a good job."

"You do not miss your children?"

"Yes Seydi. Very much. They are cared for by my sister. They will not miss me. They are small. The money I earn will help us for many months. I do more for them here working, then in my sister's home taking care of my boys and her girl. Here I can provide much more."

"If you like, my men can escort you back to town so you can bring your pay to your sister."

Kris looked up with wide amazed tearful eyes. "Oh Seydi, I would be so grateful. I miss my boys and they must be wondering what happened to their mother. And the money will help my sister with the extra mouths to feed."

"We shall arrange it soon."

"Dera Manana." Kris fell to her knees and kissed his shoe. It was hard playing the subservient female. She rose and tidied her head covering. It took all of her will to keep her head down without harming him.

"You may go."

She left the room and a man sitting in a highbacked chair in the corner out of sight rose and stood in front of the desk. He looked like Aziz but considerably more worn and older.

"I told you Amir, she does not speak it."

"Hmm. Maybe. I believe she understands all too well." He indicated the door and followed behind the younger man. They moved into the adjacent room where several men were standing and sitting. Amir addressed a western man in khaki shirt and pants with a kerchief around his neck.

"Well, my friend, it seems as if you are mistaken. She did not understand a word of what was said."

The man adjusted the red kerchief around his neck and said in English "I doubt that, Amir. She was too smug- too certain."

"What new information do you bring me Briggs? Surely you have something to come all this way."

"I brought you Cole. That was the deal. You pay me the bounty on her head plus my usual fee and I deliver Cole."

"My men found this woman in the bazaar. How do you claim to have brought her?"

"I pulled her into this op and placed her in the bazaar for your men to find. I paid the spice stall owner to make her known to your men so they would bring her here. I did this. I made it so you finally have Cole."

"Hmmm. We seem to differ in opinion in this."

The man's face grew red which lowered the contrast between his pale lower face and sunburned nose and forehead.

"Listen Amir, we had a deal! I deliver Cole- you pay me. I have done my part now it's time for you to pay up."

"I would be very careful of my tone if I were you Briggs. You are dangerously close to becoming insulting."

"Don't give me that Amir! Like I am one of your lackeys. I have kept your family one step ahead of the American authorities for the last twenty years! Your organization would have finished years ago if not for me. All I want is what I am due. Cole is the last loose end. And she is in your kitchen as we speak. She is in possession of all your trade routes and organizational structure. She's responsible for all the close calls you've had in the last ten years. Torture the information out of her."

"Marines of her ilk do not break Briggs."

"Then use her weakness. Amalia. No way your niece is dead if she was willing to go to prison rather than give up any information she has. She's still protecting her. Which means she's still alive. Cole wouldn't care about holding on to it if she wasn't."

"I pray you are correct. We shall see. We will have your money for you. I will give you directions on where to pick it up. By then we will have Cole in chains and hopefully some of the answers we seek."

"I will be expecting your call." Briggs nodded to the brothers and left.

"Are you really going to pay him Amir, or are we just going to kill him?"

Amir leveled his younger brother with a hard stare.

"Briggs will be more valuable to us alive. If he is found dead, there will be an investigation. Alive they will be too busy hunting him down and making him pay for his treason to bother with us. Ma ta ghwag sha roor, chess sometimes requires playing pawns rather than sacrificing them. If it gains us Amalia all the better. She is the only child in our family. She is the heir. Once she is back in our fold we can undo your rash actions. Her marriage to the Gharghashti tribe heir will ensure our future. With access to their trade routes, we can substantially compound our profits and eliminate our risks."

"Our trade routes are successful now. Why change them?"

"The only constant in the world is change brother. We have stayed out of sight because we are not predictable, nor do we allow those that would subvert our efforts to catch us staying still too long. Briggs is arrogant and self-important. He is not the reason we have kept ahead of our enemies. We do so because we do not allow the sand to settle under our feet. We are smarter and more cunning. They will be chasing us for many years to come. Let us dine. I would like to discuss how we will torture the information out of that Marine on a full stomach."

Kris ate dinner in the kitchen with the other servants. The last few weeks since her conversation with Aziz went slowly. She wasn't taken to her 'children.' She hoped she would be taken back to the village she started in so she could contact the team, but there was always an excuse as to why she couldn't leave. She went over the conversation with Aziz. Every time Aziz opened his mouth her dick twitched. Even from the first moment she was brought in he seemed to be amused by his own private joke. He seemed more gleeful every interaction they had. Which told her- her cover was blown. Probably had been from the get-go. Which meant her list of five possible options for who was responsible for all the leaked plans, failed missions and blown intel just got shortened to one. Knowing that meant her being here was not part of the JSOC plan but part of El Moufas' plan.

She got up and returned to the stove to refill her plate after everyone had served themselves. She figured her time was up based on the look on Aziz' face and she was going to face what was next with a full belly. Chances are it would be the last food she would get for a while. She had barely dug into the second plate when four armed men came into the room. Chambers was one of them. They looked right at her. One motioned with his weapon for her to get up. Everyone in the room looked scared. She got up and backed away. Two of the men moved in behind her.

She started to go with them quietly, but her pride wouldn't let her surrender without a fight. They grabbed her arms and she flipped back pulling them into each other knocking one completely unconscious. The second she grabbed by the throat and bent down throwing her shoulder into his gut propelling him across the room to slam into the wall. Chambers covered her from the door staying far away. The fourth was bolder. He walked straight up to Kris and put his Glock right to her forehead. She spread her arms wide to show she wasn't going to challenge him. She made her point. She still had a mission which would be difficult to complete going in with a bullet wound. The two she knocked out got to their feet slowly.

The rest of the room was shocked and wide eyed at her complete change of both demeanor and skillset. The women were huddled in the corner crying. The two armed men still standing pushed her hard through the door. Chambers tried to subdue the man with the gun and get it so Kris could flee. He shouted at her to run. She wouldn't and tried to get around, but the gunman fired on Chambers. The other two went after him, beating the shit out of him. He was down and they left him in a heap on the floor knowing he wasn't going anywhere.

They repeatedly shoved her down the hallway. She walked into the family parlor but before she could get a good look at who was in the room she was blasted from behind and crumpled on the floor as the world went black.

When Kris came to, she was seated in a dim room tied to a chair. Her head lolled as she tried to get her bearings. She blinked several times and finally got the room to focus. She wasn't in the house. It looked like she was in a cave. The floor and walls were rough and in heavy shadow. Two flood lights on tripods in each corner lit the room and a table that was filled with maps and papers. Two men stood talking over it and she took the time to examine the room. The only point of egress was to her left. A narrow corridor that was dark, so it was either part of a passage or it was dark outside. There was a video camera on a tripod directly opposite her with a hard wooden chair and monitor on a table right next to it. There were crates stacked just behind her to the left of the corridor. RPGs and launchers. To the right the far side of the cave held more crates with Russian words. Kris recognized the boxes to be grenades and ground mines. Those could come in handy.

She must have made a sound as the two men turned and looked to see her examining the room. They made no attempt to stop her. Amir walked to stand by the camera and turned it on to record. He addressed her in Farsi.

"What is your name?"

Kris sat completely immobile. He walked up to her and struck her hard across the cheek.

"What is your name?"

This went on for roughly half an hour. Kris's face felt like it was ready to explode but she did not answer him.

He switched to Pashtu.

"What is your name?"

Kris groaned hard and hung her head. He yanked her up by her hair and hit her again.

"What is your name?"

Kris tried to swallow, but couldn't. "Fa... Fatima."

"What is your name?" He hit her several more times and she blubbered audibly. Tears poured down her face mixing with the blood that was coming from her nose.

"Fatima."

"Your name is Cole. Kristian Cole. You are a Marine."

"I am Fatima. Please don't hurt me. Please. I don't know...."

"Do not insult us. We know who you are."

Amir continued to hit her about the head. The second man she didn't recognize right away then he picked up what appeared to be a whip. That's when she knew it was Farouk. He had a liking for whipping. She had seen evidence of several former associates who had been flayed alive by him over the years. She heard the whip before she felt it and screamed as it bit into her back. It didn't hurt as bad as she feared. He must have been plying it. Yet she screamed like it was killing her. Better for them not to know she had a very high pain tolerance. She could use that to her advantage. Every time the sound of the whip came she prepared to scream. Her cries echoed through the cave and filled the room. After two more hits her head fell forward and stopped moving. He stuck her two more times before his brother called him off. They reconvened at the table while she looked over the room under her lashes. If she learned anything about the brothers is that they had a very low opinion about women. They considered them weak and inferior. They did not expect her be their equal. They knew she was a Marine and that she had been trained in counterintelligence and counterinterrogation yet still they believed her weak. She would use that against them. Lull them into a false sense of security.

The next several days took on took on a sameness. They would queue up the camera and begin. Beatings and whippings with endless questions. They would continue to talk amongst themselves when she appeared senseless. They talked about locations, shipments, and routes. She sat and she listened filing all the information away. One day a third man entered, Saiyid. He brought with him another smaller old man. The man brought over a small table and opened a leather bag. She recognized him as Zahid Orakzai a professional torturer. She'd seen many examples of his work over the years. Great.

They asked her to sign a confession. She knew exactly why. They told her once she did the pain would stop. She grabbed the pen with her left hand and wrote a pithy and insulting phrase on the page. They took the paper away and she found her left hand looped with a rope and tied down to the arm of the chair they had her tied to. Her right arm was wrenched behind her as the torturer systematically broke the fingers on her left hand. She screamed and screamed. For several hours as he continued. After her head lolled to her chest the torturer broke one more finger just to verify, she was out.

She sat very still so that he would not know she was still conscious. He walked around her. He leaned down as if to check on her and whispered in her ear.

"My dear I have been doing this for many years, longer than you have been alive. You are quite simply the best I have come across. I am sorry I have to cause you pain. I hope that whatever the reason is that you are here you complete your task so you can go home."

He walked around her. Checking her bonds.

"I never wanted this. I was a doctor. Dedicated to easing pain. They took my family. I had no choice. But they killed them anyway. I could not go back after. My path was set. Do not let what has been done to you take you down the wrong path. Learn from an old man's mistakes."

She nodded infinitesimally. He saw.

The others nodded to him, and he left. Kris took a long deep breath but very slowly inhaled and exhaled so the brothers would not hear her. She grits her teeth as the pain in her hand swamped her and actually did blacken her vision for a moment. She would not give into it. She pushed through and pulled herself back.

They spoke and argued for the remainder of the evening. Constantly refining their plan for the coming weeks. What they were shipping and where. Kris knew one thing. They were not planning on letting her live if they were discussing everything so openly in front of her. Even if they didn't know she could understand them. Maybe they did. She didn't know what Briggs had told them. If they knew then they weren't intending on her leaving alive. She slept when she could. The brothers would alternate questioning her making it so she was not left alone for long.

The next few days brought more people into the cave. Two men she didn't know followed by Aziz and Briggs. One of the men looked vaguely familiar. Like Kris had seen him before but couldn't place him. Kris had been sitting with her head down letting the blood from her nose and the cut on her eye to drip in her lap. She hated the feeling of it running down her face. After the first beating they threw a bucket of water on her to rinse her off. It felt good to be rinsed. She gasped and struggled. They continued to bombard her with more questions. The torturer came back in and she got to experience being waterboarded. They kept asking questions she didn't answer. The only vocalizations they got from her were screams. She screamed loud and long. Each one more intense than the last.

Briggs seemed a bit put off by her condition. Strange. The prick hated her and was glad to turn her over to them but seemed horrified by what they had done to her. Aziz was gleeful. The more she screamed the happier he became. She guessed it was because he believed her near breaking. She made sure to beg and plead. Also, to cry. Briggs seemed uncomfortable. I think it may have occurred to him that he could have been in that chair just as easily. The brothers thanked him for his assistance and expressed their sorrow that their long partnership was ending. Two men grabbed several containers that she knew were filled with money and brought them out of the cave to a waiting truck. She looked up at Briggs with udder loathing.

"There is no place on this Earth you will hide I will not find you."

He smirked. "You'll be dead by sundown and won't be my problem anymore. Semper Fi Bitch." He left with the men and she heard the truck start and pull away. The familiar man left as well.

Aziz walked around her several times slowly circling her chair. Her ass was very numb from being strapped to it for the last three days. They only untied her every few days to clean up the mess of urine, blood and excrement. He continued to circle with a little half smile on his face.

"I amuse you Aziz?"

He smiled at the tone in Kris's voice.

"Oh yes. It has been wonderful seeing you beg and plead. You will do more before we are through with you. Oh yes. But first you will eat. You must keep your strength up." He signaled to someone out of her line of sight. A young man stood in front of her with a plate. She glared at Aziz and didn't pay him much mind. She looked at the food then looked at the young man holding the plate. It was Fazil.

Chapter Twenty Eight

A routine patrol came in at 1530 carrying a wounded man they'd found out in the desert about two kilometers from the base. He was alone and on foot. The tracks showed that he had walked and sometimes crawled alone. No vehicle tracks indicated he was dumped there. With his dark hair and dark skin they originally thought he was a local. He was in Eastern clothing but the man appeared to be Western and his speech proclaimed him American. He was badly messed up; covered in blood from multiple wounds. Three bullet wounds, four broken ribs, a punctured lung, broken arm and leg and massive head trauma. He was moaning and speaking incoherently on the ride in. When they got him into medical and started assessing his wounds he came around and started ranting and thrashing. The corpsman where trying to get through to him.

"Sir you are at United States Marine Corps Camp Delta and we are going to take care of you. You need to calm down so we can assess the damage."

"You need to tell them! She's been made. They know who she is. You have to get her out. They'll kill her."

The man thrashed some more until he seized and all the monitors they just got attached to him went berserk. The team worked like mad to get him back. They fought hard but it was a losing battle. The damage was too bad. They continued to work but after about twenty minutes they had to call it. He was gone.

The doctor documented all the information from the wounds and everything the man said in the chart while they gave the information to Security Forces to run the prints. Strangely the scan pulled up nothing. The guy had what was to their trained eye a US military themed tattoo on his shoulder that had been removed and vaccination scars that were consistent with military requirements for overseas deployed troops. That he wasn't in the system didn't make sense. They finished the report and submitted the paperwork listing him as a John Doe and putting him on ice in the freezer unit to store the dead.

***

Justin sat on a crate looking at the area he and Kris sparred at. He had his MP3 player listening to some music. It had been weeks since Kris left and there was no word. He knew this kind of deep cover assignment wouldn't give her many opportunities to contact if any, but his gut told him something was off. Javier came over holding a couple of bottles of water, handing one to Justin.

"Why are you listening to your breakup music? C'mon man. Don't do this to yourself. She's going to contact us soon. I know it."

Justin drank from the bottle and said nothing. The song continued.

"Why are you listening to this sad stuff man? It's gonna mess with your head."

Justin smiled. "You ever really listened to the words in this song? It's not sad; it's actually very poignant for me."

They continued to listen to Amber Run singing about finding love where it wasn't supposed to be and Javier grunted.

"Hmm. I guess I never listened before. That song sounds like it was written about your feelings for Kris! No wonder you played it so much."

Justin handed Javier a package that had just arrived for Kris. It was the calendar. Previously it had been the Men of MARSOC calendar. The organizers changed it to The Magnificent MARSOC calendar out of deference for Kris. Javier whistled and smiled. Wow they were a bunch of sexy beasts. He flipped to February and laughed. The picture of Justin and Kris graced the top spot as the sexual tension from the lovers just about leap from the page.

"You hear anything new?"

"No man I just came from the Comm and nothing. It's like she vanished."

"No way. If something happened to her, I'd feel it. I also know she would never let us sit and spin like this either. If there was any way to signal us even with a 'stand by' she'd do it. I don't like this. I'm going to talk to the Colonel. See if anything's come down."

The two men left the area and walked over to Stirling's office. They went in and he looked up from his desk. He'd been going over intel and calling anyone and everyone that may have heard anything. And nothing.

"I have nothing new to tell you Justin."

Justin closed both the doors to the office and locked the inner door.

"No Sir, but I have a lot to tell you. Javier, there are some things you need to know. Kris only held this information to protect your family and for no other reason. We clear?"

Javier nodded his face becoming hard with anticipation of what Justin was about to say.

"This is not a regular JSOC mission. Kris was pulled into an op with the CIA in order to stay out of Leavenworth. They were going to charge her with treason and collusion with an enemy combatant."

Javier sat there with a bemused expression before he burst out laughing. He was rolling with tears in his eyes. After a minute he stopped and quipped, "Geez man, you almost had me. C'mon! What's really...."

He took a look at the hard somber looks on the two men's faces and realized this was no joke.

"What are you talking about man? Kris is no traitor! And she'd never collude with anyone!"

"Kris was charged with aiding and abetting and falsifying government documents. As well as withholding information from the United States Government about a terrorist organization operating on US soil. She's guilty Javi. She's done that and more. But not for what they think. Kris ever talk to you about her sister?"

"Emily? No man, just that she was adopted when they were twelve or so and that she ran off after their mom died. I know she keeps in contact but they aren't close."

"That's actually incorrect. They are incredibly close. So much so they have stayed deliberately apart for over ten years. They've kept apart to protect one another. Javi before Kris and her mom adopted Emily her name was Amalia El Moufas."

Javier sat stunned. He knew exactly who she was as did everyone in Spec Ops. Intel was constantly pulling up tidbits on nefarious people and groups trying to locate Aziz El Moufas' missing daughter. Information for anything to do with her was worth a fortune. Chatter was constantly being intercepted by communications about people who knew people who knew information that would pay.

Justin went to tell both Nathan and Javier how Kris and Jenna worked to hide and build a plausible background for Emily and why Kris really joined the Corps. He explained why she studied all the martial arts disciplines, why she studied language, and tactics. How she learned to become a sniper before she was old enough to drive. The survivalists skills, Parkour, learning all aspects of mechanics, computers, counterintelligence, camouflage, even cooking was all to survive against an all-out constant war against terrorists. How she rose through the ranks for the sole purpose of getting right to where she was today in order to get into position to finally use all the information and knowledge she gathered in order to take them out.

He gave Nathan information that Kris had left out such as the knowledge that Jenna was murdered. The older man staggered at that and sank to his knees on the floor. Kris and Emily didn't confirm that for more than six years after it happened, but they suspected which put them to employ their exit strategy. It was like losing Jenna all over again. It also surged a strong measure of fear for their daughter as he knew the men she was facing, and the will Kris employed to protect those she loved. He knew she would never stop and never give in until her family was safe.

That now included Nathan, Justin, Javier, and the rest of the team and their families. She had stayed a lone wolf for a long time, but that was no longer the case, and she would not give up or give in if it meant protecting them. Which also meant if she had an out, she wouldn't take it to save herself if it meant keeping them in danger.

Javier had a lot of questions. Over the next hour he grilled Justin for every bit of information he could get. Javier was good at extrapolating patterns out of seemingly unrelated pieces. He used the information that they had on file with what Justin filled in. Kris had studied her adversary well. They decided to take this to SOC so Javier could pull up some data. Justin hugged the man in both apology and thanks for his understanding and his steadfast loyalty to Kris. He returned the embrace hard and fast in order to get to work. They had a friend to save. Javier went into intelligence to gather a couple of people and Justin and Nathan to communications.

Several hours later Javier came up for air with an excited look on his face.

"I've been going over the transmissions from several bases over the last few days added in to chatter from several agencies and it appears there is activity in the mountains about 10 clicks from here. The area is sparsely populated by migrant tribes that roam the area. No permanent settlements and they use natural and manmade caves as shelter. It has become popular with smugglers and weapons dealers because it is heavily protected by topography and satellites can't get good readings in there. According to the intel that area is in the Gharghashti tribe control and they are known to support El Moufas."

Javier spent the next several days working with SOC trying to get any plausible intel to show that is where El Moufas was operating. They needed that if they were going to be able to schedule an op to go in.

Justin was in and out working with the teams and SOC to verify the identity of whoever was working in those mountains. He was sitting at the console logged into his system when the icon signaling an incoming video message popped up. He sighed when he saw the address it was coming from.

"Hey Mel. What's going on?"

"Justin you are avoiding me. Don't deny it. Kris hasn't answered and you sign off as soon as I connect. What is going on?!"

"We are not avoiding you Mel. Kris isn't here. She's still on a JSOC mission. I know you are calling for an update and I don't have anything for you. We don't have anything."

"Justin, she's been gone for weeks. She hasn't contacted at all?"

"It's deep cover Mel. She can't. I don't have anything for you. I'm sorry."

"Are you ok? Justin I can see by the look on your face you are not good. Talk to me!"

"Mel, it's not that I don't want to; I can't. I don't want to leave you hanging- that's not my intent but I can't really talk right now."

He could see the stress on her face and the worry. He knew she needed to talk. Javi called Justin from the other side of the room and he looked around for someone to talk to her. His eye's clapped on someone approaching and he grabbed the Marine and pushed him into the chair.

"Here talk to her for a minute. I'll be back."

Noah Miller sat looking at the woman on the screen. She was the most beautiful woman he'd ever seen. She looked at him curiously.

"Hi."

"Um hi. I am Sergeant Noah Miller."

"I'm Mel. You on the teams?"

"Um yes. Alpha team. EOD."

"So you work with Kris!"

"Yes. Captain Cole is my team leader."

"Do you know anything about where she is and when she's getting back?"

"Um no. I haven't been read into her mission so I don't have that information."

Mel looked amused. "Noah, you don't have to be so formal. There isn't a test. Can you just talk to me? I hate not knowing where Kris is and what's going on. I know you guys can't really talk about what you are doing, but not knowing where she is it's so hard. I get scared when I can't see her. Seeing Justin so stressed out and upset makes it worse. He tries to hide it, but he really can't hide it from me. I know him too well."

"He is worried. And scared but he won't admit this to anyone or himself. He doesn't like it when he can't see her either. He's trying to believe she is fine and she's doing what she is trained for. But he can't help but think something is wrong because she hasn't been in contact. All of us are."

"You sound like you care for her? A bit of a crush there Noah?" Mel said teasingly.

"She's my sister."

Mel could see he meant exactly that. That made her like him instantly.

They sat and talked for almost an hour before someone called to Noah.

"Listen I have to go now."

"Can I call you? I really want to talk to you again. Is that ok?"

"Mel, I'd like that very, very much."

He could see the sincerity on her face and he smiled. Her breath stopped in her chest at the sheer beauty of his face lit up. She gave him all her contact information. He sent her an email while they were chatting and she answered to confirm. He didn't want to disconnect. The Major called him again, and he turned to acknowledge the man.

"I have to go. I will call you tomorrow-same time?"

"I can't wait. Bye Noah."

"Bye Mel."

Noah sat a moment thinking about her. She was beautiful and kind. Sweet and smart. He moved quickly to the Major to see what he needed.

"Sorry about that Miller. I didn't mean to dump that on you. I just can't talk to her right now."

"I understand Sir. I don't mind. She's really great. Who is she?"

"She's Kris's ex-wife."

Noah was a little alarmed at that. That is not the vibe he got from Mel. He would have sworn she was Kris or Justin's sister.

"Will the Captain be mad I am talking to her? I really want to talk to her again."

"No Miller, Kris wouldn't mind. She likes you. And Mel can take care of herself. She doesn't answer to Kris or vice versa."

"Good."

Justin looked at the younger man and saw he was looking like a man in pursuit. Well that would keep Mel busy.

Over the next couple of days all hands were on deck looking for any intel that pointed to Kris. The teams were due to rotate back to the states in two days. No one said anything, but there was no way in hell anyone was leaving without her. No one packed and if they were ordered, there would be a mutiny. Colonel Stirling met with General Adams to discuss the situation.

"Good to see you Sir."

"Sit down Nate."

The General picked up several files and booted up his computer.

"You and your men are due to head out Tuesday?"

"About that Sir. I am going to extend the rotation for Alpha and Bravo as well as myself."

"Extend?"

"Yes Sir. There is no way those men are leaving without Kris Sir. Nor will I. I have the capability to extend the mission for due cause for up to three months and I am exercising that right. I am not leaving my daughter behind Sir. Her men haven't said anything, but I tell you if you suggest they leave they will have something to say."

"Well then. Let's see what that is."

Adams gathered his paperwork and put on his lid gesturing to Nathan to precede him out of the door. They moved into the Comm and he called the teams to assemble. They gathered with a Corporal leaving to get the few members not in the room. Gentry came in from the showers and Tomball from the mess hall. The General stood in front and addressed the group.

"The mission parameters have been met; Alpha and Bravo pack up. Transport leaves in 38 hours."

No one made any move to leave. And the mutinous looks on the faces of the men answered for him. They wouldn't leave without a fight.

Justin stood and addressed the General.
"Permission to speak, Sir?" Once the General nodded his ascent he continued.

"I think I can speak for all the men here Sir, but if any of you disagree please speak up, but it will be a cold day in hell before we leave without Captain Cole. We've spent the last thousand man hours trying to locate where she could be and we suspect she is in the mountain region roughly ten clicks from here. There has been activity in that region and we believe that is where El Moufas is hiding. I believe with a few more days intel and some scouting missions we can determine if that is indeed where she is and we can plan an op to infiltrate the area."

Gentry stood and spoke next. "We will not leave here without her Sir. If that means we all go AWOL then so be it." He sat down. Most of the men nodded their agreement.

The General looked around the room. "Anyone here ready to pack up and go?"

No one responded. The looks ranged from a plain no to you've got to be kidding. He turned to Stirling.

"Ok Nate. You got your extension. 90 days. Find something. After that it is out of my hands and you and your men will be stateside." He looked over the relieved faces of the men and the determination to make sure they were able to get it done. They all stood and saluted the General as he exited the room.

Justin crossed over to Nate and hugged the older man. The men were doing the same and congratulating themselves for getting the extension.

"Alright. Everyone listen up. This time is going to go fast. We need to make the most of it. 'A' games all of you. Bring my little girl home!" To this the men let out a loud cheer. They dispersed pretty quick and made a concentrated effort to meet the deadline. No one wanted to say what would happen if they couldn't.

Noah went to the bank of computers and pulled up his login information. Out of the corner of his eye Justin could see Mel on the screen. Noah and Mel had talked every night. He couldn't imagine what they were talking about. Justin made a mental note to keep an eye on that. The look on Noah's face was not that of a Marine just keeping a friend in the loop.

"Justin you come with me. I am going to place a video call stateside. I am not happy that we've been largely ignored by NCIS. That worries me."

The two men left to the Comm and had communications contact the field office in Virginia that Booker was attached to. They had to wait nearly an hour, but Booker finally got on the line.

"Sorry gentlemen. I was on with SECNAV. We have a nightmare here. Ok this is what we know. On Captain Cole's advice we came back to investigate the claims made by Briggs. We found her contact. Retired Justice Deputy Division Chief Martin Banning. He was in charge of Amalia El Moufas' case. He confirmed that he got official documentation and records for a minor child Emily Cole. He actually had several identities for her over the years. He refused to give over the other names she has posed under. Only the one we inquired with. He confirmed he provided the Cole's with a birth certificate, school records, social security numbers, and medical records; any normal documentation that was necessary for a person. He confirmed she has lived under several identities and is currently under another one that he worked with Kris and Emily to protect her. Her death however he was not part of. Though he did assign a new identity to them at that time.

He investigated Amalia's death and using her original documentation confirmed that the body found was that of Amalia El Moufas. The body was unrecognizable but the dental records matched. He also confirmed that Kris has intel that she got from the inside of El Moufas that has details of the organization from the ground up. She wouldn't turn it over with the mole still in play because she knew it was disappear. She worked with Banning to 'leak' pieces to various agencies to see what made it up the chain and what disappeared to find where the leak was. They both knew it was very high up, but couldn't trace it back. So she held onto it. According to Banning what she has in her possession will show exactly where and how they operate as well as a comprehensive listing of every member of the organization. I don't suppose she gave either of you this intel before she left?"

"No nothing. But if I know Kris she has a failsafe and if anything happens to her she'll have a way to get it to someone who can act on it."

"Dammit. I was hoping you'd tell me she turned it over but it has a passcode to break. I have a team that could handle that on standby."

"What is the nightmare you referred to? Is it about Kris?"

"Yes and no. Briggs. I contacted the region chief here for a meet and was told the happy news. Briggs has been suspended."

"Because of trying to blackmailing a Marine?"

"No, because they suspected him of treason. So they suspended under full investigation six months ago."

The look of horror on the two men's faces needed no words. They all knew what that meant.

"They followed him; wanted to see what he was up to. So they held off grabbing him. When he met with us they were in a 'watch and see' phase. They didn't read us in. So we had no idea he was working outside the lines. Once he got over there he disappeared. He fell off the radar about ten seconds after leaving the base. He and Chambers are gone."

Justin walked closer to the screen. "So those bastards knew he was unsanctioned and let him leave the country? They suspected him and just let him go? They let him run this op and take my wife so they could what? Get actionable intel? If they suspected he was working with El Moufas and let him continue the operation..... They threw my wife to the wolves!" He slammed his fist on the console so hard it broke the shelf holding the keyboards which clattered loudly to the ground.

Nathan put a hand on Justin's shoulder to calm him.

"Tell me you had men on him and intel gathered on where he was operating before he went dark."

"No. All of the intel he provided has just been proven bogus. We have nothing."

Nathan closed his eyes hard and hung his head. When he looked up it was with the wrath of hell in his eyes.

"What do you have? Tell me what we can use to get her back. Tell me you have something!"

"I'm sorry Colonel. I don't. I am meeting with CIA in the morning and if I get anything you will be the first to know."

Booker turned to nod to the satellite operator to cut the link and the screen went dark. Justin sat with his hands fisted on the console bent over in agony. When he stood his stance said it all.

"We can't depend on them for help or intel, so we will get it ourselves. We are bringing her home Sir or die trying."

Justin stormed out of the room and yelled for the teams for a sitrep. Nathan just stood there frozen. He was a strong man and a superior Marine. He never feared a mission or an op. He counted on his training and his skill to get him through. But for the first time in his life, he started to pray.

Chapter Twenty Nine

Several days passed and the teams were getting ready for a scouting op into the mountains. The intel they gathered showed three possible locations for El Moufas to be operating. They would go in systematically. The first op enabled them to bust smuggling operation in the area that had been giving the military forces quite a bit of trouble over the last several months. No one in the camp was affiliated with El Moufas, however. Several had worked for them in the past and interrogations gained a bit more intel regarding their base of operations. But nothing they could act on. They confiscated several crates of RPGs and semi-automatic rifles with ammo. All Russian.

The next op was to a location that was strongly favored by most of them to be the mostly likely spot. They went in hard. They were able to grab a ton of electronics that linked the group to El Moufas. They were a splinter cell and had no direct contact with the main group but they did operate for them. They knew taking that area would require them to move fast onto the next. Alpha team stayed on point to secure the area in case any of the parent group came calling while Bravo went back with the prisoners and electronics. They stayed two days to allow intelligence to be gathered from the men and the computers found.

Justin was crossing the compound from SOC to the mess hall when he was hailed. Lieutenant Commander Campbell was jogging toward him. He and Justin clapped hands.

"Hey man it's good to see you! I heard a rumor you are transferring to medical is that right? Tell me it's so!"

Justin laughed. "Yeah, once we complete this mission I am transitioning. Be good to settle down for a change. Still lots of action, but all in one place!" Campbell laughed with him.

"Good to hear it. Hey, I heard Captain Cole is MIA."

"Yeah. That's the mission. We think we know where they are holding her. We're going in."

"Glad to hear that man. I really like her. She's quite the Marine. You heading over for chow?"

"Yeah. You?"

"No cold storage. We got a John Doe in there I have to sign out for transport stateside. I hope somebody at home has better luck identifying him."

"He didn't have prints in the system?"

"No and it's weird. The trauma team that worked on him said he sounded American even though he was in Eastern clothing. No prints or dental in the system. But the scars on his arm are consistent with US Military vaccinations. No DNA either. It's like this guy is a ghost."

All the hair stood up on Justin's neck. He turned and grabbed Campbell's arm.

"Can you take me to him?"

"Yeah, I don't see why not. You think you might know him?"

"I pray I don't. Let's go."

Justin and Campbell walked quickly to the cold storage locker in the back of the mess hall. Campbell signed the log for both of them and went in. The file regarding the incident, injuries, and death was on the body bag. Justin pulled out the records and started reading them. He blanched and paled when he got the area where they documented the patient's last words. Justin handed the file to Campbell and opened the body bag. Even with the damage to the face he recognized Chambers.

"We have to tell Colonel Stirling now! Bring that file."

Justin rezipped the bag and he and Campbell ran to the Division Command where Nathan was getting a sitrep. They ran in and everyone in the room was silent.

"Major, Lieutenant Commander? " General Adams looked up thoughtfully without rancor at the interruption.

"General we have news. While I was heading to chow I ran into Lieutenant Commander Campbell on his way to sign out a DOA John Doe. After hearing a little of the DB's story I asked to see the body. It's Chambers Sir."

Justin held out the file and gave it to the General who read through and handed it off to Stirling. His face tightened and paled as he read.

"Sir we need to question the team who picked him up as to exactly where they got him. We need to find out where he came from. Can you get authorization for satellite imagery of his exfil spot and see if we can trace him back to an origin point?"

The General pointed to two Staff Sergeants who sprung from their chairs and ran to a nearby terminal. Another man left to find out who was on the patrol and get them in. While they looked into pulling up the data Nathan came over to Justin.

"Did you eat son?"

"No, didn't make it to the mess."

"Go. This will take a bit and you need to fuel up. If this ends up in an op you have to be strong enough to face it. Go. Eat something." He turned Justin and pushed him out of the door. Campbell went with him. He grabbed a coffee while Justin filled his plate with everything and they sat down.

"Who is this Chambers? Is he a Marine, civilian?"

"Former Marine recruited by the CIA. He went in deep cover with Kris. He was her back up. If he was right, and considering his condition when he arrived he probably was, then the group they infiltrated knows Kris is a Marine and she is now a POW. It also explains her lack of contact. If she's being held she can't reach out. When did that file say he got here?"

"Ten days ago. That is the max we hold bodies. The wounds he had looked older. Close to a week. If he was on foot and staying hidden until he intersected with military that could mean he wasn't far. I can't imagine him being able to go more than a few kilometers in his condition. Even crawling. Unless them drove him into the desert and dumped him, which I can't see them doing, he had to have gotten here on his own."

Justin smiled and put down his fork. "Why can't you see them dumping him?"

"Too much trouble. They'd just put a bullet in his head and throw him in a corner. They wouldn't leave a wounded man as a loose end. If he could give intel on their location they wouldn't want him alive."

Justin sat smiling before he started eating at a break-neck pace. Shaking his head he pointed his fork at the Lieutenant Commander.

"You think like a Marine. That doesn't sound like a doctor talking."

"Well. I wanted to be a detective when I grew up and read every detective novel ever written. Easy to put all that knowledge together after being out here for long enough."

"So what made you become a doctor?"

"Read true crime novel about a mob hit in Chicago that featured your dad as an expert medical witness for the prosecution. How he described the scene was awesome. I looked him up and read a bunch on him and was hooked. He became my hero. I gave up the idea of being a detective and became a doctor instead."

"One day I hope to introduce you to him and I'd really like you to tell him that story."

"If you could arrange that I'd be glad to."

Justin cleaned his plate and left the mess hall running back to SOC. He got there right as the men returned to say the squad that was out that night is on patrol, but they were being called back as they speak and would be there in 20 minutes. Justin got to work with the squad's report marking their location and started to work backward from there. Kris was close, he knew it.

Chapter Thirty

Kris could not believe her eyes. What in the hell was Fazil doing here? Aziz untied her left arm feeling that she would not be able to attack them with most of her fingers broken. The only ones intact were her thumb and pointer. Good enough to pick up food with so they didn't have to feed her. Her right arm was tied to the chair behind her back.

He stood back from the table facing her. She looked up to Aziz who was deep in conversation with Amir. She nodded to Fazil to move over so his body blocked the brothers view of what she was doing. They had their backs to her but she didn't want them to see her talking to him. They'd kill him. She looked back to Fazil and mouthed to him.

You need to get the hell out of here!

I am your team.

Kris just looked at him with a hard look shaking her head in disbelief. This kid had no idea what he had gotten himself into. The minute Aziz figured the kid had feelings for Kris or vice versa he was dead. Kris wasn't going to have that boy's death on her conscious.

She picked up some food and put it in her mouth to chew so Aziz would not know they were communicating.

The man you left with brought me here to help you. He said you needed backup. I can help.

She continued to eat as she kept an eye on the brothers. She looked at Fazil with a glare.

You do whatever they ask. Do you understand?

Yes.

Even if they ask you to hurt me, you do it! Do you understand?

He stood looking uncertain and scared.

You do it! Prove your loyalty to them no matter what! If you don't we are both dead. Do you understand?!

Fazil gulped audibly and backed away slightly. Aziz came over to check on them.

"You do not look so well my young friend. What is the problem?"

He gazed at Fazil with fatherly concern and wrapped his arm around his shoulders.

"The man is disgusting. He smells really bad."

Aziz laughed and ruffled the boys hair.

"Yes. Infidels are quite disgusting. They do not adhere to the teachings of Allah. They are dirty and foul. This one particularly so. This person pretended to be one of us but is really an American Marine. This Marine is a thief. A thief that has stolen from us. We will find where this Marine has hidden our most precious treasure. And you will help us. Didn't you tell me you hate the Marines?"

Fazil drew deep down from strength he didn't know he had. He would not let them see his fear so he would get Kris home.

"Yes I hate Marines. They pretend to be our friends then they kill our families. They said my family was killed by Taliban but I know that is not true! I saw them. Marines killed them. Then they took me away and pretended to be my friends. They lie!"

Fazil grabbed a handful of sand and rock from the floor and threw it forcefully at Kris. It hit her right in the face sticking to the blood and rained down into her food. She looked at it for a moment and then looked up at the kid with nothing but loathing in her face. She spit at him spraying dirt, spittle and blood. She continued to spit out the dirt until she got most of it and dug back into the plate and continued eating the dirt covered food. She knew she wouldn't get anything for several more days so she continued to eat until the plate was empty. Aziz grabbed her hand making sure to squeeze the broken fingers so she screamed loud and long as he tied her hand back to the chair.

Aziz smiled as Kris sat in the chair and gasped for air. He pulled up a chair and sat down opposite her at the table. It appeared they were going to have a pleasant chat.

"Now that is better. I know our young friend here will tolerate your smell a bit longer. Take the Marine's plate. That's a good boy." He looked at Kris with great amusement. Blood had run down from the cut over her eye had bled down her face. Now covered with dirt she looked hideous.

"Not quite Mr. February at the moment are you my dear?" He laughed at his own joke. Kris sat very still. If he knew that then he knew of her team.

"Still I won't mess you up too badly. I want those fools you operate with to be able to recognize you. It would hardly do to leave any doubt they were inept and bumbling. It's quite obvious you were the brains behind that operation. Which makes me wonder at how truly stupid the rest of the Marine Special Operations are. If you are the smartest among them and you were captured so easily they must be chasing their tails all over the desert if after all this time they haven't found you. It's sad really that they have to depend on a *woman* to lead them. Women are good for many things but leading an army is not one of them. I suspect you understood this while on your hands and knees cleaning toilets these many weeks. You did an amazing job by the way. The Marines taught you well."

He picked up a stack of papers. Flipping through them Kris could see photos of her men. All were the official military shot that appeared on their ID and CAC cards. Seeing them after so long wrenched Kris's gut. She looked down so Aziz wouldn't see how that affected her.

"Major Justin Alario. Executive officer. He's a big one. Should be easy to have a sniper take him out. He's too lumbering to be able to hide well. Lieutenant Davis Gentry. Communications. We'll give him something good to listen to. Captain Javier Juarez. IT Specialist. We'll make sure we have some good information on file for him to find. Lieutenant Daniel Jenkins. Explosive Ordinance Disposal. We'll give him something fun to play with." He chuckled as he continued to name off the team and make comments.

Kris sat very still once he mentioned Jenkins. He wasn't on the team any longer. He hadn't been when Kris left. That meant any information he had was either public knowledge or from Briggs that was way out of date. Which meant anything he said about her team or anything he alluded to in regard to having them would be bluffing.

As he kept going Farouk, Amir, and Saiyid came in. With all of them here in the room Kris had to act. She needed to take them out.

"You will never get my team! I will kill you myself!"

"Yes you are so intimidating bleeding in that chair."

"The only way you will keep me from killing you is if you nail my hands to this table."

Aziz and Amir looked up. Aziz had a huge smile on his face. He went over to the crates along the far side of the cave. He came back with a hammer and two very long nails.

"Boy! Come here!"

Fazil came in from the mouth of the cave. He stopped in front of Aziz. The older man handed him the hammer and nails. Fazil stood very still not understanding having not been privy to their conversation from his perch outside the cave. Aziz loosened Kris's bonds and she hit him knocking him to the ground. Both Amir and Farouk came up to wrestle her to the table. Aziz held her from behind.

"Alright boy. Come here." Fazil came up to the table with some hesitancy. "Take that hammer and nail the Marine's hands to the table."

Fazil stood with a look of horror on his young face. She couldn't see Aziz's face behind her but his body stiffened. If Fazil hesitated he'd be dead. Kris looked at him and with the barest of movements nodded at him to do it. She looked at him hard and pointedly. Seeing the other men were looking at Aziz and arguing with him about tying her back up she looked at Fazil and mouthed the words.

Prove your loyalty.

He gulped and moved over to the table. He stood in front of Kris in between the other men and put the nail on top of her hand. He looked at Aziz who had an unholy light in his eyes. Kris slightly moved her hand so when the kid hit the nail it would miss any nerves or tendons. He hit and the nail went into her hand. She screamed long and loud. It barely went in. She looked at him and said *again harder* under her breath. He hit it much harder this time and the nail went through and impacted the table. He hit again and the nail was firmly into the wood and only a small piece showed above her hand. She wrenched her other hand from Aziz and lashed out at both Amir and Farouk leveling a strong shot to the near man's nose bridge killing him instantly and crushing the windpipe of the far man as he gasped for air he couldn't get. He gasped for several minutes until he lay still on the floor. Saiyid grabbed her arm and held it to the table as Fazil nailed the other hand down.

The boy was shaken and pale but he was holding. Kris was slumped over fighting off the pain. Saiyid checked his brothers and discovered they were both dead. He went to the far table and grabbed a handgun and started for Kris as Aziz tried to hold him off. Aziz wasn't done with her yet. Kris looked at Fazil and nodded toward the RPG's next the cave entrance as the two brothers fought over killing Kris. He ran and grabbed a loaded RPG and backing down the entrance to the cave he sat it on his shoulder.

"Now Fazil. Blow the cave!"

Fazil pressed the trigger as Saiyid pushed Aziz away and headed for Kris. Before he could get his firearm level the RPG flew between them and impacted the crates of mines. The explosion filled the cave. Prepared, Kris closed her eyes and lay as tight to the table as she could. She could feel the heat washing over her. When the dust settled she saw Aziz on his back across the cave and Saiyid on his face on the floor. His head was partially toward her and it was obvious he was dead. Aziz groaned and rolled slightly. Kris looked around and the mouth of the cave was completely caved in. She couldn't hear Fazil and hoped he was far enough down the tunnel to get out. One thing was for sure. She and Aziz weren't going anywhere.

Aziz coughed and rolled around on the ground moaning. He went onto his side and tried several times to get to his knees. He got up and promptly fell back to his stomach coughing. Kris shook her head several times to clear the ringing. She could feel fresh blood dripping down her face and wondered where she was hit and how bad it was. She took a look around. Somehow the blast missed the two flood lights in the far corners. And strangely the camera tripod was still standing. It was sound activated so the green light at the top was on indicating it was recording. Debris was all around it. Tough little bastard.

A couple of hours passed as Kris watched for any movement from Aziz. She tested her hands and found the right one could slip off the nail. She lifted her hand to wipe the blood out of one eye. Aziz groaned and stirred so she replaced her hand back onto the nail. He staggered to his feet weaving and looked around. His three brothers lay on the floor. He went to check on Saiyid. His open opaque eyes told the tale. He looked at Kris who had been watching him.

"So you are still alive. Not for long."

He staggered around for a moment looking for Saiyid's gun. It had been blown across the room. He picked it up and pointed it straight at Kris. Kris could see that the barrel was slightly bent. Aziz didn't notice. If he tried to fire it the pistol would most likely blow his hand clean off. If he decided to put the gun her head it would eventually kill her, but it wouldn't be clean. It would be a slow painful way to slowly bleed out. Not gonna happen. She looked him in the eye.

"You're gutless Aziz. You won't last ten minutes now that your brothers are gone. You don't have the brains or the backbone to run this operation. And you don't have the balls to kill me."

"I will put this bullet in your head and dig my way out of here. Then the world will see my brothers may have run this operation before, but I am the real brains here. I guess I should thank you for taking them out for me. I was getting tired of playing the buffoon. I had been planning for months to take this from them. I figured it would take me a year, but you saved me from the wait."

"You don't use guns that often Aziz. If you want to make sure that hits me, you better come closer."

"Giving up Marine?" He laughed. "Finally ready to go to hell?"

Aziz started slowly walking toward Kris. Kris prepared to engage. She lifted off the chair slightly pushing it carefully backwards. Aziz didn't notice. He was too wrapped up in the glee of his kill. He got up to the table and placed both hands, including the one holding the gun, on the table as he leaned into her face.

"Any last words Marine?"

"Yeah. I said the only way you'd keep me from killing you was if you nailed my hands to the table. I lied."

Kris braced her elbows on the table and whipped her body up so she was balancing on her forearms. She grabbed Aziz with her legs before he registered her movement and flipped him over the table. She secured his neck tightly between her thighs as she bear down. He fought for breath. She heard the gun clatter as he lost it from his grip. She continued to strangle him. He lashed out punching her twice in the rips almost stealing her breath. She pushed through knowing she had to stay strong. He beat against her leg trying in vain to get free.

Kris clenched her thighs harder as he redoubled his efforts and she jerked sharply cleanly snapping his neck. The sound seemed to echo in the small space as he fell to the ground. It was a clean break but not a kill. His paralyzed body fell to the floor of the cave as he lay gasping. He wasn't dead but soon would be.

"I can still kill you even nailed to the table. You know Aziz. It's funny really. You actually thinking that I was weak. And that you were a match for me. That's kept my humor up during our time together. I want you to know before you die that you could never beat me. Even if you killed me in here, I have still won.

Because everything you value, everything you have ever wanted I have. I just wanted these last moments to thank you. I have concentrated so hard all my life on hating you because of what you took from me I couldn't see the big picture. But our quality time together has changed my perspective. I started thinking of what I do have. And I realized that everything good in my life and everything I value is because of you. Funny huh? I thought so. And so will Amalia when I tell her. That's right. She is still alive. I wanted you to know that. Not only have you lost. But she is happy and free and always will be."

Aziz continued to gasp as his respiration became harsh and labored. After a minute that stopped. She watched as the life drained out of him. She looked in the camera and said, "Inshallah."

She looked at the camera. Fatigue swamped her. She looked over at the collapsed entry and knew she'd need her strength to dig herself out. She looked back into the camera. She wanted to say something to her men before she passed out.

"I have had the honor of working with the finest Marines in the world. My team, my family, is made up of the bravest and toughest men I have ever had the privilege of working with. Our Colonel has been like a father to me for most of my life and I have always considered him such. My IT Specialist is a wise ass that never fails to make us laugh. My Communications Officer lives for gossip but never fails to lend an ear if you need someone to talk to. My Logistics Specialist always makes sure we have everything we need but more importantly is always there when you need him. My Recon Specialist is a big guy with a bigger heart and an amazing soul. My Fire Control Specialist is quiet but steady. Always ready to lend a hand no matter what. Never fails to be there. My two EOD guys. The first is strong and steady. He's a warrior through and through regardless of how he sometimes feels. The second is largely underestimated but is one of the smartest guys I've ever met. My SOO is everything to me. My whole world and everything good in my life."

Kris laid her head down on the table and closed her eyes as the fatigue finally caught up with her. After a minute she lifted her head and looked at the camera again.

"Don't think for a minute that was my goodbye. I still fully expect you to have figured out where I am and get me out of this hell hole. Right now I need a nap. And if you haven't come for me by the time I finish, I'm breaking out of here myself. I just need forty winks first."

She lay her head back on the table and became very still.

Chapter Thirty One

Fazil ran as fast as he could as the light started to fade. He knew the general direction of the base from the mountains but that was in a vehicle. He had to stay off the roads to avoid capture. Once he got to the base of the mountain he took a large breath and closed his eyes. He heard a helicopter. He ran toward the sound. He could see it growing smaller in the sky and adjusted his path toward where it was disappearing from view. Kris never gave up on him. He wasn't giving up on her. He continue to run as night fell and he kept running.

***

The team had gathered in SOC as they analyzed the aerial surveillance the Blackhawk scouting the area for the third OP returned with. The gunship flew a low level circuit around showing the best way in and out since that area of the mountain couldn't be penetrated with satellite imaging. That is why Justin favored it for their location. Since it was the furthest out they saved it for last for the tactical advantage gained by clearing out the two previous locations. Now that they were shut down they couldn't send up an alarm or offer any kind of aid to the third area and if the third group tried to scatter they didn't have anywhere to hide. Intel just reported some strange seismic activity there they were also looking into.

If she wasn't there they'd run out of options. Their time was coming to an end. Between mission planning, wind and sandstorms, equipment and transport delays only a month remained on the extension. He didn't want to think about what would happen if they had to leave her behind.

Justin pulled up the data they had when two heavily armed men came into the room. They were from 2nd Battalion 8th Marines. They addressed the room at large.

"Is there a Major Justin in this command?"

Colonel Stirling looked up and spoke.

"What is this about Corporal?"

They saluted the Colonel. "We were on patrol in the northwest at the base of the mountains when we were hailed by a kid, Sir. He's a local and says he's part of one of your Ops, Sir and has to report. He begged us to give him a ride to the base. We searched him and he was clean for weapons. Made him strip in case his clothes were wired or bugged. He was pretty beat up. So we treated his wounds and have him at an outpost station about a click from here."

Justin stepped forward.

"Did the kid say anything else?"

"No Sir. He said it was a need to know mission and he didn't have the clearance to read us in. That gave us a bit of a laugh. Kid's only about 14 or 15." He continued to laugh but the faces of the team all zeroed in on him. He stopped abruptly and swallowed.

"Did the kid give his name?"

"Yeah, he said his name was Fazil Answari."

"You have got to be kidding!"

"Mother of God!"

"Son of Bitch."

Justin waved to the team to quiet down. "That explains why the kid was nowhere to be found."

Stirling asked the team, "Why would Kris bring a civilian kid onto an operation?"

Javier spoke up. "Colonel if I know that kid, he followed Kris out or hid in the back of the transport. Kris would never put that kid in harm's way. Never. She's real protective of him. No way."

"If he was there, he somehow got in. And if he did, he knows where Kris is."

"Bring that kid back here now!"

"Yes Sir! Protocol states we have to have him vetted before we bring him on base, and he said he'll only speak to Major Justin."

386

"Alario go with them. Find out if this kid is our kid and what he knows."

"Yes Sir!" Justin ran to get his gear and left with the patrol. They got in a Humvee parked outside and made the 15 minute drive to the outpost. The guys yelled over the vehicle noise.

"So are you Major Justin Sir?"

"Yeah. He called all of us by our rank and first name. The team practically raised that kid. He's especially close to our team leader who has been missing for months. JSOC mission went bad. She went dark and we've been trying to find her ever since."

"She Sir?"

"Our team leader Captain Kris Cole."

"Huh, the kid talks about a Gunny Kris."

"She was promoted. That's what he knew her by."

"Shit! From a Gunny to a Captain. That is a hell of a promotion."

"She's a hell of a Marine!"

"This is us up ahead Sir."

The Humvee pulled up to a sentry and was waved through. They went to a temporary structure in the center of the camp and went inside. Justin was immediately rushed with 110 pounds of naked teenager. He threw his arms around him and started to cry. Justin gathered him in tight for a minute and then pulled the kid away.

"Get him something to wear and an MRE." Justin held him at arm's length. The kid was dirty and banged up but otherwise ok.

"Report!"

"Yes Major. I was approached by a man called Chambers to help on a mission with Gunny Kris. He said she needed me to be her team because you couldn't come. We were going to be with some very bad men and he needed ears and eyes. I could help because no one looks at children. And these bad men would be happy to have me because they want young people they can make into terrorists. I wanted to protect Gunny Kris so I went with him. The men were very bad. I was going to sneak out and get the team and one of them caught me. I had to pretend. I told him I was trying to find the Marine I heard was being held so I could kill him. He laughed and told me to come with him. We traveled in a truck for many hours into the mountains and he took me to a cave. Gunny Kris was there. So was one of the men Gunny Kris left with. The mean one who looked at her with death in his eyes. They were hurting her."

He stopped there and started to cry again. Justin knew better than to comfort the kid. He needed that report. So, he commanded in a hard voice.

"Continue your report Private!"

Fazil sniffed and wiped his nose. He looked back at Justin.

"They hurt her over and over. They tied her to a chair. They made me hurt her. She used the hand language to tell me how to get the men to show me how to use the rocket that was in there. They liked showing me. How to load and how to fire. They said when they were done, I could use it to blow up the cave. Gunny Kris told me to wait for her signal. They hurt her again and this time when they got close, she killed some of them. And when the other two were arguing over killing her she told me to grab the rocket and fire it into the cave. The entry caved in with Gunny Kris and the men inside. We must get her out Major Justin! I promised her I would take care of her. We must go now!"

Justin looked at the men who were wearing grim faces. If he fired an RPG into a cave with an explosion big enough to collapse the entry, chances are all the people inside were dead too.

"You have the coordinates where you picked him up?"

"Yes Sir here is mission report with all the data."

"I'm taking him with me back to Delta. Get dressed kid. We leave now. You can eat on the way."

By the time Justin and Fazil got back to the base all the intel from the Blackhawk had been gathered. He added the information from the kid.

"Do you have the coordinates for the seismic activity detected earlier?"

"Yes here."

"Fazil when did you launch that RPG?"

"It knocked me backwards. I woke up and the cave was filled up. There was no one around. The bad men did not keep anyone else there. Days ago they were sent to another place and they had not come back. The oldest man was not happy about that before Kris killed him. It was just getting dark when I started to run."

"Sergeant! Does that coincide with the timing of the seismic activity?"

"Yes Major."

"Pinpoint the exact area. We are going in."

Normally the team would be briefed with a five paragraph operations order that would detail their mission and equipment needs. They all went into action knowing exactly what they would need for this mission and geared up.

Once they were all ready Fazil went up to them as they were getting ready to board the transport.

"I am coming with you Sir."

"No way kid. You sit tight. We'll bring her home."

"No. You don't know the area and you will waste time looking for the cave and I know right where it is. I am not staying behind. You take me!" He hit Justin in the chest with both fists.

He didn't have the time to argue. And the kid was right. If there was no air in the cave every second counted. Justin grabbed the kid by his shoulder and pushed him into the helicopter. Javier worked on getting the kid strapped in. He finished and looked at Justin. Then he started to sign.

Are you nuts Sir? Bringing the kid?

He wasn't staying behind. And he's right. He knows where the cave is and can lead us right to it. We waste time that could be costing Kris air if we have to search.

The team looked at one another. They knew that the chances of finding her alive were getting slim. She may have been alive when the kid left, but she could have be taken out in the blast. If she survived that she could have been wounded and bled out. Or killed by the terrorists still alive when the kid acted. They were going in blind.

The helicopter hovered about two hundred yards from where Fazil said the cave was. They went down a rope with Davis carrying Fazil. They set off with Fazil running ahead. The sun was about to come up making the route easier to see in the pearly predawn. The team stayed on alert. Just because there was no one here when Fazil left didn't mean someone hadn't come in since. They swept through the area. As they got closer to the cave Justin's heart began to beat faster. Noah came up behind him and grabbed him by the shoulder. Justin turned as the younger man looked at him intently. Noah pushed him back behind Javier and took point. Justin started to take issue but Javier shook his head at him shutting him down. They continued to push through the brush. Fazil stopped and looked around for a minute. He turned to the left and started up a slight incline. The path was well worn. It curved around and came to a flat area big enough for a truck. Next to a pile of rubble was a spent RPG launcher. This was the place.

Jenkins and Miller got together to rig the charge needed to clear the debris from the mouth of the cave. The team got back as Justin radioed their coordinates back to base and gave command a sitrep. He paused as the charges blew raining dirt and rocks everywhere. Gentry and Jeffries held point and covered the cave. Justin made for the mouth determined to be the first in the door. Miller held him off. Noah shook his head and motioned for the Major to go in behind him. Noah didn't want the Major to go in and see Kris without someone covering him. If the terrorists were still in there he'd be vulnerable if he broke protocol looking for Kris.

The team covered with Jenkins taking up a tactical position outside covering the team and Javier pulling out equipment to scan the cave. They slowly made their way inside as they walked into the light cast by the flood lights in the corner. They scanned the cave. Kris was just ahead of them with her head down on the table. Her eyes were closed. Four bodies were on the ground. Justin stopped dead seeing Kris.

"Sir. She's alive. She's just sleeping. She's exhausted. You have to clear the room. Follow procedure. She's fine."

Justin looked at Noah with blazing eyes. "Are you lying to me Marine?"

Noah flashed a brief smile. "No Sir! I swear to you. She's alive. But we have to clear the room."

Miller and Justin continued their circuit of the room looking for any other entry points in the cave that could be hiding more insurgents. Nothing. The room was big, but it was a single chamber.

Jenkins walked over to the table where Kris was laying. He squatted down so she was at eye level.

"They nailed her hands to the table Sir." He looked back toward Alario with glassy eyes.

He turned back to Kris and as he looked back at her face her eyes popped open scaring the shit out of him. He yelled and fell over backwards scooting on his hands and feet like a crab. Kris looked at him a second then snorted. Her soft laughter filled the cave.

"Jesus Dan, you could always make me laugh at the worst times!" She chuckled some more.

"You crazy bastard! You made me piss my pants!"

Kris snorted again. "Sorry dude. Change of clothes and a shower you'll be good as new. Hell I've been sitting in my own piss for days. Builds character."

He got up and went back to the table. She looked over to the camera still on in the corner.

"How did you find me?"

"The kid."

"You mean to tell me that traitor is here? Bring him to me!"

Fazil had already started down the tunnel when he heard the team talking. He walked into the cave to see Kris staring at him from the table.

"Didn't figure I'd still be alive did you, you little bastard? Figured you'd lead them here and be a hero so they didn't know your part huh? Too bad, because you're mine now. Restrain that traitor now."

Reineke produced some zip ties and tied the kid's hands together behind his back. He led the kid outside where Tomball was covering the mouth of the cave. Javier went to the video camera and found it to be recording. He shut it down. He looked and found a mangled laptop it was hooked to and bagged it. They gathered up all the electronics and equipment. Justin spoke to Tomball over the mike to call in for transport to come pick up the munitions and equipment still left in the cave.

Kris called out to Javier. "Is that camera shut down?"

"Yeah Kris it's down. Anything else we should be looking for?"

"No. They didn't keep a lot here. Four laptops. The table over there held maps if they weren't destroyed in the blast. You'll want to grab those. Then make sure you take pictures of every one of them. The one by my feet is Aziz. On my 9 o'clock is Saiyid. In front of the table is Amir on the right and Farouk on the left. In the back corner over there out of sight is a black bag. Get that too. Not sure what's in it though."

Kris closed her eyes again. Jenkins was looking at how to get the nails out of her hands. He found the hammer and was going to hit the nails from under the table back through Kris's hands. She shook him off.

"Work smarter not harder Marine. Reineke-bolt cutters."

He grabbed the tool from Reineke and worked them into the nail on her left hand.

"I need someone to hold her hand flat so I don't clip it."

Kris lifted her right hand and pushed down on her left hand giving him room to maneuver. He clipped the head off the nail.

"Thanks Captain." He looked nonplussed at Kris as she nonchalantly placed her right hand back on the nail and adopted an innocent expression. Dan started laughing. "You crazy bastard."

Kris wiggled her eyebrows. "Can I have some water?"

Justin came over after completing his assigned task and pulled out his canteen.

"Can you lift your head Kris?"

"Uh no, that's why I need the water. I'm stuck to the table."

Justin realized the blood had congealed effectively gluing her to the surface. He poured water all around her face as she wiggled her facial muscles to loosen the skin without causing any more damage.

"Is the kid ok?"

"Yeah. He's outside."

"He had anything to eat? I don't remember when he ate last."

"Tender feelings for the traitor Kris?"

"I only said that for the camera. It was still running. Was it broadcasting?"

"Not sure. Didn't look like it but Javi will check it out when we get back."

The rest of the team bagged up the bodies and prepared them for transport by piling them outside the cave. The helicopter was returning to them. It was able to land just below where the entrance was located. There was a place large enough for a chopper to land and take off. They loaded up the kid and the equipment they were taking. Jeffries, Tomball, and Jenkins were staying back to wait for the truck and team that was getting the rest of the stuff in the cave along with the bodies. It was about

20 minutes out. Miller and Jenkins looked over all the munitions still stacked along the cave walls. Only one mine exploded which explained why the cave didn't collapse. They were either unstable or duds. The RPG's were carried out. The mines would be exploded in place once the photos were completed and the cave emptied.

Justin was finally able to work Kris's face off the table. He sat her up in the chair and used a cloth to wipe the blood from her face. He stayed away from the contusion on her temple since the dried blood was keeping it closed. He carefully bandaged her hands being careful not to aggravate the broken fingers on her left hand.

"Carry me?" She looked at him questioningly. He raised an eyebrow but didn't say a word. With most of the blood off he lifted her from the chair and carried her outside to the chopper. Fazil was already inside. The team heading back came with the last of the equipment and boarded. Kris and Justin were the last to board. He sat her on the seat across from him as he closed the door. Javier strapped her in. She leaned over him to speak with Fazil.

"You good kid?"

He leaned forward and put his forehead against hers. Javier in between them seemed confused. She sat with their heads touching for a minute until the whine of the blades indicated they were about to lift off. When they pulled apart the kid was beaming.

"I am good now because my family is safe and together."

Kris smiled that grin and turned to face the guys. She looked at every one of them ending with Justin. They sat and stared into each other's eyes for quite a while. Suddenly Kris wrinkled her nose. Justin cocked his head in question. The noise in the chopper was too much for him to hear her without a comm so she signed to him, *all I smell is death* as she wrinkled her nose again. He got up from his seat and unclipped her harness picking her up and putting her in his lap. He opened the top of his fatigues and pulled them apart. She pressed her face into the hollow of his throat and breathed in deep. She missed his smell.

She'd never take it for granted. She just breathed deeply in and out with her eyes closed. He wrapped his arms around her tightly and rest his cheek on the top of her head. He squeezed his eyes shut tightly but it didn't stop the moisture from escaping. Two tears crept out from under his tightly closed lashes. Now that he had Kris back and they were going home he could indulge in a little release. Javier raised his camera and snapped a picture of them.

The helicopter banked as it circled to the LZ. When they touched down Justin moved to carry Kris out. She shook him off. She leaned over to his ear.

"I am walking into that hospital."

He gave her a look that needed no interpretation.

"I need to do this. To prove to myself that I can."

When she pulled away from him the second time his look was filled with understanding. When the door opened, she saw her dad coming out to the pad. Justin carried her from the helicopter, but then placed her feet on the ground once they'd reached safe distance. Nathan grabbed Kris in a hug. She gasped as he hit her battered ribs.

"Let's get you to medical." He motioned for a gurney but the stubborn ass Kris was, she just walked right by it. Limping hard she was determined to walk. Nathan and Justin just looked at each other and walked to either side of her putting an arm each around her waist. It was slow going but she was not going to be carried in. A line had formed just outside the medical building doors with SOC, MSOTs, and support personnel. They all looked on with dozens of emotions playing over their faces from relief to admiration. General Adams looked at her with pride.

"Get cleaned up Cole. Then I want your report."

"Yes Sir General. Can you get me a couple of stenographers Sir?" She held up her hands. "Can't type right now Sir."

"Get fixed up. Let the medics look you over. I'll have them over to you in an hour."

"General she needs to rest. She's not in any shape to give a report now."

He looked to Stirling who, while relieved his daughter was safe, was pale looking at her in the bright light of the treatment room. Her injuries were much more glorious in the LED lights.

"I'd agree with you Stirling, but I've seen that look on her face before and I'm not coming out on the losing end of it.' The General said with more than a little bit of humor. Stirling let out a humorless laugh. He saw the hard set of Kris's face. She wouldn't rest until the job was done. So, he stepped back and let them tend to her.

Chapter Thirty Two

When Kris's eyes finally opened it was dark. The only light was from a small desk lamp on the nurses station table on the far side of the room. She lay there minute letting her mind process. After being treated for the most severe wounds she insisted on sitting with a stenographer who took her debrief and wrote out her after action report for the mission. It took almost 11 hours of continuous talking to set down everything she could remember; all of the conversations and intel she was able to come in contact with in the last six months. They actually found two more stenographers as she was talking so fast one could not keep up.

She wanted to make sure the information was given to Command so they could get started on it immediately. She also translated all of the conversations between her and El Moufas that were on the video. The videos were being reviewed by SOC for actionable intel. She asked Carter in Communications, a wizard with video, to make her a specific cut of certain clips for the debrief she intended to give once she'd rested up. She wanted them to be able to act on the intel so they would not miss the opportunity to shut them down.

Then she met with the CIA region director who replaced Briggs through teleconference. A tough and knowledgeable former Army Intel Specialist named Riley. She gave her the real information on Fazil and made sure she ensured his safety. He was still being detained as an enemy combatant. Riley was on the next flight to the base. She still needed to speak with Justin about him. She looked around getting her bearings stopping on the shadowy figure next to the bed. Justin sat on a hard chair with his legs slightly spread; one hand on his thigh and the other under hers on the bed. She blinked a few times to clear her vision and he was still there.

"Are you awake this time?"

She looked at him a minute and then smiled a huge wide smile.

"I'm awake."

He was holding her hand. His hand was warm and strong. The bandages around her palm were warm from his heat which told her he'd been holding it for a while. Her left hand was on the bed next to her in a splint.

"What time is it?"

"It's 0300. Sunday morning."

"So, I've been out of it for a while."

"Yeah."

Déjà vu. Only this time Justin looked rested. He had several day's growth of beard but she could smell that he'd freshly showered.

"You been here long?"

"A couple of hours. Listening to you snore."

She belly laughed so hard she rolled around a little. "You didn't need to do that man."

"I didn't want you to wake up alone."

She just chuckled. "So I take it you have some heavy news to impart? I'm trying to remember the script."

"Nope. Just wanted to watch you sleep. Missed it. But I do have some news. Your fingers didn't heal clean so we have to rebreak three of them and set them."

"Yeah. They were just snapped until a certain asshole, who will remain six feet under, crushed my hand to feel superior. They were good until then."

"Well I'm sure he regrets it now." He said with a completely straight face.

Kris just snorted and snickered trying not to bust up again. She felt really good. Light. Free. It was almost like being high. Only this high was from feeling relief from anger, hatred, fear, and anxiety for the first time in 18 years. She felt like a completely different person. Someone she'd never met before. Someone she felt she was going to like having around.

Justin grinned at her and moved over to the bed gathering Kris up in his arms and placing her on his lap as he leaned back against the elevated part of the bed and cuddled her close. He was careful not to tangle her in the IV that had been giving her saline for the last 20 hours. She also had a catheter since she was so deeply unconscious, they couldn't wake her to urinate.

He just inhaled deeply and tightened his hold on her.

"Not too hard. I really have to pee."

"You have a catheter."

"Oh. I think I'd rather just go pee. Can you take it out?"

Justin pushed the button for the nurse and when she came in asked for the doctor. Kris also had a request.

"Lieutenant can you please contact Colonel Stirling and tell him his daughter is awake?"

She looked like her eyes were going to pop out of her head, but she nodded and sent in the doctor.

Campbell came in.

"Welcome back Cole! We love having you here! Always some new fascinating stories to tell. You look good and hydrated finally. Three cracked ribs, massive contusions on your back, significant facial contusions, every finger on the left hand broken, bruised kidneys, UTI, massive congestion, and according to your Communications Specialist disgraceful split ends that need to be dealt with immediately."

Kris laughed with Campbell as she curled up in Justin's embrace.

"No doubt you'll have me sorted out soon Sir."

"Well everything but the split ends you are already being treated for. Broad spectrum antibiotics and some mild pain killers. The bruising will fade on its own."

"Sir about that, can you locate some apple cider vinegar and gauze and I'll take care of the bruising and swelling."

"So you were being held by radical herbalist healers who tortured you until you denounced Western medicine?"

Kris snorted trying not to laugh. Her ribs still hurt.

"No Sir. Old remedy. The ACV breaks up the blood under the surface of the skin and dissolves the bruise. The PH also helps the body reduce the amount of acid from the stress of the injuries."

"Well I learned something new today. I'll get some over and we'll try this miracle cure of yours. Meanwhile I suppose you want the catheter out?"

"Yes Sir. I really need to urinate Sir."

He and Justin worked together to remove it and Justin carried Kris to the lavatory. She didn't comment when he decided to carry her back to bed. Considering what she'd put him through her ego could handle him coddling her. Campbell looked her over and took her vitals. Everything was good.

Stirling came in a bit out of breath. He obviously ran to get there. Kris smiled a huge smile happy to see her dad. He sat on the bed and grabbed her in a tight embrace. Justin was still holding her left hand which he had removed from the splint. He looked at Nathan and then jerked one of Kris's fingers sharply. The sharp snap of the bone was joined by a hiss from Kris. She looked at Justin with a 'seriously- right now?' look as he pulled the appendage and straightened it out. The finger needed to be fractured several times to fix the unnatural shape. She turned back to Nathan and started asking him questions about what had happened in her absence. Nathan was amazed. Kris didn't flinch as her husband rebroke the battered fingers. Nathan winced as he did the same to the second and third fingers. Finally, all her fingers were straight and he placed them back in the splint and rewrapped her hand. Kris didn't make any noise or even show that the action hurt her as she spoke to her dad. Even Campbell was impressed. Then he'd seen her through much worse.

Kris noticed a few more faces had entered the room. General Adams and Colonel Matthews had come in while Justin was fixing Kris's fingers. Adams looked a little green. Matthews eyes were so big Kris thought he was going to pass out. They recovered themselves quickly.

"Sirs, as soon as you can arrange it we need to have a debrief. I have a lot to tell you."

"Rest up Kris. It can wait. We've got people reading your AAR."

"Actually, Sirs it can't. We must act fast. In less than 72 hours El Moufas is moving the largest shipment they have ever attempted into Syria. If we don't mobilize now, we will lose it and the advantage we have."

"What advantage?"

"I have the one piece of information I have been searching for the last ten years that ties everything together. I have the name of the legitimate businessman that enables the entire operation to function and stay funded. It was the only thing I have been missing all these years. Without it, we could never stop them. Through him all their funds get washed, and their trail gets cleaned. Now that I have the name, it all ends. It was the last piece of the puzzle to not only stop the organization but to destroy every cell, operative, contact, and business that has been enabling El Moufas to survive."

"Who is this businessman?"

"Yusef Ben David Mondalvi."

Adams looked incredulous. "The billionaire philanthropist?"

Kris smiled. "Yes and no. That will take some explaining. Which I can do in the debrief." She turned to Justin. "You have my lucky radiation detection device?"

Justin reached into the top pocket of his utilities and gave it to Kris. She put it between her teeth and bit down resulting in a loud crack as the case broke and a swear from Kris.

"You forgot to mention loose teeth sir!" She wiggled one with her tongue that seemed a bit worse for her action. She spit out the top and dumped a black and silver object out of the casing. A memory stick. She held it out to Adams.

"General. I have one back up in the states, but please don't mess this one up it'll take too long to get it here. Let's go. You'll need my password to open it. SOC everyone?"

Adams nodded and Justin picked Kris up and put her in a nearby wheelchair.

"Dude, I can walk!"

"Sure with the wind everyone will get a nice view of your black and blue backside in that hospital gown. Take the ride Kris and shut up."

She leaned her head back to rest against his stomach as he grabbed the handles. "Sir, Yes Sir!"

He leaned down and kissed her lightly on the mouth. Then pushed her out laughing.

As they rolled up into SOC many people called out to Kris and came over. Kris accepted the welcome but then motioned for Justin to come get her. He pushed her into a secure room where she sat down at a computer and went over her after action report. Justin printed off three copies and put them in binders. She talked for three straight hours. Kris kept one, Justin gave one to the General, and dropped the last in Intelligence for them to get started on confirming the information and formulating the next op. While Justin called the teams to assemble in the ready room, Kris went to the console to make a quick phone call. Reineke started over then turned around and headed off toward the barracks.

 The General gathered the division commanders and the team leaders to pull them in with SOC command armed with his copy. Kris explained that most of the intel in the report he would hear for himself in the video. She just wanted to get it down on paper in case any of it was not intelligible on the audio. As they were getting settled Reineke came back in with underwear, a pair of shorts, and a T-shirt for Kris. Justin helped her dress in the corner out of sight of the room. The shorts fit but the shirt was huge. Good thing since she wasn't wearing a bra. Kris was grateful to the very astute man for realizing she didn't want to give a brief in gown with her naked backside hanging out. She wondered if he and Sue had ever been to Hawaii. If not, she was going to arrange it first thing.

While all the men were gathering, she rolled the chair over to the console to confer with Javier who was setting up the computer and downloading the data of the memory stick. His eyes widened a little over the amount of data on the thing. Documents, photos, and scans started whipping over the monitor. A couple of minutes later the download was complete. Kris turned to the room. Javi walked over and gave her a remote to pull the data onto the large display screen behind her. She had looked over this information so many times she knew exactly what each document and photo she needed to pull was from memory. Good thing as there was over 2,000 items on the drive. Two last people came into the room. One was Lieutenant Cook. And the other was CIA Director Riley. The door to the room shut and locked. The light dimmed and took a red tinge indicating the room was electronically sealed. No one outside could get in or access the information she was about to impart.

"Sirs thank you for setting up this briefing quickly. Action will need to be swift and clean. So everyone listen and hold any questions. I will repeat anything after the debrief. The last six months I have been on a JSOC mission with the CIA. Only the CIA never sanctioned a mission."

She looked at Justin for the confirmation and got a nod in return.

"What you don't know I have been working with a contact in the Justice Department for the last 18 years. Wit Sec Division. There was a mole in the US government who was aiding El Moufas and hunting my family which kept me from turning over the information I have been stockpiling since 2000. Everything I have learned, and every track of my career has been for one purpose; use this information to destroy Aziz El Moufas and his family and their organization before he takes me out.

I discovered during this mission CIA Director Tom Briggs, who recruited me for the mission, has been the government mole aiding and abetting El Moufas for the better part of twenty years. His only intention for recruiting me was to turn me over to El Moufas for the bounty they had placed on my head so he could take his money and disappear. We won't worry about him, he's Homeland's problem. But he is central to this intel.

I never intended to withhold this information. It was always my plan to turn it over once I got into MARSOC. Over the years I have with my contact's help leaked key pieces of intel to help us fight these bastards. Much of what I leaked over the years has been scrubbed or altered. I've never been able to backstop to its source. CIA Director Riley informed me earlier that they were able to trace it all back to Briggs. Now that he's gone I can get this out and we can finally act on it. 17 SEALS, Rangers, and Raiders died in last 10 years from information this traitor either withheld or twisted that I have leaked to help take them down.

Many of you are probably wondering why terrorists had targeted a United States Marine. It's a long story. Most of the details I am going to skip for expediencies sake. Well they say a picture is worth a thousand words. Let's start with these."

Kris clicked the remote and pulled up four pictures. The first of what appeared to be two little girls in dresses and pig tails. One dark haired and darker skinned and one fair and blonde. It didn't take much to see Kris in the blonde child's features. After they moved to California Kris became a skater. Including having shoulder length hair. The Major always required her hair to be high and tight. Gentry snorted. "Pigtails sir?"

Kris didn't respond, but clicked to pull up the rest and let them all take the pictures in. The second was of a younger Aziz El Moufas and the two girls each holding his hand at what appeared to be a zoo. This elicited a much stronger response. The third was a family picture showing the four El Moufas brothers, the dark-haired child, and a beautiful dark haired woman taken at dining table. The fourth was of the two children and an older boy who was about twenty five but appeared very childlike. Several of the men glared at Kris waiting for an explanation for why she was in pictures with a terrorist.

"A nice picture and the only one if I am not mistaken of the entire El Moufas clan. This was at dinner at Aziz's California house. I took that picture. I wanted one we could use later the identify these bastards. They didn't know I saved it to the sim card and then switched it out and resaved the photos to the duplicate before they deleted it. I saw Amir delete it after pretending to admire it. The third was at Sea World. That was a fun day. The last is what I want to bring your attention to. You no doubt recognize me even dressed as a girl. The other girl in the photo is Amalia El Moufas-Aziz's only child. In fact the only child any of them had. My best friend. The older boy is the man you all know as Yusef Ben David Mondalvi."

The muttering started in earnest again as many were able to see the familiar features of the notoriously reclusive billionaire who was known for the many financial donations to multiple foundations and charities worldwide.

General Adams spoke up, "Captain Cole you want us to believe that the financier of the largest terrorist weapons faction in the world is also the biggest philanthropist in the world?"

Kris smiled a cold smile. Justin caught on quickly.

"What do you mean the man we all know as Mondalvi? That is not Yusef Ben David Mondalvi?"

"No. The person in this picture is Abraham Mondalvi. Yusef's son."

"Hold on here. Mondalvi doesn't have any children."

"That is actually incorrect. He had his information scrubbed. His son Abraham was born in 1979. His mother died during the birth and Abraham was deprived of oxygen. Because of that he is mentally retarded. High functioning, but only the intellectual equivalent of about a 13-year-old. He was mute most of his childhood until Amalia and I taught him to speak. He communicates through mimicry; he is not able to articulate sentences on his own. He can say some things; names or isolated words. But his primary communication is to repeat lines from movies. When we found he could repeat lines we made a game out of it. We would have entire conversations in nothing but movie quotes. He watched endless movies. The trick was finding something we all knew. Or we'd have to watch a movie together and the next time we saw each other we would speak in dialog. That is how he can function. His father makes a 'movie' of what he wants him to say, and they sit him in front of it for hours until he will repeat the dialog. Like a parrot."

Kris shook her head in complete disgust.

"Those bastards took the game that me and Amalia created to allow him to have a voice and they used it to turn him into a puppet. They took a kind and sweetly clueless boy and made him into a monster."

Kris rolled over to the console. "Keep an open mind. And watch carefully what you see."

Kris queued up the video. It was one of the segments of her interrogation. Her head was back resting on her shoulders. Her eyelashes were fluttering. A man walked around the chair holding a whip. It whistled before cracking into her back. She screamed. The man cracked the whip several times and Kris screamed more. After four or five times the screaming stopped. He kept laying into her until a man to the side of the camera called him off. He gathered up the whip and walked to a table. The light from the camera illuminated Farouk, Amir, and a third man. They spoke softly. Discussing transportation routes and shipping schedules. The third man, who had been in shadow, stepped into the light. It was clear how much he resembled the younger man known as Mondalvi. They spoke in Pashtu which everyone in the room understood.

"Amir, if we route the ammunition through this pass, we can cut three days off the delivery time. We have contacts that will ensure its safe arrival. They will only require a modest cut that allows us to generate a greater return with the early delivery bonus."

"Yusef, my friend you are invaluable to me! We shall do this. If it works as advertised, then we can use this route for the smaller munitions and cargos. It will keep our costs lower and our revenue up."

Kris groaned low. They stopped talking and looked over at her.

"How much longer will you play with this Marine? You should kill her now and cut your losses here. You play a dangerous game."

"No one knows where she is or that she is even missing. Our friend Briggs brought her to us, and her people think she is on a covert mission. They don't have any details and they will not come looking for her. Do not concern yourself my friend. She is no danger to us." Several snorts and chuckles cropped up from all over the room.

Every shipment and route were discussed. Yusef outlined how the money would be washed and distributed. They discussed the buyers and the points of contact as well as the sale locations. 16 deals in all going simultaneously all over the world. They clapped one another on the back and the man they called Yusef called out to someone. From behind Kris footsteps. Abraham Mondalvi entered the cave. His father kissed him on both cheeks and sat him on a chair with Kris behind him. It was as if he didn't even see her.

The television next to the video recorder turned on and the older man stepped back as a video of him played telling the younger man what his next role to play was. This time it was a video for the Tajiks. Over the next hour the video which was about three minutes long ran on a loop until by the fifteenth time the younger man started speaking along with the tape. By the time he ran it through five more times the younger man had perfected the verbiage and tone. He was saying the lines as if he were speaking them himself. The lines that brokered the deal for weapons and future supplies to fund their crusade. And created a plausible patsy for the group. Anyone captured or tortured would give the name Yusef Ben David Mondalvi as the man responsible for the sale. The person responsible for the crime.

It was disgusting. Abraham was not able to comprehend what was happening or what he was doing. They had the perfect system. He would take the fall, and couldn't turn them over because he wasn't able to talk. The older men left the cave to walk outside while the younger man continued to watch. Kris lifted her head and looked at the man in the chair. She glanced slightly to the mouth of the cave. From behind him Kris spoke.

Abraham always liked the riveting you can't handle the truth scene of their mutually favorite military courtroom movie. Amalia liked it for the lead actor.

The man turned in the seat and looked at Kris for the first time. He seemed confused by her being there. He responded.

They kept the back-and-forth dialog of the famous courtroom scene going in soft tones. Abraham got up out of the chair and walked to stand in front of Kris. Their voices slowly grew until the climax of the scene was reached. Abraham's voice steadily rose with the same steel Jack Nicholson delivered the original lines in the infamous scene. He stood in front of Kris and delivered the soliloquy with a great depth of passion and commitment. Once he reached the conclusion he stopped and stared. He smiled a shy smile.

"Hi Faith."

Kris smiled at the older man. Somehow that simple man remembered her from the little girl he used to play with. Figuring the man kept up with all the top movies, especially the animated ones, Kris heard movement outside she whispered, "Andy's coming."

Abraham moved quickly into the chair and sat down watching the video speaking the lines. Kris let her head fall forward again lolling into her chest. Yusef grabbed her by the hair and yanked her head back striking her across the face viciously. Kris groaned but otherwise didn't make a sound.

"She is still unconscious Yusef. She won't rouse for quite some time. She has little tolerance for pain."

He smirked and walked away.

The cacophony in the room after that comment was audible. The Marines laughed and hooted while tossing out snarky comments on the stupidity of the men in that cave. Kris paused the video and turned to the room.

"Why did he call you Faith, Sir?" Gentry was having a hard time keeping in his amusement at the whole thing.

"That is the name they knew me by. Aziz was lazy and entitled. When told his daughter's friend was called Faith he never looked further. There was a girl in our school who was born in Afghanistan of an American mother and Afghan father who were killed in a roadside bombing when she was three. She came to California to live with her mother's sister. Her name was Faith Qureshi. Amalia overheard the school councilor talking to someone on the phone while she was in the office. When I first showed up at the house that was the name she gave her father for me. She was afraid if I told him my name he would find out I was really a boy and he would no longer allow us to be friends. She was not allowed to socialize with boys. At all.

In the end it was what saved all of us. He never knew the real name of the friend who became like a 'second daughter to him.' So, when we took in Amalia in he had no idea where to look. He sent men to Faith's house, and they didn't know anything. The men knew that she wasn't the girl who was always at the house. No girls at the school matched my description. Luckily that year I missed picture day because of a doctor's appointment so my photo was never in the yearbook. My name was listed in the back in the 'not pictured' section. And our names were redacted off of every bit of paperwork. It wasn't until last year when he came back to the states for the first time in years, he found the truth. Every time he came stateside, he would search Amalia's name for any mention of her. He'd look at social media, newspaper articles, and public records.

It was in a hometown salute to alumni who served in the military that our former school paper wrote that gave me away. A picture of me and the story of my becoming a Marine in SOC appeared in the local paper in California where Amalia and I attended school. I was considered a local military hero even though we only lived there for two years. One of my old teachers was interviewed for the story. She mentioned how it didn't surprise her, as I was always looking to help those in need. How I always aided those smaller or weaker. How inseparable I was from Amalia and protected her from bullying. And how it was a shame she died so tragically. It did not take him long since I haven't really changed all that much to put it together. Once he saw the old yearbook photo in the article next to my official Corps photograph and realized he'd been conned by a twelve-year-old he lost it. He ordered the hit that was executed in the Kabiq mission. That IED was there specifically for me.

When it came out, I was a woman I was told he laughed himself silly. He figured by virtue of my sex that naturally made me weaker. And that I walked into a trap naturally made me dumber and less cunning. He was such an arrogant prick. In the end that arrogance is what killed him. He actually thought he was a match for me. He thought I was the one who walked into a trap. He never realized I was right where I wanted to be the entire time." Kris snorted and laughed. She reached over and started the video from the cave over.

Then men sat in silence over the next several hours as Kris's torture and questioning played out on the video. Intelligence officers were documenting locations, dates, and names furiously. Kris just tossed them a binder that had about five hundred pages in it. Her after action report that she dictated and printed out. A couple of the men got up with it and ran out of the room. Gentry laughed when Fazil nailed her hands to the table and looked at Kris saying, "You crazy, honey!" Aziz was able to secure Kris easily and hold her down to the table. It was obvious to the men she allowed him to do it. In the next segment Kris took out Farouk and Amir. Jenkins was sitting there shaking. Javier looked like he was going to kill someone. When she yelled at Fazil to blow the place everyone shifted in their seats. The two brothers Kris hadn't killed were down to one after the blast. Aziz's attempt and subsequent death made everyone sit a little taller and prouder of their place in SOC. When they got to the end where Kris had her heart to heart with Aziz everyone was on the edge of their seats.

Stirling sat with his head in his hands and eyes tightly shut. It couldn't have been easy for him to see her go through that. When Kris looked into the camera and said her not so final goodbye many of the Marines weren't even trying to hide the tears. Once Kris finished and laid her head down on the table the time elapse showed only an hour had passed when a noise activated the camera's sound activated recording feature to engage. The camera shook as the small explosion sprayed dirt over the area and showed the eight Marines entering the room in standard sweeping formation.

At that point Kris turned it off. Every man in this room was tough and highly trained. All of them knew what it took to survive what Kris went through. The looks they leveled at her conveyed respect of the ordeal she went through. Her men however had a different take. Unlike most of the Marines in that room they knew her and what she was capable of. And they knew most of that video was academy award worthy.

Her team stood up clapping and whistling.

Gentry piped up, "Well I wouldn't give it best picture, but if you don't get best actress you were robbed Sir!"

Reineke was next. "If I knew that was going to be so entertaining, I would have brought popcorn! It must have drove you crazy to stay sitting in that chair like you had to."

Jenkins looked at her with a furious expression, "I ought to kick your ass! You have no idea."

Javier followed with, "I can't believe you just sat there and allowed that to happen. What were you thinking Jefe?"

Stirling was standing there looking like he could grind glass with his teeth. His face was getting more thunderous by the second. Justin sat with his arms crossed over his chest looking like he'd just watched a mildly entertaining sitcom and not his wife getting the shit beat out of her for hours on end.

Tomball shouted over the din, "My favorite part was hearing her scream when Orakzai broke her fingers. I didn't know you knew how to scream like a girl, Captain! Mel teach you that?" He laughed clapping Kris on the shoulder.

Javier leaned in, "No the best part when Farouk was whipping her. She was concentrating so hard on screaming at just the right time. You could actually see her counting off the seconds from the whip crack until she opened her mouth. You were off a bit by the way. Not your best performance."

"Oh c'mon! You guys! It was all those times she pretended to be passed out. You could see her eyes moving-watching those pricks under her eyelashes." Jeffries added with glee.

Justin wasn't not going to not comment, however.

"What I would like to know, is why you told that asshole to nail you to the table? Playing possum not enough of a challenge for you?"

Kris did have the sense to look a little abashed at that one.

Adam's eyebrows drew together. He signaled for quiet in the room. He looked at Kris.

"Wait a minute. Are you all implying she sat there and let those men torture her? That she could have just left at any time?"

Looking at the faces of the men who ranged from anger to pride to hysterical laughter told the tale. He just witnessed her husband rebreak her fingers in ten places while she had a conversation with her father without so much as blinking. He read the file on her battlefield wounds and the subsequent surgery- while she watched. He'd seen her fight in the past. She was the Marine Corps only undefeated Men's MMA champion. She'd fought in dozens of matches against skilled opponents. She never uttered a sound even when taking a severe beatdown. Yet in that video she screamed nonstop.

He turned and looked at Kris with a knowing stare and she knew she had to tread carefully here. She stood tall and faced the General squarely with a look of pure steel on her face.

"Sir, before I was called into Command six months ago I had already formulated a plan to pull El Moufas out into the open and leak them my location. I intended to have them capture me during a mission. I researched all of their known tactics and studied countering techniques. I studied the psychological profiles our people made on all the known players and reviewed all of my own personal files. I also used my own personal knowledge of the men from years of being around them and formulated a series of tactics to disarm. I used my knowledge of their psychological weaknesses to my own advantage.

Sir there was no point in that mission that I was not right where I wanted and needed to be. I wasn't about to pull out until I had that final piece. Once I got it, I ended it. Only I didn't expect the kid to aim that RPG at a stack of volatile land mines causing the entry of the cave to fall in. I wasn't prepared for the kid to be there. I never would have brought the kid in, Chambers did. But I wasn't about to leave without him. He stood. The whole time. I was terrified for the first time of what could happen in there when he stood in front of me with that plate of food. I wasn't about to do anything to put that boy in jeopardy. I needed them to believe he was loyal to them. I needed him to show that he had no attachment to me. In the end everything worked out. The kid is safe, the intel is here, and they're done. Mission accomplished Sir."

"We'll discuss that at a later time Captain." He turned to the commanders in the room.

"Get your people together. I want an OP set and ready to go in 24 hours. I want that shipment they discussed taken and confiscated. I want SECDEF and SECNAV on video conference in five minutes. Stirling you come with me and help explain this. It'll give you time for your blood to stop boiling."

Kris looked at her father who was as coldly furious as she'd ever seen him.

"You are grounded. Go to your room. I don't want to see you until I call you." He turned and left with the General.

No one seemed to think it odd that the Colonel just grounded a 29-year-old Marine. As Justin and Kris stood looking at one another a familiar voice piped up from behind them.

"Well, I think all the angst and rebellion you didn't get to have as a teenager just erupted all over him and I think he acted accordingly."

Kris turned and smiled a huge smile.

"Hey Cook!" Kris pulled the unsuspecting woman into a tight hug. Shelly laughed and pulled Kris closer. This Kris was not what she was expecting. Her buoyant attitude was completely at odds with her most recent experience. She came in right as Kris started talking and stayed in the back. After watching what Kris went through and listening to her talk she had to completely readjust her professional opinion. What Kris experienced was far different than your average POW situation. She and Kris talked for several hours letting Cook really take a good look into Kris's psyche. What she saw was a carefree, happy, adjusted woman. Free from fear, anger, and the consuming mission she had taken on as a child. She was seeing a woman that Kris had never allowed herself to be. Letting her guard down and opening up to people. Cook was impressed.

"Well in my professional opinion you are in a remarkable mental place. But that doesn't mean that at some point in the future you are not going to come crashing down. If you start having nightmares, or issues with anything no matter how little-do not shrug it aside. PTSD can manifest in a myriad of ways. It can come on at any time so please. Do yourself a favor. Get counseling. Don't try to tough this out."

"I already put in a call Lieutenant. I figured that's why you were here!"

Cook laughed. "No, but if you want to talk some more..."

"You'll be the third or maybe fourth person I will come to!" Kris said with snarky grin. "Set something up. Though it will be dependent on SOC. If they need me that takes priority."

Cook left to find her quarters for the next couple of days. Justin grabbed the wheelchair and put it behind Kris to sit down and he wheeled her over to the barracks and the room they shared off the main hall. She got up out of the chair and sat on the bed.

"Wow, I've never been grounded before. How long do you think he'll be mad?"

"Oh I'd say anywhere from a couple of hours to three days after hell freezes over. You may be sitting in this room long after American troops are pulled from the theater of operations here. You may die here."

Kris laughed, shaking her head. She didn't blame her father for being pissed. She was going to have to work on how to make this right with him. 'I'm sorry' just didn't cover it. Justin had an idea of what she was thinking before she left but even he never thought she'd go to those extremes. But then he knew everything thing she'd done to get here. No way she was going to do less than everything in her power to gain the only end result she would accept. He could forgive her for all the worry because she was here now. But if she ever considered pulling anything like that again...well that was a different story.

He lay on the bed with her and pulled her into his arms. She lay on her side just looking at him. After a couple of minutes she snuggled into his neck so she could breathe in his scent. She'd never take it or him for granted.

"Justin."

"Kris."

She opened her eyes and looked at him.

"I want to have children with you."

"What right now? Well ok, but I am not going to guarantee anything."

He made moves to mount her and she hit him.

"I mean it!"

"So do I baby, so do I."

He plopped back down grinning and she moved in to kiss him slow and thoroughly. He was careful not to grab her too tight or jar her ribs or back. They just flowed into one another drinking in the closeness after so long apart. When they pulled apart they sat looking at one another quietly for several moments until Kris spoke.

"Do you ever think about adopting a child?"

"Of course."

"How about an Afghan orphan?"

"You want to bring one of those kids home with us?"

"Yeah."

"Ok."

"What? Just like that? Ok?!"

"Yeah. Did you have a particular one in mind?"

"Yeah. One very special one."

"Selima." Justin smiled remembering the sweet shy four-year-old girl that always climbed in his lap for a hug.

"No I was thinking a boy."

Justin looked at her closely. It didn't take a rocket scientist to put this together.

"A boy. Hmmm. Like a fourteen-year-old former terrorist maybe?"

Kris grinned. "Yeah. Like that one."

"Are you out of your mind? The kid nailed you to a table and you want to take him home?"

"I told him to do it. He followed orders. He can't stay here. I promised him I would protect him. I get it if you can't have him around. I really do. But I promised him. If he can't stay with us I'll see about getting him in with a good family until he can get out on his own. But I'm not leaving him here."

"I didn't say I couldn't not have him around, but Kris are you sure?"

"It won't be for long. He'll finish school and be on his own in a couple of years. But in that couple of years, we can give him a good start. Be good practice for those babies we will have someday soon."

She ran her hands up his chest and draped them around his neck as best she could with them wrapped.

"Babies huh?"

"I want to try. I know my eggs may not work, but I want to try. If they don't there are plenty of kids we can make a difference with."

"How are you going to be there for those babies if you are constantly deployed with the teams?"

"I have been giving that some thought. I had a lot of downtime pretending to be unconscious. I think I want to move to MARSOS." Marine Corps Special Operations School.

"Are you sure?"

"Yeah. I only joined the teams for one reason. Mission accomplished. Literally. Now I don't think I have the same purpose in the teams. I don't need to be out there like before. I can be just as vital and effective there as I have been downrange. Maybe even more so."

"I know you could. I will support any course you choose."

He brushed his hands through her hair.

"I do have one question, you accused the kid of treason, how are you going to fix that? They are getting ready to send him to Gitmo."

"While you were gathering the teams I made a call. I spoke to the new head of the CIA in this region. She is here and we had a chat. With Fazil. Off the record. She looked up his information and one thing Briggs did was put the kid's information in the system when Chambers pulled him in. That was CYA. No one would care if this kid was there or ever heard from again. I think he did that so he could use the kid as a scapegoat or a patsy if he needed to. It actually may help us in the long run. I have an idea that will allow the kid to come to us and keep his cover in El Moufas intact."

"Why Kris? Why does the kid need a cover?"

"He wants to come to the states and become a Marine. He wants to be part of stabilizing the region. He wants SOC but I think CIA has some ideas based on the information I saw in his file."

"You busted into his file?"

"Nope, I used the back door that Briggs put in. I heard him discussing it with Aziz. It's how no one was ever able to finger him for so long. I changed his password to a 24 digit encryption he will never break. But I still plan on informing CIA of its existence. The CIA is already thinking of formally recruiting Fazil, or was before this. That's why I need to give them a sitrep before someone screws up and that kid's life is over before it begins. I wanted it on the footage that he was a terrorist in case it was broadcasting so he wouldn't be considered a collaborator or a traitor. Now that we know it wasn't we can use it. If he really wants to make a difference, we can back story all this information until he's trained and he can assume his own identity later and use it to infiltrate. Covers don't get any tighter than that."

"What if he doesn't want this? What if he just wants to go to the states and be a normal kid with a normal life and forget this shithole?"

"Then that's what we help him do. I want him to have a life. A good life. Family. Only when I look at him, I see me at his age with that fire burning inside and no way to let it out. That drive to take back what was taken. I can't see him walking away any more than I could have then. But if that is what he wants I will help him do it. Either way. His choice, his path. Not mine. If I thought I could talk him out of it by telling him all I had to lose, I'd beat it into him. But sometimes your path is set. You can't walk away no matter what."

"You know if he stays on that path, you could lose him."

"I know. And we could get hit by bus in Chicago next week. You just gotta live your life man."

Justin pulled Kris close and she lay her head on his heart. After a few minutes she fell asleep. He lay for a long time listening to her breathing as he thought about everything. He could see them together over the years raising a family, fostering kids, mentoring youth groups. Kris couldn't stay away from kids. She needed them. They kept her grounded. Family meant stability. They couldn't both be deployed constantly and create that. He took the Lieutenant Colonel's test while she was away and passed. He was up for promotion. He really didn't want to lose that. He'd had a great career and was only eight years from retirement once he pinned that on. He already had made the decision to change his MOS to medical. He'd been approved and only needed to submit the paperwork. He was looking online and the hospital on Lejeune was looking for a civilian surgeon. If he changed to reserve status he could still work to retirement and transition to medicine while staying on Lejeune for Kris.

Tomorrow. Nothing would be finalized tonight. Once they got some more answers and more information the future would sort itself. He pulled her close and closed his eyes.

Chapter Thirty Three

The interrogation room was a sterile dismal room with a two-way glass that separated the questioning area from the observation area. General Adams, Lieutenant Colonel Frazier with antiterrorism, and Justin and Kris all stood watching the two people on the other side of the glass. Two junior Marines sat at a console monitoring the recording equipment and audio visual in the room. Kris stayed in the observation room with Justin as CIA Director Riley questioned Fazil. He sat with his gaze fixed on the window as if he was looking at her. He only uttered three phrases.

I am following the will of Allah.

I will never betray my brothers.

I have nothing to say to you.

No matter what Riley asked he only repeated these same words over and over. He'd been in the room for three hours. She threw question after question at him. He never changed his response. She was beginning to get worried they'd actually brainwashed the kid. Riley left the room and came to observation. She looked at Kris standing next to the General.

"I think your kid has been turned. No way a fourteen-year-old is that skilled at counterinterrogation without help."

Kris smiled. "He's a smart kid who has largely been raised by MARSOC Marines. Chances are he's picked up a lot of chatter. Let me have a go at him."

Kris picked up a file folder and went into the interrogation room with Justin on her heels. He wouldn't let her go alone since she was still wounded. She came in and dropped the file on the table and leaned over glaring at him.

"So you think you are tough shit now huh? You are about to find out how wrong you are."

Kris circled the table as Fazil stared into the glass as if she wasn't even there. She fired off questions regarding his involvement with El Moufas. Who recruited him, how long he'd been a member, what his tasks where. Every time he answered with the same three phrases. Finally Kris looked at Justin and nodded at him to leave.

"I need you to step out of the room Sir."

"Captain?"

"Sir I need you to leave. I am going to get through to this little bastard and you need to leave Sir."

The way Kris looked at him made him think she was going to beat the crap out of the kid the minute he was gone. He'd seen that look before and the last time it almost put her in the brig. He trusted her though and realized she had a game plan and turned and exited the room. She paused long enough to let him get back into place in the observation room. When she laid into the kid again she did so with all the fierce rage that made DI's feared in basic training. She got into his face and he didn't move. When she turned and faced the glass she did so with a grim determination.

She walked over to the camera in the corner of the room and disconnected the wire. The light went off and the feed in the next room went to static. The two Marines manning the console rose and looked into the window. She turned to the kid and glared at him for a moment then walked around the table to stand right next to him. He removed his gaze from the glass and smiled a great big smile at her as he got up from the chair and leaned into her arms which came around him tightly. The handcuffs holding him to the table did not let him move much but he was able to cuddle into her embrace as he laid his head on her breasts. He smiled up at her and she rocked him back and forth.

"That was pretty good kid."

"I did just what you told me. Stay simple. Don't ever change your story and don't elaborate. Stick as close to the truth as you can so you will be believable."

"And never waiver in your resolve; especially if a camera is on and recording you." She turned back to look at the observation glass with a smirk. Fazil just kept his head on her chest.

"That has to be uncomfortable."

"It has its compensations..." he said with a cheeky grin as looked down her utilities blouse.

She grabbed his head and pushed him away toward the chair.

"You little pervert." He just snickered and she shoved him into the chair with a chuckle. She sat Fazil back down and propped her hip on the corner of the table. "So how is what you were saying before close to the truth when the director was questioning you?"

"I am following the will of Allah. I believe Allah called my mother and father and brother and sister to paradise so I could go to that orphanage. I believe he meant for me to be there to find you. So you would be my new family and help me down my path to finally get peace for my people. I would never betray my brothers. I am a Marine now. Every Marine is my brother. I will never do anything to harm or to bring harm to my brothers. I have nothing more to say to you." He finished with a fair imitation of Kris's cheeky grin.

Kris just sat there and laughed. She threw her head back and really laughed. Fazil just sat in the chair with a cocky grin pretty pleased with himself.

"I have been talking with the CIA. What's going to happen next is you are going to be escorted to Guantanamo Bay Cuba Marine Corps detention center. You are going to be there for several weeks and you will be interrogated. Repeatedly. By people who will believe you are a terrorist. They will try to trick and to break you. They *will* scare you. Just stick with the plan. Keep those three phrases. Stick exactly to what you have been doing. You will be there for several weeks. Keep to yourself. Do not talk to the prisoners and do not talk to the Marines.

You will be put into an area of solitary for a week or so. Then you will be brought out and taken to interrogation. After that point you will be given a set of Marine Corps MCCUUs and you will be walked out of the facility in the company of a Marine who will be your handler. He will be your liaison with the CIA. He has been appraised of your mission there. For the next several years you will be escorted to Gitmo two or more times a year for two to three weeks and put into the mix with the actual terrorists. You will become one of them.

When you are 18 you will be processed into Marine Corps basic training and you will complete the course and become a Marine. Once you complete training and choose an MOS you will be sent to school and complete your duty. You will serve one year stateside in a training division learning to do just about everything. Then you will complete a tour of duty. After that you will enter MARSOC. If you pass and make it in you will be assigned a new MOS and you will receive your orders to a JSOC with CIA in which you will go deep undercover using your actual name and identity as a terrorist. You will infiltrate and eliminate it from an ironclad cover. You will do something never attempted and never achieved. Or. You walk away."

Someone started beating on the glass pretty heavily. Probably trying to get Kris to stop.

In the viewing room Riley beat her fist on the glass.

"What is she doing! We had a deal."

Justin crossed his arms over his chest. "The deal was for you to arrange for us to adopt Fazil and get him stateside. That was it. Neither Kris nor I are going to let you use that kid. He's been through enough."

Riley turned back to the window pissed. She didn't want to lose this kid as an asset. Kris continued.

"You walk away, and you come to the states and you live a normal life. You give up this crusade and you become a lawyer or a teacher or anything else. You give up this revenge and live your life as best as you can. You make a difference by being a good person and encouraging others to do the same. You get a house, a dog, a car, and family. Peace."

Fazil looked at Kris with his heart in his eyes. You'd have to be a cruel heartless bastard not to be moved by the love and dedication there.

"And I come live with you and be your brother? You and Major Justin?"

"Yeah. You come live with us. But you wouldn't be my brother. You'd be my son. Our son. We'd be your parents. You'd have rules and chores. You would be expected to go to school and study. Work hard. And if you're lucky, when you are sixteen, we will talk about a car. You go to college. You become a man we can all be proud of."

"But if I come live with you, I can't become a Marine? I can't come back with the CIA and help make peace?"

"Kid I don't want you to feel just because this is what the CIA wants you have to do it. There are no strings attached. If you want to go to the states and be a normal kid then I will support you 100%. You don't have to follow this plan. I can tell you right now from experience that the only thing you will get from this path you think you have to follow is a lot of shit you can't undo. Violence, death, and pain. It won't bring those you lost back. It won't heal the wounds of the past. It won't fix anything. You have a choice. Only you can make it."

"Captain Kris. I understand what you are telling me. I see with my eyes. I see with my brain. I cannot walk away and watch as so many die when I have the ability to save them."

"One thing I learned kid, the hard way, you can't save them. And you can't live your life for revenge. That is no life. It's an existence. You need more than that. I want more for you than that."

"I understand. I do. But I also know I need to do this. If I don't how can I face myself?"

Kris just nodded. She understood. It was like she told Justin. Just like looking at herself 15 years ago.

"Well that's it then. I'm turning the camera back on." She reached up to reattach the cable and heard a loud bang behind her. She swung around as Fazil picked his face from off the table. He grabbed his hair and yanked it and then beat his face into his fists on the table.

"Ok, now you can turn the camera back on. Do I look like you beat the crap out of me?"

She laughed. "Yeah kid. You look pretty beat up. No don't wipe your eyes. Tears are good."

He slumped back in the chair cowering. He looked a little scared. That gut checked Kris a bit. She hated that look on his face. But she schooled her features to the grim fierce mask she had on before and reengaged the camera. The feed went back to normal in the viewing room. She turned to him.

"Well that was fun. Enjoy Gitmo you little traitor. You deserve it." She gathered up the folder and walked out and entered into the viewing room. Nathan had come in while she was in the other room to watch the interrogation. He stood there thoughtful. She saluted him and handed the file to Justin.

"That was an impressive demonstration. I almost believed you were ready to kill that kid. I would believe it if I hadn't seen you with him all of these years. Are you seriously considering adopting him?"

"Yes that is the plan. He'll go to Gitmo for a while then home to us. Your first grandchild."

Nathan shook his head. He looked at the kid in the room. His nose was running and bleeding some. He looked at the glass with a fierce look of determination. Nathan had seen that look before. On Kris at that same age. He had a feeling he was seeing history repeat itself. He thought back to when Kris was that age. How he mentored her without knowing what she was facing. He encouraged her to become what she became without knowing what was really driving her. She had the advantage of knowing exactly what that kid was feeling and thinking. If anyone could get him on the right path it would be Kris.

Two Marines entered the interrogation room and escorted Fazil out. He walked with his head held high as they took him back to detainment. Riley turned and looked at Kris.

"You called that one Captain. I was ready to tear you apart when you tried talking that kid out of this."

"Then you may want to stay loose Riley, because I have every intention of doing so before he's 18. I didn't lie, I don't want this for him. I know what that life is like, and I don't want it for him. But ultimately it is his choice. I will do my best to keep him safe, teach him everything he needs to know, and give him a life he can be proud of in hopes he realizes what he'll be giving up so he'll quit this vendetta. I know it probably won't happen, but I'm going to do my damnedest to try."

"Well in the meantime I will be escorting him to the states for a briefing and then to set the stage at Gitmo. I have that paperwork you requested." Riley handed her a file.

"It's all in there. The full agreement and a copy of his visa. The papers you and Justin signed adopting him and the contact information for the division he'll be working with. Once his paperwork clears, we'll get him in DEERS. His handler will be Marine Major Tyler Jackson. He will meet Fazil in Cuba and bring him to Lejeune. He will be the liaison between Fazil and the CIA. He will be his escort to and from Cuba over the next several years."

"I want Jackson's record. I want to see who this Major is and make sure he will take care of him. And if at any time over the next few years he decides he wants out, you will make that happen. I did not risk my life for that kid only to put him in a worse situation than the one I got him out of. I love that little brat and I am not about to let him get hurt or screwed over by someone else's agenda."

"You have my word, Cole; this is a no strings attached deal. We owe that kid. Because of him we are about to take down an organization that has dogged our agency for 20 years and we dug out a thorn in our side at the same time. He also saved the life of a valuable Marine asset in the bargain."

Kris snorted. "I would have been on my way after that nap."

"Yeah, with your face and hands stuck to the table. Or were you planning on just bringing it with you?"

Justin stepped in. "Riley- Kris would have gotten herself out of there without our help. She wasn't in there because she was forced to be, she was in there because that is right where she wanted to be."

Riley looked over Kris. She was impressed with the Marine's actions and record. But she didn't believe the hype. Kris took a seat at the table and opened the file. Riley decided to test her. She walked up around Kris and cuffed her to the wooden table.

"What are you doing Riley?"

"You're tough, get out of it."

Kris just looked at her with an inscrutable expression. Kris didn't look like she was going to move but then in an action that seemed to come from nowhere she rounded the table, completely free of the cuffs and put a hand on Riley's throat. It happened so fast Riley didn't have time to even take a step back. She was on her feet and squared off in front of Riley before the table even crashed to the floor. She looked over Kris's shoulder and saw the pieces of the pen on the floor Kris used to pick the lock and undo the cuffs. Not hype.

"No one puts me where I do not want to go. And no one messes with me unless I allow it. Keep that in mind if you do one thing to put that kid in harm's way. He is mine now. And I will protect him. Keep in mind what I have done thus far to protect one of mine. And how far I will go to keep someone I love safe."

Riley's smile was blinding by the time Kris finished. Damn that was impressive. She respected the Marine for her toughness and ability. But she liked the woman for passion and her loyalty. She pulled Kris's hand away from her neck and put hers out to shake. Kris grasped it in a hard grip and nodded to the Director.

"I gotta say Cole, you have great style." She laughed a rich laugh full of humor and warmth.

"I'll keep you posted on Fazil's progress and each step of the operation until he gets back to you. We'll keep him detained until I get word from your Command you are back stateside. That will give us time to set up and you time to finish what you started."

"He'll have to pick a new name. He can't use his own if it's attached to the op. Tell him to choose. He's had little choice in his life before now. That way you can update it on all the paperwork before you bring him home to us."

They all left the room and the Marines all headed back to SOC. Earlier that day Kris wrote the warning letter for the teams. The letter outlined the mission and gear needed so the teams could prepare. Alpha and Bravo would be going. She would stay in Command monitoring the op. She had drawn up a detailed mission brief in the last couple of hours with the five-paragraph order of the task at hand. She was keeping it simple and clear so the teams could work on their infil and exfil as a unit. It wasn't as hard for her to step back as she thought it would be. The good news is that this would be Justin's last mission. His paperwork for transfer to medical had been submitted.

The op was scheduled for departure at 0300. The teams had assembled in SOC and everyone was ready. Kris walked them through the intel and the parameters. Capture Yusef Ben David Mondalvi. Rescue Abraham Mondalvi. As the teams departed Kris stood and looked hard at the men who have been her brothers and her team for the last six years. The air was ripe with anticipation. When they left it was with the knowledge that when they returned a new chapter was beginning.

She hadn't told the teams of her plans. She'd been in discussion with Nathan and Anderson regarding her transfer and why. She spoke frankly. She was open and honest with her father for the first time on everything. He knew most of it. She filled in the rest. Anderson was blown away on what she'd done. He couldn't imagine a 12-year-old with the presence of mind and strength to embark on such an undertaking. Or the understanding to face down and infiltrate a terrorist cell at such a young age. Nathan was upset at the danger Kris and Jenna had been in. But more that he hadn't been there for them when they needed him most.

He was saddened at how Jenna died. Kris apologized for not telling him. She didn't want to hurt him more than he was already hurting. Her loss was a significant turning point in his life. He dedicated his life to mentoring and watching over Kris in her memory. In the end he was able to forgive himself. As Kris pointed out, it was all El Moufas. Nothing they did or didn't do would change anything but now they had a chance at a new beginning. Free of the past.

The teams checked in once in position. Kris stood back and watched the feed and listened to the transmissions. The fight was lengthy but in the team's favor. They knew where everyone was and who all was going to be there thanks to the plans in the cave and the intel on the video. The takedown was largely bloodless. All the Tajik men still alive were rounded up. Less than half were killed in the firefight. The El Moufas men fought until the last man. No one remained alive from the group. Yusef Ben David Mondalvi was captured. Trucks arrived as the sun came up to take the men back to base. The weapons and ammo were confiscated, and everything went off without a hitch. Right up until they were ready to depart. The squad that was sent to gather men and contraband was finishing the loading and the teams were doing the last sweep. Justin went to Abraham and recited the lines Kris told him to say to get through to the man. Stephen King wrote a hell of prison escape movie regarding hope and friendship.

"Abraham, Faith told me this is your favorite." Justin quoted the hero's letter to his best friend. Left for him after being paroled; encouraging him to make one more trip and reminding him that hope was a good thing.

Abraham looked at Justin and responded with the narrator's affirmation and promise to get busy living.

Justin put his arm around the man and lead him to a Humvee and put him inside under guard. He didn't resist or struggle. Yusef watched this with a high level of awareness. Once Abraham was in the vehicle Justin approached Mondalvi. He listened to the exchange between the Marine and his son with trepidation. He knew what it meant. The Marine Amir had expected to kill had escaped. El Moufas was either dead or captured. And if they knew his son was called Abraham then they also knew who he was and his life as he knew it was over. Never one to go quietly; he barged into one of his guards attempting to grab their weapon. The infantryman who secured Mondalvi made a critical error in fastening his hands in front of him instead of behind him. Justin grabbed his weapon and shot the man in the thigh. He went down but grabbed the side arm of his guard on the way. He knew he couldn't take out enough of the Marines, but he never intended to be captured. Before any of the men could gage his intent, he put the weapon in his mouth and pulled the trigger. He was dead before his body hit the ground. Justin was running to him, and Javier had also run to intercept but it was too late.

"Kris is going to be pissed."

"Yeah. She will. She wanted him to serve time. But more over she wanted Abraham safe." He looked to the shaken guards and yelled. "When you secure a prisoner you make sure their hands are secured behind them and they have no opportunity to get ahold of weapon. That was sloppy and careless and you could have been killed or gotten someone else killed. Bag that and get your asses over to the truck. Both of you are on report."

They ran to do his bidding.

"C'mon man you are going to miss this."

"Nope. I'm not. I'm ready for the next chapter. Family. Home."

"Yeah. Home."

"Let's go. Sooner we get outta here the sooner that all happens."

The teams geared up and climbed aboard the vehicles. Three hours later they were back in the camp safe.

***

Kris was plenty pissed about the death of Yusef Mondalvi. His interrogation was supposed to go a long way toward exonerating Abraham. She observed the questioning of Abraham. He was scared and he didn't have the ability to answer them. He sat rocking for the better part of an hour. She broke protocol and entered the interrogation room. She didn't say anything just stood off to the side. She felt her presence would go a long way to keeping him calm. He was scared but when she came in he stopped rocking. Kris stood for two hours while they ran him through the standard evaluations and tests. She had briefed the psychologist of what she knew of his mental state and abilities and by the end of the questioning he concurred. When they finished he walked to Kris and pulled her into a gentle hug. She returned it with great compassion. He held onto her for a long while. One of the guards cleared his throat but Kris just stabbed a sharp look at him. Abraham pulled back and smiled at her.

"I like Faith. I miss Faith. I miss Mali. Where is Mali?"

"Mali is in Paradise."

He looked sad like he would cry. "Inshallah."

"Inshallah. Abie is going to go with these men and they will find you a room. Then Abie is going to go somewhere safe where people will take care of him. Aba is in Paradise. So Abie will have to be strong and take care of Abie."

"Faith will go too?"

"No Abie. Faith has to stay. But Faith will visit from time to time."

Abraham looked distressed. But stood. He had learned to articulate a great deal more than Kris remembered. He turned to look at the men and then addressed Kris with the wise cartoon Shaman's words to a certain young lion about facing the past. Kris responded with the signature two word phrase made popular by a meerkat and a warthog from that same movie.

He returned by saying the immortal words of everyone's favorite 1980's truant high school boy about missing life if you don't look around once in a while.

Kris actually bent over laughing. She embraced him again and whispered in his ear the phrase in the movie he said to his friend about where they would be if they had stayed in school that day. He started out the door then stopped and turned to Kris.

Abraham delivered the after credits quote at the end of that movie where the 4th wall had been broken, minus the bathrobe and towel, smiled his sweet shy smile and left with the escort. The psychologist was amazed at the discourse between them. Kris stood and grinned.

"He may be mentally retarded and inarticulate but that was a sound and thoughtful dialog full of intelligence and feeling. He has adapted remarkably to his situation thanks to you. You said this was a game you developed with him as a child?"

"I was child. He was about 23 if memory serves. That would have been around 2001. He can be taught. Yusef just didn't bother. He'd probably be pretty self-sufficient if he'd been worked with as a child. I think he just left him alone with an old woman who didn't do much other than feed him."

"I put a call in to a facility I know in Virginia. It is a home for stroke victims who need specialized care. Small and exclusive. I talked to General Adams and once the funds are seized by the government a trust is going to be set up for him with some of them. Enough to care for him the rest of his life. Publicly they will release that Yusef ben David Mondalvi had a massive stroke. He survived but will be unable to fully recover. That way he is protected. His situation is not his fault, but his face is too well known to have him disappear. This way his condition will be ramifications of the stroke. No one will have to know he's not who they thought. I'll send you the information so you can keep in contact with him. It'll be good for him to have visitors that he knows."

"That sounds good. He is a kind and gentle man. He deserves better than he got. I'm glad he will finally get it."

Kris shook the man's hand and walked him and the group of evaluators out. Abraham was being loaded into a transport. The group got in with him. He waived to Kris as they pulled away. She waved until they left sight.

Over the next three weeks the teams worked hard to aid in the assaults against the last of El Moufas' active cells. A day after the final mission after the teams completed their after action reports and the necessary paperwork for the missions they all got the word they were being sent home. They were already four months past their original return date. They were all looking forward to going home.

Kris sent word to have Nathan, Justin, Javier, Davis, Dan, Mike, John, Jack, Noah, Max and Steve meet her in the ready room. They had all packed and were waiting for the truck to take them to the airfield their transport was landing at. Javier arrived first and Kris asked him to set up the display monitor to field a Skype call. He raised an eyebrow but just set it up knowing she'd explain once the rest arrived. Justin arrived and grabbed the handful of chairs they would need. The tables had been taken down and stacked at the back of the room with the chairs stacked in several piles beside them. He set the dozen chairs up along the sides out of the camera view. They all got there and sat down.

"I wanted you all to be here to see the fruits of our labor. I wanted you to know what all this sacrifice has been for."

She turned to the computer and placed the call. She moved to stand directly in front of the monitor that hung on the wall with the camera mounted above it. It rang and didn't connect. The men muttered and talked quietly among themselves. She wasn't worried. It was prearranged protocol. She waited five minutes and dialed again. When the call connected a women wrapped in a hajib with her face covered by a thick veil filled the screen.

"Amalia."

The woman's eyes filled with tears. She spoke in Pashtu. "Kris! Oh thanks be to Allah you are ok."

"It's over. He's dead. They are all dead and you are free."

"Inshallah. Thank you, God!"

She sat with her hands up to her face crying quietly tears pouring down her face. Kris let her get it out. They had both waited for this their whole lives.

"How did he die?"

"By my hand."

"Slowly, painfully. Tell me you made him hurt. That you made him cry for every moment of pain and fear we had to endure."

"No."

She tilted her head and narrowed her eyes and in perfect unaccented English exclaimed-

"Why not Marine?! You swore to me! You swore he would pay."

"He did pay. He's dead. And he knew at the end we had beaten him."

"But why didn't you....."

"In the end I realized I owed him."

Her eyebrows disappeared under her hajib as her eyes showed her incredulousness.

"You owed him. You owed him?! You owed him pain. Lots and lots of it."

"Listen....."

"No you listen! I can't believe after all we have endured you just let him off...."
Kris got up close to the screen and yelled at the woman.

"I did not let him off dammit! I had a lot of time to think while I was tied to a chair in between torture sessions." Amalia started to speak to ask what she was talking about and Kris cut her off.

"I thought of every single time we were scared or fearful. I thought of mom. I thought of all we had lost. Then I started thinking. And I realized something. Every good thing I have in my life I got from him."

That through Amalia for a loop. She threw up her hands and sat back in the chair quietly waiting for Kris to explain.

"I have hated him for as long as I can remember. It didn't take much to dredge up all the anger and pain he'd caused. It helped remind me of why I was there. But the longer it took the more I was thinking of what I had. What I stood to lose. Then I realized all he'd given me. A family. Everything and everyone in my life that I love, that I would kill for, that I would die for. He gave me. I have spent so long reminding myself of what he's taken I never took into consideration what I got in return.

I have a sister I wouldn't have otherwise had. The first person I ever loved was you. I became stronger in martial arts so I could protect you and mom. I took on more disciplines so I could fight. I got to travel and see things I never would have seen. We were on the run, but if we hadn't been I would never had met Buck. I never would have trained to be a sniper. I never would have wanted to become a Marine. My wanting to be a Marine was why we moved to Georgia. So I could go to high school and be in ROTC.

It was there mom found dad. The man she'd been looking for years. The man who was the love of her life. She was happy finally. Then we moved to North Carolina, and I met the man who was my mentor. The man who told me for the first time my goals were attainable. The man who made it his mission to help me become a Marine. The man who I always thought of as a father. Funnily enough the man who actually was my father! He put me on the path to MARSOC. He helped guide me to a place where I could actually make good on the promise, I made you in that closet in California. To protect you from the monsters. To end them.

It was on that path I met the love of my life. The person that saw everything about me and loved me anyway. Who didn't look and see the broken kid who wasn't a boy or a girl but the person that kid had become despite it all. My best friend. The man who pushed me to be better, to do more. Someone who got me. All of me. Who shared every passion I have and helped me realize a few more. Then there are my brothers. The men who I have waded through mud and blood with. The ones who gave me roots and faith. Who brought me into their lives and made me theirs. Who gave me their families. Who made me their family. The ones who made me realize that I wasn't really living. Only getting by. The ones who made me open up for the first time in my life and let someone else in. The people I couldn't have ever done this without. It was knowing what I would do to them if I didn't come home that helped me stay strong. I could have blown that cave at any time and taken us all out. It would have ensured you would live safe. But I couldn't give up or give in. Not knowing every one of them would hunt to the ends of the earth to get me home. Not knowing that if I went down like that it would kill every one of them. They kept me straight. They kept me focused. They kept me alive.

I only have them and all of this because of that psycho. If not for him my life would be a far cry from what it is. I have lost. I know fear and pain. But I have known so much more joy and love than I would have otherwise. I also appreciate it more because I know what it is I have to lose. I sat in that cave and realized for all I have lost I have gained so much more. And in the end I knew I would have to kill him. I was ok with that; he had to die. I knew if I went down that dark path to make him pay I could never come back from it. So I killed him in a way I could live with. My act of mercy wasn't for him. It was for me. For you. For all of us in this room."

Kris stopped and faced the men she stood with. Most of them had inscrutable expressions. Some were thoughtful. Nathan looked proud. Justin looked relieved. The look Noah had confused her though. His eyes were bright and he looked like he was ready to bust out of his skin. He looked as if he had some exciting news he was dying to share and was ready to spill. Kris looked back to the screen.

Amalia's eyes were bright with unshed tears. Her expression had softened. She had let go of her earlier rancor. She wasn't angry any longer. She nodded and accepted what Kris said. But she had something to say as well.

"Ok. I understand." She shifted a bit and her arm reached down in a gesture that had Kris pausing.

Kris stood there a minute and stared. Then said in Farsi.

"Amalia. Stand up."

The woman on the screen adopted a very innocent stance. It was obvious she was trying to play dumb.

"Why?"

"Stand up!"

Amalia sighed and pushed her chair back from the desk the
computer was on and stood up in front of the camera. It was not
hard to see the obvious bulge on her abdomen. She was very
pregnant.

"You're pregnant?!"

She dipped her head shaking it slightly and looked up with
laughing eyes.

"No baby. You are."

Kris stood stock still at that bomb shell. Her face frozen. She
couldn't move. Justin came up behind her and put his hands on
her shoulders moving into the camera view.

"What did you say?"

"I said you are pregnant. You and Kris are having a baby."

They turned and looked at one another as if the world had
suddenly gone crazy.

"You left me power of attorney remember? That included
medical power of attorney. I put it to good use. I will never
forget that because of me, because of my father and his hatred
you can't have children. I know how badly you have always
wanted kids of your own. I won't get into the specifics but I will
tell you that there was an emergency and we had to act quickly.
There was no time to get ahold of you. If we didn't do this all
would be lost. I have never been able to let go of all that you have
lost because of me. This. This was easy. You would never ask.
You would never let me take that risk. But Kris I would risk
anything for you. For you and Justin."

Kris staggered back into Justin who wrapped his arms around
her stunned. She started shaking. She didn't realize she was
crying until she looked at Justin and saw the tears falling down
his face. She reached up to wipe them as he did the same for her.
Then they just pulled each other into a tight embrace. Nathan
got up and wrapped his arms around the pair. Kris grabbed him

and held him tight as she finally let go and started crying in earnest. The men didn't quite know what to do; no one had ever seen Kris cry before. John reached into his pocket and pulled out a handkerchief and put it Kris's hand. She looked at it and him and burst out laughing. Then she reached over and grabbed him in a hug. That pretty much spurred the rest of them who jumped up and reached for the couple. Everyone passed around hugging and clapping one another on the back.

"Colonel?"

Nathan pulled away from Javier and looked at the screen.

"Yes?"

"When are you sending them home? If they don't leave soon they are going to miss the birth of their child. Come to speak of it you better get here too if you want to be there for the birth of your first grandkid."

Justin spoke up. "When are you due?"

"Four weeks but I could go at any time. My doctor thinks I will deliver early." She said with a twinkle in her eye.

"I will have them out of here in two hours. Arrangements have already been made."

"Good. Come home-all of you. We will have one hell of a welcome home party."

Kris nodded and said her goodbyes. Amalia's attention was not on Kris but looking past her to the back of the room. Her eyes were bright and happy as she looked at something else. Kris turned around to see Noah standing in the rear looking at the screen with a fiercely possessive look toward the woman on the screen. She turned back to the screen only to have it go dark as the call disconnected from the other end. Everyone was still talking at once. Max left after congratulating the couple to make sure everyone else was prepped to leave.

Kris walked back over to Justin and they embraced laying their heads on each other's shoulder. They stood like that for several minutes. When they pulled back the smiles on their faces were hard to contain.

"We are going to be parents."

"Yes we are. We're having a baby Kris. A baby."

"You uh, better call your dad and get a sitrep. He has some explaining to do."

"Oh yeah."

Javier spoke up. "Anyone else recognize that voice?"

Every hand in the room, including Noah's, raised.

"After all this time. After everything." He turned to Justin and Kris for an explanation.

"Yeah. That's why I wanted you all here. Why I wanted you all to see. She couldn't show her face just in case the feed was intercepted but I wanted you to know why I risked my life and for who."

"Damn man! You should have told us!" Dan sounded a bit hurt.

Mike stepped up. "I get it man. I can't believe this though. You mean to tell me all this time your marriage was just a cover?"

"How in the hell did you manage this without anyone finding out?" John said.

"That's why your house was different. I noticed the modifications, but I forgot about them. You have bulletproof glass in the windows. The door is reinforced steel. All the walls in the front are lined with steel plates. The roof has sensors over the vents and ducts. And there is a tunnel from the basement to the sewer line."

Kris turned amazed. "How did you know that?"

"Oh c'mon man! I made that scanner that reads buildings. I tested it out on all our houses right before we left last year. We jumped straight into it when we got here. I meant to ask you about it but everything happened and I forgot about it."

"Yeah. Always prepared. I never knew where the threat was so I prepared for everything."

"Well good; now we know to go to Kris's house if it ever gets real." They all laughed and whooped.

"Ok so wait a minute." Javier stepped forward. "Let me recap-see if I have this straight. Our hero was married to a woman who is really a terrorist's daughter that he has hidden for like 17 years. His mother who he thought was killed in a car crash was really kidnapped and tortured by the terrorist looking for his daughter. The man becomes a Marine who becomes best friends with the man who would save his life; a man who divorced his wife because he fell in love with him while he was still a guy. But he is really a she. She divorces her wife who was really her sister in disguise. The star-crossed couple secretly get married and then find out their commanding officer is really her father who ordered them to marry before he knows they were related and was secretly dating her mother when she died but never told her. They go back to work and are tasked with tracking down and taking out a terrorist cell that is headed by her former father-in-law. Then the CIA shows up and she gets pulled into a covert mission to kill this terrorist. Her cover is blown, and she becomes a prisoner of war. She spends five months being tortured while she really getting information and biding her time. She strikes and kills the terrorists and destroys their cell while she is nailed to a table. She is stuck waiting for her team who swoop in but they can't find her location only to have the boy she has mentored who wants to be her little brother come in at the last second to lead the team to her and bring her back to base where she finds out her sister volunteered to be a surrogate mother and is pregnant with their child to repay her for being wounded after her father put a hit out on her for killing his daughter, who is not really dead, making it so she can't have children. She gets rescued and finds out she is going to be a mother just weeks before her sister gives birth to her child. BEST TELENOVELA EVER!"

They all laughed.

"Well we need to get mama and daddy home team! Let's go. Get your gear together and be ready to hit that transport in two hours."

Nathan held Kris and Justin back a moment.

"Kris your mom would be so proud of you both. I know she is looking down smiling at the beautiful people you have become. I am so damn proud of you. I can't believe after all this time your sister was hiding in plain sight."

"Social services messed everything up. We tried to get them off us but I couldn't risk contacting Justice right then. We had to act fast. And in such a way that would protect her. We were afraid that mom's death wasn't an accident and if not whoever killed mom would tie Emily to Amalia. So when she 'ran away' and I 'went to look for her' we actually arranged for Standish to perform plastic surgery on her. He didn't know who she was, but he must have guessed. We changed her face so no one who saw her at the funeral would recognize her later. She had two more surgeries after the original to complete the transformation. That way even Standish wouldn't recognize her. I contacted Banning, my Justice contact, right after I got to basic and he got new documents for her with a different identity and he made sure she was put into DEERS as my wife. She stayed out of sight while her face healed. That way when I finished basic she met me at my first duty station as Melody. My wife."

"It worked. I never realized. And I saw you both twice a week at school."

"I'm sorry I kept it from you. I swear to you. That is the last of it. There is nothing left that you don't know."

"Well there is one thing I don't know."

"What is that Sir?"

"How you are going to fit a new husband, a teenage boy, your sister and your baby in a three bedroom house?"

"Oh man!" She looked at Justin. "We are going to need a bigger house."

Epilogue

In the last week the house had underwent many changes. First Kris set out pictures for the first time in her life. Her favorites of her, Justin and Javier mountain climbing, when the three couples went clubbing in New York, and the last team shot with the families before deployment. They could never leave out photos before. Too dangerous; they could be used to identify them or anyone close to them if anyone got onto them. Kris took a look around the bedroom that used to be Justin's. They spent their first day home moving him into the master bedroom. Kris never had a lot of clothes or personal items in case they needed to abandon them so there was plenty of room for his things.

They donated the furniture he brought from his house with Trina to a veteran's organization and bought a new bedroom set and bedding for Fazil. Something that would be good for a growing boy and would carry him into manhood. Strong dark wood with the heavy bed frame and matching dresser. Rich green for the bedding. The matching desk had a comfortable chair good for doing homework. The computer had a 29 inch screen mounted on the wall with a PS4 hooked up to it and a couple of gaming chairs that fit in the corner when not in use. She got with Jackson and got the kid's measurements and she and Justin went to the PX to get him some American clothes and shoes. They only picked a couple of things not knowing what style he wanted to embrace. A pair of khakis, some jeans and button down shirts. T-shirts and basketball shorts. Joggers and hoodies. Tennis shoes. Good starter pieces.

She walked over to Mel's bedroom where a pack and play was placed with soft yellow bedding. A changing pad was put on the top of the dresser. They held off buying a crib. Mel's room wouldn't accommodate a crib and her bed. Kris and Justin picked up a few things. Kris's favorite was an OD green onesie with MARINES across the top. Justin picked out a couple of Corps bibs that said Oorah and one that looked like Desert Camo utilities. Mel said she would stay with them for a few months. Kris and Justin both agreed. She would stay as long as she needed to.

The call to Salvatore had been enlightening. He'd been given a call by the storage lab that Kris's eggs wouldn't survive in cold storage. They could only be stored for two more weeks before they would be nonviable. And not knowing if she was producing eggs they couldn't take the chance that letting them go. So Mel talked Sal into using her as a surrogate. Something she would have done for the couple anyway. Since Mel and Kris were the same blood type it was perfect. They tried to contact the couple but got their out of office message indicating they were in the field. When Kris was downrange, and Justin contacted them they chose not to tell Justin Mel was pregnant. Sal and Connie were told Kris was a POW. They did not tell Mel in her condition. They'd planned to tell her after the baby was born.

Kris read a baby book on the flight home that said to keep it simple. Babies mostly need love. And burp cloths. Salvatore hinted Mel and Connie had been busy since Mel conceived not knowing when the team would come home and wanting to be prepared. Yeah right. They couldn't not shop for the baby. Kris was grateful. They bought all the hard stuff; bottles, diaper bag, and all the various things and stuff babies needed on a daily basis. Keeping the parents in mind they found items created by a company that made tactical baby gear. And clothes. They couldn't resist the tiny items and tended to just pick up one every time they left the house, or went online, or inhaled, or exhaled. He or she probably wouldn't even wear them all before growing out of them.

The word went out and the families were rallying around Kris and Justin. Rosa came over with a box of onesies, blankets and bibs. She and Javier had a ton. Sue made a beautiful quilt for the bed which she brought by. Mel wouldn't tell them the sex of the baby. That was ok they really wanted it to be a surprise. Connie and Sal knew but they were careful not to say. They were supposed to arrive any minute. They said they were an hour out 45 minutes ago. A car pulled up front as Kris stepped onto the porch and Noah got out. He had flowers. Before Kris could even ask why he was there looking like he was picking up a first date an SUV pulled up with Illinois plates. Justin came out of the house behind her just as the doors opened.

Connie jumped out and ran to Justin and Kris throwing her arms around them. She held on tight. Sal got out and went around to the passenger rear door and opened it to help Mel out. She didn't get off the seat, just swung her legs around. Kris knew something was wrong. Just as she moved to the vehicle an ambulance pulled into the street with lights flashing. It stopped behind the SUV. Kris ran to Mel. She was panting.

"She's in labor!"

"Yeah. My pains started about an hour ago but I didn't tell Sal until we pulled up. He called the ambulance to meet us here. My water hasn't broke yet. We're good."

She stood up and suddenly her leggings were soaked.

"Oh well I'll take that back. There it goes."

She bent over as the contraction hit her. The EMTs were bringing over the stretcher as Mel looked around.

"Noah!"

He ran to the truck from the car with the flowers still in his hand. He looked a bit panicked.

"What can I do baby?" His eyes were wide as he grabbed Mel's hand. Kris looked at him and back to Mel. Baby?

"Just hold my hand. I'm scared." He grabbed it and held on as she squeezed it in a death grip as another contraction hit. The EMTs addressed the group.

"Folks we need to go and get her to the hospital. As close as her contractions are she may deliver in the bus."

Kris climbed on board once she was in and looked back for Justin.

"I'll drive my parents-go!"

Mel yelled from inside the ambulance, "Noah!"

Justin looked at the kid and pushed him into the back with Kris as he closed up the doors and rapped on them to let the driver know to go. He ran to the SUV pulling out his phone to call

Nathan to meet them at the hospital. He rode shotgun as his mom climbed in back.

On the drive to the hospital Kris looked at Miller.

"How the hell do you two know each other?" Miller looked scared and at first couldn't answer as he rubbed Mel's hand.

"Um I was walking by the Comm room and Major Alario grabbed me and pushed me in front of a console and said 'here talk to her' then left. I didn't know who she was but we talked. I liked her. When she asked if we could talk again I was shocked. I mean girls don't usually want to talk with me. I don't really know how to talk to girls, but Mel wasn't like a girl. I mean she was easy to talk to. She didn't make me feel stupid. We talked every day. She said you and Justin were family. When she told me she was pregnant I was sad. I liked her a lot. More than a lot. Then when she told me she was carrying for her sister who couldn't have a baby, well. That's when I realized how special she was. I knew soon after I loved her. Even though we never met. When you spoke on that Skype call and I realized who she was, I was so proud. I knew she was smart and brave. I knew she was kind and selfless. I knew she was the one for me. I couldn't wait to get home so I could tell her in person."

Mel was panting and doing her Lamaze breathing. But she looked at him with so much love in her eyes. Just as he was looking at her. Kris was having a hard time digesting this. She just got used to the idea that she and Mel could start planning for a real future. And here it looks like Mel was on her way. She wasn't sure how she felt about her sister dating a Marine in MARSOC. She wanted someone who was going to be there for her. Kris had to deploy often, but Mel had her own life. It wouldn't be like that in a real relationship. She'd be alone a lot. Well not really, Kris would be there.

Her transfer to MARSOS meant she would no longer deploy as her duty would be at the school training permanently. That meant she'd be home for her family. Justin had changed his MOS and soon would be transitioned to reserves. He was taking a full-time position at the Navy Medical Center on Camp Lejeune as a civilian reservist. He just needed to pass the boards for North Carolina.

Mel yelled as another contraction hit. Kris rubbed her shoulders. Since her hands were still healing and the bones were knitting in her left she wasn't going to risk Mel breaking them again. They pulled up to the hospital and the EMTs went into action. Kris and Noah got out as the gurney was wheeled into the elevator. Justin and Sal squeezed through the doors just as they started to close. Connie would wait downstairs for Nathan.

They got upstairs and in between contractions got Mel onto the bed. The on call OBGYN came in after being briefed by Sal as to her condition and prenatal care. The Navy Captain examined Mel while Justin scrubbed in next to his father and they both put on gowns and gloves. Kris sat next to Mel on the bed while she pushed Noah to sit behind her and support her back. He rubbed her shoulders and spoke quietly to her encouraging her and keeping her calm. Connie and Nathan came in and gathered over in the corner where they would be out of the way.

The OB took a step back letting Sal and Justin take point. She'd met Justin a couple of days before as he toured the hospital with the administrator and liked the Marine immediately. She knew Sal by reputation and had no qualms about him assisting. After a few minutes of everyone talking she figured out Justin was the father. She was a little confused as she thought the blonde woman was his wife but figured she got it wrong. She was really confused when Mel looked back at Noah and he bent down to kiss her on the lips.

"Not how I pictured our first kiss."

Mel laughed then groaned as Justin checked her out. He checked with the OB as to her progress.

"Looks like you are fully dilated and completely effaced. You can start to push."

Mel started to push holding onto Noah's hand. Push. Breathe. Push. Breathe. This went on for almost an hour until Justin announced he sees a head. The grandparents gathered around as the baby crowns and slithers out right into daddy's hands.

"Kris we have a daughter. Look at her. She is beautiful!"

Kris leaned over to kiss Justin on the mouth as he lay the beautiful little girl on Mel's chest.

"Oh baby look at you! Hi sweet baby girl. I'm your Auntie Mel. Look at her sweet little fingers and toes!"

Kris pet the back of her head and kissed Mel on the forehead.

"I'm so proud of you baby. Look what you did!"

Mel blinked rapidly and yelled again. The nurses took the baby as Justin tied off the umbilical cord.

"Is she having more contractions?" He looked at his father questioningly.

"You're not done yet son." He said with a huge smile.

Kris looked at him stunned. "More than one?"

"Yes twins."

Mel pushed again. Five minutes later a second bundle of joy came screaming into Justin's hands.

"A boy! We have a boy!" He laid him on Mel's chest where his sister had vacated as he tied off the cord.

Mel was crying and laughing. Kris whooped and hugged Mel and Noah at once. Nathan and Connie just held onto each other awed at the miracle they just witnessed. Justin and Sal helped the nurses and the OB weigh, measure, and clean the babies. Mel lay back and Noah pulled her into his arms cradling her tightly. He kept kissing her forehead, check, and lips while wiping her brow with a cloth one of the nurses handed him. She had closed her eyes and was drifting off to sleep after her ordeal. Kris walked over to the incubators as Justin and Sal removed the gloves and gowns and stepped into Justin's arms. She laid her head on his as they looked at their new family.

"We have a daughter and a son."

"We weren't even able to pick out one name much less two!"

Kris had been thinking. She wanted to name the child to honor the two responsible for it being here. This was a no brainer as far as she was concerned.

"Justin, how about Salvatore and Amalia. If you think about it, we wouldn't have this beautiful family if not for them."

Justin was very moved that Kris would want to name their son after his father. And he couldn't think of a better way to acknowledge Kris's sister for her part in creating their family.

"I think that is perfect. Salvatore Nathan Alario and Amalia Jenna Alario. What do you think?"

"I think that's perfect too. Grandma, Grandpas; come meet Sal and Mali."

The group gathered around the babies as they were swaddled in their incubators. Justin picked up their daughter, rocked her for a couple of minutes and placed her in Nathan's arms. Then he did the same with their son and put him in Connie's arms. She cried as she rocked him back and forth. Nathan looked awed. He missed this with Kris. It was one of his only regrets. Now he was there for her daughter. He smiled down into the beautiful little face. She had Justin's dark hair but was Kris in miniature. Kris came over to admire her little girl. Connie put little Sal in Kris's arms. She pulled him close. He had her blonde hair. He looked like a perfect blend of her and Justin. He had a rich pool of features to choose from and he chose wisely. He was beautiful.

Kris looked around the room at her family. Her heart was full.

***

Three days later Kris was pacing the living room like a caged lion. She kept walking to the front window and looking out.

"Geez Kris chill out! He'll get here when he gets here!" Mel was on the couch feeding Sal while Mali slept on a blanket in a little bed made up in the laundry basket on the floor nearby. Justin was upstairs showering after hitting the gym. Kris was too keyed up to go. She wasn't even this worked up when the babies were born. Probably because she didn't have time to be. She heard a car pull up and went to the window again. Two Marines in utilities got out. She went out front to meet them.

Major Tyler Jackson was a well-built good looking man in his early forties. Brown hair and hazel eyes with tanned skin. Tall and lean he stood several inches over Kris and about a foot over the young man next to him. They made their introductions. She reached out and shook the man's hand and thanked him for taking care of Fazil.

Seeing Fazil in a Marine uniform took her breath for a minute. Her heart clenched just a little with pride at seeing him standing so tall and proud. She stared at the 15 year old a moment then held her arms out to him. He didn't hesitate to dive in. She grabbed him hard around the shoulders pulling him as close as she could. She held on until he pulled away.

"Let me look at you. Damn. You must have grown half a foot in the last month. What were they feeding you?"

"Gruel and slop. I liked the slop it was good." Fazil quipped with a smart aleck grin.

Kris laughed. That was Marine food in a forward area. She looked at Jackson.

"Any problems?"

"None. Everything went off without a hitch."

Kris looked at Fazil, "Are you ok?"

"Yes. I am good." He reached for the bag that Jackson was holding with his gear and Kris saw him wince. Looking at him again there was some nearly healed bruising around his eye and jaw.

"Are you injured?"

"It is nothing. Really."

She looked to Jackson.

"Just some bruised ribs." He told Kris with a knowing look. She knew they would interrogate him. She knew some of the men got rough when they didn't get the answers they wanted. She figured they had a plan in place to keep him safe from serious harm.

"So they rough you up kid?" He shrugged.

"So what, they tie you to a chair and beat you, a little waterboarding, pull out a few fingernails?" Kris quipped.

"Nothing a Marine can't handle Captain."

Kris snorted. "You aren't a Marine yet kid!" She grabbed him in a headlock and roughed him up a bit laughing. He broke free and put his fists up like he could fend her off. She laughed at his attempt.

"We'll work on that." First thing was teaching him martial arts. He had to be able to protect himself.

He walked back and put his arms around her waist laying his head on her chest.

"I looked up the word you called me after the last time I hugged you like this."

"Yeah?"

"Um hmm. I am not a pervert. I just missed placing my head on my mother's soft breasts and knowing I was loved."

She lay her check on top of his head. She had no idea she could feel such tenderness for anyone. The babies naturally; to look at them and see both herself and Justin in their features and mannerisms constantly amazed her. Even though she didn't carry them what she felt for them was so overwhelming it frightened her how much she loved them. But that she felt the same for this boy still amazed her. The sound of a baby crying behind them made him jerk up and look behind her. Justin was coming out with both babies in his arms. He handed the crying one to Kris.

"Someone wants her mommy."

Justin grabbed Fazil in a one armed hug pulling him close and holding the boy's head to his chest. Fazil held close for a moment pulling away to look at the baby in his new father's arms.

"This is your brother and sister. They were born just three days ago. This is Salvatore. And with Kris is Amalia. Sal and Mali this is your brother Fazil."

"Not Fazil. Fazil Answari is a terrorist detained at Marine Base Guantanamo Bay Cuba." He looked at the baby and said, "I am your brother Michael. Michael Justin Cole."

Kris looked over the head of her now quiet daughter at her three men huddled together. Her husband and her two sons. She cocked her head to the side in question.

"Michael huh? Why Michael?"

"I wanted to honor my new mother. I did not know her father's name. So I chose her grandfather's name. I also wanted to honor my new father. So I chose his name as my second name. The Major said American children have a first name and middle name. So that way I didn't have to choose. I could honor both my parents. But I had to be Cole. I have wanted to be Cole since I was very little. Since I came to the orphanage. When they told me to choose it was the only choice."

Kris was overwhelmed at the boy's impassioned speech. She couldn't say anything. She just nodded. Jackson shook Justin's hand and they introduced themselves. The group spoke for several minutes before the Major took a step back.

"I'll let you all settle in. I know you have some catching up to do. I'll be in touch regularly. We'll work out a schedule regarding Michael. I'll see you all soon." He said with a touch of humor and turned to get back in the car. He honked as he drove away.

The new family walked back into the house. Michael had a great many questions. He loved his room. He exclaimed over his new clothes. He had to take off the uniform and stow it until he was due to report back to Gitmo. It was the easiest way to get him on and off the base without drawing attention to him for now. He put on the jeans and t-shirt and his first ever pair of tennis shoes then touched everything in his room. Justin showed him how to use the computer and how to turn on the video game system. He also left a list of instructions written in Arabic script on the desk to help him out until he learned how to use everything. First thing on the list was to learn how to read better in English. Kris and Justin arranged for a tutor for him.

The next couple of days were a great adjustment for them all. Michael got into a new routine. He got up early and worked out with his parents. He had chores in the house. He helped Mel with the babies. That was his favorite time. His tutor came in the afternoons and they worked on his English. He would learn to speak without an accent and how to read and write in English. He could read a little, but needed to learn a lot more. In the evenings he went to his new grandfather's dojo to learn martial arts. Nathan had put in for retirement and rented studio space to operate a dojo. He would teach full time once he finished out his duty in one more month. He put in 27 years and was ready to settle down near his daughter and grandchildren.

Mel and Michael hit it off immediately. She worked with him on languages. They would play games pointing to an object and naming it in Pashtu, Farsi, Spanish, English, and French. Michael wanted as many languages as he could learn. He already spoke Pashtu and English. Kris and Mel both took French in school since they both learned and studied Spanish in Texas. He planned on learning Spanish and French. French was used liberally in the Middle East; more so than English. Farsi he'd learn at home. He was working to talk without an accent and Mel was a great help since she had learned to do the same thing. Already his English was almost clean. Partly because Mel was a great teacher, mostly because he was incredibly motivated.

Kris and Justin were back and forth to Command filling out paperwork. They enrolled the twins in DEERS and got them and Michael ID cards. They met with the Corps career counselor so they could sort out some things. Like how two active Marines would take care to two infants while on full duty.

The answer came from an unexpected source. While they were downrange Rosa's mother came to stay and help out. She'd been there for four months. She decided to move to North Carolina from Texas to be close to her daughter. The problem was that she was only in the country on a work visa. She'd lived in Texas for thirty years but never became a citizen. If she didn't get work in the next two weeks she'd be deported. Rosa was ready to tear her hair out because living with her mother was driving her crazy. She kept trying to override her with the children and criticizing Rosa's mothering skills, cooking, cleaning, everything. She loved her mother but actually began to fantasize about ICE coming to take her away.

Abuela Carmen was wonderful with children and her grandchildren adored her. But Rosa needed her out of the house and employed. Mel came up with the solution. She was planning on moving out in a couple of weeks. Carmen could move into her room and become an au pair for the family. She could take care of the babies and the house. It would keep her busy, and more importantly employed, and out of Rosa's hair. Rosa planned on getting her mother citizenship as she should have long ago. She only hesitated because her English was poor. Michael volunteered to help her with English and she would teach him Spanish and they would learn to read and write together. Problem solved.

Noah was becoming a fixture in the house as well. He and Mel were head over heels in love. Kris worried about how fast they were moving. Noah was sure. He could see that Mel felt the same for him as he felt for her. She had no secrets from him. He knew all of her story and accepted everything she was and everything she'd gone through. His sisters were shocked when he told them he found the love of his life and was going to ask her to marry him. Almost as shocked as Mel was when he proposed with everyone on the teams and all their families present for the twins welcome home dinner. There were lots of tears and hugging involved as the family welcomed him into the fold.

The team was changing as well. Javier transferred to MARSOS with Kris wanting to be home more for Rosa and the kids. Davis was almost out. He had only three weeks left as a Marine. He'd be opening his salon in a few weeks. Kris invested in the endeavor and became a silent partner. Her help made it so Davis wouldn't have to struggle and could even consider the line of products he always wanted to create. The best part was Miracle was thrilled her dad would be home forever now. Noah, Max,

John, Jack, and Mike would be put into new teams following the more standard rotating roster. The dream team was done. They were close and would stay close even though they weren't working together anymore. They were family. Nothing would change that. They'd all been through too much together and for each other. No matter where any of their careers ended up they would still be family and stay close.

John and Sue were going to spend two weeks in St. Thomas Virgin Islands. Kris wanted to do something for the man who had bent over backwards for her for as long as she'd known him; and more so after she transitioned to female. She bought flights and booked them at an all-inclusive resort that had excellent reviews. She paid for everything including incidentals. Sue couldn't believe it. It had been her dream as long as she could remember. Kris even arranged for him to have the time off so they could enjoy themselves. They would leave in two days. No matter what John always came through for everyone. Now she was happy to come through for him. He was speechless.

Kris also paid to have Carmen moved here permanently. She already adored the fussy Mexican woman. She spoiled Michael and adored the babies. There was a great deal of protesting but the trust Kris received as damages from her lawsuit had been sitting largely untouched since she received it. She horded it in case she and Mel had to live off grid. She'd made some very wise investments over the years and even with the little she used to set up the two foundations she created, she still managed to triple her money. Even after splitting it and putting half in a trust for Mel; her family, her children, and their children would never want for a thing. She pushed away all their protests.

***

Two weeks after Michael came home the Alario household got new neighbors. Michael sat with his nose pressed to the window watching the movers load in the furniture. Mel had baked them a cake and while the babies were down for a nap she grabbed the baby monitor and took Michael over to meet them.

They walked next door after the moving van left and rang the bell. A pretty woman in her late thirties with long dark hair answered. Billie Jackson was sweet and kind and very appreciative of their welcome. She invited them in for iced tea and a piece of the cake. She called upstairs to her family and her husband and daughter came down. Michael did a great job of hiding his surprise when she introduced him to her husband Tyler and their 14-year-old daughter Tori. The Major gave him the nod behind his wife and daughter's back to acknowledge his restraint at mentioning their prior acquaintance. Michael figured they would insinuate the Major into his life somehow, but didn't expect this. He smiled at Tori and she smiled brightly back. Michael was taken aback. She was the most beautiful girl he'd ever seen. She had long dark hair like her mother and her father's hazel eyes in a heart-shaped face that filled his mind. She was tall and thin with an athletic build. She was a runner and played soccer. Those were his favorites too. She suggested they go for a run and he could show her the good paths to take. He could only nod.

Mel was amused at his dumbstruck expression. They made small talk for a bit and the family walked them out when Mel said they needed to get back to the babies. As they walked out Kris and Justin were just coming out of the house. They each had a baby and they were both in uniform. Mel introduced them both to the new neighbors. They shook hands and the girls exclaimed over the little bundles. Technically both were on leave but they had to meet with Command regarding their change of status and MOS. They filled out the paperwork that put them on parental leave for the next twelve weeks.

Tori asked if she could come over and see the babies sometime and the bold look she leveled at Michael showed they weren't the only attraction at the Cole/Alario house. They were happy to have her anytime. She came over often and helped Michael with his studies. They also played video games. Michael had played some at Camp Delta and he was hell bent on becoming as good as Tori. They both liked 'GTA' but his favorite was 'Call of Duty'. He spent time at their house often as well. Not only did the kids become almost instant best friends, but Tyler was becoming conversant in Pashtu so Michael would go help him his studies. It gave him a plausible reason to be there with the Major and allowed them to speak without the family understanding them. Everything was falling into place.

Kris and Justin marveled at how much their lives changed in the last year. They had literally everything they had ever wanted. Or ever dreamed of. Night fell as they relaxed on the couch and the slight snoring of the two babies sated with milk held in their arms could be heard over the two kids laughing in the kitchen as the Spanish Telenovela played and Abuela showed them how to make fresh tortillas for the fajitas they were having for dinner. They leaned into one another and kissed slow and long. When they pulled away to lay their heads against one another's to look at the sweet little lives their love had created it was in the secure feeling that ensured this this was only the beginning of the wonder and joy and they had many years ahead of them bringing more of the same.

About this book

This book is fiction. Many of the locations are real. All of the characters are fictional and not based on any real people living or dead. I have tried to remain as close to factual as possible when dealing with US Military bases and operations; but have adjusted some things to fit the story. If you have served in the Armed Forces you will see inconsistencies and errors.

The condition Kris is born with, Gender Dual Chromosomal Zonation (GenZ) is a fictional gender disorder that is a combination of multiple factual gender disorders. The medical information used regarding gender conditions is factual. The GenZ Foundation Symbol is fictional and not intended to represent any real organizational symbol.

Camp Delta is a fictional Marine Corps station in Afghanistan based on several actual bases in the region. All of the information regarding the Marine Corps, United States Military Bases, and MARSOC is factual and gathered from official Marine Corps websites and publications. Uses of weaponry and battle tactics may be incorrect as they have been adjusted for literary license.

The charity Corps Values is fictious and not affiliated with any existing charity of the same or similar title.

Resources used for this book

https://www.marines.mil

https://www.militaryfactory.com/special-forces/usmc-marsoc-special-forces-weapons.asp

https://www.marsoc.marines.mil/

Couch, Dick. Always Faithful, Always Forward: The Forging of a Special Operations Marine. Berkley Caliber, 2014.

www.ingramcontent.com/pod-product-compliance
Lightning Source LLC
Chambersburg PA
CBHW020248030726
47499CB00001B/113